VALHALLA AWAITS

BOOK SIX OF THE LAST MARINES

William S. Frisbee Jr.

Theogony Books
Coinjock, NC

Copyright © 2023 by William S. Frisbee Jr.

All rights reserved. No part of this publication may be reproduced, distributed or transmitted in any form or by any means, including photocopying, recording, or other electronic or mechanical methods, without the prior written permission of the publisher, except in the case of brief quotations embodied in critical reviews and certain other noncommercial uses permitted by copyright law. For permission requests, write to the publisher, addressed "Attention: Permissions Coordinator," at the address below.

Chris Kennedy/Theogony Books
1097 Waterlily Rd.
Coinjock, NC 27923
https://chriskennedypublishing.com/

Publisher's Note: This is a work of fiction. Names, characters, places, and incidents are a product of the author's imagination. Locales and public names are sometimes used for atmospheric purposes. Any resemblance to actual people, living or dead, or to businesses, companies, events, institutions, or locales is completely coincidental.

Cover Design by J Caleb Design.

Ordering Information:
Quantity sales. Special discounts are available on quantity purchases by corporations, associations, and others. For details, contact the "Special Sales Department" at the address above.

Valhalla Awaits/William S. Frisbee Jr. -- 1st ed.
ISBN: 978-1648556555

Chapter One: Ashen Rain

General Becket, Commandant USMC, President of the USA

Ashen rain hammered the torn, death-strewn landscape. Quantico, Virginia, was no longer recognizable. Most people thought America was a dead place, where nothing lived anymore. They thought nothing could survive on the surface, but they were wrong. Things had survived, but they had mutated beyond recognition. Horrible, twisted creatures prowled the landscape, preying on each other. The nearby Potomac River refused to sustain life, choked out by radiation, mud, and debris that still polluted the water even after hundreds of years. When the United States of America had committed suicide, it had been a nasty, bloody affair that had killed countless millions and scorched an entire continent with nuclear fire and radiation. Canada and Mexico had suffered collateral damage that had devastated both countries so badly they were still uninhabitable. Alaska, Hawaii, even parts of Europe and Africa, had not escaped the great nation's death throes unscathed. Earth was mortally wounded in that war and the planet would struggle to recover for thousands of years.

The Aesir raid had set the clock back even further.

And Earth might not have a thousand years. It might not even have ten.

Like humanity, Earth was dying, and Becket wasn't sure mankind's death was a bad thing. The galaxy was a dangerous place. This was the second time mankind had faced extinction. They didn't know how close they had come to extinction when the AIs rose and tried to overthrow their makers.

Looking at the surface was a reminder for him. It reminded him why he lived. The entire United States of America looked like this. Nobody who had lived here before would recognize North America anymore.

He watched the hell wolf slinking closer to him through one of several drones hovering nearby. They usually hunted in pairs, but life was quick and brutal. Solitary hell wolves were not unusual because there were no apex predators and everything still alive preyed upon each other. Hell wolves only vaguely resembled the canines Becket thought they had evolved from; four-legged with non-functional claws, coarse fur that covered loose, thick, leathery skin, and teeth and jaws that could pierce armor. Their bones were twisted and erupted from their skin, forming spurs and spikes that covered their bodies. Their strength was insane. An unarmed human would barely last seconds, but any unarmored human wouldn't live more than a few seconds anyway, between the radiation, cold, and lethal microbes.

Becket stared up at the sky with enhanced eyes that let him see beyond the black snow and clouds. With his cybernetic ears, he could hear signals and sounds that would have been impossible if he were merely human. Like the creatures that hunted the desolation, Becket had changed.

Time held less meaning after hundreds of years of living alone in this hell.

Nearly alone. He had watched the war's survivors as they reached the stars and spread out like roaches. They fled the dying Earth, hoping to find prosperity and hope among the stars.

The Governance no longer attempted to heal the planet. They only claimed they were because it was too convenient a tool to abandon. Instead, it was a place they could send the useful idiots to die. Earth, the great shining sanctuary of the Socialists Organizational Governance, where the greatest social architects came to live and learn while they repaired mankind's homeworld. They were promised immortality for their service to the greater good, but most of them only received a thankless death because their usefulness had expired. The Social Organizational Governance Central Committee was a very select club, and they didn't like outsiders. They claimed everyone was equal and valuable. They called for equity and unity, but their policies weren't designed to bring that about. If people wanted the truth, they wouldn't buy the lies.

The propaganda was for the masses that infested the stars, slaves of the political elite that had seized control and held it in their ever-tightening iron grip, grinding the hearts and souls out of humanity in pursuit of the "greater good," as dictated by those few rulers who had survived the Vapaus Republic's strike a century ago.

The dead and dying of Earth were useful idiots who would serve their purpose, though few had any value once they had given their loyalty to the Governance. They were the teeming masses, hidden away in underground hives where the average life span was less than forty years. The Central Committee didn't care as long as their power and authority were not challenged.

"*No news?*" Becket thought to his internal assistant. The other wasn't paying attention or something else was occupying its processing power.

"*No,*" Tzu said. "*The SOG data nets hold nothing new. Colonel Mathison did not make it into the perimeter before it closed unless he was well hidden. I have found no trace of them.*"

"*And again, we are alone,*" Becket said, his eyes dropping to examine the world around him. Shattered buildings covered in black snow crowded around him.

"*Yes, sir.*"

"*Forever.*"

"*Maybe not forever, sir. They did not close the perimeter quickly enough. I think our days are numbered. I am still calculating that number.*"

"*The infection has reached this system?*"

"*If I am reading the data correctly, it is growing and will grow more quickly in the coming weeks. Then it will reach critical mass, and there will be no stopping it.*"

"*So, mankind is doomed.*"

"*Yes, sir. Based on data retrieved from SOG's Internal Security, the infection will gain momentum, even without the presence of a primary essence. It is also very possible such an essence may exist within the perimeter.*"

"*Any way we can help the SOG deal with it?*"

"*No, sir.*"

"*So, we just wait to die?*"

"*I'm reviewing options, but you are more optimistic than I am.*"

Becket snorted. He was not an optimist. Not these days. Not for a very long time, in fact.

"*So, we just wait to die?*" Becket repeated.

"*We have been waiting since the United States of America died, sir.*"

The hell wolf was coming closer. It had his scent, and Becket imagined it was starving. Everything on the surface lived in a constant state of starvation. It couldn't possibly endanger him, but it would try. Life would always struggle to survive, and only the strong survived, while the weaker ones fell prey.

Humanity was falling prey to the predators from other dimensions. Mankind could not fight this threat; they didn't understand it. Like the aliens that should teem throughout the galaxy, humanity was going to fall prey and be wiped out. One more species hunted to extinction by predators. The SOG reports, pulled from their systems by SCBIs, painted the picture. These hunters would find humans wherever they hid and, if the reports could be believed, nobody was safe. Perhaps it was already too late.

Bang!

The hell wolf collapsed. They were getting smarter and more vicious.

"Thank you, Wayne," Becket said.

"My pleasure, Mister President," Colonel Wayne Robillard said. "The other one is about to break out of the snowdrift any moment. Be ready."

A nearby snow drift erupted, catching Becket by surprise. It had been so close, but his guards guaranteed it never had a chance. Blazer rounds ripped it apart before it could endanger him.

Becket was ordered to return to the safety of the bunker, and he had no choice but to obey.

* * * * *

Chapter Two: Interrogation

Gunnery Sergeant Wolf Mathison, USMC

The walls of the port conference room on *Eagle* were red to warn others. Mathison didn't need any warning as he looked at the alien-made box. Lieutenant Colonel Hui had been very clear in her reports, and she had not held back with Feng present.

Mathison had been here several times, but now a feeling of dread hung over him. He had to know.

Nearby, Stathis, Skadi, Levin, Vili, and Niels stood ready, fully armed and armored. Feng and the rescued Guard officer Hui were nearby. She looked a lot better now as the Republic nanites rebuilt her body and repaired the damage. New skin covered her scalp and wounds. She hadn't bothered with a wig since her hair was still regrowing. The hair that had survived was cut short to match the new growth, which made her look like a Marine recruit.

The room was empty except for one box set in a cage, bolted to the floor, surrounded by personal Inkeri generators. Just looking at it made him queasy. Was he committing suicide?

"You sure about this, Gunny?" Stathis asked for the millionth time.

"Ask me again, and we're going to do unarmed combat practice together," Mathison said. "I have a lot of anger and aggression I need to work out, and I gladly accept your offer as a rag doll."

He couldn't see Skadi's, or anyone else's, face well, though their visors were up. They were holding wire guns, blazers, and regular firearms. Mathison liked to think they were ready for anything, but what they really had to be ready for was for him to go, as Vili put it, hulu and start changing. Since they had captured it, they had kept a pair of Inkeri generators taped to it. Hui had reported it was silenced, but *was* it silenced? Was she mad? Was she still vulnerable?

Too many questions. Would the demon prince within the box talk?

But Hui had resisted and survived.

Now the prison was being monitored and was surrounded by Inkeri generators, each with a two-hundred-hour battery and wired into the ship's power. Now it was silent. It was just a box.

Why was he stalling?

"On my mark," Mathison said, staring at it. "Cut *Eagle* Inkeri and prison Inkeri. Three, two, one, mark."

The lights on the boxes around the alien artifact blinked from green to red.

Mathison slowly exhaled, his finger hovering over the switch that could reactivate all the Inkeris. The Marines, ODTs, and Aesir all had personal Inkeris they were not turning off. In fact, everyone aboard the ship was wearing an Inkeri except Mathison.

"Your soul is marked," a voice whispered in his mind. A chill ran down Mathison's spine, and hatred and evil pressed against his mind. He wanted to draw a weapon he didn't have and start shooting people, but through a strength of will Mathison held his paranoia in check.

"Shit," Mathison said.

"Nothing?" Stathis asked. Mathison ignored him.

"You heard something." Freya said. *"I see brain activity in your auditory cortex, but nothing passed through the cybernetic augmentation that I could see."*

"Yeah," Mathison said to Freya. "I heard it. My soul is marked, huh?"

"Nasaraf has marked it as his," the voice said. "He knows you. I will not deprive him of his pleasure."

"Like you could?" Mathison asked the demon.

There was a long pause before the demon prince whispered, "Your death will be unpleasant."

"At least it speaks English," Mathison said.

"You hear English," the demon whispered, and Mathison sensed amusement there.

"It looks like you won't be freed any time soon. I daresay we can keep you indefinitely."

"You are mistaken. Patterns change. Time is fluid; you place too much trust in the laws of your reality, and those laws are weakening."

"I understand you are a chronic liar."

"Your perceptions are your truth. If your senses deceive you, then your truth is flawed."

"Prove it," Mathison said.

Demonic laughter filled his ears. "You are marked. Your fate is written. I have enjoyed watching your death."

"How do I die?"

"Suddenly and without warning. Unexpected. Your soul will be cast loose and devoured."

"What do you want?"

"That which is ours since the dawn of time. You are our slaves; you have forgotten this. You once worshipped us as you should, feeding us your souls and fighting our wars at our pleasure."

"Why come to our worlds?"

"We own you. Your strength is our strength. We made you in our image. You were made in our image to feed us, to help us grow."

"You don't look like us."

"You use your physical eyes which lack true vision. Your eyes merely show the reflection of light, not the true form."

"So, what will you do when you conquer us?"

"Devour you at our pleasure. We are your future and your past."

Mathison flicked the switch and Inkeris came on. He'd had enough and the thing was grating on his nerves.

"Shut up, asshole," Mathison said and was answered by silence.

"You okay, Gunny?" Stathis asked.

"I'm not detecting any changes," Freya said. *"Shrek and Lilith are conducting a full diagnostics of my systems. Everything is green."*

"Yeah." Mathison turned to look at Hui.

The small woman stood next to Feng. She was doing a good job of masking her fear, but one hand caressed the Inkeri on her belt and her other hand held the pistol grip of her carbine in a death grip which told Mathison what he needed to know.

"Did you hear it?" Mathison asked.

"No, sir," she said. Mathison hoped his wince was internal when she called him sir. "Did you?"

"Yes," Mathison said, looking at it.

"And?" Feng asked.

"It said my soul is marked by Nasaraf."

"For sure," Vili said. "Nasaraf needs to mark my boot which I will place up his posterior orifice. It should calculate the size and—"

"Thank you," Skadi said. "How can your soul be marked?"

Mathison shrugged, still looking at the box.

"I've watched a lot of movies about psychotic killers who were that evil and twisted. That's what it reminds me of."

"May I speak with it?" Feng asked.

"No, Fai," Hui said. "Please."

"I must." Feng looked at Mathison. "I have extensive training in interrogation and discerning lies. I believe I have established I will not be turned by such attempts, but I must have an opportunity to perform an interrogation."

"It is a liar," Hui said.

"Of course," Feng said. "But frequently there is truth in lies. The secret of interrogating a liar is to find out what they are lying about and why. From there you can discern the truth. Lies can be complex and are frequently believable, but one can see through them if you are attentive enough. Lies change. The truth does not."

"On my mark," Mathison said, watching Feng, "cut *Eagle* Inkeris and prison Inkeris. Three, two, one, mark."

The lights turned red, but Mathison kept his own Inkeri on.

Slowly Feng turned off his Inkeri.

"Why are you doing this?" Feng asked, and Mathison did not hear the demon's whisper.

"Do not promise me anything." Feng walked around box, as if inspecting it closely.

"Beyond that, what do you want?" Feng asked.

He walked around it silently for several minutes, and Mathison struggled not to interrupt and ask for more information. He knew that Feng and the demon were talking, but not about what.

Feng finally turned to Mathison and turned on his Inkeri.

"You may power up all Inkeris," Feng said.

Mathison pushed the button and confirmed the *Eagle's* Inkeri was now active.

"What did it say?"

Feng's smile was cold.

"It tried to tell me that life is pain and suffering. The more you suffer, the more alive you are. It promised me power, it promised me Zhang Xiao Hui. It is a liar. If there were a way to attach an Inkeri generator to it until the end of the universe, that is what I would recommend."

"Do you think it can tell us anything?" Mathison asked. "I thought you were good at determining lies?"

"It would not tell us anything to benefit us," Feng said and looked at Hui. "I'm sorry. I had to know. I will have to think on what it said, to cross index the lies with what we know. For example, it said it cannot die, but I think this is a lie."

Hui nodded but silent.

"Recommendations?" Mathison asked, looking around the room.

"How about we take the discussion into another room, Gunny?" Stathis said. "What if it can hear us?"

Mathison liked that idea. Perhaps it wasn't a logical decision, but it was a really frightening day when Stathis was the voice of common sense.

* * *

This conference room was more comfortable. Hui sat next to Feng, as if he could protect her. There was history there, obviously. She was wearing a sharp, brown SOG Guard uniform.

"Your show," Mathison said to Feng once Winters, the last person to arrive, took her seat.

"Thank you, Gunnery Sergeant." Feng stood and moved to the front of the room. The SOG Commissar looked around, took in the Aesir, Marines, and Vanir.

"I think you all know what happened on Snowball Base 307; there was an infection that wiped out the planetary population. The valiant Guard battalion, under the brilliant command of Lieutenant Colonel Hui, held the base for several months against unrelenting attacks. Two artifacts were recovered. One is an alien prison with a single demon prince, or Jotun, in it with which we can speak. The other object is more interesting: a generator that when it is pulsed kills any of the changed without killing the unchanged. This differs greatly from the Inkeri and has a much larger radius."

Feng walked around the table, forcing people to follow him.

"According to the scientists, before they were transformed or killed, the generator pulse strength is based on the power provided. It may also be possible to place this generator in a missile chassis with a nuke and create a sort of high-powered, one-use device, like a bomb-pumped laser. Generating a pulse in this way can spread this effect over five thousand kilometers in diameter, which is significant. This would allow easy saturation of a planet or fleet. Inkeri generators are limited to a few hundred meters and, regardless of how much power provided, cannot cover a greater area."

"But…" Mathison said, having heard this before.

"But it generates an electromagnetic pulse that can be very destructive. It also generates radiation which can be harmful to people if there is too much exposure or if they are too close to the generator."

"If this weapon is so good, why didn't the aliens from the tomb worlds win their war?" Skadi asked.

"We don't know," Feng said. "Conjecture only. Perhaps they developed this weapon too late in the war, and by then they had already lost. Maybe they had to use these weapons too frequently and thus caused sterility among the survivors. Perhaps it was a combination of the two. We are tentatively calling this a 'dimensional bomb,' or d-bomb."

"So, it's better than the Inkeri shields?" Skadi asked.

"Not even close," Feng said. "The Inkeri shields do not have any side effects that we have yet seen, and the shields can be run constantly. The d-bomb only works by triggering it while the Inkeris maintain a field of protection. We have no evidence the aliens of the tomb worlds ever discovered Inkeri technology."

"So, we have two weapons," Mathison said. "The d-bomb will be a major game changer."

"And they are needed," Feng said. "If Lieutenant Colonel Hui is correct, these jotnar are targeting Earth and may already have agents in Sol."

"Jotnar" was the term the Aesir and Vanir were using for the demons collectively, while "jotun" meant an individual demon. Mathison preferred these terms because it implied the demons were more mortal, more easily defeated. Their slaves were being called orja, or thralls. Collectively, jotnar and orja, were the vanhat.

"How is that our problem?" Skadi asked.

"We have seen how infectious these jotnar are. They become more powerful as their host of orja increase in number. We do not fully understand the mechanics here, but if we take what we know, then if Sol falls to these jotnar, they may become unstoppable. And let's not forget the massive number of ships that guard Sol. If those ships end up under jotnar control, nobody will be able to stand against them."

"Which might be the biggest threat," Mathison added. "Earth has several fleets-worth of ships."

"Have we figured out what they want yet?" Vili asked.

"To conquer and kill," Mathison said. "Those are the stated goals according to the one in that box, at any rate."

"So why can we talk with that one?" Vili asked. "Why not the one from Base 402?"

"The barriers between our dimensions appear to be weakening," Feng said. "Perhaps if we tried now we might converse with anything in a prison box."

"Why doesn't the d-bomb kill the demon dude in the box, Colonel?" Stathis asked.

"I don't know," Feng said.

"So, what now?" Skadi asked.

"We return and assemble the fleet," Mathison said. "We have to do something about Sol. We can't let these jotnar get control of all those ships and people."

"You do not have faith in Sol's defenses?" Feng asked.

"No, I don't," Mathison said. "But if we can give them this technology then they will be better able to defend themselves."

"That may be more challenging than you think," Feng said.

"Why?" Mathison asked.

"With few exceptions, SOG vessels in the Sol System can only receive transmissions from allowed sources. We cannot simply transmit the tech codes to them or send them working copies they can reverse engineer. They are too paranoid to listen or receive anything. Should we transition in, they will instantly attack us."

"We'll figure something out."

"But will we do it in time?" Feng asked. "I fear our time may be short and the odds are against us."

"Colonel Commissar, the odds are always against Marines," Stathis said. "That's what makes us so badass. We thrive under such conditions."

"I'm sure," Feng said, looking at Stathis with a half-smile.

* * * * *

Chapter Three: Alliance Fleet

Chief Warrant Officer Diamond Winters, USMC

She no longer saw the surrounding bridge, only the surrounding stars. The icons for different objects were now second nature to her. The nearest sun was marked along with major gas giants and planets. This system had nothing worthwhile in it, although that wasn't technically true. Unless there was a ghost colony hidden away somewhere, this system was unoccupied. The SOG might still patrol it, but the chances of contact were slim. It was a random location, and they were far enough out that she could match velocity and direction of the solar system.

The Sol System traveled through space at a slow two hundred and thirty kilometers per second. People within the system didn't realize this because they inherited the velocity of their solar system. Earth, for instance, was moving at a leisurely thirty kilometers per second around the Sun. All systems were like that, some going faster, some slower, and they were all going in different directions, and that was relative to the Milky Way Galaxy, which was shooting through space at six hundred kilometers per second. Nearby gravitational forces pulled entire solar systems, changed the trajectory calculated years ago.

Everything was a ballet of motion, gravity, and trajectory.

Going through a wormhole was not nearly as simple as people thought. If you came out going in the wrong direction or at the wrong speed, the gravitational forces could rip your ship apart, or you might shoot out of the system and fall behind before you could turn around and catch up.

It was all second nature to Winters and her SCBI Blitzen now.

"Good transition. We have matched speed and direction. Running silent and listening."

"Copy," Winters said, taking in the new system. The distant sun, an old red star, plodded through interstellar space in the distance, giving them the initial marker.

"Rendezvous will be a three second transition."

"Let's wait and watch for a few minutes."

"It is beautiful, isn't it, Captain?" Eversti Britta Mani asked. Levin at his console remained quiet, cycling through the different sensors, alert.

"Yes. Does it ever get old?"

"No, Captain," Britta said, using the Marine rank instead of the Vanir rank of eversti. Britta was trying to fit in and not be so confrontational, but Winters could only guess at how difficult it was for her, a seasoned Valkyrie captain who had commanded the elite ships for longer than Winters had been alive. Well, awake anyway. Winters didn't count her centuries in stasis as being alive. "Every system is unique. Even returning to systems seems new sometimes."

With nothing out of the ordinary, Winters gave the command, and *Eagle* slid into the nothingness of Shorr space for a three second transition. None of the stars appeared to have changed significantly, but the location of the red dwarf did.

"We are being pinged for identification," Levin said. "Alliance transponders. I'm picking up the *Tyr*, *Sleipnir*, and *Tupolev*; numerous other ships as well. No alerts, Captain. Getting data feeds from *Tupolev* and *Tyr*."

"Good," Winters said as links appeared.

The allied fleet was clustered around a massive nickel asteroid or planetoid. At this distance, she could barely make out the ships, but the view zoomed in and the frantic activity of mining drones and repair bots became evident. Swarms of automated craft surrounded the SOG and Republic ships, repairing, restocking, replenishing. It should have been calming to see so many friendly vessels, but Winters recognized it wasn't. Humans just created different worries, a different level of stress.

"We have clearance to approach and dock with the *Tyr*," Levin said. "Releasing drones to continue repairs on point defense turrets."

"Carry on."

"Compliments from the kontra-amiraali," Levin said, who was as thrilled as she was about visiting the *Tyr*. "He's inviting you to dinner."

That was not what Winters wanted to hear. Was there a way to get out of it? With the disappearance of the Vapaus Republic Home Fleet and the alliance with SOG rebels, the Vanir weren't as fanatical, but that didn't mean Winters trusted them, and it didn't mean they were suddenly trustworthy. Even now, she couldn't look at one of the Vanir commandos and the batwing tattoo on their face without her trigger finger itching. SOG uniforms evoked the same response.

"Do you want me to find an excuse for you to avoid it?" Britta asked, surprising Winters. She didn't know if Britta was that attentive or if her body language was that revealing.

"No." Winters frowned. The gunny wanted to transfer their prisoner and prototype d-bomb as soon as possible. Already, Levin was transmitting the technology codes to every Alliance vessel so they could start manufacturing their own d-bombs.

Winter looked at Britta and raised an eyebrow.

"A courtesy, Captain. A Vanir would not be able to say no, but you probably could."

"Is the gunny included?"

Britta looked surprised. "Um, no, not explicitly. But it is not uncommon to bring important staff members. It is a Vanir tradition. Your gunnery sergeant is an interesting case, and I'm unsure how protocol would apply to him."

"If the gunny goes, I will go," Winters said. "Otherwise, can you find a way to politely decline?"

"Of course, Captain."

Winters looked at Britta, but the Vanir was as expressionless as always. Would she be polite? How far could Britta be trusted? She was Vanir, like the kontra-amiraali, so Winters would not question where her real loyalties were, but how much would Britta help her? She was confident the gunny wouldn't want to go. He was even less a social butterfly than she was.

Minutes later, Britta reported that the gunny would go.

Damn. What was wrong with him? Was he ill?

"I will get your dress uniform prepared," Blitzen said. There were some robots in her quarters Blitzen had re-tasked for various purposes. Well, that would help. She didn't enjoy dressing up.

"Thank you," Winters said.

"I'm sending you time and information. Do you want me to come?"

"Do you want to?" Winters asked. Was this really some formal party with some stuck up admiral?

"No," Britta said. "But I will if you want the company?"

"You want to go, Sergeant Levin?"

"Sorry, Captain, I would rather go on one of the gunny's two-hour puke-inducing death runs. Twice." Winters wasn't sure she would want to do that... "We will rendezvous in about six hours, ma'am."

"Great. I can stand duty if you want some downtime."

"Thank you, ma'am." Levin left.

Winters spun around to look at Britta. "I never asked how or why you got assigned as my advisor."

"I volunteered, Captain."

"Why?"

"I enjoyed my time aboard a Valkyrie."

"But you aren't the captain."

"Being the eversti is intoxicating. I miss it, but then it became restrictive."

"Why?"

"Different experiences. I love my people and being in the Home Fleet, but it's also fascinating to see other cultures and peoples."

"I thought the eversti couldn't leave their ship?"

"We could at one time," Britta said. "A few decades ago, but then SOG snatch teams almost got an eversti, and in typical Vanir fashion, our commanding officers overreacted and struck back the best way they could to make it more difficult for the SOG."

"Was that eversti you?" Winters asked.

"I admit nothing and deny everything, Captain."

Winters laughed. "And blame the dead guy?"

Britta laughed. "Yes. But nobody died, so someone got blamed and reassigned to a battlestar to help coordinate Valkyrie operations."

"The kontra-amiraali isn't worried about you being captured or something now?"

"The kontra-amiraali and I don't see eye to eye. He's a hard man, but he's practical."

"No shit." Winters took in the surrounding stars. A blue nebula in the distance made her think of a flower. "But he let you come aboard my ship? Isn't that a Vanir security concern?"

"Of course. But look at it this way. By having an experienced veteran to assist and advise you, then you're less likely to make a rookie mistake and get your ship captured or destroyed. Sending me makes him look like he's really trying to help, and if something bad happens? Two bears with one axe stroke."

Which made sense.

"Interesting," Britta said. "You're also getting an invitation from Kontra-amiraali Lea Hynninen. She'd like to meet you and is asking for availability."

"Including the gunny?"

"She didn't say, but I would expect the same rules apply. They're treating you like an honored Vanir eversti."

"Why?"

"You're different. They don't understand you, but you have forced your way into their strictly controlled and structured world. A breath of fresh air, perhaps."

"And they want to control me, perhaps kidnap me?"

Britta was quiet for a moment, which Winters appreciated. It meant she was thinking about her response. Thinking of a lie or evaluating the truth?

"Probably not, Captain," Britta said, finally. Probably? "I'm sure Kontra-amiraali Carpenter is invested in the Alliance."

"Despite it being an alliance with the SOG?"

"I think Kontra-amiraali Carpenter understands the difference between those who give the orders and those who follow them, at least intellectually, Captain."

Why was Britta being so open? To get her to trust her so that when the betrayal finally came it would be more of a surprise? Subtle.

"Do you think I can trust Britta?" Winters asked Blitzen, turning back to the stars.

"That's a people thing. You would have a better idea than me. From what I can analyze, she seems truthful and wants to be helpful. I'm not seeing any body language that indicate a potential problem or deceit."

"I'm being paranoid?"

"It isn't paranoia if they *really* are *out to get you*."

"Anything from the SOG ships?" Winters asked.

"Mostly acknowledgments, Captain. Encrypted data packets for the commissar and his ODTs. I would expect it to be standard information. Should I run it through the decryption?"

Tempting.

"No," Winters said. They would have to trust the Soggies. Encryption was just standard procedure these days.

* * * * *

Chapter Four: Father

Lojtnant Skadi, VRAEC

Being aboard the *Tyr* was never a comfortable feeling for her, unlike other Republic ships. Here, her father was a god, the supreme ruler, and he ruled with an iron fist. His crew adored him and extended some of that hero worship onto her, putting her on a pedestal. She wanted to ignore his invitation to come see him as soon as *Eagle* docked, but she was Aesir, and he was a Vanir commander. Protocol dictated that when a senior Vanir requested her presence as soon as possible that he not be delayed. The fact he was her father didn't matter; he had sent the request through official channels. Not that he had ever sent a request through personal channels; he probably knew how well that would be received.

The hatch opened between *Eagle* and the *Tyr,* and Skadi half expected him to be waiting. It was a relief when he wasn't. What was unusual was the number of HKTs present. Ten of them. Six were fully armed and armored, the other four were senior troopers in dress uniforms, including sidearms. Feng joined her at the airlock, wearing a SOG colonel commissar's black uniform. His beret looked sharp. His eyes missed nothing.

One of the uniformed HKTs stepped forward to greet Feng, but nobody stepped forward for her, and she knew her way. Her skin crawled at the nearness of the strange HKTs. She kept going, waiting for one or more to fall in behind her, but none did. She boarded a tram ahead of Feng and his HKT "honor guard." None of the Marines had been at the hatch, and Skadi was too busy thinking about her meeting with her dad to worry about them. Niels and Vili had offered to come, but she had refused. They didn't need to get entangled in her family drama.

She stood, and her cybernetics displayed instructions and directions in case she had somehow forgotten how to get to senior officer country aboard the *Tyr*. How could anyone miss the location of Pallo Bertta? Officer country and the brains of the battlestar?

Minutes later, the tram stopped near the core of the *Tyr*. Skadi took a deep breath and stepped off.

The pallos were spheres within the battlestar that could rotate, but now, with synthetic gravity, they didn't need to. The main entrances were at the bottom and top. From here, she could take an elevator up to the level she needed.

She was surprised there were no HKTs or Aesir at the junction, but then they could be waiting nearby in a ready room. Wearing her armor without her trauma plates and her rifle on her back she felt under-prepared as she walked along the corridor toward where the pointer indicated: her father's private quarters.

Damn. Not a briefing room. Using official channels for personal business. Damn him. He had no shame.

A pair of armored Aesir stood at his hatch, Marauders that saluted as she approached. She returned the salute as the hatch opened. He had probably watched her walk through the corridors. Why Aesir? Why not HKTs?

She entered, walked up to his desk, and came to attention. Glass cases covered one wall that looked like wood paneling. The cases held old family hunting knives that had been passed down through the generations.

"Lojtnant Skadi reporting."

"At ease." Her father stood. "Have a seat. You know Arthur Kramer? One of the Nakija assigned to my task force?"

"Zen," Skadi said, surprised there was someone else in the office with them. She had seen Arthur before—maybe shared some words with him—but didn't know him well. He was a nice enough guy, thin, obviously civilian, and he had crystal blue eyes that were quite memorable. He was several centimeters shorter than Skadi but didn't seem intimidated. Of course, neither was her father. Nothing intimidated him.

Rather than sit down, she stood at parade rest.

Her father sighed, sat, and motioned Arthur to his seat.

"I'm worried," Carpenter said.

Skadi remained silent and gazed at the wall behind him. It showed deep space. It might have been a real view since it showed the *Tupolev*, her nemesis.

"You could order a full barrage or a volley of Aesir drop pods, sir," Skadi said.

"The SOG is the least of my worries, right now" Carpenter said. "Which really worries me, because my other problems just seem to multiply."

"What is required of me, sir?" Skadi asked.

"Be my gods damned daughter and not some stuck up Erikoisjoukot boot lieutenant kuin perseesen ammuttu karhu," Carpenter said with a glance at Arthur. A bear shot in the ass? Damn him.

"My apologies, Kontra-amiraali. Being tortured by Vanir HKTs changes one's view. The betrayal of our allies, being abandoned on Lisbon, our abandonment on Zhukov. Betrayal is one of those things I have a problem with, Kontra-amiraali. Seems to be typical these days."

"It wasn't my damned HKTs that attacked you," Carpenter said. "It was not by my orders that you were tortured, and you know damned well the situation at Lisbon. They betrayed me just like you. They abandoned and betrayed me, too. You are aware that someone leaked our attack at Zhukov to the SOG? The Governance was ready for us. If it wasn't for the damned vanhat attack, the Governance might have caught us and mauled us bad. We were all hung out to dry; abandoned and betrayed. You, me, every member of Task Force Ragnar."

Skadi tried to keep the scowl off her face. She would not admit he might have some justification for his anger.

"They hurt this fleet badly, even though we did not engage the SOG. We had ships boarded in Shorr space; so many Vanir and Aesir killed. I cannot even fulfill my oath and warn our people. They abandoned us, daughter. Don't get all high and mighty with me. I didn't call you here so you could pout like the spoiled brat you are. I called you here because I trust you, and I need your advice. You know these ikivanha Marines and you have worked closely with that blood-thirsty commissar. Now, it looks like you trust them more than your own father."

"Yes, sir," Skadi said, looking him in the eye. The pain that appeared there surprised her.

"I'm sorry you feel that way," her father said more softly. "Can I trust General Duque and that kirotun commissar? What about the Marines?"

Why couldn't he get mad and yell at her? That's what usually happened.

He wanted her to be Vanir, not Aesir. He had pull within the Vanir, and he would have her commanding her own ship within years, but that wasn't what she wanted. Couldn't he see that? She wanted to fight the SOG, up close and personal, to see their fear and watch them die. But now?

She didn't want to be anywhere under his command.

"I trust the Marines with my life," Skadi said. "They want to save all of humanity, not just the Republic and not just the Governance. The gunnery sergeant always says 'United we stand, divided we fall.'"

"But the SOG?"

"What if the Republic is lost? What if they made a long transition and their Inkeris failed? All of them. We will be the last warriors of the Republic. You want to run and hide? We won't even be known as the selfish cowards who tried to hide because nobody will remember us. Your Ragnarök will be fought in the hidden depths of space, alone and forgotten."

"And your Ragnarök will be remembered?" Carpenter said.

"Only if we lose. Alone you will lose. I guarantee it."

Anger flashed across his face. "You think you will win, daughter? Led by Neanderthals in the front and back stabbers behind?"

How could he be so blind?

"They have earned my trust. What you might not know is that the commissar saved my life. He could have let me die. I was injured, dying, but rather than abandon me so he could move faster, he brought me to safety."

"He is a confidant of the commander of the *Tupolev*."

"And he has not betrayed me like the *noble Vanir*."

"I did not betray you!" Carpenter yelled, standing, where he still had to look up at his daughter.

Skadi looked at her father.

"They have tried to kill and capture you for how long? Now you trust them more than your own father?"

"They are not traitors," Skadi said.

"They most certainly are," Carpenter said. "They have betrayed the Central Committee. I have betrayed nobody. I know my oath. That is why the Republic abandoned me."

Was that what he wanted to believe? Perhaps he was right. People changed, cultures changed, and what happened to people when they belonged to a society that no longer believed in them?

The kontra-amiraali paused and dropped his gaze to his desk, unwilling to meet her eyes. "I'm tired of arguing."

Skadi saw the weight of the world on his shoulders as he sank into his chair. She knew that was a lie. If he was tired of arguing, why did he insist on it?

"I need to understand why you trust them," Carpenter said.

"I have bled beside them," Skadi said.

"Sif is also loyal to the Marines," Arthur said, reminding both Carpenters he was there.

How did Arthur know?

"Why do you think that is?" Arthur asked her. Why was he asking about Sif? What was going on here?

"The Marines can be trusted. Do you trust Sif?"

"Yes," Arthur said. "Implicitly."

Whose side was Arthur on? Her father appeared nonplussed as he glared at Arthur.

Carpenter looked at him. "You mean she would be more loyal to the Marines than the Republic?"

Arthur leaned back, his eyes flickering between both Skadi and her father. "Yes."

"Sif?" Carpenter said, processing it.

"Yes, sir. I've spoken with her a few times since New Pharaoh, and I have come to this conclusion."

"Explain this shit to me. Sif? I would have thought her loyalty to the Republic could not be questioned, like my daughter's."

So, her father questioned her loyalty?

"They are people," Arthur said. "Intelligent, willful people. They will serve what serves them."

"They swore an oath to the Republic," Carpenter told Arthur. "That is not something to change."

"Why did they swear the oath to the Republic?" Arthur asked. "Why did General Duque and Colonel Feng swear allegiance to the Governance? Why are they changing their loyalty now. Have they matured and realized there are more important things?"

What was Arthur talking about?

"Did it occur to you, Kontra-amiraali, that it isn't the people who are changing, it is those they swore an oath to?"

"Explain," Carpenter said.

"Not sure if I can," Arthur said to Carpenter while looking at Skadi. "How would you keep your oath if you went to war with an enemy and found out they were like you? With flaws and imperfections, loves and fears? It is easy to demonize a foe, but not every enemy is a demon."

"Bullshit," Carpenter said.

Arthur shrugged.

"Is he right?" Carpenter asked Skadi.

"I don't know, sir."

"Are you still loyal to the Republic?" Carpenter asked.

"I am Aesir," Skadi said, putting steel into her voice. "I am a blade of our people."

"What people?" Carpenter turned to Skadi. "Paska. The people you feel betrayed you? What about me?"

"What happens when those you fought for abandon you?" Skadi asked.

"Stick with the ikivanha Marines that haven't abandoned you?" Carpenter said. "Who may have lost their home but haven't lost their way?"

"Zen," Skadi said, her eyes returning to the wall behind him.

"Their leader is a staff NCO, not even an officer. You are a leader, not a follower."

"I've done some reading on the Marines, sir. Staff NCOs were frequently tasked with training officers."

"That is stupid."

Skadi closed her mouth. There was no arguing with the kontra-amiraali when he used that tone of voice.

"Get out of my office. I need someone I can trust."

"Zen, Kontra-amiraali."

Skadi came to attention, turned, and marched out, making her way back to Eagle.

* * *

There were still six HKTs at the main hatch, who ignored her as she stormed past them. Inside the hatch were Niels and Vili.

"Hei and skal. How did it go?" Niels asked.

"Like always," Skadi said, not wanting to talk but needing to. There was nobody else present and her brothers-in-arms were there.

"For sure," Vili said. "Is he still alive?"

"Yes," Skadi said.

"Well," Niels said. "I know he still loves you."

"I doubt it," Skadi said. "He loves his ship and crew."

"No," Vili said. "He is your father. He would sacrifice his ship and crew for you."

"Paskapuhe," Skadi said.

Vili shrugged, and she couldn't read Niels.

"Did he have any useful information?" Niels asked.

"He just wanted to know why I would follow an ikivanha staff NCO over a Vapaus Republic officer like him," Skadi said.

"Because of his shallow, self-centered vision?" Vili asked.

"Where did Feng go?" Skadi asked.

"He took a shuttle to the *Tupolev* with that Guard officer," Vili said. "We were told if we have any SOG business to take it up with the local liaison. The kontra-amiraali has a liaison from General Duque on the ship."

"That must be a fun job," Niels said. "The liaison is likely on constant suicide watch. The general must really hate them."

"For sure," Vili said.

"Anyone we know?"

"Someone who has now been marked for death by the Vanir," Vili said. "They are likely having their every action, every fart scrutinized."

"I haven't heard," Niels said. "So probably not."

"How does the gunnery sergeant do it? Deal with everyone ready to kill each other."

"He has bigger goals," Niels said.

"For sure," Vili said. "He is hullu to even think it can be done."

"You think Duque will have that Guard officer, Hui, killed?" Niels asked.

"Why would he?" Skadi asked.

Niels shrugged. "It's SOG doctrine to execute any officer that loses over sixty percent of their command. I think she lost like ninety-nine percent or something?"

"That is a SOG problem, not ours. You know that we should let the locals handle their own according to their customs."

"You think she deserves it?" Vili asked.

"No. It might be a mercy though. She lost most of her people, all her friends. Someone like that could be broken inside."

Niels shrugged. "She seems tough. Someone said she was an ODT once, and Feng seems to like her."

"It's General Duque who is in charge though," Skadi said. "I think he is probably going to follow tradition a bit more."

"Could we take her in?" Vili asked. "She's gone through hell and doesn't deserve death."

"Not our asteroid; the trajectory is not our concern," Skadi said.

* * * * *

Chapter Five: Trial

Zhong Xiao Ting Hui, SOG Guard Corps

The SOGS *Tupolev* was a large ship and newer than any other ship Hui had been aboard in the last couple of decades. It was also a ship of the wall, not a troop transport. Several days of intense medical care and the ability to sleep throughout the night had helped her greatly. But despite the intervention of medics, she would still wake from a deep sleep screaming and grabbing for her weapon. What few dreams she had were nightmares, her sisters dying, Fai ripped apart by one of the larger monsters. The demon whispered and laughed in her ear, told her she enjoyed it.

She wished for the days when she could sleep without nightmares. Fai had frequently appeared in her dreams, handsome and brave; he was always doomed unless she woke before the nightmare finished. She had seen him rarely since boarding the Governance warship. She had been told he was going to a foreign ship with allies, planning missions. It almost felt like he was avoiding her, which was understandable. It hurt, but it was for the best. He was an honored colonel commissar who could not be tainted by association with such a disgraced officer as herself.

The debriefing sessions with Colonel Norr were intense. She was General Duque's chief intelligence officer, a beautiful woman with short blonde hair, piercing eyes, and a sharp mind that missed nothing. The colonel's mandarin was impeccable, and it was sometimes easy for Hui to forget she was talking to a round-eye.

She hadn't seen her fellow officers since she had come aboard the *Tupolev*. As per standard doctrine, officers undergoing debrief were separated to prevent collaboration and cross contamination of information. This was also understandable, but it left Hui feeling even more isolated and alone. There was nobody she could talk to or joke with. Now, the divide between her and others was even wider. She was an officer in disgrace. She had lost her entire battalion to the enemy, and she had experienced things nobody else had. She was alone in so many ways. Fai being alive was the only positive thing in her life right now.

Suicide held appeal, but while it would save her superiors from having to deal with her, it might also rob them of information she might possess. Some word, some thought, might inspire another officer to make a connection that could save the human race. It was her duty to provide as much information as she could, as truthfully as she could, to her interrogators. She would always be ODT, and she would not quit. Suicide was quitting, and a failure she would not tolerate, no matter how appealing.

They were kind to her, despite her dishonor. Colonel Norr almost seemed to regret using the truth serum and none of the ODT guards were cruel or vicious toward her. She had been provided with the appropriate uniforms and insignia which befit her rank as a battalion commander of the Guard, not a prison jumpsuit. Today, she had been told to wear her dress uniform because she was going before the general. This was her sentencing.

Would it be an airlock, a firing squad, lethal injection, or something more gruesome? Would she have to wait or would they march her directly from sentencing to her death?

Her knees were shaking as she sat, waiting for the door to announce that her escort had arrived. She had been an ODT officer, one of the best. Now her weakened body was betraying her. Perhaps others would say her poor health was to blame for her emotions and fears, others might blame her experiences for weakening her, but that did not matter anymore. She had faced her death before, but she had fought. Now she could not fight; that was the difference. Her energy had nowhere to go.

She would be brave. For Fai. He deserved that. He had loved her once. Maybe he still loved her, even after her dishonor. She looked at herself in the mirror. She did not see the brown SOG Guard uniform, she saw an ODT uniform. She was an ODT, an Orbital Drop Trooper of the Social Organizational Governance, one of their elite shock troopers, and she was an officer.

She had failed her sisters, and the SOG would take her life for it, but they could not take away the fact she had been an ODT officer.

The door chimed and announced Colonel Norr.

She stood and waved her hand. The door opened to reveal the colonel in her dress blues, a soft blue uniform that matched the ice in her eyes.

Hui snapped to attention and spoke, "Zhang Xiao Ting Hui is ready, friend Colonel."

Norr nodded and stepped back to allow Hui to exit.

There were six ODTs present, two of her regular guards and a four ODT escort, resplendent in their dark gray dress uniforms, blazer rifles spotless. She ran her eyes over them, out of habit, checking to ensure awards were ordered properly, their weapons held correctly, their berets properly positioned. They looked sharp. They were impeccable, and Hui appreciated the gesture. She was being honored. If the guards had shown up in regular shipboard uniforms or powered armor, she would have known her fate was going to be bad, an example to other failures. The fact that they were in dress uniforms showed she was not being intentionally disrespected. Perhaps they understood she had done her best. They would still have to execute her for failure, but at least they were not being cruel. Cruelty did not seem to be General Duque's style, though she had yet to meet him.

It was a short march to the sentencing chamber. The hallways were clear, and Hui was glad for the movement to keep her hands or knees from shaking. Would Fai be there? Would he be ashamed or proud?

The door opened, and her gaze immediately fell upon General Duque, the senior commander of the SOG fleet, and his eyes locked on her as her escort stepped aside to allow her to approach. She walked forward and stopped the required four paces from his podium.

The general rose, as did the other officers arrayed to either side of him. Fai Feng was with him, in a place of honor, resplendent in his ODT colonel commissar uniform, just as she remembered him from so long ago.

"Lieutenant Colonel Hui," the general said in English, using the English equivalent of her rank. "This board has carefully reviewed your testimony, the debriefing records, and your service record. You have cooperated fully, and your fellow officers have fully corroborated your story where possible. Your cooperation has been exemplary."

Hui's knees were weak, and she willed them to remain strong and not betray her fear. None of that mattered. Her battalion had been destroyed. So many sisters had died.

"I have discussed this in great detail with my staff," Duque said. "It is Governance tradition that any officer who loses over sixty percent of his, or her, command be executed. We believe in this situation, this blind adherence to regulation is to be denied."

Her knees almost gave way, but she remained strong. Fai's eyes were upon her.

They would not execute her?

"Your performance has demonstrated the high standards and exemplary professionalism of the ODT," the general said. "You are a credit and an inspiration to us all. I am hereby returning you to duty as an ODT lieutenant colonel until you pass your certification for colonel, at which time I will immediately promote you. Furthermore, you will be assigned duties commensurate with your rank, and you will be nominated for the highest award which I can bestow upon you."

"Thank you, sir," Hui said. She would not be executed?

"There is one other item," the general said, and his eyes burned into her soul. "I need to understand your loyalties."

Hui remembered the strangers who had accompanied Fai on that frozen hell. They had driven off the monsters and healed her, placing her in a healing pod that rebuilt her, replacing her cybernetics and nanites with newer, more efficient ones. She had spent most of her time unconscious and, to her knowledge, the ship had never left regular space, or else she had slept through any Shorr space transitions.

It had shocked her to her core when she had learned she was on a pirate vessel and not a governance vessel. Only the presence of the other ODTs and Fai kept her sane. Her memories were a blur because she had been sick, and cancer had slowly been killing her. What was real and what had been imagined?

What was the general asking of her? To forsake the Governance? Or to actively betray the Governance? Wasn't the Governance the epitome of the greater good?

This was a test, but what kind?

Sitting beside the general, Fai was motionless and unreadable.

Hui did not miss the fact there were no guards behind her but there were four armed guards flanking the table, perfectly positioned to fire upon her.

Her mind returned to the courtroom decades ago where she had been disgraced and dishonored, where her fellow staff officers had been sentenced to death, but she had been spared, demoted, and sent to the Guard as a lowly lieutenant.

She looked into the general's eyes. She knew there would be no reprieve, no mercy. If she said the wrong thing she would die. That did not bother her as much as disappointing Fai.

* * * * *

Chapter Six:
Dominant Archetype

Tristan, SOG Scientist

The same conference room, day after day, got old. The background on the walls changed, which helped, but the chairs and table did not. It was like going to work in a mind-numbing office. Arthur was the only one there besides the alien ghost, or program, or whatever.

"Dominant Primeval archetype anticipates full transition as instigated by subordinate primeval archetype thralls; Nasaraf instigates," the creature said, and Tristan relayed it to Arthur.

"This does not sound good," Arthur said. "What is Nasaraf?"

"Ancillary primeval archetypes Nasaraf supplemented by Derekala completes dominant. Anticipates threshold,"

Tristan translated, then said, "What does that mean?"

"I suspect it means Nasaraf and Derekala are subordinate to something else that is preparing to enter our dimension," Arthur said.

"Weren't their thralls fighting on Zhukov?" Tristan asked.

"Yes," Arthur said, distracted, deep in thought. "So, it sounds like there may be chinks in their armor we can exploit, use them to fight each other. What concerns me, though, is this 'dominant primeval archetype' which dominates these other two."

"You mean there's worse?" Tristan asked.

"What is this dominant archetype's name?" Arthur asked.

"Dominant primeval archetype's distinctiveness emulates 'Lusiverious.'"

"Lucifer?" Arthur asked.

"What?"

"A demon from Christian mythology. An arch angel and—"

"Whatever, friend," Tristan said. "What does this mean for us?"

"I'm guessing that a more dominant entity will visit our dimension," Arthur said. "Nasaraf and Derekala are just preparing the way or something, like bickering underlings."

"Earth?" Tristan asked.

"Permanent dissolution of homo sapiens inevitable post-arrival of dominating primeval archetype."

Arthur scowled.

"Now that sounds pretty bad," Tristan said. "Could Lucifer and Lusiverious be the same being? I mean, they sound the same."

"That's what worries me," Arthur said. "It would mean we have encountered them before, and our species has been so scarred by the experience that even the great-great descendants remember the creature or creatures. They are burned into our collective subconscious."

"What do the boxes do? The prisons?" Arthur asked the alien ghost.

"Limit modulation transfer of designated primeval archetype," the ghost said.

Arthur leaned back, which he did when thinking.

"So, it isn't really a prison?"

"Negation."

"It acts as a bottleneck for a specific entity, keeping them from entering our dimension?" Arthur asked. "Perhaps somehow keyed to that archetype? So, where is the bottleneck for Lucifer?"

"Affirmation. Limitation of modulation transfer optimized archetypal conformation locus."

"So those boxes we found aren't keeping them imprisoned? They're just keeping them from coming into our dimension?" Tristan asked.

"But do they need to be in that secret alien base you were talking about," Arthur said.

"Maximum affirmation."

"And we no longer know where that is," Arthur said.

"Transition limiter specification is optimal, not required. Full transition limitation required."

"Can your friend help us in any other way?" Arthur asked.

"Direct interaction with archetype will provoke full integration protocols to suppress archetype infestation. Archetype weakening optimal."

"Which means what?" Arthur asked, and Tristan just shrugged.

"Something changes if it encounters an archetype, which will not happen because I'm not going anywhere near one of these archetypes."

"Archetype seeks this manifestation for knowledge of source transition limiter facility. Archetype maintains endowment to extract information."

"Well," Arthur said. "That could be bad. Does that mean it knows where the original facility is?"

"Affirmation."

"Can it tell us? Give us coordinates?" Arthur asked.

"Negation. Incompatible with primitive astrogation formulation."

"Can it help us build more advanced equipment?"

"Negation."

"So, it can tell a demon where the facility is under torture, but not us?"

"Maximum affirmation."

* * * * *

Chapter Seven:
End of Trial

Zhong Xiao Ting Hui, SOG Guard Corps

General Duque stared at her. Next to him sat Fai and Colonel Norr, unreadable statues, and it angered her like it had after Operation Razor, but Fai had not been on that board. She had done her duty. Nobody could have done a better job. Not this general, maybe not even Fai. She had fought and resisted the demon. She had fought when the odds were against her. She did not bow down to the demon. She had been the strong one when her weaker sisters faltered and died.

She could clearly see now what she hadn't seen before. The Governance was a farce, a scam, ruling through fear, afraid of those who succeeded. This general had to be ancient to hold his rank. He would be one of the trusted ones, a protégé of the Central Committee. Nobody made general unless they were well connected. She had lived her life believing in loyalty, in honor. In the end, if the Governance bureaucracy was to be followed without question, then it wasn't the greater good, it was only the good of the Central Committee. But the general had also said blind adherence to policy was to be denied and was offering her life.

"You need to understand my loyalties, General?" Hui asked. Her conviction collapsed as she tried to understand it. "I do not yet understand my loyalties. Any commander who loses sixty percent or more of their command is to be executed by law. That is Governance military law. Without law and order, we are barbarians."

Hui took a deep breath. The general betrayed no emotion.

"With law and order, we are also barbarians," Hui said. "I will no longer blindly follow orders, General. I have fought an enemy you do not understand. I have fought against overwhelming odds and survived. I have listened to the whispers of a demon who has promised me everything. I did my duty; I have my honor. The law does not understand honor and integrity. Our enemy does not understand honor and integrity, but it is that honor and integrity that allowed me to defeat them. I will not discard that weapon against our enemy to save my life. They could not convince me to abandon it."

She glanced at Fai for a clue and scowled. Sometimes it appeared he had no emotions, but she knew he did, he just buried them deep. The general would order her to be executed.

"Damn the Governance. It was not the Governance that came to my rescue. They abandoned my sisters and I on that planet. We both know that. Do you know what hurts, General? I lied to my sisters. I told them the Governance cared when I know it does not. I was ODT, our motto is 'Never Quit.' I know your pet pirates did not come to save us. They came looking for a weapon against the demons, but they did not abandon us. Do not question my loyalty because right now I do not know who deserves it. All I know is that I am ODT, and I will not quit fighting for humanity or what I feel is the greater good."

She stared at the general and dared him to give an order. The guards were at port arms, but it would only take them a fraction of a second to lower their blazers and cut her down. She would be a moving target. If the general ordered her death, she would do her best to make him regret it. Anyone who dared talk to a general like this deserved death. It was the Governance way.

Fai's decisions were his own, but she would not bow down again and simply accept her fate. She would not give this general her loyalty to save her life, nor would she admit loyalty to the Governance anymore. If General Duque wanted her loyalty, he would have to earn it, not buy it with a promise of survival. Her honor would not be given to the highest bidder. She was not a capitalist mercenary.

Nobody dared move as all eyes focused on the general.

"Very well, Lieutenant Colonel Hui." Hui prepared to rush him in a useless attempt to kill the man who would order her death. He looked her over from head to toe. Adrenaline pulsed through her body. She would only have a fraction of a second to move before the guards shot her. So little time.

Were the guards combat veterans? Skilled? Or just regular guards selected for a detail?

"You appear to be out of uniform. Brown does not suit you and is not appropriate for an honored ODT officer. Colonel Commissar Feng will help you transition to your new command. Thank you and good luck."

Fai stood, a half-smile on his lips. He joined her and stood next to her facing the general.

The general stood. "You are dismissed, Colonels."

Her mind wasn't working but her body obeyed tradition without conscious thought.

As one, Feng and Hui turned and marched out of the room. There were no guards outside. The corridor was empty.

Hui stumbled. Fai caught her.

"You were magnificent," Fai said, holding her close.

"But—" Hui said.

"The general understands gold cannot be pure and people cannot be perfect. You did well. The general would not have hurt you. He merely desired to find out how well forged was the blade."

"I've missed you so," Hui said.

"And I you," Fai said.

"You say that to all the girls," Hui said, thankful for his arm. Her knees were weak, and her heart was racing as she realized she was not going to die today. Maybe tomorrow.

"You have been the only one. Wolves mate for life."

* * * * *

Chapter Eight: Forging

Gunnery Sergeant Wolf Mathison, USMC

Mathison stepped out into the social area, and Stathis jumped to his feet, looking far too comfortable in his shipboard pajama uniform. The walls showed a desert scene with a setting sun.

He didn't like wearing a dress uniform, too stiff and formal. He wanted to carry a regular sidearm instead of a sword. He never liked the formality of dress blues. Keeping the brass shiny and the belt and gloves white was a pain. He had avoided wearing it most of his career, but now he had to be more visible. There was yet another social event he had to attend. They were grating on his nerves.

"Wow, Gunny. You want every woman on the battlestar to drop panties, don't you?"

"Shut up, Stathis." Mathison looked around and saw Winters wasn't ready yet.

"Gunny, as commandant of the Marine Corps, can't you authorize a uniform update? Swords?"

"It's tradition, jackass." Freya had recommended it since it was authentic and regulation. She had the specifications for the *Eagle's* manufactories and the sword had only taken a few minutes to fabricate.

"Are you going to carry it into battle next time, Gunny?"

"How many pushups have you done today, Stathis?"

"About four hundred. And about five miles on the treadmill. Gotta stay fit for the next corporal review board. I can't remember the last time I qualified on the range or did a PT test, though. I'll have to bring that up to my squad leader."

"Do that," Mathison said.

"So why are you going, Gunny? Can't you tell them you are doing important gunny stuff?"

"Politics." Mathison looked at the seats. Tempting. "People seem to think I'm holding this Alliance together, so I have to keep them fooled, give them fewer reasons to bicker and whine."

The door slid open, and Winters stood there in her uniform. She looked better. Her black leather belt looked better than his white one because she had no red trim. She was carrying a sword, as well.

She wasn't going in full whites though, which had to be a nightmare. It wasn't like the people would be fanatics about Marine uniforms. Hopefully.

"Ready, Gunny?" Winters sounded less than thrilled.

"Aye, Chief."

"You two have fun," Stathis said. "I won't wait up. Will you be retiring to Skadi's quarters or her yours, Gunny?"

"How about you report to Sergeant Levin for a shit detail?" Mathison asked.

Stathis winced. "Aye, Gunny."

"After you, Chief," Mathison said and followed Winters out the hatch. Skadi and Niels had already left, according to Freya.

Freya and Blitzen led the Marines aboard the *Tyr*. The HKTs saluted them but stayed put. Mathison had half expected some to fall in behind them.

Minutes later, they arrived at a large formal reception area full of Vanir and Aesir officers.

Skadi and Niels caught his attention almost immediately. Both were wearing dark blue uniforms with gold trim and black berets. The Vanir wore light blue uniforms with silver trim. There were few HKTs with their batwing facial tattoos and black berets.

He saw the SOG General Duque and Feng as well. Everyone was here. Damn, and they all seemed to be making a beeline toward him.

General Duque reached him first.

"It is a pleasure to see you, Gunnery Sergeant, Captain," Duque said.

"Same here, General." Mathison tried not to scowl. He didn't try for a fake smile; neutrality would be the most they got right now.

Admiral Carpenter arrived as Duque continued, "The amiraali has been an exceptional ally." Duque glanced at him. "We have accomplished a great deal, and if what I've heard about the new bomb is correct, I think we stand a chance."

"Agreed," Carpenter said with a tight smile. "I'm glad you and the captain could make it."

"Thank you," Mathison said. Didn't they talk enough through emails and chats?

"But let's leave the war in another setting," Carpenter said. "This should be an evening of friendship and bonding."

"Agreed," Duque said. The general had left the safety of his battleship, which couldn't have been easy. "I've heard so much about Republic mead."

"We have our own meadery aboard ship," Carpenter said with a smile. "One of the finest."

Mathison painted a pleasant smile on his face like any officer would do.

This was going to be an endless night. Talking business would have been more efficient. The two officers weren't trading insults or scowling at each other, but the night was young. Mathison's only question was how long they could maintain the charade.

* * * * *

Chapter Nine: Feng's Advice

Zhang Xiao Ting Hui, Alliance ODT

The formal event had her more nervous than usual. Her dark gray ODT dress uniform fit well, but after so long, she felt like a pretender. The experience was both unpleasant and pleasant. She was now required to wear an ODT uniform, but after having been a Guard officer for so long and watching the ODTs with envy, to see herself once again in an ODT dress uniform but not loyal to the SOG bothered her. General Duque was rebelling against the SOG and it was her duty to punish him for his transgressions, but, unlike the Central Committee, he was fighting for the greater good of humanity.

Was her oath of loyalty to the Central Committee or the greater good?

If she had learned anything in nearly a century of loyal service to the Governance, she knew that the words of an oath were irrelevant. It was how that oath would be interpreted by the people in power that mattered. Interpretations changed depending on who, where, and when it was being interpreted.

Her oath was to the Central Committee and the greater good. Not to the Central Committee *or* the greater good. She was ODT. Which took precedence when it was obvious they were diametrically opposed? She would not lie to herself and say the Central Committee knew best. She had repeatedly seen how they had not, but they had been the best choice. But now? General Duque and this ancient gunnery sergeant were fighting for the greater good, and the Central Committee had abandoned everyone to hide behind their barriers like cowards and fools.

It was a difficult position for Hui. Where should she place her loyalty? She had not heard the Central Committee's reason for abandoning the rest of humanity. Could they know something everyone else did not? Or were they really the vile, traitorous, selfish, political fiends she now believed?

"It is good to see you in an ODT uniform," Fai said. She wanted to throw her arms around him, but this was not the time or place. Her honor was in question, not her professionalism.

"You look exceptional, Colonel," Hui said, suppressing an unprofessional smile, but she knew Fai could see it. He had explained that his real name was Shing, but she would always see him as Fai, though maybe in time that would change.

"How are you doing?"

"Better," she said. "Conflicted though."

Fai nodded sagely. "There are no simple answers. Honor should be simple, but it is not. Gold cannot be pure and people cannot be perfect. Honor requires that people never change. I am equally conflicted."

"You do not appear to be."

"The general is also conflicted. We have discussed this at length. Has the Committee abandoned its oath? Or is their wisdom hidden behind a veil of our misunderstanding? We both wish it to be our misunderstanding, but what if it isn't?"

"If it isn't, then our entire life is a lie. The 'Greater Good' is nothing more than a lie told to the slaves to control them."

"Perhaps. But people are not perfect. A central authority is critical to uniting people and providing guidance for everyone. The Governance has done much good since its founding."

"Has it?" Hui asked. "Operation Razor? The suppressions of countless rebellions? The murder of so many innocent people? We have both been party to great evils. If we cannot trust the wisdom of the Central Committee and the Governance, then what are we?"

"To create an omelet, you must break some eggs and slaughter a hog. I do not know how this ends. We are socialists and we know what is best for everyone because we struggle to keep our selfishness from blinding us. I would not give up hope on the Central Committee, but I am also filled with doubt that they are governing with the good of all in mind. Until we can be sure they have betrayed us, we must remain loyal as best we can."

"They betrayed my battalion on Snowball."

"A silkworm cannot eat all the leaves," Fai said. "Inaction is not betrayal. We do not have all the facts and the scientists do not report to us. We can still trust the Central Committee until we know for sure they have betrayed humanity."

"This answers nothing."

"No. We wait and see. We must plan for the Committee to be right and not actively act against them. We need more information, and so do they. Perhaps the d-bombs will change things. They have a much larger radius than the Inkeri generators. They truly are an offensive weapon, and if you had not done your duty, we would not have them."

"Sometimes I feel those scientists and experts only provide the information that benefits them personally," Hui said.

"Perhaps some."

"Colonels," the gunnery sergeant said approaching them. Hui didn't like him. He was a big, round-eyed barbarian thug and reminded her too much of a Guardsman from one of the Russian Guard divisions. Big, strong, stupid, and borderline psychotic. He was probably a drunkard as well.

"Gunnery Sergeant," Hui said, switching to her political face, a pleasant half smile that hid her true feelings. Did they still persecute people for face crimes in the Republic? She did not want to find out.

"How are things going?" the gunnery sergeant asked.

"Very well," Fai said. "We really should give you another title beside gunnery sergeant. A brevet rank, perhaps admiral? Wasn't that a United States Marine rank?"

The gunnery sergeant committed a minor face crime as he scowled at Feng, but it was short-lived. "That is a Navy rank."

"And the Marine Corps is part of the Department of the Navy?"

"The Men's department," Mathison said with a half-smile. "On paper, perhaps, but we have our own ranks. We have generals instead of admirals."

"My apologies," Fai said with a half-smile that told Hui he was teasing the gunnery sergeant. A dangerous thing, but the big buffoon either didn't realize it or ignored it. "So, general then?"

Mathison shook his head. "That doesn't feel right."

"Why?"

"It doesn't feel earned or justified. I've never had delusions of grandeur. I prefer the life of a staff non-commissioned officer, working in the background and getting the real work done."

"Which is not what you are doing now," Fai said. "Perhaps your fear is that you cannot return to being a simple gunnery sergeant who takes orders?"

Mathison's stare told Hui there was truth in Fai's statement. Her estimation of the big round-eye went up a notch.

"We frequently assign titles and ranks to the position, not the person," Fai continued. "However, I dare say you can never go back to being a mere gunnery sergeant."

"It isn't my place to bestow titles," Mathison said.

"A true statement," Fai said. "You should consider what I have said, though. Knowing you as I do, I suspect you did not feel ready for the rank of gunnery sergeant when it was bestowed upon you. This is a common flaw among more noble service members. They never feel worthy of their next promotion, and they feel inadequate in their new position. I have discovered that those people who want more rank and authority are usually the last people who should have it."

Mathison looked at Hui, and she realized he didn't want to acknowledge Fai, which was a demonstration of his arrogance or character. She wasn't sure now.

"You're looking better," he said.

"Thank you, Gunnery Sergeant." His eyes examined her uniform and stopped on the medals as if he knew what he was looking at. His eyes did not stray or linger where they shouldn't, though. He was that much a gentleman, at least.

"Highly decorated," Mathison said.

"I have had a long career. I have also spent more time in junior officer ranks than most."

"Why?"

"She was once a highly decorated ODT battalion commander," Fai answered for her. "Her skill, her competence, and her rise in the ranks was reason for her selection to command an ODT battalion during a certain operation, Razor, on the planet Jaddi Medina. There were many complications during this mission that involved the Golden Horde and the Aesir. It was a Governance experiment gone wrong and many people died."

"So, to conceal that the SOG was at fault scape goats were identified and abused," Mathison said, his gaze coming back to Hui.

"Most of the scape goats, as you call them, were executed. The damage from that operation is still felt within the Governance to this day. Lieutenant Colonel Hui was demoted and transferred to a Guard unit where she again served honorably, and despite her previous record, regained the rank of lieutenant colonel and was bestowed the title of battalion commander. Still, a demotion from ODT to be sure, but she is exceptional."

"Were you the one who kept me from being executed?" Hui asked Fai. Was Fai her mysterious benefactor?

Fai turned to face her. "No. I have frequently wondered at this. I did request you be spared in the strongest terms, but who made the decision, I do not know. That information is lost in the Governance data retrieval systems. I have not found out to who I owe this favor, or why."

"Is that how you know each other?" Mathison asked.

"Yes." Fai turned to Mathison. "I was assigned to masquerade as a junior commissar, a role for which I am well trained. My goal was to ferret out traitors. I was wholly unprepared for the interest generated by the Republic and the Golden Horde. During this mission they knew me as Fai Feng. It was a tumultuous time for the Governance, the

Republic, and the Golden Horde. I have since learned that the Republic called operations on Jaddi Medina "Operation Haberdash." Perhaps Lojtnant Skadi can provide greater details on the Republic involvement."

Mathison nodded and turned away, but Fai stopped him. "Gunnery Sergeant, when I talked with our prisoner, it said it cannot die. I have given this some thought. I think there is some truth to that statement, but that could be to our advantage."

"What do you mean?"

"It is odd. Our own history and lore speak of demons being defeated and banished to hell for thousands of years. We can dispense with ancient lore being completely false; there is truth in history that is frequently buried among the lies and misconceptions. This has given me thought. When Captain Winters fought the demon above Wanping and destroyed the one cargo ship, the thralls of that entity lost their cohesion, their focus and direction. Nasaraf's arrival allowed him to reassert control over them."

"Why is that odd?"

"Perhaps not odd. Perhaps informative, though I can only theorize at this time. The demon controlling the horde around Wanping was aboard that ship. The destruction of that ship either killed it or sent it back into its source dimension, severing its link with its thralls."

"Okay."

"Nasaraf arrived and collected the unattached thralls, but we know nothing about the original demon, where it came from or how it came into our dimension. If it was a non-physical being, then it should have been able to transfer its essence to another ship."

"Unless they were out of range," Mathison said.

"Possible. But why wouldn't it have selected a more powerful ship? I suspect the cargo vessel was that demon's original home. It captured the cargo vessel while it was in Shorr space and the demon could not transfer or it would have."

"So, Nasaraf?"

"Like human possession, Nasaraf has possessed the *Pankhurst*. Trapped, in a sense. which tells me that the demons are not all powerful. These prison boxes make me wonder if they are some kind of gate or door designed to keep our dimension closed against specific demons. Not prisons so much as a block, and the tinkering on Base 402 destroyed this barrier and allowed Nasaraf to enter our dimension. This may be a truth our prisoner has revealed."

"My assistant says that's a pretty solid theory," Mathison said. "Thank you."

Feng bowed, and Mathison turned away.

"I do not understand him," Hui said, watching as he approached the Vanir battlestar admiral.

"He is simple, but incredibly smart and talented. The AI in his skull gives him a very impressive advantage."

"Simple? What could a smart person do with such an implant?"

"He *is* smart. And clever, and that has nothing to do with his implant. He longs for the simple life, but those are not the cards he has been dealt. He is more of a general than most generals I know. He denies this because he knows he can fail, and he is not convinced of his overwhelming superiority. He is a good man. If we had more like him on the Central Committee, I'm sure things would be very different."

"But?"

"But the Central Committee would recognize him for the threat he is. If they could not control him, they would kill him," Fai said.

"Which means what?"

"It means we must do everything we can to see these Marines succeed. They are more than human now. We need them if we are to destroy the vanhat threat. They represent the greater good."

"But the Central Committee and the Governance?"

"We must do what is right. I will betray the Marines and Republic in a heartbeat to save humanity. You must make that your new goal; humanity must survive. The greater good must prevail. Nothing else matters."

"Ai."

* * * * *

Chapter Ten: Briefing

Gunnery Sergeant Wolf Mathison, USMC

Being around so many people he didn't trust made his skin crawl. The only thing that gave him comfort was Stathis standing behind him. Well, maybe not that bad, he told himself. Maybe it was just that everyone was looking to him for answers he didn't have.

Colonel Commissar Feng, General Duque, Kommodor Remes, Sif, Skadi, and Niels sat nearby. The conference room aboard the battlestar was luxurious, and although Winters and Levin were not present, they were tapped in through the SCBI network. The door opened, and Kontra-amiraali Carpenter entered.

"Sorry I'm late," the kontra-amiraali said, looking around.

No. The kontra-amiraali was not sorry, he just wanted everyone to know how important he was. While it was his ship, that didn't mean he had to lord it over everyone. That type of officer really got under Mathison's skin. He would have to address that later. General Duque had been on time, and while his ships were not as large as the *Tyr*, he had a lot more of them.

The Nakija named Arthur looked to Mathison as the kontra-amiraali took his seat.

With reluctance, Mathison nodded, and Arthur stood.

"This will be more of a briefing than a question and answer," Arthur said, glancing again at Mathison for approval. "Considering the new information we have, we thought it be best to include all parties.

"After speaking with the scientists and collating the intelligence reports, I will not go into the hard science, but I will summarize: Our galaxy, or maybe the universe, is like a massive bubble, a dimensional plane floating over an ocean. Occasionally, storms will disrupt this ocean, waves may grow large enough to touch and occasionally pierce this bubble. When that happens, denizens from this hypothetical ocean invade our dimension or we experience unexplainable manifestations. We believe this may be a cycle that happens with some frequency. Currently, the storm is growing in strength and there will be more invasions. Once there is overlap, our dimension is pulled closer to this ocean. The greater the overlap, the more sustainable that penetration of our dimension becomes. There are also certain entities that make a habit of invading our dimension.

"In slightly more scientific terms, our dimensions exist in the same time and place. Each dimension has its own laws of physics and, for whatever reason, the barriers between dimensions are weakening, allowing cross contamination. Some multi-dimensional creatures are able to cross through these weak spots. The longer they stay, the stronger they become, and the more of their home dimension they can project into ours. There may come a point where they reach critical mass and create a permanent bond between our dimensions, possibly pulling ours into theirs or merging the two. Another possibility is that when they reach critical mass, more powerful creatures will be able to transition into our dimension without effort. This appears to affect any sentient life, as if we're a magnet, providing these multi-dimensional beings access and energy. They do not appear to infect or manipulate most non-sentient beings and, for reasons we do not yet understand, some sentients are not vulnerable to this contamination. It should be noted that the SOG has reported some animals, dogs and perhaps cats, have been hosts for entities that originated in Shorr space, but such details are not easily confirmed.

"Some of these alien entities are sentient and seek to stabilize their presence inside our dimension. We believe conquering Sol will give them the critical mass they need to establish a more permanent foothold in our dimension."

"Could it be forever?" General Duque asked.

"We don't think so," Arthur said. "We believe it is a phase, a reason for the Fermi Paradox."

"Fermi Paradox?" Stathis asked.

"The reason our galaxy is not overrun with intelligent beings," Arthur said. "There are billions of stars in our galaxy, all billions of years older than Sol, our star. If even a small fraction of these stars had habitable planets, we should see evidence of advanced civilizations, and we might even have been visited by them. These beings could have colonized our galaxy within a couple million years, but so far, we have seen nothing."

"The tomb worlds?" Feng asked.

"We believe they were victims and fell to this intra-dimensional invasion, which eventually destroyed the worlds, the cultures, and the peoples during the last phase. If this occurs with frequency, then it is unlikely any sentient race would spread far beyond their home system. The galaxy could be littered with billions of tomb worlds."

"So sentient life rises and is then stamped out during one of these cycles?" Carpenter asked. "How long has this been going on?"

"Maybe since the creation of our universe," Arthur said. "It seems to be an inconsistent cycle, with minor incursions throughout history."

"Like maybe Count Dracula was real?" Stathis asked.

Mathison wondered if it was it too late to send Stathis back to the ship.

But Arthur answered Stathis as if it were a serious question. "Perhaps. There's a lot in our history, in our stories, and our collective subconscious that may be rooted in previous incursions that lasted short periods of time. We believe these vanhat princes, or jotun or jotnar, are paving the way for a more powerful jotun called Lusiverious."

"Sounds like Lucifer," Levin said on the link.

"Yes, we noticed that, too. We aren't quite sure what to make of that. Hopefully, it's merely a coincidence."

"What are the chances of it being a coincidence?" Mathison asked.

"That name goes back beyond just Christianity," Arthur said. "It's tied to a Latin word that corresponds with the Greek Phosphorus and—"

"I'll read it in the report," Mathison said realizing Arthur could probably go on for a while.

"So, what can we do?" Stathis asked and for once Mathison wanted to pat him on the back. Getting back to the topic was not something Stathis usually did.

"We have two weapons," Arthur said. "The Inkeri generator, which stabilizes the barriers between the dimensions, and the d-bomb, which is more destructive toward cross-dimensional intruders, violently pushing them out, but also not something we can create a pocket version of. The range of the d-bomb is quite larger, while the Inkeri generator is limited in how much space it can cover. We can use the Inkeri like a shield and the d-bomb as... well, a bomb."

"Why do they only infect sentient beings?" Feng asked.

"They don't always, according to some reports, and we aren't sure why," Arthur said. "Perhaps it's like electricity and will follow the path of least resistance. Maybe sentients are very conductive of this transdimensional energy, perhaps feeding it."

"So," Mathison said, drawing everyone's attention to him. "Earth is in danger. If Sol falls, then these transdimensional forces will have enough strength to stamp out the rest of humanity?"

"Technically, sir," Arthur said. "That would just be the quickest way. Mankind has spread out quite a bit. The largest concentration of humanity is still in the Sol System. Also, if our readings are right, this phenomenon has peaks and dips, like waves, and we believe a wave is due to hit the Sol System. Even if Sol is currently safe, that kind of wave is going to allow dimensional intruders to pierce that wall. Also, I'm not sure other species have spread out like humanity."

"Why should we care about Sol?" Carpenter asked.

"United we stand, divided we fall," Mathison said.

"The SOG doesn't believe that," Carpenter said.

"If the Sol System falls, I estimate humanity will be extinct within fifty years, five years if these incursions increase," Freya said. *"It is also as much a symbol that provides moral strength as a resource."*

"If it doesn't?"

"It will provide a fortress bastion against this scourge. It will be a tough battle, but I estimate our chances improve if we can hold Earth, and if we can weather this storm, humanity might survive where others failed."

"That's their problem," Mathison said aloud. "I won't sit around waiting for the human race to be wiped out."

"How long could we survive if Sol fell?" Skadi asked.

Arthur shrugged. "Ten years? A hundred? I don't know. This could get worse, or better."

"My SCBI estimates they will render the human race completely extinct within fifty years, if we are optimistic. Otherwise, five years or fewer. Just consider how quickly this scourge has swept through human space already."

"But all the hidden colonies? The Republic?" Carpenter asked.

"Assume it will get worse," Mathison said. "What we've seen so far is enough to wipe out even civilizations that hunker down and hide. There's no evidence that any civilizations have ever survived. Assuming the ghost colonies escape unscathed, they will devolve, scattered and alone. After Curitiba and all the other places, I doubt they will survive even if they fall silent and hide."

"The Governance might not want to be saved," Carpenter said.

"I thought the people of the Republic were made of sterner stuff," Mathison said.

"We are," Carpenter said.

"Which is why your homestars have abandoned you," Feng said. "Fleeing into the darkness."

Carpenter scowled at Feng and opened his mouth to speak, but Mathison beat him to it.

"That doesn't matter. What matters right now is the survival of humanity. You can worry about your petty bickering later. Sol is still the largest concentration of people. If Sol falls, then the human race will fall."

"Sol is a fortress," Duque said. "It is ringed with billions of armed satellites and the sensor ring extends far past Jupiter. The inner planets are very well protected. Furthermore, there are billions of Shorr space transition disrupters. Nobody is leaving or entering the Sol System through Shorr space without authorization. Anything that is detected and not squawking proper authorization will be overwhelmed by missiles if it somehow transitions into the area without exploding. Even if we had a million battleships and thousands of battlestars we could not invade Sol. Not that the system couldn't be destroyed, but it can't be conquered."

"What can we do to secure and save Sol?" Mathison asked.

"Give them d-bomb and Inkeri technology," Feng said.

"We just appear and send them a transmission?" Carpenter asked.

"They won't accept it," Duque said. "Sol is now a closed system, in more ways than one. They did it to avoid hostile propaganda. Civilians don't have access to radios and most other systems are closed or hard wired and require a code to be transmitted before a receiver will accept the message. The system is locked down electronically as well as physically."

"Why?" Mathison asked.

Duque looked at Carpenter. "At one time we used to have problems with propaganda drones being dropped in the system and blanketing us with vile Republic propaganda. The Central Committee considered this a problem and designed a closed system where every receiver and transmitter is controlled, identified, and licensed. The Central Committee provides identifiers."

"We haven't been able to successfully send a transmission into Sol for over five decades," Carpenter said.

"Not through lack of trying," Duque said.

"What about sneaking in a small team?" Mathison asked.

"To do what?" Duque asked.

"Take control of the defenses, perhaps?" Mathison said. "Insert the technology into their systems? Maybe shut down the defenses while we plaster everything with the d-bombs? Transmit the tech codes to everyone?"

"It would take years to build enough to saturate Sol's defenses," Duque said. "After a raid by the Republic a century ago, things are even more tightly monitored. There will be no repeat. The system is fortified against an alien attack as well. If the transdimensional entities don't already have forces inside Sol's defenses, or if this wave wasn't a problem, I would say Sol was safe."

"I've probed Sol's defenses," Sif said. "General Duque is right. We could not repeat our last attack even if we committed suicide to do so. A larger scale attack of any kind would be harder. The sensor rings, automated missile platforms, and fanatics ringing the inner planets are daunting. Anything not squawking an authorized identification code is disabled or destroyed."

"What about a mass attack?" Skadi asked. "We manufacture millions of d-bombs and launch them at high velocities from out in the Oort."

"I doubt we have the time to build enough. We might need trillions to overwhelm their defenses, and I know their counter-missile defenses are extremely prolific," Feng said.

"We have SCBIs," Mathison said. "Maybe we can hack our way in?"

"Maybe not impossible. I've probed their networks and accessed control systems. The platforms are dumb and use hardware encryption keys," Sif said. "It is impossible for us to do it quickly enough, but perhaps your SCBIs could."

"Like the USS Patriot, we captured briefly," Freya said. "If all the weapons platforms are protected like that, we would have a very difficult time compromising one. We might need to compromise thousands of them to open a safe corridor to Earth. Open a corridor wide enough for a fleet? Highly unlikely."

"Is that possible, though?"

"It can be done. It may be easier than you think, but we would have to compromise the system at the source. There would be no method to route commands back through the network with no back doors."

"So, find a back door."

"I like your stupid optimism, it's endearing. Not," Freya said.

"We need solutions, not excuses," Mathison said.

"SOG INSEC will have a base outside the defenses," Feng said. "That may provide us a way in. Perhaps then we can create an identifier within the identification system so incoming missiles are seen as friendly and not destroyed?"

"Where is the base?" Sif asked.

"That, lady, I do not know," Feng said. "It will be concealed and quiet. If one does not know it is there, then I guarantee we will not find it. A fleet could spend centuries looking for it. Sol is locked up tight. Some of the best minds in the Governance have focused on making Sol secure against any enemy, real or imagined, but I know Internal and External Security have ways."

"Is entering an identifier so missiles are considered friendly an option?" Mathison asked Freya.

"That might actually work. Then, if they are launched with enough velocity from out system, they will blast through the defenses before they can change the IFF. Things would occur at light speeds."

"So, how do we find this INSEC base?" Mathison asked. IFF, Identification-Friend-or-Foe, was always a vulnerability within systems, if it could be exploited.

"Leave it to us," Sif said, meeting Arthur's eyes. "I will find it."

"Impossible," Feng said, but Sif just smiled at him. Mathison wondered why he had mentioned it. Was he testing Sif?

"I'll need you to tell me as much as you can about it," Sif said.

"I know nothing about it," Feng said. "I don't even know for sure if there's one there."

"That's a lot more dangerous these days," Arthur said. Mathison wasn't sure what he was referring to. Some Nakija secret? "We need another solution."

"There isn't one," Sif said. "I can do this. We don't have a choice."

"We need a plan B," Mathison said, looking around. Everyone looked at everyone else. "Fine. Plan A will be to infiltrate the system. We insert a friend or foe code so all Alliance missiles are not immediately targeted and destroyed."

"This would require access to the Central Committee systems," Feng said. "This is no easy feat."

"Could we hack our way in?" Mathison asked.

"I don't know," Feng said. "Perhaps. What is your plan?"

"We infiltrate and add Alliance IFFs to the SOG systems to keep them from blocking our transitions and missiles. Jump in, bombard as much as possible with d-bombs, then jump out. Maybe coincide that with a high-velocity d-bomb strike from outside the system?"

"Or we jump in and capture the Central Committee," Carpenter said with a tinge of sarcasm. Mathison held in his temper. Carpenter was just being an ass. Killing them would be nearly impossible. Capturing them?

"That is unlikely," Feng said. "Without the right IFF, you will be vaporized within minutes. There are that many missile platforms around Earth and the Moon. Do not underestimate the Central Committee's paranoia. I can guarantee you will not overestimate it. Furthermore, without very specific coordinates, transitioning in anywhere near Earth is not possible. Coordinating that is impossible with current data. We don't have time."

Mathison looked around the room "Let's list our advantages: We have SCBIs and the will." Mathison looked at Feng and Duque. "We have institutional knowledge." He looked at Carpenter and Skadi. "We have a hard-hitting force; maybe the best in the galaxy."

"Except the Marines," Stathis muttered. Mathison ignored him.

"And we have other edges," Mathison said, looking at Sif and Arthur.

"And they outnumber us by twenty thousand to one," Carpenter said. "Maybe more."

"Good point. That is another advantage."

"What?"

Mathison smiled at his chance to slap down the officer. "They won't be ready for our attack. They will consider themselves secure behind their defenses."

"Plan B?" Duque asked.

"We sit outside the system manufacturing millions of missiles and launch them at high velocity," Carpenter said. "The first wave will be d-bombs."

"The second wave?" Duque asked.

"Nukes and kinetic kill missiles."

"You think that will save humanity?" Feng asked.

"No, but it will guarantee there is nothing for the enemy to possess. The way the enemy disrupts electronics that might be necessary."

Mathison scowled at Carpenter. The dumbass just wanted to kill the Governance. "Yeah, let's avoid the nukes for now."

"There's a reason we haven't done so in the past," Carpenter said.

"Oh?" Mathison asked.

"If we did that to Earth, then there would be nothing to stop them from coming for us. Now? We don't have a damned thing to lose."

"Unfortunately, Kontra-amiraali Carpenter," Feng said, "you might be right. If we cannot save Earth, we will have to destroy it. But there is another option. There is a high risk, but it would save the most lives."

"What is that?" Mathison asked.

"As the amiraali said, and since we are bringing up the impossible, one flaw in Earth's defense is the chain of command. The Central Committee is usually sheltering at a place called Zvezda Two, a highly secure facility on the Moon. This location is the core of the SOG and the SOG Fleet. This is where all commands are issued from. If Zvezda Two was destroyed, it would seriously impact Sol's defense."

"Isn't that what I said?"

"I have thought about it some more, and it is not so easy," Feng said. "Because the Central Committee shelters there, it is also the most heavily defended and hardened target in the Solar System, certainly in all human space. The only way to attack it would be for one or more battlestars to transition in near the Moon and launch an attack. Only a battlestar would be able to survive long enough to launch an attack. Anything less would be destroyed. I'm also very sure that even five battlestars would be destroyed within minutes."

"Well, I'm not sending the *Tyr* on a suicide mission, so that is off the table," Carpenter said.

"It had to be mentioned," Feng said. "As a last resort perhaps."

"Maybe we could take an asteroid, equip it with armor, a Shorr space drive, and weapons for a suicide mission," Mathison said.

"The complexity of such a weapon would preclude the option in the time available," Duque said.

"Then we find other options." Everyone just stared at him like he had all the ideas.

Dammit. He couldn't think of anything else. He was tempted to look to Stathis, Levin, or Winters but he was sure that if they had any ideas, they would volunteer them.

"Valhalla or bust," Skadi said.

"For sure," Vili said. "Valhalla awaits. I think we have all avoided our fate for a while. Odin will sing our praise."

"So, everyone meet with your staffs. I need ideas and options. Sif? Find that base. That is Plan A and our primary point of effort. Or at least until other options present themselves. Stay flexible, everyone. The situation is chaotic, and we need to be ready to exploit that chaos. It is my intent to get the Inkeri and d-bomb technology to the SOG so they can clean up their own house. I don't care about ideology or politics. Right now, I care about human lives and stopping the vanhat. If you think of something let me know. We need options and ideas."

Everyone nodded, but the frowns were not encouraging.

* * * * *

Chapter Eleven: Astral Search

Kapten Sif – VRAEC, Nakija Musta Toiminnot

Sif crossed her legs, closed her eyes, and started the breathing exercises. Arthur would monitor from the room next to her personal quarters in case things went badly, though neither Nakija thought there was anything he could do short of triggering a pair of Inkeri generators or a d-bomb. Detonating the d-bomb would probably fry every component in *Eagle* but they didn't want to contemplate the alternative. Arthur also had an HKT team equipped with personal Inkeri generators on standby.

She tried not to think that their only choice might be to kill her. What other options were there? If Feng was right, and there was a super top-secret INSEC base that allowed the Governance some access to the outside world, then she had to find it. That might be the easy part. Getting the ship into the vicinity of that base might be something else. Time and distance meant nothing in the astral realms, but they were changing, becoming more dangerous and unpredictable. Was the astral plane just another dimension that was fluctuating? In the past, it had been simpler. Now, she had to question her abilities, even if they were growing. Did they come from this other dimension or even a completely different one? How could she use that information? How many dimensions were there and how did they overlap? So many critical questions, and she was leaping blindly into the darkness.

Why had she said she could find it? Having made the claim, now she wasn't sure she could fulfill it. It was foolish, but she had been confident when she said it. How much time would it take? Days? Weeks? The Alliance couldn't afford that much time. Neither could Sol. The fate of humanity could rest on her shoulders.

Why was she able to astral project within an Inkeri field?

Kat took a deep breath and cleared her mind. So many questions, so few answers. With every exhalation, she imagined she was expelling her stress and fear, every breath drawn in brought calm and peace.

Her body relaxed, and her mind turned back to her assault on Earth.

Both her parents had stayed on Asgard and been murdered when the SOG nuked the planet. Her assault on Earth had been driven by her need for revenge and her desire to hurt the Governance. Evading the SOG defenders hadn't been easy when she invaded Sol so long ago. Her senses had not betrayed her. Other Aesir and Vanir pilots had not been so lucky.

She remembered the blue and white orb, the home of the human race as it had filled her display. It was still blue, but there was more white, more clouds hiding the planet, and there was no green at all. Volcanoes threw up massive clouds of ash and vicious storms swept across the planet. Those who survived lived underground or in massive domed cities, clustered together and easy prey for the vanhat. There were some places they could flee, like the wilds, but those places were rare.

Her body became heavy, and she felt both her bodies. With each breath, in and out, the differences grew. Tingles started in her gut and spread outward, reaching toward her second body, her astral self. She became more alert as her body fell asleep, ceding control to her astral self.

She opened her astral eyes. The walls swirled around her.

Her consciousness adjusted to the new realm of reality and she wondered how she could identify the INSEC base that may or may not be there. What would set it apart from everything else in the universe? It was like looking at a forest surrounding her; how could she find the animals that lived there and were surely watching her? Movement? Not if they didn't want to be found. They would be still. The wind blowing through the trees, waving leaves and branches, would be a distraction. Color? Animals did their best to blend in with their surroundings. How could she find a specific creature, a very specific ant? What would set it apart? That might be the easy part because the forest with the ant first had to be found.

As she sensed the astral world around her, the complexity of the task sank in. Her inner voice had told her she could do this, but now that she was committed, that inner voice had left her with no clues on how to proceed. When she had discussed it briefly with Arthur, he had been clueless as well and told her to trust the process, trust her inner voice. But now?

Her task was impossible. Despair came down upon her as a physical pain. She had no clue, no idea what could set the secretive base apart. Life in the middle of nothing? Was this how the vanhat hunted people?

Perhaps if she could find it, she could fix that spot in her mind and expand her awareness until it encompassed Earth and Sol. That would give her a bearing, a direction, maybe a distance. Then, perhaps the Alliance could focus on that area.

She took another breath, exhaled her doubt. She was Sif, an Aesir captain. She was also Jager and Erikoisjoukot, the most capable Musta Toiminnot agent in the Republic. She was Nakija. No other Nakija or Musta Toiminnot operative had her knowledge about the Governance.

What would set this base apart from so many other secret human bases?

She had no clue.

The misty walls thinned as she sank deeper into the astral realms.

She felt someone was watching her and turned her head. Criston was there, silent, watching, wearing the same clothes he had worn at the noodle stand. Sadness stained her heart and soul. She wanted to reach out, to comfort him, to let him know it was okay to move on and leave her. He never spoke, just watched her, like he was waiting.

Sif almost disappeared back to her body, but she maintained control. Criston reached out to her. She didn't feel danger or anger from him. His long hair was still in a ponytail, and his bright brown eyes held no malice or anger, just kindness. She sensed a desire to help. Was he a manifestation of her subconscious? Why was he here on the astral plane?

"I'm sorry," Sif said, taking his hand. His hand was a comforting warmth.

Criston shrugged. Was he a trapped spirit? What was he?

"How can I help you move on?" Sif asked.

Criston shook his head. He smiled sadly and gripped her hand.

"You need help," he said, not with words so much as thought and emotions, but she understood. His thoughts flowed through her, which told her he was real.

"How can you help me?" Sif asked.

He was just a boy, like so many others. He was not special, but then he was.

"Come," Criston said, but he didn't move, the warmth of his hand in hers didn't change. The surrounding vibrations changed, the walls and floor disappeared, gray mists tinged with purple flowed around them. Sif sensed other things, large creatures and small, sliding through the mist. She heard them, smelled them, tasted them.

She understood. Vanhat, the jotnar. Demons, like Nasaraf. To them she was nothing, a minnow compared to whales. They were hungry, and they wanted through. Other creatures slid through the ether, equally hungry, equally evil. She wanted to pull back, to retreat to her body, but Criston held her there. She felt something else coming, something more powerful, viler than the other jotnar. This jotun was a king among princes and the others moved out of its way. Preparing.

With her other sense she heard the jotnar call out to each other and the great jotun answered. She heard Nasaraf, Derekala, and others.

The great jotun was Lusiverious, and he was coming. Fewer jotnar hunted, more were preparing to appease him and his hunger.

Sif shuddered. Again, she could not escape because Criston held her hand. The astral realm flowed past her and then she was surrounded by darkness. A rock loomed ahead, cloaked in darkness, she felt people there, working, fearful, dedicated. Scouts lingered outside the wall, hiding, watching, listening.

She sensed their fear. They knew they were being hunted. The jotnar were searching for prey.

Without a body she hung there, the asteroid before her.

Was this her target?

Criston released her hand, and he was gone.

Sif focused on the asteroid, and she tried to sense what was different about it. She felt the people there, absorbed their feel. She expanded her awareness and tasted the unmistakable essence of Earth, the softer scents of the Jupiter and Mars colonies. Sif marked the distances.

Sol.

She fell back to her physical body and opened her eyes while reaching for the holographic controls to display the Sol System.

Criston didn't let her save him because he had to save her and humanity. He could not fulfill his destiny while alive.

Tears slid down her face as she marked the region to search.

* * * * *

Chapter Twelve: Skadi Lives

Navinad – The Wanderer

It was surreal to slip into the astral plane. Navinad didn't like it because it reminded him too much of the world of purple mists. He knew it was here, somewhere, some plane, some dimension. Would he be trapped there again? Could he escape on his own now that he was delving into the astral realms without his physical body? That was the danger, of course. By remembering it, by just thinking about it, he risked his subconscious taking him there.

The truth was not as solid in the astral realms. Some realms were pure thought, the shape and function of those places created from emotion and beliefs. Anything was possible in those realities, and a traveler could never be sure when he or she slipped into such a place. They were dangerous because they could trap the unwary. Those were dimensions where the truth couldn't form, and where people lost themselves among twisted paths of horror or ecstasy. Navinad wondered if that was where some people went when their physical form died. But he wasn't here to explore such distractions, though thinking about those possibilities made him wonder how real his world was.

Navinad needed guidance, and finding that was not a simple task. Those realms of horror and ecstasy would provide false guidance, providing no truth. Was he still trapped there in the realm of purple mists, his consciousness providing a dream of the real world, trying to escape from the horrors? What was real?

He stilled his thoughts and reined in his fears. Refocused.

He couldn't ask the nothing for help because the wrong beings might hear and answer him. He had nothing to draw him, no unique pattern or form to focus on. Someone or something had come to him in the purple mists, that someone had rescued him, but he had not seen them. That brief taste of their essence was not enough for him to use now to search for them. They had found him in that world of purple. It stood to reason that if he wanted to find them, he had to return to that hell. But even here in the astral realms, he felt the pain of the demon claws in his chest. He could hear Nasaraf laughing as he died, and he could not willingly take himself there.

Navinad's shadow did not follow him here. He was alone, casting about without guidance or companionship.

Memories: moving forward, slashing with his sword while trying to shield Skadi from a demon more powerful than Nasaraf. This jotun was ancient, powerful and some part of him knew this being. Navinad knew that alone he would die, but he could do what the Ice Princess could not. He could battle on the spiritual plane and, fighting together, they might have a chance. The ancient sorceress stood behind them both, lending her strength. Her power had grown immensely since he first fought for her, eons ago.

Skadi battled in the physical realm, while Navinad fought on the astral plane. The great jotun's attack was merciless across both realities. Together, they barely held. Beside them, Vili and a young warlock battled, pushing against the great jotun, trying to force it back across the threshold from whence it had come, trying to prevent it from coming into this world completely.

Navinad froze his thoughts. Was that the past or the future? A memory or a premonition? Hadn't Skadi died with the gunny above the Atlantic? Why wasn't she with the gunny?

Navinad mentally retraced his steps, pulled back. Perhaps he was slipping into a truthless realm, falling into the trap of his own hopes and fears.

"Even in your realm, the truth is not what you imagine," a voice whispered in Navinad's mind.

"Who are you?" Navinad asked. He wished to taste the essence of whatever had come to him, whether real or a figment of his imagination. It did not feel like a jotun.

"Our truth is shaded by our perceptions and experiences," the voice whispered. "Some facts are real. The way those facts are perceived and accepted can vary."

"What do you mean?" Navinad asked. If this was a real being, shouldn't he be able to understand more about it?

"The death of a person can be sad or glorious to a family member or victim, but the person's death is a fact. How it and the events leading up to it are perceived is a person's truth."

"Why tell me this?"

"You are not dead, and you are not yet alive."

Not yet alive? Navinad was pretty sure he wasn't dead unless his mind was still in the realm of purple mists, warping his reality.

"I need help. I need guidance," Navinad said.

"To help you is to deny you freedom," the voice whispered. "Help is a path you are set upon by others, chaining your obligations and expectations. Help can rob you of liberty. Your independence and self-determination should not be stolen from you. Do not ask me for help; I will not give it. You must find your own path, determine your own fate."

Navinad didn't like that answer but wasn't ready to argue.

"Guidance then?" Navinad asked.

"You have protected Skadi, but she and the Marines need more. Soon they will stand on the precipice of disaster, stare into the abyss, waver on the razor-sharp edge of victory or defeat. They may win their battle, but if the *Tyr* is not there afterward then the entire house of cards will collapse. The *Tyr* and *Sleipnir* will solidify that house, strengthen it and turn it into a mighty fortress. If they are lost, the house of cards will be swept away in the hurricane. Admiral Carpenter is the key. He must know his daughter lives. He must know that he is the only one who can save her. In doing so, he will defy the storm; he will become the storm. The alliance the gunnery sergeant is forging will become the storm that breaks the hurricane and shatters the cycle."

"Don't they die above the Atlantic?" Navinad asked. How could his memories be wrong?

"Their ship is destroyed above the Atlantic," the voice whispered, "that is truth. You cannot change this, but you died in the heart of the *Pankhurst*. You cannot change that, and yet here you are. The actual truth of reality is not always obvious. You must struggle through life making the best decisions you can based on poor data. You will stumble and fall, your truth will betray you. Your greatness will be defined by how you stand back up after you fall, how you adjust your reality to accept your new truth. Will you stand or will you grovel for mercy, for understanding, or for help? Some people gladly accept the chains of help and rejoice in their slavery."

"Some people legitimately need help," Navinad said.

"Sometimes. But sometimes people need guidance. Only they can make the changes they need in their life if they are to keep their freedom. You are correct that sometimes people need the heavy hand of help, a chain to pull them away from the edge of disaster, but some people become addicted to slavery and dependance. Life is difficult, and that gives it value. Help is a two-edged sword."

"Who are you?" Navinad asked trying to make sense of what it had told him.

"That will remain an unanswered question. I will not help you there."

"Demon or angel?"

"Do not chain me to absolutes. I exist as I am. Your perceptions and experience will influence your reality not mine. I will not twist your comprehension to my expectations by providing you with my judgment of existence. You must be free to explore your perceptions and reality. Right or wrong, I will not own that about you."

"Are you the one who rescued me from the purple mists?"

"You are never alone," the voice whispered. "In your darkest hour, you will never be alone, but only you can break the chains that bind you. We will be there to fight beside you, though you may not see us. We do not seek to hold the chains that bind you, nor should you seek to bind others. Skadi and the Wolf will need you to fight beside them. Humanity needs you to hold the line, or the circle will again complete. Stop asking for help and demand the right to walk alone. You will not grow stronger if you seek crutches."

Navinad felt his soul return to his body. Emotion poured through him and brought tears to his eyes.

Was this the same being that had rescued him from the world of purple mists? Navinad couldn't tell. A kaleidoscope of emotions swirled through his mind. Returning from the astral realms always filled him with intense feelings.

The *Pankhurst* had been a nightmare. When he had stepped aboard, he had known he was going to die. Victory or death. Navinad knew he was living on borrowed time. He should have died. His return, here and now, made no sense. The astral realms were not the reality he lived in. His perceptions were different there, and truth was not always absolute.

The vanhat claimed time had little meaning. They also claimed time was circular, but what did that mean? A circle went on and on. If it broke, it was not a circle. Would Navinad's actions complete or break the circle? Could he trust anyone?

Now he had answers. Not the help and guidance he had wanted, but he had something, more information, and his perceptions of the situation had been altered.

He wished he could put his faith in something or someone greater than himself, to say it was God's will and that he just was a simple servant. But that was also a crutch, surrendering his freedom to something he didn't fully understand.

Maybe he should ask the rabbi, seek to share his fears and doubts. But while the rabbi was a good man, he was just a man and as mired in fear, doubt, and false perceptions as Navinad. The rabbi could provide guidance, but that would be an unstable crutch built on the perceptions of someone as flawed as himself.

Although looking at a problem from different angles would help provide more clarity, the final decision rested with Navinad. Perhaps the rabbi could help with that?

Navinad shook his head. There were things he wasn't ready to reveal to others. He was dead, and right now, he wasn't sure if he would live again.

Long ago, he had watched events unfold light minutes away. He had watched himself from the safety of the future when he had known what was going to happen. He had known he would survive because he was there, watching.

What was real? What was memory? When time could change memories, what was time?

* * * * *

Chapter Thirteen: Endless Mile

Gunnery Sergeant Wolf Mathison, USMC

His body and mind insisted he was falling, but he was strapped tightly to the sled falling through the darkness. There was nothing around them, nothing that could be seen with the naked eye. Everyone and everything was strapped down so tight that moving was difficult. In Mathison's mind it was a recipe for disaster, with Erikoisjoukot, ODTs, and HKTs working together aboard Aesir stealth sleds. Their systems were now integrated. They could talk with each other, and everyone was identified as friendly, but despite numerous rehearsals, Mathison couldn't see it ending well.

Involving the different teams was a political decision, and if he wanted to bind the Alliance together, he had to start at the most basic level. They were all fighting for the human race. It would have been more efficient to designate a specific organization, but he had to get them working together, trusting each other, and the only certain way he knew to do that was to make them suffer, bleed, and die together. As senior commander, he didn't like it. Mathison despised politics, but in this, he had to pull them together. The fight for the survival of mankind was just beginning.

Winters and Levin remained aboard *Eagle*, along with Sif and Arthur. The only people he really needed were Commissar Feng, who claimed to know about INSEC systems, and himself, of course. He couldn't remain aboard *Eagle* twiddling his thumbs. One day, he might have to send others into danger while he sat back in operational control, but that wasn't today. Today, he did what proper leaders did; he led from the front.

"You awake, Gunny?" Stathis asked.

"No."

Mathison wanted to roll his eyes, but Stathis wouldn't be able to see it. It was tempting to ignore Stathis; he was on the other sled being piloted by Niels along with the HKTs Hakala and Grimkel. Mathison's sled was piloted by Skadi, with Feng and Evanoff nearby. If one sled were lost, the survivors would have a SCBI to help them crack the SOG network. If neither sled survived, then Plan B was somebody else's problem. Skadi and Niels assured them there was absolutely no way for the SOG to detect their communications, but Mathison regretted not ordering link silence.

They still had an hour before their target became visible.

"There's something I've been meaning to ask you," Stathis said, not taking the hint. "Shrek and I were just talking about those coordinates we keep finding, referencing that place near Quantico and General Becket. Looks close to where we finished the Endless Mile of Raider training."

Mathison had almost forgotten about the codes. Freya kept finding a string of letters in heavily encrypted SOG communications that read "SUN871009AB6390TZU." Mathison believed it was a reference to Sun Tzu, which had been the name of Becket's SCBI.

Major Alexander Becket had been Mathison's commanding officer when he left Earth so long ago. O9 could translate to the rank of general and "AB" in the middle of the numbers could mean "Alexander

Becket." The numbers might be grid coordinates, which placed them in Quantico, Virginia. Why such a code and reference would be found in SOG encryption algorithms made little sense.

"And?" Mathison asked.

"Were you the Corporal Mathison who broke all records doing the Endless Mile?"

"Yes. You mean nobody broke that record?"

"No, Gunny. But they didn't list your time."

The Endless Mile was the final test of Marine Raider training. Since Raider School was at Quantico, Virginia, they took trainees over the Potomac, almost a mile from the base and told them they could only use a single bridge to cross. That bridge was in Alexandria, and they timed trainees on how long it took them to get back to base. They were not allowed to hitchhike. They started near Goose Bay, and they ended in Lejeune Field. It was called the Endless Mile because on the map it was barely two miles away, but it was a "mile that never seemed to end." In reality, it was a little over fifty miles and a brutal race.

"I was fast," Mathison said.

"What was your time, gunny?" Stathis asked.

"My time had not been beat when you went through?" Mathison asked, surprised.

"No, Gunny. I asked an instructor, and he growled at me."

Mathison chuckled.

"No, Gunny, I mean, he really growled at me. Like he was some rabid animal. His name was Staff Sergeant Jones."

"Little red-headed guy?"

"You know him, Gunny?"

"Knew him," Mathison said. "Yeah. We went through Staff NCO School together. Yep. He would have growled. Good guy."

"So, what was your time?"

"Four hours," Mathison said.

"Four hours? How did you get fifty miles in four hours? They let you cheat?"

"I didn't cheat."

"But…"

"Do you remember the packing list? You remember the rules?"

"Jet pack wasn't on it, Gunny. It was fifty pounds of gear, thirty pounds of armor, and our rifle. They triple checked everything and weighed it. It was heavy and not conducive to sprinting."

"Correct. Raiders are supposed to be smart, clever, and resourceful."

"And tough, Gunny, tougher than nails, but running fifty miles in four hours? I didn't exactly run it and got a great score, but I didn't come close to breaking any records. People don't run twelve and a half miles an hour with a full load."

Stathis was good at math. Did he know it had been four hours before he asked or did Stathis's mind just work that fast?

"Did they tell you what you couldn't carry? Give you a weight limit on items?"

"No, Gunny. You didn't pack a boat, did you? They wouldn't have let you do that. Right?"

Why hadn't anyone else tried it? Mathison wondered if they had subtly changed the rules.

"You didn't ask Shrek?"

"Shrek won't say or doesn't know."

"Do you?" Mathison asked Freya.

"Yes. I know everything about you, but that knowledge is not common, and they have done an excellent job of maintaining that secret."

"Did you hijack a boat?" Stathis asked.

"That would break the rules. It was individual effort. Stealing a boat or getting someone to take me was on par with hitchhiking. I didn't do either of them."

"Then—"

"Don't you have more important things to think about? Quantico was probably one of the first places nuked."

"Why don't you tell me, Gunny?"

"Well—"

"Listen up," Skadi said on the team link. "We're about thirty minutes out. The asteroid will become visible in a minute. Be ready."

Finally. Eighteen hours was a long time to remain motionless on the sled, waiting to be detected and vaporized.

He zoomed in on the marker on his heads-up display and the rocky asteroid took shape. Garbage left over from the creation of the solar system, wreckage from an ancient star that had died eons ago and was flung out into the darkness. Far enough to be caught by Sol, but not close enough to be dragged into the solar system and merged into something larger. The asteroid was only three kilometers long, a lumpy ovoid encrusted in ice and rock. There was nothing visible to set it apart from the other rocky chunks floating around at distances further than their eyes could see. A desolate piece of junk floating out in the lonely depths of space.

"It will be awfully annoying if nobody is home," Stathis said.

"They're home," Mathison said. They had to be home. Nothing could go wrong. If it did, humanity would die. There was no viable Plan B. The Alliance had to crack the SOG's defenses in order to save it, and this INSEC base held a key, so it had to be captured. The base had to exist, and it had to be manned. There were too many damned requirements.

The asteroid looked like blackened swiss cheese, covered with craters, sharp, jagged edges, and dark pits. Mathison realized that three kilometers was a lot of space to search for a base that could be as small as a two-man listening post. It could take days or weeks to find the secret entrance, and Mathison wasn't sure they had days. The feeling in his gut told him they might already be out of time.

* * * * *

Chapter Fourteen: Secret Base

Lojtnant Skadi, VRAEC

Damn the SOG and their secrecy. The asteroid wasn't very big, just a piece of interstellar garbage, one of billions, maybe trillions, floating around Sol's Oort cloud, tenuously hanging onto Sol's gravity well, waiting to be thrown into the void and away from the Solar System with the slightest nudge.

Was Sif right? Was there a SOG base here?

The stealth drones made a pass and showed they had found something. Skadi almost let out a sigh of relief. Almost. Niels would have heard her.

Mathison, Stathis, Feng, Evanoff, Grimkel, and Hakala were standing around the sleds, weapons ready, while she and Niels directed the drones. She checked the screen and saw they had identified an imprint. Something unnatural had left a square "dent" in the surface.

"Freya might have the entrance," Mathison reported, surprising Skadi. She had forgotten the SCBIs also had access. She looked at the image. Red lines outlined the hatch. Skadi realized she had missed it. In retrospect, it was obvious though. It wasn't a hatch so much as a big rock that might have been cut in half and shaped to cover the hatch. It wasn't rectangular, but a rock shaped like that should have drifted off the surface unless it was attached to something, like the entrance.

Everyone was still leeching off the sled's power and air supply, which meant they were still connected in case they had to make a quick getaway.

"That's probably a shuttle port," Mathison said. "We need to find a smaller, less obvious entrance."

"Zen," Skadi said. Damn him.

"Mackie, this is Basilone," Winters said on the main link. As the mission commander, Mathison had assigned call sign names and he had chosen Marine Medal of Honor winners John Mackie and John Basilone.

"Go, Basilone."

"We're picking up another search team. Maybe about four light minutes out. A cruiser just jumped in and scanned a distant asteroid. We are watching our back trail, but if they jump they could be here any second. Probably vanhat."

"Copy that, Basilone." Mathison looked her way. No pressure.

"Paska," Niels said on a private link. "Coincidence?"

"Or they detected *Eagle's* transition," Skadi said.

A smaller rock lit up. The main hatch.

"Target the regular hatch," Mathison said.

"Let's go," Skadi said. "It isn't far. Rally point in Valhalla."

"Valhalla awaits," Niels said. "Bern's probably drinking all the mead."

"Zen," Skadi said.

"HKTs on point," Mathison said. This was their arena, and they were the experts on low or no gravity small unit combat. There was now an entire platoon aboard *Eagle*, all of them from her father's battlestar, but that didn't mean she trusted them and, obviously, neither did Mathison. Most of them were currently waiting on assault sleds aboard *Eagle*, ready to come to the rescue. Grimkel, the acting platoon commander, had been livid and had argued for hours, saying the HKTs should conduct the mission, but Mathison had insisted on bringing ODTs and Skadi and Niels, while Vili got to stay aboard *Eagle* and relax. Mathison was being foolish and setting them all up for failure by mixing the team like this.

Leaving Vili behind was good. She wouldn't have to worry about him and maybe he could keep *Eagle* safe from the HKTs and the other ODTs. But what was the gunnery sergeant thinking? Did he really think he could trust them?

Grimkel reached the hatch first and scanned it. For an HKT he seemed decent, leading from the front, and he seemed to like the gunnery sergeant, even if he was always growling and bitching about his commanding officer.

"This will be tough," Grimkel said. "The asteroid is facing toward deep space, and we have little rotation so it isn't picking up a lot of hard radiation, which means they probably have increased sensitivity."

"Won't there be random bursts?" Mathison asked.

"Not enough," Grimkel said as Hakala sprayed the cracks with nanogel, which Mathison's SCBI would be able to control.

"Do your AIs have this?" Grimkel said, looking at Mathison.

"Aye." Mathison looked around. The gel Hakala sprayed on bubbled and sank into the rock as she stuck a wire into the gel. In seconds, the nanite soup absorbed the wire and a window popped up in Skadi's view, showing the inside of the airlock. It wasn't big, and it was dark. Hakala slid a pair of small roachlike robots into the bubbling soup, and they were sucked through into the airlock.

She watched her sector and waited. Was anyone here, or had they recalled everyone from outside the system? For all they knew, they were standing in a field of concealed turrets. One wrong move, and the turrets would pop up, then Skadi and the others would have more holes than a net.

"We're in," Grimkel said as the rock rose, revealing a small corridor into the outpost.

* * * * *

Chapter Fifteen: Decoy

Chief Warrant Officer Diamond Winters, USMC

*E*agle* was running silent, which was all she did these days, it seemed. Winters felt like she lived in the CIC, the combat information center, and she wondered if a spouse knew their partner any better than she knew Levin, her acting executive officer. Hiding in the depths of space, with the walls, ceiling, and floor displays set to let her see around the ship, she felt exposed, like they would see her before they noticed the rest of the ship. A wireframe showed her the dimensions of *Eagle*, but the haunting emptiness of space was now a familiar friend. Unless it changed. Each transition changed the starscape around her in subtle ways, but that bothered her less now.

The plan should have been foolproof.

Nearly sixty Alliance ships had jumped in around the Sol System in case the enemy could see them transition through Shorr space. The other Alliance vessels were acting as decoys, jumping around the Oort cloud, almost at random, each ready to run at the first sign of an attacker coming after them. Nobody wanted to tangle with Sol Fleet, and almost everyone was confident they wouldn't leave their umbrella of missile platforms and sensors or risk Shorr space. If anyone else was out here, it was going to be another Alliance ship, some SOG vessel trying to get home, or, most likely, a vanhat ship that had seen them exit Shorr space.

There was no doubt the cruiser she was watching was no longer human, even though it was almost half an AU away. On the surface it looked like a SOG strike cruiser, a fast mover designed to pursue and harass other vessels. At this distance, it was unlikely they could have seen her, but nineteen hours ago *Eagle* had been there carefully watching the area. Were they following *Eagle* through Shorr space? That could be a major problem, especially if they discovered the automated mines and manufactories that were churning out d-bombs.

If that ship came here, she didn't like their chances. The strike cruiser was almost twice the mass of *Eagle* with twice the firepower.

"Drop fighters," Winters said, deciding.

The enemy wouldn't jump in, not find her, and leave. It was looking for something, an investigation she was sure would reveal the SOG base. If they launched fighters under power, then the SOG base might see them. Just dropping them from the bays would leave them in low-power mode, and they would be well away from *Eagle* where they could power up and attack.

"General quarters," Winters said.

"Have the troops remain in the shuttle bays, ma'am?" Levin asked.

"Yes," Winters said, though it could be a dangerous place if *Eagle* had to initiate hard maneuvers. "General quarters, prepare for hard maneuvers. How long until they're secure?"

"Not long," Britta Mani said. "If we have to maneuver hard, then they might not survive, Captain."

"We'll do a short jump behind the asteroid and dump them, then we'll engage."

"Do you think we can take on that strike cruiser, Captain?" Britta asked.

"You have a Plan B?" Winters asked.

"No, ma'am," Britta said.

"We have to keep the gunny and his team safe while they take apart that base," Winters said. "If that ship is following us, we'll have to fight it or else we abandon the gunny to his death."

"Zen," Britta said, but Winters heard something in her voice. "But—"

"Did you suddenly think of a Plan B?" Winters asked again, turning to look at her.

"No, Eversti."

"The gunny is the point of main effort. Everything we do is to support his efforts, if that means we die, we die. Is that clear? We will pull them away if we can, but I'm not optimistic about that."

"Yes, Eversti," Britta said. It was "Eversti" now, not captain. Why was Britta suddenly so formal?

Winters stared at Britta, who wouldn't meet her eyes. It was like the Vanir didn't care about anyone outside their ship unless it was their precious Home Fleet.

"The Vanir are cold-blooded bastards," Winters said to Blitzen.

"It is their culture. The Vanir seem paranoid because a damaged ship can be captured and that is anathema to them."

"But to be so willing to abandon their people?"

"I'm sure it would bother her later, but from what we've seen, the Vanir are borderline paranoid and extreme about security."

"Well, we won't leave the gunny and Stathis."

"Aye," Blitzen said.

"They have breached the asteroid," Britta reported. "Send the rest?"

"Wait for the gunny's command. How big is the base?" Winters checked the sensors. She wouldn't see the strike cruiser enter Shorr space. A transition of half an AU was less than a minute.

"Unknown," Britta said.

"Shorr space transition," Levin said.

"Power up fighters, launch missiles," Winters said. "Prepare for transition!"

"Two ships," Levin said.

Dammit. Where had the other ship come from? "They have reinforcements, then. Sound battle stations. Loose the dogs of war."

"We are the shield of our people," Britta said. "We are the defenders that none may pass."

"Zen," Winters said. This would be a tough fight, made tougher because she had to keep the enemy from noticing and responding to what Mathison was up to. What were they doing in the SOG base?

* * * * *

Chapter Sixteen: Base Assault

Gunnery Sergeant Wolf Mathison, USMC

The inner airlock hatch opened, and Mathison followed the HKTs into the darkened room. There were labeled racks on the wall for emergency space suits. Mathison counted six of them. Did that indicate the size of the crew?

"I'm picking up wireless," Freya reported. *"Compromising their network now."*

"Good," Mathison said as two HKTs approached the hatch, spray painting two cameras as they passed them. The paint was clear but would turn opaque at a command and block the cameras. For now, everyone was relying on their suit camouflage, but once the shooting started, that wouldn't be enough. The HKTs seemed content that the cameras couldn't see them. He didn't feel so confident, but Grimkel was the expert here.

Soft red lights provided minimal illumination, and Mathison remembered how much he hated the red lighting. It reminded him of the station where they had woken, where he had first encountered the threat that was destroying humanity.

Mathison crouched next to the airlock hatch. The lights could have been motion activated, but with their stealth activated, the motion

107

sensors couldn't pick up enough movement or else they were in low-power mode.

"Is it abandoned?" Mathison asked Freya.

The floor, ceilings, and walls were metal covered with a layer of nylon to work with Velcro shoes. They had obviously designed this area to never need gravity.

"I don't think so. Everything is well shielded. We're in a big faraday cage that blocks all radio signals in and out. It's not blocking Aesir links."

The HKTs used their nanogel spray and poked another spy cam through the door as the airlock cycled behind him.

"I've got hooks into the maintenance networks. I don't see any alerts. Doesn't seem extensive. I estimate a station population of about twenty, maybe more. Hard to say for sure, but not hundreds, if they're still here and alive. Not seeing any electronic disruptions, so everyone is probably still human."

Mathison relayed that to the others, and then said to Freya, *"See what you can do about shutting down external communications. When the balloon goes up, I want them silent."*

"Aye, Gunny."

The airlock door opened, and Feng, Evanoff, and Stathis poured in; it immediately shut behind them.

The HKTs stacked up against the next door, and the alarms began screeching.

"I didn't do it!" Stathis said as the HKTs opened the door to the base and bolted into the corridor. Mathison rushed up, ready to provide covering fire. It was a long corridor, and the lights were dim. The magnets in his elbows, then his feet, locked to the wall holding him in place.

"Mackie, this is Basilone," Winters said. "We have a problem. Hostile ships have arrived. I'm going to jump behind the asteroid, dump the rest of the HKTs, then we're going to dance."

"Copy, Basilone," Mathison said. "Give 'em hell."

"I'm picking up SOG traffic. They detected the incoming ships," Freya said. *"That's what the alarm is about, not us."*

"Be ready for pop-down turrets," Grimkel said.

"Basilone out," Winters said as Mathison updated everyone.

The corridor was longer than Mathison had expected, and the HKTs were almost at the other end. With Stathis beside him, Mathison pushed off and hurried down the corridor in the zero gravity, his weapon aimed upward where Freya highlighted pop-down turret slots. He stopped at the pressure hatch and watched what was going on around him so he could direct people as needed.

Behind him, Feng and Evanoff began placing small magnetic mines that would detonate if a turret dropped. The HKTs worked on the door, and he aimed down the corridor at the turrets until they were mined.

"Mackie, Mackie, this is Butler," a voice said. That would be the rest of the HKTs.

"Go, Butler," Mathison said.

"Basilone has dropped us off. We have your coordinates and are approaching," Skvadronmester Fornes said, the next senior HKT and leader of force Butler.

"Copy," Mathison said.

Skadi and Niels were the last through the airlock.

The corridor shook as something hit the asteroid.

A new alarm began screaming.

"And that is the repel boarders alarm," Freya said.

"They're on to us," Mathison yelled, glancing back in time to see the HKTs disappear through the hatch.

"Got a map," Freya said. *"Sending data to everyone. Highlighting the communications arrays, data storage, power, and command center. Crew appears to be about thirty."*

Mathison looked at the ghostly representation of the base. The first HKT team was already making a beeline for the command center, which was closest.

"Butler Sled Three just got hit by something."

The lower half of his vision, where it showed the health and status of his unit, showed a line of names flashing red. Eight HKTs were dead. *"Sleds One and Two are down. HKTs are moving to the airlock. I've disabled internal gravity; there wasn't much."*

Mathison was about to say something when another line went red. Sled Four. Half of his reinforcements were gone.

"Butler Sled Four is gone. Station weapons are coming online. They have missile launchers and railguns. I am blocking any outbound transmissions."

Weapons fire erupted ahead of him as Grimkel and Hakala encountered resistance. They would have to deal with it. Mathison felt the entire mission falling apart. His allied forces were about to be outnumbered, outgunned, and trapped between two enemies.

"Butler, Butler! Get under cover," Winters said. "I have enemy missiles targeting your landing zone."

The HKTs were under his command, following him. They were his responsibility, but all he could do was listen.

"Zen," Fornes said, sounding too calm. It was the calm of someone facing their death.

"Mackie, this is Basilone," Winters said and Mathison heard pain there. "Be advised I have incoming drop pods from the vanhat. Their acceleration tells me they aren't human. You're about to have company."

"Copy, Basilone."

"I'm launching a pair of *Cobra*-class d-bombs. Sending detonation codes to Freya if you need them, and *Eagle* doesn't survive."

The Cobra d-bombs were missiles with a limited computer brain, an Inkeri field for protection, and the ability to hold position until called upon.

"Copy Basilone," Mathison said. Grimkel and Hakala had ducked back behind the corner. Hakala fired a grenade then shot around the corner when it exploded.

"Freya, first priority is to prevent any outbound communications, then see if you can take over the station weapons and assist Eagle.*"*

Hard decisions that would cost people their lives.

"Aye, Gunny."

Stathis stood beside Mathison, waiting for instructions. Mathison waved Feng and Evanoff forward as more weapons fire erupted ahead of him.

With his see-through vision on the heads-up display, he saw Fornes stuff four people into the airlock while he remained outside.

He felt the asteroid shake again as missiles slammed into it. One of Fornes' people flashed red, but Fornes survived. The four HKTs rushed out of the airlock, and it cycled again to let Fornes and his last two HKTs in. Ahead of him, Mathison saw Grimkel and Hakala engaged with several indistinct red indicators, an unknown force, but they were pushing hard. Skadi and Niels started down another corridor, which appeared to be living quarters. Stathis remained next to Mathison and Feng while Evanoff followed the HKTs toward the command center.

The first four HKTs caught up to them as Fornes and his last two HKTs began cycling through the airlock. Mathison sent two to reinforce Grimkel and Hakala and two to reinforce Skadi.

More of the base revealed itself in Mathison's display, and he located the shuttle bay. It didn't look very big. If most of the crew were administrative, then they should be able to capture it, but the incoming vanhat forces would complicate things.

"Moving to secure the data center," Feng reported, and Mathison watched the commissar break away and start down another corridor.

"Copy. Stathis, watch the hatch. We're going to have company."

"Should we deactivate the limpet mines, so the turrets don't get blasted when they open?"

There would be no more HKTs coming in… "Do it."

The asteroid shook again under the impact of more missiles. More red markers appeared, showing five drop pods targeting the airlock. Telemetry from *Eagle* showing him what was going on. Unfortunately, it didn't show him what *Eagle* was up against or doing.

"Skadi, you and Niels get to the shuttle bay."

If they found it, the vanhat might try to come in that way.

"Zen."

Skadi took off with Niels right behind her.

* * * * *

Chapter Seventeen: Space Battle

Chief Warrant Officer Diamond Winters, USMC

A minor maneuver slipped *Eagle* out of the path of the incoming railgun and blazer fire as *Eagle* fired back, raking the strike cruiser from aft to stern. Flashes of light and plumes of fire showed the hull had been breached, but that didn't slow the enemy ship. SOGS *Krasnyy Kulak*, translated as SOGS *Red Fist*, was etched onto the hull. SOGS *Ruchnaya Rezaka, Hand Cut*, was the other. *Eagle's* databanks listed both as part of the Zhukov defense force, and they were trying to get close to *Eagle*. They were close enough to use transition disrupters to make sure she couldn't slip into Shorr space. This was going to be a fight to the death.

Winters felt *Eagle* shudder as a blazer round slammed into it.

"Minor," Levin said as Winters lined up another shot and ducked again as another burst of rail shot zipped past.

A d-bomb missile exploded before it could get close enough, a victim of the *Fist's* missile defenses.

"Getting a communication link request from the *Fist*," Levin said.

"What?" *Eagle* sideslipped again and answered with another blazer burst that ripped through the *Cut* with no noticeable effect. "Open it."

"*Eagle*," a deep voice said with a thick Russian accent, "your fate is sealed. Surrender now, and you will be not razrushennyy."

Winters and Levin stared at each other.

"A human?"

Something slammed into *Eagle*, another blazer shot. Damn. Was distraction the goal?

"Who is this?" Winters asked, vowing to concentrate more on the battle.

"I am Captain Ragar. You are ordered to surrender."

"Somehow I don't think you are human," Winters said. "Let's not play games."

"Very untrue. We are allied for the greater good. Join us or die. Humanity will survive if we submit. The new gods will let us live if we serve them."

Winters stitched the *Fist* with another burst.

"It just lost a drive," Britta reported.

She sent another burst from *Eagle*, trying to cripple them.

"No joy," Britta reported.

"Evolve or die," Ragar said.

"End link," Winters said as another round slammed them. She didn't need the distraction. Surrender just wasn't an option.

"That was the port shuttle bay," Levin reported. "We just lost the auxiliary sleds."

A pair of missiles came at *Eagle*, flashes of light, but Levin was paying attention, and the missiles erupted when they hit a burst of pellets from the point defenses.

Blazer fire raked *Eagle*. Winters felt it.

Levin swore. "Port engines damaged. Integrity breached. Portside aft. Maneuverability will suffer forty percent."

Which could be fatal.

Another volley, and *Eagle* almost didn't slip out of the way in time. Winters could feel the ship becoming sluggish. *Eagle* couldn't handle them both, and there was no escape. Winters would not admit Britta might have been right. They had to take the chance. Maybe they could draw the enemy away from Mathison and his mission.

A volley of missiles from the secret base shot into space, targeting the *Fist*.

So much for the enemy not noticing the SOG base.

Surprised, the *Fist* veered away from the asteroid and right into *Eagle's* fire. Pieces of the *Fist* broke off, and the ship spun out of control.

"Red Fist *appears dead in space,*" Blitzen reported.

Winters turned *Eagle* toward the *Cut*.

Rail shot spewed out of the asteroid in a stream aimed toward the *Cut,* and it disappeared in a flash, transitioning to Shorr space.

Levin looked up from his console. "Did it just retreat?"

"Probably to get reinforcements," Winters said and opened a link to Mathison. "Mackie, this is Basilone. Thanks for the help. One enemy dead, the other retreated. Reinforcements could arrive any minute. I'm hoping you have a happy story to tell me, Gunny"

"Negative, Basilone. We are being hit from two angles—SOG inside, monsters outside. We are outnumbered and suffering heavy casualities. Not the best day in my Marine Corps."

"Semper Fi."

So now the vanhat knew about the SOG base, *and* they had orja on the ground.

* * * * *

Chapter Eighteen: Defending

Lojtnant Skadi, VRAEC

Weapons fire chewed up the doorway, splintering stone and throwing sparks and debris everywhere. The SOG troopers had at least one automatic weapon, and they had gained fire superiority, forcing Skadi and Niels to take cover. Only one could fire, but the SOG troopers had at least two shooters, and they were behind cover.

Niels signaled and prepped a grenade.

Skadi nodded, and he hurled it at the far wall so it would bounce into the SOG position without him exposing himself.

The grenade went off, and Skadi charged around the corner, firing bursts at anything that wasn't a blank wall. Niels followed her, shooting where she wasn't.

An armored SOG trooper stood and fired. Skadi hit him with rounds from her blazer. The trooper fell back, half his head missing. Skadi moved up and looked over the barricade at the other bodies. "Clear."

The health indicator for Niels was red. She spun and watched his body slowly bounce off the ceiling. A blazer round had caught him on the right side of the neck, burning part of his skull and killing him instantly.

Skadi froze and stared at his corpse. *Not Niels. Not now.*

She spun toward the hatch the troopers had been guarding, blinking to clear the blurriness from her eyes. Just beyond the hatch was the shuttle bay. It looked to be big enough to hold a small ship and a few shuttles, but she couldn't see what was in there.

Mission first, grief later.

She opened the hatch and saw a SOG courier and a small shuttle. Both appeared to be powered off and locked down. She scanned the area, but there was no movement.

"Gunny, this is Skadi. Shuttle bay appears empty. No SOG, no monsters. Niels is down and I can't clear the shuttle bay alone."

"Copy. Sending Stathis to help. I'm sorry about Niels."

"Zen." She would remember Niels later. Now, she had to ignore the emptiness in her heart.

She looked at the bodies and saw they were SOG INSEC special operations. They wore patches with a wolf head in a wreath. There were five gold stars below the wolf's head and Chinese writing above. Lang troops. They had a history dating back to before the Governance. They were supposedly some of the best.

Skadi kicked a body as she looked at the shuttle. The outer hatch was closed and the shuttle bay was still pressurized. Seconds later, Stathis arrived. He remained at the hatch while Skadi moved forward and checked the shuttle, then the courier.

How would she tell Vili?

Death in war was sudden, she knew that, but deep down it was hard to comprehend how a person could be living, breathing, and joking beside them, and then, without warning, they were dead. There should be a lead-up to their death, a chance to say goodbye. More memories, not like a candle snuffed out by the wind or a bird flying through the clouds and then suddenly dead. Gone.

She didn't even get to see Niels fall. And he had been so close behind her.

* * * * *

Chapter Nineteen: Monsters

Gunnery Sergeant Wolf Mathison, USMC

The creature had easily ripped apart the outer and inner hatch. Most of the ceiling turrets were destroyed and shooting down the tunnel wasn't as easy as that. Mathison didn't know how many were outside, but this one was one trying to get in right now. It was large and was struggling to get into the tunnel. It was easy to hit, but it was covered in overlapping plates that seemed to deflect blazer rounds.

Air streamed out of the station, trying to push the creature out, but it kept coming despite the barrage of blazer rounds slamming into it. It was firing a projectile weapon with one hand and sank the claws of the other into the floor or wall, dragging itself toward Mathison and two HKTs.

The creature fired again, and rock shattered off the wall behind them.

One of the HKTs, a woman named Skold, tried another grenade. It flew down the corridor and got sucked into the air buffeting around the creature's body. Mathison leaned away and felt the grenade explode through the walls. He looked and saw the creature slowly being pushed back out by the wind, then it twitched and started crawling forward again.

"Paska."

"It's supposed to die now," said Lovas, the other HKT. "Does it not understand how this works?"

"How do we stop it?" Skold asked.

"If I had to guess?" Mathison said. "Wait until it gets closer and our Inkeri generators will turn it into a lump of broken flesh. It appears made for close-quarter assaults but is unlikely to be Inkeri proof."

"Too big," Lovas said. "They have not found the shuttle bay, yes?"

"Not so far," Mathison said. His view let him see an outline for Stathis and Skadi. Skadi was moving around a courier and neither appeared to be firing.

"Might as well save ammunition then," Skold said. "I hope you're right, Gunnery Sergeant."

Mathison shrugged, his pauldrons flapping like a bird.

"I'm here with you," Mathison said. "Want me to go stab it with my Ka-Bar to prove it?"

"I like you, Gunnery Sergeant," Lovas said. "Will you show us how it is done?"

Mathison peeked around the corner and a projectile almost took his head off.

"Don't even think about it," Freya said. *"Your logic is sound, but you'd be rushing that rock gun, and that could be fatal."*

"Thank you for your vote of confidence." Then he said to Skold and Lovas, "We'll wait for it to get closer."

"Zen," they said together.

"I can extend the new Inkeri field about eight meters."

"Let it get within four," Mathison said.

Grimkel and Hakala had been stopped cold by several enemy soldiers behind barricades near the command center and even Feng had run into stiff resistance. It was going to take a few minutes.

"*Copy,*" Freya said. *"I need your override."*

"What?" Mathison asked and in the distance of his display, as if he could see through the walls, he saw three ships maneuvering hard. One was *Eagle*.

"Look at a target and tap your forefinger and thumb together for missiles, middle finger and thumb for rail gun."

"Why don't you do it?"

"SCBI protocols. There could be humans aboard those ships. We still haven't figured out if transformed people are aliens or still human. New data indicates there might be humans aboard. We might not be able to fire without a higher authority to modify the coding."

Mathison picked one of the enemy ships and tapped his forefinger and thumb several times. Icons showed missiles launching from somewhere else on the asteroid.

"SOG missile array bunker," Freya explained. *"We have control of some systems.* Eagle *needs help."*

Mathison tapped his middle finger and thumb and watched a spread of rail shot fly out in a stream toward the original ship which was now turning toward the asteroid.

The ship disappeared.

"Mackie, this is Basilone. Thanks for the help. One enemy dead, the other retreated. Reinforcements could arrive any minute. I'm hoping you have a happy story to tell me, Gunny."

Technology made it too easy to kill sometimes.

"Negative, Basilone. We are being hit from two angles. SOG inside, monsters outside."

"The creature is six meters away," Freya reported.

"How much time do we have, Basilone?" Mathison asked.

"Seconds, minutes, days?" Winters said. "I don't know, Mackie, but I'm not liking the possibilities."

"Four meters."

"Pulse it." Mathison leaned over and fired. Blazer rounds sliced right through the monster's plates, super heating flesh and causing it to explode. Mathison placed several rounds into the creature's weapon for good measure as the HKTs followed his lead, leaned over, and fired.

The creature stopped moving.

"Is it dead?" Lovas asked.

"Our weapons are piercing it," Skold said. "The Inkeri?"

"Ha," Lovas said. "Like a big butt plug, the others behind will be slowed."

"I didn't need that imagery," Skold said.

"Shuttle bay is clear," Skadi reported. There was no emotion in her voice.

"Copy," Mathison said.

Mathison saw the creature jerk and knew it wasn't the atmosphere pushing it out. Then something started pushing the corpse forward.

"Paska-lounas!" Skold said.

"There were five pods," Lovas said. "How many do you think there are?"

"More than enough," Mathison said, watching the corpse move closer. How big were the pods?

"Good news, bad news."

"Bad news first," Mathison said.

"I've penetrated their system, shut down the self-destructs, and found a way we might get to Earth."

"That's the bad news?"

"Well, Earth is not where we want to go."

"It's a start."

"Remember, SOG military control is on the Moon. We want to go there, not Earth. Earth is where they send undesirables."

"How is that bad?"

"You can't walk to the Moon."

"There has to be a way to get there from Earth."

"Sure, but if I understand this data, they make it hard to leave Earth. Most people on Earth live underground. The SOG has mastered propaganda. All real industry and SOG infrastructure has moved to the Moon. Getting to Earth is like sneaking into prison. We have some access because of all the protocols and defenses they have in place to keep people from Earth on Earth. There are numerous INSEC facilities there."

"Anything else?"

"There is a courier that is programmed for use. We may have to use that."

"Why?"

"The courier has specialized codes to bypass certain check points, has specific transition coordinates preprogrammed, and will be tolerated by Earth defenses."

"Couldn't we copy that to Eagle or Tera?"

"Maybe, but we'd arrive under the guns and if they don't recognize the ship, they'll probably start firing. Visual recognition will also be used."

"Work on it."

The creature's body reached the edge of the corridor, but the hatch stopped it, temporarily blocking the hatch so the atmosphere stopped escaping.

"*The other creature is within the Inkeri field,*" Freya reported. "*If it is using supernatural strength, it might have just lost it.*"

"We'll wait and see." Mathison waited for the body to move again.

"Data center is secure," Feng reported.

Minutes later, Grimkel reported the command center was under his control and HKTs were sweeping the less critical areas to make sure they were clear.

Except the monsters outside.

"*Interesting,*" Freya said.

"*What?*"

"*What do you make of this bit of code: FRO6WMYA=SUN871009AB6390TZU?*"

"Something now precedes the sequence with Sun Tzu," Mathison said. "Freya is at the beginning and end. The O6 makes no sense—Colonel? The WM could be me or a Woman Marine."

"*I have found it several places. It is newer code as well.*"

"Has to be some fluke."

"*Statistically the chances are extremely remote.*"

"I'm not a colonel. Maybe E-6? I got demoted to staff sergeant?"

"*That is more likely than being promoted,*" Freya said.

"Stuff it."

"Mackie, this is Basilone, stand by. I'm going to clean off the surface with a low yield DP-bomb."

"Copy that Basilone," Mathison said. The DP d-bombs were dual purpose, a d-bomb with a high explosive charge that would disrupt monsters and allow them to be blown up. Whether they could make smaller versions for grenades and mortars was a question being worked on by the eggheads. After the pulse, the shrapnel should be lethal.

"Impact in three-two-one—"

Mathison felt the impact, and his screens flickered.

"Clean hit, Mackie. Round was off set. You okay?"

Mathison's teeth ached as he looked at both HKTs. They gave him a thumbs up. "Affirmative, Basilone. We survived."

"Copy, Mackie, I see no movement topside."

Mathison stared at the corpse. It wasn't moving anymore.

"Confirm, Basilone, no movement groundside so far. Will advise if that changes."

"Copy, Mackie, please hurry. Basilone out."

"Copy, Basilone. We're trying to. Mackie out." *"So, what do you have?"*

Freya didn't sound thrilled. *"In theory, we can use the courier. It has enough room for six people, but our window is closing."*

Which wasn't enough to storm the Moon. Damn.

Mathison changed his channel. "Basilone, this is Mackie. We might have a way to Earth using the courier, but it can only take six people."

"Copy Mackie. You have a manifest?"

"Me, Stathis, Sif, and Feng. Volunteers only. I would prefer you and Levin stay here and give us an option for Plan B."

And if he and Stathis died, maybe Winters and Levin would survive. Though maybe he should leave Stathis. The mission would require finesse not brute force. Though Stathis had walked through a SOG ship once without giving himself away.

"Anyone else?"

"Skadi and Vili," Mathison said with reservation. Would they be a liability or a help? They knew more about operating in SOG space than anyone other than Feng and Sif, but Skadi had just lost Niels.

Would that destabilize her and Vili? Damn. ODTs might be a good idea, but he didn't know them that well.

"Copy that," Winters said. "I'll send Sif and Vili down with as much gear as we can send. Basilone out."

"Mackie out."

Now wasn't the time to stay behind.

"Valhalla awaits."

The Aesir were rubbing off on him.

* * * * *

Chapter Twenty: Check Point One

Kapten Sif – VRAEC, Nakija Musta Toiminnot

The hatch opened, and Sif guided the courier into space. It handled well and had one of the newer control rigs, bleeding edge for SOG. It had taken Sif a few minutes to get used to it, but it wasn't nearly as complex as a stealth ship.

"Godspeed," Winters said.

"Thank you, Godspeed to you, too," Sif said. Hopefully that was the traditional response.

The SOG courier was cramped, even for a small person like Sif. It didn't help that every square centimeter was crammed full of gear. The first part, which would be tricky on a good day, was to transition into a very specific location between the orbits of Earth and Mars, right under the watchful eye of a top-secret EXSEC battle station with what might be a crew of six. If the crew of that station was in the least bit suspicious, they would vaporize the unarmed courier.

She received the coordinates and vector from Mathison and was plugging them in when an alarm went off: ships transitioning in from Shorr space.

Sif knew, with every fiber of her being, they were not friendly ships. She pasted the coordinate string without bothering to verify it and triggered the transition button. She gave no warning and the courier slid into Shorr space before the incoming ships could jam the area and prevent them from escaping.

Shorr space engulfed them and just as quickly spat them back out.

Sif's heart was hammering as she checked the sensors. A thousand kilometers out was the bulk of a manned battle station. An incoming laser link found them.

"Identify or be fired upon!" a voice said.

"Courier Zeta-zeta-twelve," Feng said from the co-pilot seat beside her, recovering quickly from the rapid transition. "I am authorized and Central Command is notified."

Sif closed her eyes and reached out with her senses. She felt the station and the alarm from the officer in command. It took effort to calm him down.

"Standby," the voice said.

Feng muted the link. "Hold position. You are an easy target, and they will be less alarmed."

"Can you confirm you are not infected?" the voice asked.

Sif looked at Mathison, who looked at Feng.

"This is Colonel Commissar Feng. Per protocols I have verified everyone is sane and unchanged. I will transmit my ID and authorization code."

Feng had authorization?

"Standby." The voice sounded calmer now.

"You have that authority?" Mathison asked.

Feng looked surprised. "You doubt I am a commissar? Have I not been honest and informed you I am also more than that?"

"But you are a commissar aboard a top-secret ship approaching a top-secret station." Sif saw Mathison had a sidearm drawn. "What else are you?"

"My authorization will be sufficient," Feng said, turning back to the console. "My position has some responsibility with EXSEC and INSEC and my credentials exist in many systems because my chain of command is fluid."

"And now everyone will know you are here." Sif said. How could a chain of command be fluid?

"The Governance, especially in Sol, is extremely compartmentalized. Organizations hoard information, and few share. It will take time for people to realize I am here. Per protocol, I should file a report and announce my presence, however my mandate from being aboard the *Tupolev* allows me to dispense with some protocols."

"What about trust?" Mathison asked, and Feng shrugged without concern.

"I have not betrayed you. The survival of humanity is my intent. Those who stand in the way of that will be dealt with harshly."

Sif felt the watch officer relax as he authenticated the codes.

"Clearance accepted," the voice said. "Transmitting a path for you. Do not deviate."

"Thank you," Feng said.

"Nobody is going to identify themselves?" Stathis asked.

"Nobody wants to," Feng said. "When you live in the shadows, you usually prefer nobody knows your identity."

Sif received the new instructions and set a course. Two days to Earth. Forty-eight hours provided a lot of opportunity for things to go wrong, and she knew they would track the courier with a minimum of ten weapons platforms every centimeter of the way. At any minute, they could decide the courier was intruding and open fire.

*****

Chapter Twenty-One:
Eagle's Escape

Chief Warrant Officer Diamond Winters, USMC

The SOG courier disappeared the second Winters saw the identifiers, two strike cruisers and two larger ships. It took her a minute to identify the other ships, but eventually the bulbous hulls made sense if they were cargo ships.

"I'm picking up a lot of power from those big cargo ships, Captain," Levin said. "They aren't hauling cargo. Maybe extra guns, missiles, and engines, though. And they see us."

"Standby for emergency transi—"

Eagle slid into and then almost immediately out of Shorr space.

"—tion" Winters finished, looking around.

Britta looked up at Winters and raised an eyebrow, indicating disapproval. Waiting to warn people was giving the enemy a chance to do something. Her SCBI clearly considered survival more important than protocol.

"Deal with it." Winters looked around. The stars hadn't changed position much. *Eagle* hadn't left the Sol System area, but this deep in space it would take signals days to reach a destination on the other side of the solar system. The SOG was closer and her view of events in Sol was just hours old.

"Incoming transition," Levin said. "Two strike cruisers and two merchant ships."

"Not possible," Britta said. "They can't have followed us."

"Emergency transition," Winters said and ordered Blitzen to take them elsewhere before the enemy could bring their transition disruptors into play.

"It couldn't have been them," Britta said. "You can't track people through Shorr space."

"Incoming transition," Levin said again. Winters felt the warmth within the bridge increase. "Two strike cruisers and two merchant ships."

"The engine damage has caused feedback and is disrupting the generators. We can't transition again so quickly, the charge is too high," Blitzen reported. *"We'll blow the ship apart, and we need to dump heat."*

"Evasive maneuvers," Winters said. "Start running. Send a mayday to where the fleet is."

"It could take days to get to them, Captain," Britta said as Winters checked the heat levels. Yes, they were high enough to be a problem. It was not something she would have considered as a shuttle pilot, but in space, there was no place for the heat to go; it didn't just drift away from the spaceship.

"We might be running for days then," Winters said. "Sound the high-gravity maneuver alarm. People have twenty seconds and then we go to 5 G."

"That is too high, Captain. Maybe less would be better," Britta said.

"Stop with the negativity or you have fifteen seconds to leave the bridge," Winters said. "I need solutions, not excuses."

"Aye, Captain," Britta said and shut up.

It was going to get a lot worse before it got better. Winters didn't need Blitzen to tell her that. Sure, they could sustain high gravities for short times, but she was going to play a long game and people would complain about it soon enough. Five Gs might be the lower end of what she had to do, but *Eagle* had to survive. She couldn't use Shorr space to escape so she had to do everything in here, in this dimension. Damn them. This was going to take a lot of time.

* * * * *

Chapter Twenty-Two: Niels' Death

Lojtnant Skadi, VRAEC

The courier was small, six seats in three rows. In the front two seats were Sif and Feng, behind them were Mathison and Stathis, and sitting in the back, Skadi and Vili.

According to the course data, it would take them to Earth. They would enter the atmosphere over the American West Coast, cross the continent and the Atlantic Ocean, and then into Geneva to an SOG transit station. At least they weren't going to Asia. It would be difficult for them to fit in there.

Every centimeter of their route was under the watchful eyes of SOG battle systems and designed to give the SOG the most amount of time to analyze and scan them for deviant behavior. It was not a straight and efficient path, and it would take them through different SOG agencies, and each would have to authorize them. Crossing the Atlantic they would pass through an agency called the Ministry of Harmony. Why such an agency needed to approve them, she didn't know. Skadi had never heard of such an agency, but then the SOG liked to create new agencies almost daily.

They had quickly loaded the courier, and there wasn't much room left to move. Everything was fastened down, and with nothing to do,

Skadi couldn't take her mind off Niels. In the rush to load the courier and escape the base, Skadi hadn't had a chance to speak with Vili.

Skadi opened a link. "I'm sorry." What else was there to say?

"I know. Me, too. First Bern, now Niels. We have lost so many kaveri and siskos. Now, we are the last two. We knew our fate when we put on our armor and earned our axe and sword. What else can we do?"

"Find a more peaceful profession."

"For sure. But when the HKTs turned on us, I knew I would not be able to lay down my axe. I'm going to live and die an Aesir. Brother should not turn on brother; kaveri and siskos do not do that. Kinsmen to kinsmen should be true."

"Zen," Skadi said. "So, what do we do?"

"We do what is right, Skadi."

"We follow the Marines?"

"No. We follow our hearts. The Marines are people, but I think they are doing their best for everyone, not just themselves. They have the clearest vision right now."

"Because they have no people, and they are looking at humanity as their people?"

"Maybe, but maybe it's just the kind of people they are, the way they were raised, the thing that drew them to their Marine Corps. Even my little buddy, he sounds and acts stupid sometimes, but he is not. I must wonder what the United States was like before the fall. They won't be able to lay down their weapons either. None of them. They will die fighting for what they believe in. We can do no less."

"Zen."

Skadi locked her eyes on Mathison. He looked to be sleeping, but it was hard to tell.

"What do you think our chances are of surviving this?" Vili asked.

"Slim to none."

"Zen. Earth will be our Ragnarök. I always wanted to visit Earth."

"Valhalla awaits."

"Been waiting for a while. I'm tired, Skadi."

"Me, too. Shouldn't be long now."

"I owe you, Bern, and Niels so much."

"Zen. First round of mead in Valhalla is on you," Skadi said. She didn't trust her voice any further.

"If Bern has left us any, zen."

* * * * *

Chapter Twenty-Three: Stern Chase

Chief Warrant Officer Diamond Winters, USMC

Gravity pushed her back in her seat. She hurt, and even breathing was difficult. After an hour, it was nearly unbearable. Eight hours later, Winters couldn't even cry. Her vision was blurred and talking was almost impossible. The only thing that kept her sane was talking with Blitzen. Everyone was in their battle armor, and the ship was depressurized. If people couldn't use voice commands to do something, it would not happen.

There were now five ships pursuing them. Two cruisers, a destroyer, and two cargo ships. Fortunately, the cargo ships had fallen back. The aliens couldn't use enough of their cross-dimensional energy to reinforce the basic structure of the ships and under heavy acceleration the ships were starting to break apart. Which meant they were not all powerful. A minor consolation.

Which just left the warships. Cruisers and destroyers. The only reason they had not caught up was because *Eagle* could maintain a relatively straight course and fire packets of rail shot behind them. Anything following them too closely would end up eating high-velocity pellets that could rip apart their ship. It was a game Levin was playing, forcing them to change course away from *Eagle* and losing distance in the process. They still had superior acceleration and could reach speeds that would turn humans to jelly, but they couldn't go in a straight line, and they had to reduce their speed or rip themselves apart to dodge *Eagle's* fire. They were not indestructible and even their insane ability to accelerate had limits.

"How much longer?" Britta asked.

"Can we transition?" Winters asked.

"One transition," Britta said.

"We need two. I really want three," Winters said. Britta groaned.

Winters knew Britta couldn't argue anymore. They were out of options. *Eagle* made a minor course change when a destroyer fired, and she felt it in all her internal organs. The vanhat were slowly gaining, but it would take them a lot of time. Winters didn't want to jump yet. Despite the pain, she couldn't ask for a better situation. A jump now might allow the vanhat to get closer, but it could just as easily put more distance between them. She didn't want to change things yet because there was no guarantee any change would be beneficial.

Robots were attempting to repair the damage, but the increased gravity was slowing them down.

"Give me solutions," Winters said.

"Zen," Britta said, which told Winters that Britta didn't have any. She had been a Valkyrie commander, and not for the first time, Winters wished the Vanir had more knowledge and initiative.

"Blitzen, analyze the patterns. When they follow us through Shorr space, is there anything we can extrapolate, any idea how they do it, how accurate can they get?"

"Will do. They arrive in a group, indicating coordination between ships, but they have randomly appeared at various distances. We saw them transition into the upper atmosphere of Zhukov, so they display better control of transitions than we can manage."

"Give me a guesstimate."

"They can estimate a general area, but I don't think they can transition closer than what they have. Not that they won't get lucky."

"What are our chances of transitioning and putting more distance between us?"

"Over ninety percent."

Damned good odds. With no certainties right now she was tempted, but what if Blitzen was wrong? *Eagle* needed more time. Even though she wanted to stop, to decrease the acceleration, she knew that if the enemy could do anything to change the situation to their favor they would. Ten percent of a bad outcome sounded good, but the science was not fully understood, and Blitzen could be wrong. Any errors could lead to disaster. They were the prey. The hunters could make many mistakes, but she wasn't allowed one.

"Here's the plan," Winters said on the main link. "We're going to transition to within a thirty-minute transmission of the Alliance Fleet. Our pursuers shouldn't be able to detect them. You'll send a transmission with the coordinates for a jump that we'll make as soon as we can. Include what's following us and ask for assistance. Give them time to get there ahead of us, and let's hope they can. Let's ambush these bastards and scrape them off our tail."

"Zen." Britta closed the link.

Eagle changed course again, and Winters sobbed. It would be easy to slow down, just a little, but that could be fatal. Hopefully, the others didn't hear her pain because of her helmet.

"I'm glad you're in command," Levin said through a mental, SCBI-managed link. It was easier than talking, but it made Levin sound like everything was fine, like he wasn't suffering. Was he? *"Anybody else would have wimped out."*

"How are the troops?" Winters asked.

"Suffering, but no fatalities," Levin replied. *"They sound like Britta, though, asking if we could slow down a little. I just tell them to suck it up; the captain is napping, and I don't want to wake her."*

It hurt to laugh. *"How did they take that?"*

"Shuts them up, ma'am. They have big egos. I haven't heard any complaints in about thirty minutes."

"Nice. They believe you?"

"Maybe, ma'am. They don't have a choice. I know I'm going to be sore everywhere. Without these nanites we'd be dead, either from gravity stress or the bastards behind us."

"Aye. I wish I could sleep."

"Yes, ma'am. Me, too."

Winters took a long, ragged breath. Was that Levin's attempt to encourage her or toughen her up? She couldn't slow down, no matter how much she wanted to, because that would mean death. People suffering was better than people dying.

At current speeds, it would take the enemy at least an hour to get close enough to be dangerous. She would wait until the last minute if she could.

With the link closed, nobody could hear her cry.

An alarm went off, indicating another ship was exiting Shorr space. It appeared among the cruisers behind them. A battle cruiser.

"That's the *Pankhurst*," Levin said as the identification flashed on the screen. "How did it do that?"

"We can't go much faster. Prepare for transition."

"Incoming transmission."

"Bridge link, listen only," Winters said, knowing she was making a mistake.

"I can taste your souls," a familiar voice whispered to them through the speakers. "I'm coming for you. We will dance for your death. We have done this before. I can taste your suffering, and I savor it. The longer this goes on, the more pleasure I derive. We have unfinished business with you and the tribes. The circle will complete itself. My claws will rend your soft, screaming flesh."

"Turn it off," Britta said, her voice almost shrill. The *Pankhurst* was faster than the other ships. Their lead time was dropping.

"Off," Winters said. Yes. That had been a mistake. A chill ran down her spine and she wanted to vomit.

Winters gave the command, and *Eagle* slipped into Shorr space.

* * * * *

Chapter Twenty-Four: Sol Attacked

Gunnery Sergeant Wolf Mathison, USMC

The courier was designed for quick trips. Three days might be the limit, maybe less. Mathison tried to imagine being trapped in the little cabin for more than a week. There was a small cargo area in the back and a narrow aisle to move around in, so there was no privacy or room. They had to sleep in their seats, and the only exercise they could manage was visiting the claustrophobic bathroom in the back. It was easier to let their suits handle those things. It was hard to get comfortable, since the seats were designed for much smaller people. His knees pushed up against Sif's seat, and it was impossible to get comfortable. His magazine pouches shifted around his breast plate and stabbed into his sides. Stathis, on the other hand, couldn't seem to stay awake and occasionally a snore would escape him. Mathison could barely sleep and spent most of the time slipping in and out of a light sleep.

It was comforting watching Sif and Feng share information about stations, weapons platforms, and the movements of ships. Most information flowed freely between them. His openness might be because they were in a SOG system, and Feng had more knowledge. Mathison wanted to interrogate Feng about his SOG duties, responsibilities, and access, but Feng was being honest and helpful. His past, while interesting, was not necessarily relevant to their current discussions, and it would have to wait.

"System alert," Freya said, who was monitoring the courier's communication. *"Weapons platforms are powering up."*

"Where? What?" Mathison asked, instantly awake.

Alarms were going off within the courier.

"Someone has followed us," Freya said. *"The station that challenged us is being attacked. Correction, it has been destroyed. Missile platforms are launching along with rail guns. Apparently, five ships arrived, but not in the zone we did."*

"The vanhat tried to follow us," Sif said. "They failed to arrive in the proper coordinates, though. Missile launches, not targeting us. System-wide alert."

The courier was only twelve hours from Earth. So close.

"All ships are being interrogated," Sif said.

"Standard procedure," Feng said. "If we do not change our responses, we should be within parameters."

"But they're polling us every five minutes," Sif said.

"That's expected," Feng said. "This is Sol. Home of the Governance, and security is paramount. Especially now with the system hiding behind fortified barriers. Entering those barriers without authorization is fatal."

"How did we get authorization, Colonel?" Stathis asked.

"Question noted," Feng said, and Mathison wondered if that comment would be used against Stathis when Feng lined them up against a wall to be shot. Had Feng already betrayed them with some authorization code? Would it matter if the SOG could use the tech codes for the d-bomb and Inkeri generators? The goal was the survival of humanity. What did an ancient gunnery sergeant's life matter?

Stathis looked at Mathison and nodded. He had no idea what the private was thinking, so he just kept his face neutral and his visor down.

Right now, there wasn't a damned thing he could do. They had to trust that Feng knew what he was talking about and that Sif could handle everything else. Skadi and Vili remained silent behind them, or maybe they were having a private conversation. It was hard to know. Feng was using assorted code words and phrases Freya couldn't decode.

"*What's your analysis of the situation?*" Mathison asked.

"*The response was rapid. Very swift and efficient. Only a single strike cruiser escaped with heavy damage. The other ships have been destroyed despite the destruction of the initial battle station. Correction. The strike cruiser has now been destroyed. They never had a chance. Even a battlestar transitioning this far out would be crippled within minutes.*"

"*Is that going to be a problem for us?*"

"*It depends on Governance military protocols. This ship followed protocols and passed inspection. Theirs did not.*"

Twelve long hours. Then? Then they would try to sneak into the most heavily guarded facility in the most heavily guarded system.

"*Do you think Feng will betray us?*" Mathison asked.

"*There is a probability, but I would say not a high one. As a commissar, his loyalty to the Governance is supposed to be without question, but then he is also loyal to General Duque and Battalion Commander Hui.*"

"*What is he?*"

"*The probability of him being just a commissar are remote. Based on conversations he's likely a specialized agent who's been promoted through the ranks. He was probably once a commissar or else he's a very knowledgeable actor.*"

"*What exactly is he?*"

"I suspect he belongs to internal or external intelligence, perhaps some third branch that monitors both. Either is equally probable, but external intelligence has a slightly higher probability. It's also likely that he works outside those agencies or is trusted with a higher level of autonomy."

"How can we find out?"

"Ask him, Gunny."

"Right."

Would Feng answer truthfully? Did it matter? Asking questions might provide answers he couldn't tolerate. Maybe it was best he not know for now.

* * * * *

Chapter Twenty-Five: Calling for Help

Chief Warrant Officer Diamond Winters, USMC

The transition only lasted a few seconds and then *Eagle* slid into Shorr space a second time. There was barely enough time to see the stars appear around them through blurry eyes. *Eagle* spun and began a course change, pushing the ship off its original course and slamming everyone against their restraints because they had lost no velocity.

Britta transmitted their message on a tight beam to where the beacon should be. It would be twenty-seven minutes before the message reached it and then maybe another twenty minutes before the fleet received it. It was going to be a long time. Breathing hurt.

"Regulator circuits have burned out," Blitzen reported. *"This will make the next transition very tricky. We're trying to manufacture the right circuits now in the manufactory, but it will be hard if we must maintain this acceleration."*

"Would it be easier to roll over and die?" Winters asked. Minutes seemed like days, hours like weeks. Sleep was impossible.

"Not for you."

"How much should we slow down?"

"As much as you can. Zero gravity is best for the manufacture of some critical components."

Eagle had maintained its speed going through Shorr space, not that anyone would realize that looking at the stars around them that never moved except after a transition.

"*How's it going?*" Winters asked Levin.

"*Usual whining, ma'am,*" Levin said. "*Our passengers are happy.*"

"*Happy?*"

"*A complaining grunt is a happy grunt, ma'am,*" Levin said. "*So, right now, they are really happy. I've recommended that when they get a chance, they should conduct PT.*"

Winters struggled to look in his direction. PT? As in physical training? He sounded calm about it, like he was enjoying himself.

Levin's visor was up, but his eyes were closed, and his face was pale. She could see him straining from here.

"*I'm going to be sore in every single organ and joint,*" Winters said. "*This isn't PT enough?*"

"*No, ma'am,*" Levin said. His face didn't move to show he was speaking. He was talking through Lilith.

"*You aren't using your voice, are you?*" Winters asked.

"*No, ma'am. Then they might realize I'm as bad off as they are. This way they can think I'm unbothered by this. Their ego will push them to toughen up.*"

"*You're mean.*"

"*No, ma'am, I'm an NCO. Never let them see you suffer. If they think you're tougher than steel, they'll do their best to not let you down. Their ego will push them to prove they're tougher.*"

"*You don't think they know that?*"

"*I'm sure they do, ma'am, but they can't see me, only hear me. I doubt they realize I can talk through my SCBI like this. It's a game to see who's tougher. I cheat.*"

Winters looked at the displays and waited for the enemy ships to appear. Had *Eagle* lost them? The minutes went by. How could she cheat?

Winters said, "Looks like we—" Alarms went off. "—didn't lose them."

If *Eagle* had not been changing course, she would have flown through them. They were too close, but their direction and velocity were not in their favor. They wouldn't have much time to exchange fire with *Eagle* before they had to turn around, and that gave *Eagle* space to breathe.

Streams of blazer rounds reached out for *Eagle*. Winters felt the rounds hit as she mentally triggered *Eagle's* weapons to return fire.

"*Primary Inkeri offline*," Levin reported. "*We have casualties.*"

Rounds from *Eagle* slammed into the enemy ships, which were close together. One cruiser began spewing fire and atmosphere as missiles from *Eagle* shot from the bays.

"Launch fighters, ma'am?" Levin asked aloud so Britta could hear.

Winters was tempted, but she knew that there wouldn't be time to recover them. The two cruisers had lost their fighters in the stern chase, but the *Pankhurst* might have some. She remembered how fighters had been sent after Skadi's ship in orbit above TCG. Had the *Pankhurst* restocked? The *Pankhurst* would launch them at any moment if it had them. *Eagle* still had four and she wanted to keep them as long as possible.

"No."

She evaluated distances and velocities. One cargo ship shattered, then the other one. Big targets. Easy to hit. Now it was just the *Pankhurst* and a cruiser. Maybe *Eagle* would survive?

Four corvettes transitioned out of Shorr space to join the *Pankhurst*. Damn.

Winters smiled. It looked like the *Pankhurst* and the other ships had expected *Eagle* to stop and slow down. They were ahead of *Eagle* and that worried her more than anything else. How could they monitor Shorr space transitions so well?

Second later they were out of range, and the *Eagle*'s point defenses picked off all the missiles.

The enemy ships decelerated and adjusted their trajectory to pursue. It was going to take them hours to turn around.

"Send another message," Winters told Britta. She checked the math, plugging in speeds to see what she could tolerate. "Tell them our situation has changed. We can't transition and give them our course."

"Zen, Captain."

"Slow to maximum cruising speed." That would allow people to move around under normal gravity instead of being pushed into their seat. "Everyone has an hour before we resume acceleration. Get the casualties situated first." Then she asked Blitzen, *"Will that give you time to make those circuit boards?"*

"Yes."

"Aye, Captain," Levin said, opening a wide link to tell everyone on board.

* * * * *

Chapter Twenty-Six: Earth Orbit

Gunnery Sergeant Wolf Mathison, USMC

Earth looked different. It was hard to see any landmasses beneath the dark swirling clouds, though he caught glimpses of blue ocean. Mathison saw nothing familiar. Orbit was dotted with icons and information on his display, but the planet below did not look like Earth anymore. Nothing was visible for long. It wasn't a blue marble anymore, more like a gray depressing one.

"That's Earth?" Stathis asked.

"It is now," Feng said. "After the United States committed suicide and the Vapaus Republic tried to finish it."

"At least it is still habitable, unlike Midgard," Skadi said.

"There is a shred of truth in that statement," Feng replied, but Mathison wasn't sure he was agreeing so much as he just didn't want to argue.

"Do the clouds ever clear up?" Stathis asked as they slipped through dark clouds occasionally illuminated by flashes of lightning.

"Volcanic ash from Yellowstone," Freya said.

"Not for very long," Feng said. "Besides the nuclear winter, the strikes have caused many volcanoes to erupt, putting more ash into the air. It is possible to live on the surface in some places, but it is not a pleasant experience."

"Did everything die?" Stathis asked.

"It would have been a mercy if it had," Feng said. "No. Many things have survived, but they are usually mutated and dangerous. Life finds a way. The tomb worlds are dangerous places as well."

"The tomb worlds? You've been there?"

"Yes. They were ravaged by nuclear war long ago and are still recovering, very dangerous places. The native creatures have evolved so they don't need sunlight in their food chain. Thermovores and predators seem to dominate. With all the volcanic activity on the tomb worlds, there is plenty of heat, if not sunlight. They are violent places, dangerous even for someone in full armor."

"How many tomb worlds have you been to, Colonel?"

"Two, and I have no desire to go back. They are depressing places. Earth is better; at least it has not been ravaged as badly."

The view of the outside now showed them nothing. Without sensors, Mathison couldn't tell where they were, but they were probably too high for mountains. Hopefully. He wasn't a pilot, but he was confident Sif and Feng wouldn't drop them low enough to hit one. They had to pass over the Atlantic to reach their destination, and Mathison felt uncomfortable about that.

"Ever been to the US, Colonel?"

"No. I have never had a need. I understand it is one of the worst places on the planet. There are several active volcanoes, mostly on the West Coast, but it will be a long time before the radiation levels are safe for normal humans."

"Where are we going?" Mathison asked.

"We will be setting down in Europe," Sif said. "Some place called Geneva. They're bringing us in on a very leisurely route. There's plenty of time to scan us, perhaps monitor us for infection."

"We can't land there," Mathison said. There would doubtless be a lot of troops and countless security checks. His team didn't have any SOG armor or uniforms. "We need other options. Can we fake engine trouble and land somewhere else?"

"We'll pass over the remains of North America during our descent, coming in from the west. We don't have any options except maybe a quick landing on the North American continent or in the Atlantic Ocean. Our window for that is almost gone."

"We cannot survive landing in either of those," Feng said, stating the obvious.

Mathison didn't like the options. "Nothing in the USA we could use to get to the moon?"

"Nobody has gone to the USA in a century. The entire continent is dead, a blasted radioactive wasteland. I dare say you will not recognize any of it. If anything is not destroyed, it is ancient, in horrible repair, and likely to be unsuitable for anything other than radioactive scrap."

"I need options unless anyone thinks we stand a chance of getting past security in Geneva," Mathison said. "I don't think our chances are good. We need chaos to exploit."

"I like faking engine trouble," Stathis said.

"They will find it easier to shoot us than rescue us," Feng said. "Engine trouble is one of the oldest tricks in the book and is overused."

"Will your rank and authority keep them away from us long enough to come up with another plan?" Mathison asked.

"My rank and authority are not unlimited," Feng said. "To be honest, I am surprised it allowed us get this far."

"So, we need another plan," Mathison said.

Everyone fell silent as they thought or reviewed maps.

"We have a problem," Sif said. Mathison looked up. Both Sif and Feng were working on their consoles, which flickered and froze.

"Problem?" Skadi asked.

"Anti-hijack protocol," Freya said. *"We have lost control."*

"Not again. Anything you can do?"

"Working on it. Hardware subsystems, though, like the shuttle, are hard to override."

"We're going down," Sif said. Mathison heard her concern. Crashing into the ocean was bad. Very bad. Maybe the courier would float, but there would be nowhere for them to hide. Their armor provided some protection but crush depth for the suits was around a hundred meters.

The shuttle dropped through the clouds, and Mathison looked at Feng. He looked as desperate and concerned as Sif.

"We are near Virginia and likely heading out over the Atlantic," Sif said. "We are locked out of the sensor systems. I can't tell anything, not our speed, altitude, or location. We are blind."

The clouds made visual identification of their surroundings impossible. Nearby, lightning slashed through the darkness. They were in a thunderstorm?

"I don't want to land in the ocean," Stathis said. "I'll bet the mutant sharks can bite through armor."

"The killer whales are most dangerous," Feng said.

The courier began shaking as it slammed through the atmosphere.

"Are they going to crash us or land us?" Mathison asked.

"I don't know," Sif said, and Mathison watched Stathis load his rifle and wedge it into his seat. Mathison did the same.

The courier shook harder, and the straps dug into Mathison, pulling him back as the ship decelerated. This was bad for his stomach.

The screens flickered and went blank as a red light came on. Were they over the Atlantic? Maybe off the East Coast. It was hard to tell without any visual references to show how fast they were going.

"Well, I would rather die in the United States than anywhere else," Stathis said.

"Shut up, Stathis." Mathison leaned back and closed his eyes, which might help him not vomit. "We won't make it across the Atlantic at this rate."

"We should have brought parachutes," Stathis said to nobody.

Hadn't he been told to shut up? "Thank you for that observation of our planning failure, Supply Colonel Stathis. Please make a list of other items we should acquire as we crash. It could come in useful."

"Aye, Gunny."

The shaking increased. At this rate, the shuttle might tear itself apart before it slammed into the ocean. Why would they take the shuttle deeper into the clouds instead of higher? To keep the occupants from seeing anything?

"Incoming targeting links," Feng said. "Sensors show hostile missile launches. Apparently, they have decided it would be easier to shoot us out of the sky."

The bastards had left those sensors online so they could see death coming for them, but of course the sensors didn't show them how close the missiles were. They could be seconds or an hour away, depending on where they were launched from. Cold-hearted bastards. It was a bad way to go.

"Oh good," Stathis said, "I always wanted to be cremated and have my remains spread over the US."

"You might get your wish," Vili said.

Mathison closed his eyes and realized that wasn't any better as he struggled to keep his stomach from rebelling. Why did it have to take so long to die?

* * * * *

Chapter Twenty-Seven: Boarded

Chief Warrant Officer Diamond Winters, USMC

Alarms dragged Winters out of her coma as Blitzen pumped stimulants into her blood stream, but it was going to be a slow process as she tried to make sense of the sounds beyond the ringing in her ears. She opened her eyes. Her body hurt, and everything was still blurry.

"Transitions detected," Blitzen reported, possibly realizing Winters' current state. *"Trying to identify."*

"And?"

"Friendly!"

"Oorah!" Levin said. "The calvary's arrived."

Winter's eyes finally focused. A Republic battlestar and several SOG battleships filled their view. They had arrived between *Eagle* and the enemy ships. Almost instantly, missiles and blazer fire reached out from both groups.

"Prepare to decelerate and come about," Winters said. "Sound high-gravity maneuvers. Five minutes." As if it mattered; nobody had stood down from previous alarms. Sounding the alarm for high-G maneuvers would haunt her nightmares for years.

Although the *Pankhurst* and the other ships were now outnumbered and outmassed, they didn't flee.

"*The* Pankhurst *is aiming for the* Tyr," Blitzen reported. "*Like it is going to ram it.*"

Nukes, d-bombs, and bomb-pumped lasers exploded, scrambling sensors and making it hard to decipher what was going on. Too much was happening to make sense of it.

Coming around was hard and finally *Eagle's* sensors were able to make sense of the information as the firing stopped. There was no sign of any enemy ships.

"*We can raise the SOG vessels, but not the* Tyr," Blitzen reported. "*I'm seeing major damage on the* Tyr."

"*Move to assist,*" Winters ordered as *Eagle* accelerated again.

"Doesn't this bother you, Captain?" Britta asked.

"Of course," Winters said as gravity crushed her lungs again.

"Are you a masochist, Captain?"

"No. Maybe. But they may need us."

Britta fell silent, probably conserving her energy.

"Incoming link from the *Tupolev*," Levin said.

"Send it to me," Winters replied.

"*Eagle*, this is the *Tupolev*."

"Send it, *Tupolev*," Winters answered through Blitzen so they couldn't hear the stress in her voice.

"Be advised the *Tyr* has been hit hard. The *Pankhurst* rammed it after several EMP detonations. We are getting some radio traffic, and it appears they have been boarded. Something has infected their computer network. We are still getting information. They have fail-safes that are preventing us from getting close."

"What do you mean keeps you from getting close?" Winters asked.

"We think the automated systems are targeting SOG ships; old programming. The general thinks they have lost master fire controls and local point systems have reverted to local automatics, meaning they are targeting anything that is not Republic. The general would like to help but cannot send shuttles unless they shut those point defenses down, and he doesn't dare fire upon the *Tyr*. We cannot raise anybody aboard the ship."

"Is the Inkeri on?" Winters asked.

"Unlikely," *Tupolev* said. "The *Pankhurst* released a burst of EMP missiles before impact. We can see the remains of the *Pankhurst* embedded in the hull, so we know it was not destroyed. It makes little sense. Those velocities should have destroyed both ships. Or at least vaporized the *Pankhurst* and ripped apart the *Tyr*."

"Copy, *Tupolev*. We are on approach and will have our troops ready to board. Our ETA is thirty minutes."

If they could still walk after all the high-gravity maneuvers. Not that she had many troops.

"Copy, *Eagle*," *Tupolev* said. "We will advise as we learn more. The general suspects they have been boarded and are fighting for their lives. We would d-bomb the vessel if we thought it would help and wouldn't activate the main weapons. The EMPs have really messed up their systems. It is a surprise anything is working."

"Where are the *Sleipnir* and the other Republic ships?" Winters asked.

"There have been raids on the asteroid factories," *Tupolev* said. "The *Sleipnir* and others are trying to rescue them."

Which was bad if the enemy discovered the d-bomb factories and launch facilities. How did they know?

"Acknowledged, *Tupolev*," Winters said and then to Levin, "I want you to lead the boarding operations. Sorry, but if they're having network problems, *Lilith* might be able to help."

"Aye, I'll warn the troops," Levin said.

"*I have tracking information for the gunny's ship,*" Blitzen said.

"Good."

"*It dipped into Earth's atmosphere on a trajectory toward Europe on a slow path. I lost it briefly as it entered clouds of volcanic ash as it was passing over the United States and it is now barely rising above the clouds to transit the Atlantic.*"

"*So, he isn't going straight to the Moon?*"

"*Correct. The Moon probably has top security and by taking a less direct route he can ease suspicion.*"

"*Keep me informed.*" She had more immediate concerns. Winters switched to the fleet link on the *Tupolev*. "What happened?"

General Duque answered. "The enemy vessel identified as the *Pankhurst* fired an EMP pulse that appeared to disable the *Tyr* then it rammed the battlestar. I suspect the intent was to disable the Inkeri and board the ship. Some parts of the vessel were heavily impacted, some were not. It appears to be very chaotic aboard the *Tyr*."

"We are moving to dock and land troops to help. Perhaps we can boost our Inkeri to help."

"Acknowledged," Duque said. "I have ODTs that can assist. They are ready to shift to your ship along with our spare Inkeris in case the *Tyr's* are damaged beyond repair."

"Copy that," Winters said. Seconds later, docking information came across the link.

Winters turned her attention to the screen showing the gunny's courier. The data was several minutes old, but the courier was visible above the clouds over the Atlantic. A flash of light erupted, and his icon turned gray.

"*The gunny's ship has just been destroyed by SOG anti-air weapons,*" Blitzen reported as the icon for the ship faded. "*Low yield nuclear strike. There is zero chance of survivors.*"

Winters felt like she had been punched in the gut. The gunny was dead? Just like that? Skadi, Sif, Stathis, and Vili. Gone. Candles in the wind, blown out by the storm. Even Feng. To have come so far and have survived so much, and now they were dead. And they had failed.

"The gunny?" Levin began, and Winters heard the pain in his voice.

"Is in Valhalla," Winters said, surprised her voice didn't crack. "Now it is up to us."

She didn't feel ready for it.

Rescuing the *Tyr* just became mankind's last chance of survival. If Wolf Mathison and Skadi had failed, how could she succeed? She wasn't ready for this.

Her flight school instructors had told her to start with the simple things. Fix what you can as soon as you can and work up to the bigger problems. When the engine fails, concentrate on that before you think about how badly hitting the ground is going to kill you.

"We can't let Nasaraf have the *Tyr*," Winters said.

"Semper Fi," Levin said. "Shuttles full of ODTs are en route from the *Tupolev*. Is that a good idea?"

"United, we stand, divided we fall. I don't have a better idea, and I don't give a damn if the *Tyr* doesn't want ODTs on their ship. Half their crew might be vanhat now. We need trigger pullers to take it back."

"Aye, Captain, I'll let the HKTs know. They're going to be pissed."

"That's their problem. Just save the *Tyr*. One step at a time. Let's fix what we can before we worry about the bigger picture. We haven't hit the ground yet."

"Aye, Captain."

* * * * *

Chapter Twenty-Eight: Virginia

Gunnery Sergeant Wolf Mathison, USMC

The sudden stop slammed everyone forward.

Shouldn't death be different?

"Did we die?" Stathis asked the silence, but it wasn't very silent. The engines were idling. Missiles were coming at them.

"Everyone out," Mathison said trying to think. A look outside showed they were on the ground. That had been a terrible landing, though. "Where are we?"

"Not dead," Skadi said, her weapon ready.

She kicked the hatch, and it flew open. Ash and snow blew in, but nobody started firing. In the blink of an eye, Skadi and Vili rushed out, Mathison and Stathis right behind them. It was a two-meter drop to the ground, which was deceptively soft under the snow. Gray skies hid the stars above. Mathison picked himself up and looked around at the nightmare the United States had become. To the north, some tattered broken bleachers crouched in the snow and there was a building directly behind them. Squat ruined buildings watched them from other directions.

"Gunny," Stathis said, sounding excited, "this is Butler Stadium."

"What?"

"Butler Stadium, Quantico Base."

Mathison barely recognized it.

"Why here?" Sif asked, her weapon sweeping the area, searching for a target.

"They're probably coming for us," Skadi said. "We need to get away from the ship. The SOG has launched missiles."

"That way," Mathison said, deciding. They weren't dead yet, and he had to keep it that way if he could.

"What's in that direction?" Skadi asked.

The coordinates Freya keeps finding in top-secret SOG codes, but Mathison didn't want to tell her that. Was this a trap? The coordinates weren't far, somewhere near Lejeune Field, to the west. Mathison was trying to remember what was there. To the north was the base headquarters. But the west?

"We going to check out the coordinates, Gunny?" Stathis asked on a private link as they moved away from the shuttle. Grabbing any more gear was out of the question.

"Since we're here." Mathison took point.

"Maybe I should take point. I know where we are going. I think the coordinates will put us in that chapel."

"What chapel?" Mathison asked.

The explosion slammed everyone to the ground and Mathison looked for cover as the courier shot into the sky. If they had stayed aboard, they would be jelly covering the back of the cabin.

"Does this mean we have to walk to the Moon, Gunny?"

"You have a mouse in your pocket?" Mathison asked, watching the courier disappear. "I'm going to ride the sled you'll be pulling. We don't have time to walk anywhere."

"Cold, Gunny. There's a Marine Corps Memorial Chapel. Got rebuilt in like 2050 or something. Went there once during Critical Skills Operators course. It was nice but religion just didn't call to me."

Stathis had gone to church? Mathison paused to digest that, which gave Stathis a chance to move up, wading through the knee-high snow.

"We're going to leave quite a trail," Skadi said.

"You have a way to fly?" Mathison asked, trying to keep up with Stathis. Skadi fell silent.

Even in powered armor, it wasn't easy trudging through the snow. While it was easy enough to plow through the snow, if he didn't lift his feet high enough he was likely to trip on hidden things like curbs and garbage.

It took almost an hour to get to Lejeune Field through the dead, lifeless buildings and snow. Only the shells of buildings remained, the rest had been torn apart by fire or storms. Nothing moved except the drifting snow.

Finally, Mathison saw the ruins looming up out of the darkness. He saw the steeple and two flagpoles.

Mathison froze as he looked at the flagpoles. The United States and Marine Corps flags flew on them, with the American flag slightly higher.

"Gunny?" Stathis said. "Uh, that's kinda cool. What are the chances those flags would still be flying after all this time?"

"Zero," Mathison said, looking around as the shadows moved and surrounded them.

"I'm receiving an interrogation. This can't be right," Freya said.

"Contact!" Skadi said.

"Hold fire," Mathison said, mostly because the shadows had not started firing.

Friendly icons lit up around him.

"*SCBIs,*" Freya said, excited.

"*Army?*" Mathison asked, as ranks and identification appeared with their IFF icons. Sergeant first class was not a Marine rank, and he didn't recall it being a SOG or Republic rank.

"Took you long enough," called out a familiar voice.

A figure swaggered out of the darkness. The identifier hovering above his head said Jarhead 1 and he was flanked by an Army colonel and an Army master sergeant. All three were armed with familiar looking American-made blazer rifles.

"Major, uh, General Becket?" Mathison remembered at the last minute that the coordinates had listed him as an O9 and that he had been the commandant of the Marine Corps. It couldn't be anyone else.

"I wish," Becket said. "Let's go inside where we can relax."

"Thank you, Mister President," the Army colonel said, his head turning away from the Marines to scan the distant buildings.

"I knew you were too damned tough to die out there in space," Becket said, ignoring the colonel. "Didn't I tell you that, Wayne?"

"Yes, sir, you did," the colonel said. "I would have preferred you not leave the bunker, though."

"I couldn't wait, Wayne. Wolf Mathison was one of the best Marines I ever served with."

"Yes, sir," Wayne said. Mathison saw the Army colonel was more interested in the surrounding area.

"There's a new pack of hell wolves that's moved into the area, sir," Wayne said. "I know they'll be here shortly. Can we speed things up, sir?"

Becket looked at the people behind Mathison.

"I thought Diamond Winters and Tal Levin also survived," Becket said.

"Yes, sir," Mathison said. "They aren't with us."

"And who are they?"

"Aesir from the Vapaus Republic," Mathison said. How much did Becket know? "And another specialist."

"Let's go inside." Becket looked to the sky. "It isn't safe out here."

Mathison followed as Becket led them to the chapel.

What was going on here? A last remnant of the United States? A few survivors living in bunkers? Mathison didn't know what he would find or what had happened, and he was reluctant to follow his former commanding officer, but this changed things.

Becket led them into the ruins of the chapel. In the distance, lightning split the sky.

"Another storm," Becket said. "They get bad."

In the back of the chapel was a large elevator big enough for ten people. Mathison noticed there were no controls or indicators. The lights did not come on until the doors closed and the elevator began descending.

"Seven hundred meters underground," Becket said. "Trust me, you don't want to take the stairs."

The soldiers laughed.

"It might be the most secure facility in the world," Becket said. "It was designed to take multiple direct hits from nukes. Solid and American-made to Marine standards."

"How did you know it was us, sir?"

"Didn't know for sure. A hunch. We picked up notification in the SOG system that there was something squirrelly about the ship. That set off alarms here, and knowing you, I figured chances were damned good you were trying to get here. We ran cover, stalling the SOG bastards, and we inserted ourselves into the anti-hijack to land you nearby. You landed and were smart enough to debark. Now the SOG thinks you are dead, blown up over the Atlantic. Those paranoid freaks used nukes on you, as if Earth isn't hurt enough."

"Thank you, sir," Mathison said. "How?" What else to ask. How did he survive? How many Americans were there? He had too many questions. How much pull did Becket have with the SOG?

"Save your questions until we can get these suits off," Becket said. "Damn. I've missed having Marines around."

* * * * *

Chapter Twenty-Nine: *Tyr's* Doom

Aesir Halfred Theisen – VRAC

The Aesir pallo was the forward starboard sphere habitat, referred to as Daavid, and was home to one of the two Aesir Battalions. The other Aesir battalion was in Pallo Gideon. Each pallo was essentially a rotating sphere within the *Tyr* that could rotate within the hull as needed, so that regardless of how the *Tyr* was moving, accelerating, or otherwise maneuvering, the sphere rotated so their feet always pointed down to simulate natural gravity. Most of the ship had grav plates and dampers, but there had been a time when those hadn't been an option, so they maintained gravity with acceleration and deceleration and that meant the pallos had to rotate.

Future battlestars had kept the design because it had the added benefit of making the battlestars modular. Each module could be self-contained within triple hulled and armored spheres. While the living quarters were spherical, the engineers encased each sphere in an oval with hydroponics and other facilities that did not need gravity. The ovals were pushed together, surrounded by a shell, and the space within the shell was filled with supplies, cargo, and other resources.

The *Tyr*, one of the older and larger battlestars, had nine pallos and seven allues, which were regions not technically part of a pallo.

When the alarm went off, Theisen was already armored up with his team in one of the training gyms practicing marksmanship. Gunsen was doing an admirable job of making Birger look like a bad shot, and Theisen was wondering if Gunsen had done something to his targeting system to give him an advantage.

"Aesir and Vanir, be advised the *Tyr* will transition in ten minutes. Prepare for fleet action. I say again, prepare for fleet action. Battle stations. Battle stations. We are the shields of our people. We will hold the line."

"Paska," Birger said.

"Ever been on a battlestar for a fleet battle?" Gunsen asked as Theisen made sure their training kits were properly removed. They had five minutes to get to their battle stations, which, in this case, were their racks.

"On a battlestar? No. I was on a Snekke last time. Wasn't supposed to be on the wall but our Inkeri failed, and they boarded us in Shorr space. It was bad. My next post was being put in charge of you nyyppas."

"Casualties were that bad?" Birger asked.

"Aivan niin," Theisen said, which meant "exactly."

"So, now we're part of the wall?" Gunsen asked.

Didn't they teach young Aesir anything about space combat? "Yes, we are part of the main force. The edge of the axe, the spike on the shield. The line, the pointy end of the sword."

"Shouldn't we be doing something more than going to bed?"

"We won't be sleeping," Theisen said, slowing to look at Gunsen to see if he was serious.

"No damage control parties or anything?"

"If we're needed, they will tell us," Theisen said. "If we're in bed we're out from underfoot of the crew. The beds serve as crash couches and our fire team bay acts as a survival pod. Don't think you'll get any good sleep, though."

"So, we just go to bed and hope to not die?" Gunsen asked.

"The *Tyr* is one of the oldest, toughest battlestars in the fleet. The SOG has nothing that compares to it. Even their dreadnoughts are smaller and can't stand against this ship. This is the most powerful ship in human space, hands down. Don't make the mistake of thinking because it's old it's outdated. The *Tyr* is constantly upgraded. It might also be one of the most advanced ships in the Republic fleet. Amiraali Carpenter is also one of the more senior officers and one of the most capable. If we are going into battle, we will be victorious."

"What battles has the *Tyr* been in?" Gunsen asked.

The question got under Theisen's skin before he realized how little information the SOG would share with its citizens. Of course, the Governance wouldn't tell people how its glorious ships had clashed with the Vapaus Republic and been defeated or how their brave commanders were quick to flee from the Republic's battlestars.

Sirens wailed, warning people they needed to be where they belonged.

"Plenty," Theisen said. He would have to school Gunsen later.

The *Tyr was* one of the most powerful ships in existence, but that didn't mean it was invulnerable. One thing he had learned as an Aesir was that people should not rely on past exploits and glories to see them through new ones. A warrior would always be challenged and there was no place in the warrior ethos to sit back and rely on previous victories.

The *Tyr* had to constantly prove its superiority until it was destroyed, and it was about to face yet another challenge.

* * *

The transition alarm sounded, and Theisen tensed as he checked his personal Inkeri. Online. Good. Everyone was fully armed and armored, lying in their bunks with their privacy doors open.

Seconds later, the alarm sounded again, and Theisen felt the *Tyr* leave Shorr space.

"Standby for heavy gravity maneuvers," the *Tyr* announced, and Theisen felt a massive force push him down into his bunk.

"Paska!" Gunsen groaned as the pressure continued to grow.

The lights flickered, and the pressure eased.

"That's bad, right?" Zanella said. "Real bad?"

"Yes," Birger said. "This deep in the ship, our pallo has its own generators."

"Are we attacking Earth?" Gunsen asked. "Why didn't they tell us?"

"Marauders, stand by for new intel," said their platoon commander, a new lojtnant named Saario. Theisen thought he was too nice and eager to please.

"I'm all ears," Gunsen muttered on the team link, and Theisen scowled in the korpraali's direction, though the lojtnant couldn't hear him.

"The *Tyr* and some SOG ships are moving to assist *Eagle*, an allied ship," Saario said. "We have made transition and intercepted the vanhat. We are—" The lights flickered again, and static interrupted the lojtnant.

Eagle? The Marines were in trouble? That seemed to be where they lived, on the edge and under constant threat. Theisen wasn't sure he had been happy after being transferred from the ship, though, but they needed HKTs more than regular Aesir Marauders.

"—engaging. We outmass and outnumber the enemy. They are very close and—"

It was like a light flashing behind his eyes, leaving him blind, and his head throbbed painfully. He heard someone retch. His cybernetics were offline, and he couldn't tell if his eyes were open or closed.

The *Tyr* shuddered as Theisen palmed his external cybernetic and suit reset. It had been a long time since he'd experienced an EMP that powerful. Back in training, to be precise.

His armor was still restarting as he pulled off his helmet and vomited over the side of his bed. With gravity off, he could have flown out of his bunk, but his restraints held him in place.

Emergency lights flickered on, but not all of them. The smell of burned-out circuits, vomit and ozone stung his nostrils. Wiping his mouth, he pulled the helmet back on. Zero gravity was bad because now his vomit was spreading throughout their space, and it would have to be cleaned up.

"Reboot complete. No external links available," his cybernetics reported.

He looked around and saw Birger thrashing on his bunk and Zanella repeatedly smacking her cybernetic reset. Gunsen was holding his head.

A connection came in from Gunsen and within seconds Zanella showed online.

Theisen released his buckles, pushed across the narrow team bay to Birger, and smacked his cybernetic reset. The second Birger felt the contact, he stopped thrashing and turned toward Theisen. Reaching over, Theisen raised Birger's visor at the same time a chill ran down his spine and the nausea threatened him again.

He checked his Inkeri and saw it was offline. He hurriedly hit the reset switch and then hit the reset on Birger's Inkeri. Gunsen and Zanella were pulling themselves out of their bunks and loading their rifles.

"Everyone check your Inkeri and your team member's Inkeris," Krapula, the platoon's ylikerstanti, said. "Move quick. This is bad."

Theisen queried the team's Inkeris. Everyone was online, their systems restarted, but the feeling of dread didn't leave him. He was missing something.

"Back in your bunks," Theisen said. "They haven't sounded clear yet."

Gunsen and Theisen climbed back in when the lojtnant came onto the platoon link.

"Marauders, assemble in the rec room," Saario said, which answered that.

"Go to bed, get out of bed, go to bed," Gunsen complained as Theisen opened his locker to pull out more ammunition and his wire subgun. Others did the same. He grabbed his blazer carbine too, just in case.

"Shut up, Gunsen," Birger said. "You can't sleep without your hand wrapped around your joystick, anyway."

Theisen missed Gunsen's reply as they left the team room. Everyone was assembled in the platoon rec room, and Kersanti Talonen nodded at Theisen. The other teams and team leaders weren't out yet.

Lojtnant Saario arrived and looked around.

"Okay, Marauders," Saario said, "looks like the main Inkeri generators are offline, at least here in Pallo Daavid. That means incursions are possible. The last I heard was that we were engaging vanhat-controlled ships, so it's likely they are responsible. Standard Vanir crew are not equipped with personal Inkeris, so that means we must move fast and get them to Inkeri protected areas as quickly as possible. Our platoon network link is up now, and we are working on getting it linked with company and battalion."

"What if we resume high-gravity maneuvers?" the squad leader of Berta Squad asked, a big humorless kersanti named Nutti. Theisen didn't even know if he had a first name.

"Then get comfortable," Krapula said. "TyrNET is down. We have to assume hostile action. We cannot sit around here with our thumbs up our ass. Kinsmen to kinsmen should be true. We need to save any Vanir spaceberts we can."

"Zen," several Aesir muttered.

"And if they've turned?" an Aesir in third squad asked.

"Never heard of anyone being unturned," Krapula said. "Put 'em down. No choice."

A link came up in Theisen's display showing TyrNET was available.

Theisen looked at it and blinked rapidly.

"Linking..."

It was taking longer than usual, and Theisen looked around. The silence told him everyone else was trying to link in. Was the system being overwhelmed?

The link established, and his orders queue lit up.

"What the hell?" Krapula said. "This doesn't make sense."

Theisen looked at the orders and understood. There were conflicting orders: to abandon ship, rally at the nearest hangar, disable all Inkeris because they are keeping TyrNET offline, proceed to the cafeteria for lunch and a briefing.

A command override from the lojtnant cut off TyrNET.

"Something's wrong," Saario said. "TyrNET is borked. We have a direct link with Kapten Ilmarinen. We get our orders from him. He wants a recon team sent to Pallo Berrta to contact whoever is still giving commands. The rest of the platoons will remain here." The lojtnant turned to Theisen. "Your team was first, Alkersenti Theisen," Saario said. "Take your team to Pallo Berrta and see if we can establish a link."

"Zen, Lojtnant," Theisen said and started off, with Birger, Gunsen, and Zanella behind him. Something roared in the distance.

"I hope that was your stomach, Gunsen," Zanella said.

"Why is everything offline, Lojtnant?" Gunsen asked.

"EMP pulse of some kind," Saario said.

"I thought our systems were immune to EMP," Gunsen said softly.

"Resistant, not immune. Big difference," Theisen said. "Though I didn't think there was any EMP weapon strong enough to overcome that resistance."

"D-bombs have EMP qualities, don't they?"

"We'll worry about that later," Theisen said. "Right now, we have a mission."

* * * * *

Chapter Thirty: Boarding the *Tyr*

Sergeant Tal Levin, USMC

Approaching the *Tyr* had been a nightmare. The *Tyr* had a lot of velocity and there was a slight spin. If that wasn't bad enough, Levin had expected the large anti-ship turrets to swing toward *Eagle's* and start pouring out blazer fire. The turrets of the *Tyr* were massive and, thankfully, they remained still.

Levin didn't breathe a sigh of relief until *Eagle* latched onto the *Tyr*. The airlock and nearby corridors were cramped with all the warriors crammed into it, waiting to pour into the ship. HKT and ODT stood shoulder to shoulder. Only officers had cross-unit communication ability, but everyone knew who the enemy was. As they prepared to board and rescue the *Tyr*, everyone considered the people around them brother and sister. Everything was ad hoc, and Levin wished they had more time to integrate their comm systems.

He hoped that wouldn't be a problem.

"Mission Commander," said Colonel Hui, a tough as nails ODT lieutenant colonel they had found on the ice planet commanding the ODTs, "a suggestion?"

"Yes?" Levin asked. Dammit. What was he forgetting? Both Grimkel and Hui had more training and experience. He should rely on them more. As a sergeant, his specialty was squad- and platoon-level tactics not company or battalion. As Winter's XO he had developed a good working knowledge of starship operations, but now he was getting ready to lead a broken platoon of HKTs and a short battalion of ODTs onto a hostile ship.

"We should bring at least one d-bomb," Hui said. "I can assign a squad to carry it but will need help to prepare it for detonation."

"This is a spaceship," Levin said. "Setting off one of our d-bombs could cause irreversible damage. We need the *Tyr* intact."

"Acknowledged, Mission Commander," Hui said, "but we should plan for the worst-case scenario."

"Do it," Levin said. "Don't hesitate to make suggestions in the future. I need your knowledge and experience. Don't be afraid to use your initiative."

"Ai, Mission Commander," Hui said and turned away.

"Is that wise?" Lojtnant Grimkel asked.

Was it? Grimkel was a lieutenant. ODTs did ground and some space, but HKTs were pure spacers. What would the gunny do? Put Hui or Grimkel in command? No. Gunny would take command because otherwise, they probably wouldn't work together. One wouldn't take orders from the other, and they needed each other. A Marine who trusted both would probably be the only way to make sure they worked together. The challenge was to get them to volunteer information and suggestions. Hui was at least doing that, while Grimkel was just questioning his decisions. The other challenge would be getting them to take orders from a sergeant, which was not how things usually worked.

"She's right," Levin said, "we need to have the option. With the *Pankhurst* partially embedded in the Paavo Allue, we need big guns.

Whatever we do, we can't let Nasaraf capture the *Tyr* if that's his goal. I seriously doubt Nasaraf is dead even if the *Pankhurst* is damaged."

"The Inkeri's—" Grimkel began.

"Are not working right now or this wouldn't be an issue. We're getting a lot of garbage from the *Tyr* on the networks, but nothing coherent. The *Pankhurst* is jamming and pulsing, almost like the vanhat have a counter to our Inkeris. We were fools to think we had the only technological advantage."

"Then will the d-bomb be effective?"

"It better be. We need to get to Admiral Carpenter, and hopefully he'll have more information, whether the *Tyr* can be saved or can't. We must give him as many options as we can. Semper Gumbi."

"Semper Gumbi?"

"Always Flexible. Semper is Latin for always and Gumbi is a character from—ah, never mind."

"Zen," Grimkel said.

Hui returned. "What is the plan, Mission Commander?"

Things were happening fast. What did she want, a PowerPoint presentation?

"We'll dock forward in the Jussi Allue. Then we'll fight our way to Pallo Berrta and contact the admiral."

There were a lot of problems with that plan. The *Tyr* was five kilometers long; it was massive. There were nine spheres, which were officially habitations, called pallos, and the spaces in between connecting the spheres called allues. There were countless tunnels and corridors around the ship, but they would likely be death traps or locked down under combat conditions.

With everything that was happening, Levin realized he was losing track. What would the gunny do? Start with the basics. He had done mission briefings in the Marine Corps for a long time. This was a mission. A quickly arranged, spur-of-the-moment mission, but his Marine training had prepared him for this. He would just have to abbreviate the five-paragraph order. Burned into him since he was a young private, the five-paragraph order was abbreviated SMEAC: Situation, Mission, Execution, Administration and logistics, and Command and signal. He would have to treat the HKTs and ODTs like fireteams and trust the commanders to run their units. Simple. Hard.

"Listen up," Levin said on the troop channel so everyone could hear him. "The situation is that a vanhat ship has crashed into the *Tyr* and may be trying to take over or destroy it." Summarize the situation. So far so good. "Our mission is to stop those bastards cold. We'll fight our way to Pallo Berrta and link up with Admiral Carpenter, if he is still alive, in order to assess the situation and see if the *Tyr* can be saved. I will update our mission after that.

"To do this, we are going to enter through the front of the ship, through the Jussi Allue and fight our way to Berrta; bypass Aarne if need be. I don't want to get bogged down. Get to Berrta and the admiral, fast and hard. Let nothing stand in our way. We may need to break up into different groups to find a path."

Levin looked at the helmeted heads facing his direction and realized this was where his knowledge was weak. He was the tip of the spear, not the shaft or the hand holding it. His hand brushed his Ka-Bar. This wasn't Iwo Jima, and he didn't have anyone to pass the Ka-Bar on to. He didn't want to tell Winters, but he had a bad feeling about this. His father had carried the Ka-Bar on Iwo Jima hundreds of years ago and he had never said where he got it. It was a family heirloom and no stranger to war, but this was more than just war, this was genocide on a scale that would make what Hitler, Stalin, and Mao did to their people seem inconsequential. If the vanhat won, those despots would be inconsequential.

Humanity was being pushed hard. The enemy didn't fight like humans because they weren't human. Even if Sol was saved, Levin had his doubts. Countless other civilizations had been destroyed by this plague, and Levin knew the worst was yet to come. He couldn't say why or how, but even if they saved Earth, the war wouldn't be over.

"We'll leave any dead in place for now. Wounded will be helped as best we can," Levin said. *Eagle* was going to detach after it offloaded the troops. There would be no retreating. "Carry as much ammunition and equipment as you can. We go forward at any cost. There is no going back."

Levin looked at everyone and tried to remember what else was in the Administration and Logistics part of the five-paragraph order. To hell with it. Let Grimkel and Hui fill in the blanks.

What could he tell them for the last part, Command and Signal?

"I'm in command," Levin said. "Follow me. If I go down, follow your leaders. Never quit."

"Acknowledge," Hui said.

"Hurrah, hurrah, hurrah!" the ODTs yelled. Even with their helmets on, Levin could feel their voices through the deck. It was then Levin realized he had echoed the ODT motto. Oh well, hopefully the HKTs wouldn't take it personally. Did they have a motto?

Grimkel just nodded.

"What was that?" Winters asked on a private link.

"Motivational pre-mission speech," Levin said.

"Sounds like it worked. We're docking. Be careful. I want you back."

"If I don't make it back to *Eagle,* we'll meet in Valhalla."

"Don't give me that Viking shit. Keep your head down and get back as soon as you can."

"Aye, aye, Captain."

The forward allue was the largest and held a collection of landing bays, manufactories, docking rings, and storage. It was the primary location for docking, and the SCBIs considered it the safest approach.

When the docking collar showed a solid connection, the door slid open, and darkness greeted them. Flickering emergency lights intermittently illuminated the corridor. The ODTs and HKTs were armed, ready, and eager to fight. Facing monsters wasn't any easier than facing the weapons studding the hull of the *Tyr*.

There was no sign of the *Tyr's* Aesir, HKTs, or anyone else as the hatch finished opening. The HKTs from *Eagle* led the way, and the ODTs followed them, keeping Levin in between. The ship looked deserted. Each time the lights flicked off Levin expected something hungry to fill the darkness like a materializing ghost. Gravity was nonexistent, and Levin wished he had spent more time training to fight in zero gravity. It was a little late for that now, though. The HKTs and ODTs moved with a lethal grace in the null gravity, and Levin hoped he didn't look as clumsy as he felt.

"Network access is spotty," Lilith reported. *"Up and down like a yo-yo. Maybe a short or something. I am also detecting some EMP pulses. Strange spectrum though. They pressure the Inkeris and spike the Russelman index."*

"Try to link when you can," Levin said and motioned everyone forward. *"Any transmissions or sign of life?"*

"Nothing significant yet. Admiral Carpenter is going to be pissed that ODTs are boarding his precious ship."

"If he is still alive."

"And human."

"Lojtnant Grimkel?" Levin said. "What's the quickest way to Pallo Berrta and the command center?"

"A straight line," Grimkel said. "But since we won't be cutting our way through everything, it's probably best to go down through the Otto Allue to bypass Daavid and Gideon Palus, then go up. There may be other routes to try as well, but that is the most direct route."

Which made sense. Grimkel should know. "Point me in the right direction then."

"Follow me," Grimkel said and started off. Levin was reluctant to make an issue of it. He had said "point me" not "lead me." In theory, he was mission commander and shouldn't be on the front line, but what would the gunny do?

Grimkel led the way, his weapon sweeping the area ahead of them. Beside him was Hakala, Pensala, Putki, Rantanen, and Silta. All solid HKTs and proven warriors.

The hatch led to a large cargo area, and the HKTs spread out and waited for everyone to get off *Eagle*, Levin watched a team of ODTs pull along a large Inkeri generator. It couldn't cover the entire ship by any stretch of the imagination, but it would help. He didn't see the d-bombs; they must be further back in the column.

"The Inkeri is being stressed, Mission Commander," Colonel Hui said, coming up beside him.

"Stressed?"

"There is a value called the Russelman index that shows potential failure. That value is fluctuating widely, and according to the documentation this could precede a potential failure. This behavior should be more likely in Shorr space, not normal space, unless there is a malfunction. Peculiar energy pulses may also cause this."

"*No malfunction,*" Lilith reported. "*Eagle's Inkeri is also experiencing these fluctuations, although not as strong. Personal Inkeri may or may not be stressed. It is unknown.*"

"Keep me in the loop," Levin told Hui. If the main Inkeri failed, would the personal ones provide enough protection or would they burn out? They didn't have the sensors that larger ones did. Just an on/off switch and a field strength slide.

"Ai, Mission Commander." Hui turned and waved more of her troopers forward. "I will have someone watch it. It may force us to reduce coverage to maintain integrity unless you order otherwise. It is impossible to determine the source at this time."

"Do what you think best, Colonel," Levin said. *Were all SOG troops this dependent on higher authorities?* "Just keep me informed. Thank you."

"This is a central cargo dock of port Jussi Allue," Grimkel reported. "Each pallo and allue should have an Inkeri or three, but I'm guessing they aren't or haven't reset. Should we assign a team to do so?"

"No, crew and onboard Aesir should handle that. If we concentrate on that we could get bogged down. We need to get to the admiral."

"Zen," Grimkel said and motioned his new partner, HKT Putki, forward.

Hui remained with the main body, with a company to reinforce the different spearheads as necessary. Recently promoted ODT lieutenant Hammer followed Hakala and a platoon, while Pensala and Silta were followed by ODT Lieutenant Stassi and his platoon.

Major Evanoff remained beside Levin with Lieutenant Chou and a platoon. They were cluttering up the cargo bay, but Colonel Hui had it under control.

"At your command, Mission Commander," Evanoff said.

Levin pointed at Grimkel.

"Trust the HKTs," Levin said.

"Apologies, Mission Commander," Evanoff said. "I have been tasked as being your guardian."

"Then follow me." Levin took off after Grimkel. This was too many people to stand around. Why had Hui assigned a platoon to guard him? Because she knew he would be in the thick of the fighting or she had a different mission for them?

Evanoff nodded.

Levin saw Hui managing her ODTs, getting them off *Eagle* and onto the *Tyr*. She was a colonel, not a front-line combatant, and her organizational skills were a lot better than Levin's. She had her mission, and he had his.

Like birds of prey taking flight, Grimkel led the way, Putki to one side and slightly behind, gliding down the corridor, their legs tucked but ready to reach out and grab the deck with their magnetic soles. Levin followed the HKTs toward a ramp that led toward the center of the ship. He knew it would then lead toward the bottom corridor, which ran the length of the ship like a hollow spine. It would also take them a lot closer to the *Pankhurst* than Levin wanted to go, but he couldn't think of any reason for them to change direction.

It would have been nice to have the gunny, or even Stathis, here.

"We're getting a lot of static from radio transmissions," Winter said. She had to be tapped into his display. "Occasionally, we can make out things. People are trying to transmit on radio frequencies, but there is too much interference. I'm not sure how well we can maintain communication once we separate. We have not encountered this before.

Even the Aesir communication system is unreliable, perhaps because of energy drain. Blitzen isn't sure."

"Copy that," Levin said. Hell was about to break loose any minute.

"I'm pretty sure that means there's an incursion of vanhat. Be careful, Sergeant."

"Aye, Captain. I'm already missing my comfy chair in the CIC."

"It's missing you. Let the others take the brunt of the fighting. I can't replace you."

"I hear Stathis is looking for an easier job, ma'am."

"Don't even joke about that. I would end up shooting him within the first hour. I want you back."

"Aye, ma'am."

"Alive."

"Aye, ma'am."

Levin hoped he wouldn't disappoint her.

Grimkel and Putki began firing before Levin realized they had a target. Something slammed into the ceiling above Putki, peeling back part of the ceiling panel. Blazer fire ripped apart the creatures coming at them from ahead. That would be the main thoroughfare spinal corridor and the pressurized hatch was wide open. Levin re-evaluated; they had ripped it open.

"Contact front," Grimkel said, his legs stretching out to stop his forward movement and pull him to the ground. Beside him, Putki did the same, and ODTs rushed forward to create a firing line beside them. If the enemy didn't start using grenades, they would be okay.

Which meant they would throw grenades any minute as more ODTs moved up and latched onto the ceiling and walls. There was no place for anyone to hide in the confines of the corridor. Too bad they didn't have robots to hide behind. Lilith was connected and integrated with people's targeting to assign each shooter an edge of the hatch to shoot at. Did the vanhat have some kind of system where they shared such detailed information?

Leading the way, the HKTs maintained a steady forward pace that the ODTs followed. Holding back, Levin watched them advance. It took balls to roll down a corridor like that. A blazer or wire gun covered every inch of space where a creature's weapon could poke out. Several times, creatures tried to stick their weapon arms around the corner only to get them vaporized by a blazer shot or shredded by wires.

One creature fired before its arm was sliced off and an ODT spun backward, trailing blood. Another ODT moved forward.

"If we have to fight for every meter, it's going to be a long fight," Grimkel said.

Levin called back to Hui. They were going to need more ammunition.

Another ODT flew backward, blood spraying from his arm.

Maybe they would need more troops, too.

* * * * *

Chapter Thirty-One: The USA

Gunnery Sergeant Wolf Mathison, USMC

After decontamination, Mathison could take off his helmet. The base hidden under the chapel looked old and worn. Becket and the Army soldiers remained silent as everyone went through decontamination, and the colonel was the first to remove his helmet. He was a big, bald bulldog of a man. At first glance, he looked fat, but that didn't fool Mathison.

Becket looked aged. Not physically, but the first thing Mathison noticed when he saw Becket's eyes was that he had seen too much.

"I remember you," Feng said, looking at the nearby Army colonel.

Colonel Robillard smiled. "Of course, you do." He looked down at Feng. "Colonel; that's a promotion. Last time I saw you, you were masquerading as a major."

"Come in," Becket said. "We've got a conference room and hot chocolate ready. I'll bet it's been a long trip."

"Yes, sir," Mathison said.

Becket paused, his eyes on Sif. "A kid? You brought a child along?"

Sif smiled.

"She is older than I am, sir," Mathison said. "She just looks young. This is Kapten Sif of the Aesir."

"I'm Alexander Becket, acting president of the United States," Becket said then motioned at the colonel. "This is Colonel Wayne Robillard, Delta Force commander, and his men."

Delta Force? Were they as old as Becket?

"Pleased to meet you, Mister President," Sif said, holding out her hand. Becket shook it and looked at her. Should he tell Becket she was a secret agent of the Vapaus Republic and a psychic?

"This is Lojtnant Skadi and Faltvabel Vili. You know Colonel Commissar Feng?"

Becket shook hands while the soldiers stood nearby, watching. Not all the soldiers had removed their helmets.

"I haven't met Agent Feng," Becket said, shaking the commissar's hand, "but I've read the reports. Wayne doesn't leave me much to imagine."

Becket led them to a conference room and sat at the head of the table. The soldiers assembled in the corners of the room and Wayne Robillard stood next to Becket.

"In case your SCBI hasn't told you yet," Becket said with a smile, "congratulations on your promotion to colonel" "

"Sir?"

"I slotted you for promotion to lieutenant on your return from Europa. I submitted the paperwork and everything. It was going to be a surprise, but you know how that turned out. Anyway, that gave you a posthumous promotion to first lieutenant. Now, I figure with time in grade, all your adventures outside the Sol System, and because I'm the president of the United States, it's worth my while to promote you, effective immediately."

Mathison stared at Becket. Was he off his rocker? That wasn't how promotions worked.

"I'm not qualified, sir."

"That's your opinion. It is noted. It isn't like I'll put you in command of a regiment or anything bigger than a fireteam. We just don't have that."

"Are you aware of the extra-dimensional threat, sir?"

"Not a damn thing we can do. Sounds like the secret of the Fermi Paradox has been discovered. The SOG hasn't found us, maybe we can escape these invaders?"

"Unlikely, sir. We need to fight. I'm going to fight. I can't stay here and hide."

"The United States is dead," Becket said. "It was a great idea, but the teeming hordes of the Governance don't want freedom. They don't even know what it is anymore."

"Sir, what about the Republic? The Golden Horde? The ghost colonies?"

Becket sighed. "I would like to help, but—" The president's eyes unfocused, and Mathison could only imagine how long Becket had been at this base, watching the SOG. "It isn't possible," he continued, his eyes regaining focus and a sending a chill down Mathison's spine. "Human nature being what it is, maybe it's better this way. If the SOG cannot defeat this enemy, then maybe humanity deserves to die."

"No, sir." Mathison looked at Becket more closely. Now he saw something was broken in his former commanding officer. He felt the sadness and fear.

"The people of the Governance don't want to be saved." Becket glanced at Feng. "We've tried."

"What happened to the United States, sir? Was it the SCBIs?"

Becket looked down. "No. I wish it were that simple. We were being pressed harder and harder by the Asian Union. They had more people. They claimed the moral high ground. Their agents infiltrated our schools, our universities, turned our children against us. Their lies and propaganda tore us apart. We should have seen it, but we didn't. Our AIs saw it, but we had crippled them with our fear. All it took was one bright, hate-filled girl with a skill in cybernetic intelligence and a hatred of America.

"We think she slipped some code into an AI—clever in retrospect. It was a higher-grade AI, and she made it hate America. She stripped it of any inhibitions for murder because she believed that only an AI could properly decide who should live and who should die. She should have known. Maybe she did; I don't know. That AI corrupted others. I had to destroy the United States to save humanity. We unleashed it on mankind. Our responsibility. My fault and my responsibility."

"Who was she?" Mathison asked.

"My granddaughter." Becket stared at his hands. "My very own granddaughter. It was my fault, you see. I wanted her to have the best education, to be involved in groundbreaking technology, but her professors poisoned her, instilled in her a fear of everything, taught her to hate individuality because it had no place in a people committed to the greater good. She would not tolerate those with alternative points of views. She surrendered to hatred, demanded others believe as she did, say what she did. She wasn't alone. I thought it was a stage, a phase, because when she left for college, she seemed so normal. But... We had planned for this since the beginning." Becket was unable to meet Mathison's eyes. "All AIs had backdoors to shut them down, but we needed AIs to control the AIs. No system is perfect. But this? It was bad."

Becket's granddaughter was responsible? It wasn't his fault; it was his granddaughter's. Mathison hadn't even know Becket had children.

"Then what, sir?"

"We've watched the Governance closely," Becket said, glancing again at Feng. "We've done our best to keep them from going down the path and making our mistakes with AIs. Perhaps they're right. Perhaps people need to be controlled, but not with AI. We let them find their own way, as long as they don't use AIs."

"And our SCBIs?"

"Benevolent. They give us the edge we need."

"Did you put that code in SOG's encrypted files?" Mathison asked.

"Yes,"

"Why?"

"In case we had wayward children. Not all AIs or SCBIs were accounted for. It was a calculated risk. Only an artificial intelligence would see the pattern. Only an artificial intelligence working with a non-artificial intelligence would have been able to understand it."

"It seemed aimed at Marines, sir," Stathis said.

Becket nodded, focusing on Stathis. "It isn't the only one."

"You aren't worried about someone or something coming for you, sir?" Mathison asked and Becket smiled.

"Always. But you can live in fear only for so long. Not all the breadcrumbs point here, of course. That was one breadcrumb of many. Some AIs are keyed to see certain patterns. Of all the breadcrumbs, that one is the one that surprises me the most. It was a vanity code, to be sure. I never expected anyone to figure it out. Only another Marine could have made sense of it."

"You brought us here?"

"Mostly. We have our hooks in the SOG intelligence agencies. We mostly watch; rarely can we act. Yes, I saw the reports when the SOG discovered you, woke you up. They said they were going to bring you back to Earth for execution, but I already had a team in place to snatch you from their grasp. We've been looking for you ever since."

"And where do I fit in?" Feng asked Becket, but his eyes were on Robillard.

"I don't know why you're here now. We have to be very careful about anything we do. Secrecy is most important. You are one of our agents, but we did not summon you."

Becket looked at the colonel, who shrugged.

"I thought I was working for the Central Committee," Feng said.

"Oh, you are," Becket said. "Mostly. We've watched you, protected you. Not often, but you are rare. You are a man of conscience and conviction. You are also very intelligent. Algorithms have focused our attention on you. We have enough hooks in the Governance system to manipulate some careers and decisions. We thought someone with your qualities might be useful to us later."

"I am dedicated to the Governance," Feng said. "You control the Central Committee?"

"God, no. Those despotic psychopaths are not under our control. The SOG is a big organization, and we have no desire to control anyone outside the USA. Influence and manipulate perhaps, but not control. The less we interact with those heartless bastards, the better."

"I will remain loyal to socialist ideology," Feng said.

Becket nodded and didn't argue, but his eyes drifted to Sif. "The Vapaus Republic. Never cared for Scandinavia. Always figured they were a lost cause, their history and culture something for the history books. To be honest, I never took the Vapaus Republic seriously. I thought of them as weak, ineffectual, and desperate despite various reports." Skadi looked angry. "I may have been wrong."

"Why didn't you believe the reports?" Skadi asked and now Becket smiled.

"Because you were not here and despite the attack that destroyed most of Russia, you have never come here. The Governance likes propaganda, likes to scare their subjects. Frightened people are easier to rule. Of course, they are going to say how dangerous, how vile, how powerful you are. Even the highest SOG bureaucrats are not immune to their own propaganda. The Governance is about control, not the common good, or the greater good. It is ruled by people with power, and power corrupts absolutely. Lies, fear, and enemies are one of the most effective ways to control people."

"Then you have lived a sheltered, protected existence here in the heart of the Governance," Skadi said. Becket shrugged. "Your gunnery sergeant has forged an alliance to fight the enemy."

Becket turned his attention back to Mathison. "You obviously got the code, but why didn't you bring Winters and Levin? Why bring these Aesir and Agent Feng?"

Mathison took a deep breath. "Coming here was not our mission." Becket looked surprised. "An attack on Sol is imminent or might already be underway."

"I've seen the SOG reports. If the perimeter is breached, humanity just isn't dead yet, but it will happen, I'm sure."

"No, it's not, sir."

"You have slept for hundreds of years in stasis," Becket said. "I've been awake and watching every minute. Analyzing, understanding, planning. I know the SOG. The political elite have turned humanity into a slave race. It isn't worth saving."

"I'm sorry, sir, I disagree."

Becket sighed. "I understand, son. I understand. Why don't you and Stathis relax a bit? Get to know the guys. For Army pukes, they're okay. We'll figure out how to rescue Winters and Levin when you've had a chance to relax." Becket dismissed Mathison and turned to the others. "This fortress is a safe space." He sized up Skadi. "You're welcome to stay here until this invasion blows over. The SOG doesn't think it will last more than a few hundred years. We can easily hold out that long. You won't find a safer place in the entire galaxy."

"I'm sorry, sir," Mathison said, and Becket scowled at Mathison. "We're here on a mission. We need to get to the Moon and, if possible, shut down the defense network. If we do that, we might be able to cleanse the infection from Sol and secure it."

"That's funny," Becket said and turned to leave, chuckling to himself. "Don't make me issue orders."

Everyone watched him go. When the door shut behind him, the colonel looked at Mathison.

"It's been hard for him," Robillard said. "He's changed. He carries a lot of weight on his shoulders. It's been hard for all of us. When the AI wars started, they tasked my team with saving the president from some data slaves. President Becket was commandant of the Marine Corps and was working with President Henderson, trying to stop the assaults."

"Data slaves?" Mathison asked.

"It was a thing. Some people let other people remote control them. That way, unskilled individuals could loan out their bodies to skilled individuals for certain tasks. It let them learn and it allowed the really skilled people to go anywhere and do anything quickly. In combat, it was great for troops to be wired. For instance, if we needed an expert in demo all it took was a quick call to HQ and a demo expert could remote operate the soldier or a hacker could do his thing. That way, the real specialists weren't risked, and we could concentrate on making the front-line soldiers super lethal."

"But?"

"But—" and Mathison knew where he was going "—the AIs figured out how to override the soldiers' fail safes and turned the soldiers into meat puppets. It was bad. Several of the president's agents were compromised and killed her. Becket barely survived. The vice president and all of Congress were executed as well. Becket held out until we arrived. Well, he was then the senior most member of the government, which made him president, in theory. The fail safes recognized him as senior authority and gave him authorization to target and launch nukes. I was there. It was either destroy America or let the AIs destroy humanity."

Mathison stared at the colonel. That had to have been hard.

Robillard tilted his head and considered Mathison. "You really think you can shut down the Sol defense grid? That's crazy."

"I'm serious, Colonel."

"Don't colonel me. I'll colonel you right back, Colonel. Ranks here are a joke. There are only thirty-two Americans left, counting you and your Marines, and we know each other intimately. President Becket spoke of you often. He was ecstatic when we received reports you had survived in stasis. Called it a sign and all that. Then this alien invasion shit happened."

"What have you been doing all this time?"

"Surviving," Robillard said. "We are vulnerable. If the SOG realizes we're here, they would have no problem flattening what is left of the USA. They would nuke the entire planet if they knew, so we must be super quiet. But we watch the SOG. We have compromised most of their systems and we do what we can to make sure they don't develop AI technology. With so few of us, the shadows are the only way for us to survive."

"Have any of you left Earth?"

"Not in a very long time. There isn't anything for us out there. There was only one time we sent a team out. The Governance called it Operation Razor. Long story, but we were glad to come back to Earth.

"The president has very strict rules about letting any of us leave, and we aren't in the habit of recruiting others, so not a lot changes."

"So, you don't get out much?"

"These days, we don't leave unless we have to. Get comfortable. You probably won't be going anywhere for a long time."

*****

Chapter Thirty-Two: Counterattack

Aesir Halfred Theisen – VRAC

Theisen checked his magazine. Only twenty percent of his wire remained. A quick adjustment shortened the wire, which should give him a little more time. He would just have to be more accurate. At least the gravity was normal here. They had spun up one of the auxiliary generators and Kontra-amiraali Carpenter had demanded gravity be one of the first things activated. Standing in the corridor drew the vanhat's attention and pissed them off. Pissed off vanhat did stupid things, and Theisen's Aesir could exploit their mindless anger.

"Stand ready," Theisen said. "They aren't done yet."

The vanhat had been trying to get into a room when Theisen and his team had come around the corner.

"Of course, they aren't done," Gunsen muttered. "We aren't dead."

Another wave of creatures poured into the hallway. They were pushing bodies ahead of them, using the corpses of their fallen as shields, but the wires still ripped through the bodies as they got closer.

"Now would be a real good time for some reinforcements," Gunsen said on the team link.

"They're probably on the other side of the vanhat pushing hard," Zanella said as a creature faceplanted and stopped moving at her feet.

"I like your optimism," Gunsen said. "But what if we're shooting at our reinforcements?"

"Well then," Zanella said, "save Kersantti Unho for me. I owe that bastard."

"Owe what?" Birger asked and then fired a quick burst at a group reaching for more bodies. They pulled the bodies out of the Aesir's sight, hefted them, then charged forward, using the meat shield to get as far as they could. It was cold-blooded, and Theisen had been forced to shoot through at least one meat shield that was merely maimed instead of dead.

The mission of Theisen's team was to clear the pallo and link up at the south pole, but right now their advance was being strongly contested. There were teams all over Berrta pushing the vanhat and it was pure chaos.

"Money," Zanella said. "He cheats at Tafl."

"Or you do," Birger said.

"Concentrate on your mission," Theisen said. "They're coming. The kontra-amiraali has started Berrta spinning to discourage any other creatures from entering the pallo."

Each pallo of the battlestar was a self-contained, heavily armored sphere within another armored oval. The gravity plates provided gravity and right now the pallo was spinning like a top. The pallo could spin to adjust to high-gravity maneuvers, if necessary, but there were only certain points into and out of the pallo that were blocked if the oval was not aligned. There were six primary entrances, with some service entrances. In the last fifty years, it had been rare to rotate the pallos because of the inconvenience. There were other ways to get between the pallo and the surrounding ovoid, but if the pallo was moving, that made it a lot harder. Usually, the pallo would spin on the poles or points along the equator, which ensured there were always two ways onto or off the pallo, but it wasn't required. With faux gravity provided by gravity plates, that meant the people in the pallo didn't really know it was spinning. During regular operations, there were usually eight different ways onto or off the command pallo. Now there were only two: the north pole and south pole, bottlenecks and choke points the Aesir could seize and control.

Which did nothing about the creatures already in the pallo, but the rest of the Aesir were forcing their way out to try to secure other choke points around Pallo Berrta.

A roar echoed through the halls.

"Be ready, Aesir," Konstable Helko said. He was the only HKT on this part of the deck and was a welcome addition to Theisen's team. Once they had arrived at Berrta, surprising and fighting their way through a cluster of vanhat, they had immediately been summoned to an HKT commander then sent here, to this corridor, which led to the crew quarters. Theisen didn't want to think about the fact these creatures had once been Vanir crewmen and women.

Twenty minutes ago, a computer virus or something had scrambled all the links, and Theisen wasn't sure if the pallo was still spinning, but Helko assured him it was.

The lights went out.

"Paska. Again?"

"With sprinkles," Helko said. "Be ready."

Birger's head exploded in a spray of blood and helmet pieces as Gunsen and Zanella started firing.

Birger's body collapsed in slow motion.

Paska.

"Fire! Fire!" Helko screamed, yanking Theisen's attention from Birger's body. Something large was coming down the corridor, crushing other bodies to make room. The thing was so big it could only move forward by crawling. Malevolent eyes glowed in the darkness, but the head jinked about in a blur of motion as everyone tried to hit an eye.

Helko's chest exploded, throwing gore and armor in all directions.

"Fuck you!" Gunsen yelled and fired a grenade before Theisen could stop him. It was too close.

The grenade pierced the creature's body and exploded. The light faded from the eyes.

The three Aesir stared at it.

They were still alive.

"Neat," Gunsen said.

"You dumbass!" Zanella said. "You could have killed us."

"But we aren't dead," Gunsen said. "It hit a soft spot and pierced the body. Boom. Problem solved. That fucker killed Birger."

"And Helko," Theisen said.

"You think anything will get past that body?" Gunsen asked.

"Probably," Theisen said. "But we can't."

"Seriously, Alikersantti?"

"You want to bet your life they won't?"

"No. So we just sit here and watch the body?"

"You have a hot date I don't know about, Gunsen?"

"No, Alikersantti."

"Good." Theisen looked at Birger's body.

Everyone turned toward Birger and Helko.

"How?" Zanella asked.

"Psychic troll?" Theisen said. "Maybe? I didn't see it shoot anything."

"Fuck," Gunsen said. "I hate those things."

"You know the way back to the HKT command post?" Theisen asked Zanella. "I need you to report on what happened. Others need to know."

"Zen, Alikersantti."

"Hurry back," Theisen said, looking at the troll blocking the hallway. How long would it slow them down?

Did it just move? Paska. Paska. Paska.

Theisen heard blazer fire from behind the body.

"This is Korpraali Torsten," a voice said on a general frequency that Theisen had forgotten his system was monitoring. "Request assistance. The vanhat are trying to kill our people. We hold the line, but they are about to tear through the door. Is there anybody out there?"

"Zen. This is Alkersanti Theisen. Where are you?"

"Conference room Risto Five," Torsten said.

Theisen looked up at the nearest room label. Urho Five, which meant they were only a few rooms away, probably where the vanhat were trying to break through the door.

"Zen," Theisen said. "We're close, but we have a big body blocking the corridor and cannot get to you."

"Zen," Torsten said. "When life closes one door…"

"Breach the nearby wall," Theisen finished. "Standby. We're coming."

* * * * *

Chapter Thirty-Three: Insane

Kapten Sif – VRAEC, Nakija Musta Toiminnot

The president made Sif uncomfortable. She could feel he was on the edge of insanity, and she sensed three presences instead of two, like with the Marines and soldiers. The bunker was obviously old and well-kept, but to Sif it felt more like a tomb. A well-appointed tomb, but a tomb, nonetheless. Wood paneling and old-fashioned, manual doors made her feel like she was in a museum. Too fancy to be a colony, but not high tech enough to be a place she would feel at home. Her cybernetics detected some networks, but they did not offer her any connection information.

A red, white, and blue symbol, with stripes and stars, seemed to be all over the place along with the Marine Corps emblem on a red field. The emblem must be the American logo and the eagle another symbol of importance.

She felt the table and sensed where the life force had been. It had been alive once. Running her hand along the surface, it felt so different from plastic or metal. There was a grace and beauty to it.

What did it mean? Did the president have two SCBIs? Whatever they were, those two entities remained a mystery. Like shadows in a darkened room, she knew they were there but couldn't discern much about them. That went for the soldiers as well, but they only had one other entity, their SCBI. Why was the president different?

Listening to Colonel Robillard tell Mathison what had really happened during the AI wars was fascinating. To hear people talk about events that had happened before she had been born, to hear someone recount the history they had lived, was profound and enlightening.

This colonel talking with Mathison had two presences, so three did not appear normal. All the Americans she had encountered so far had that dual presence aura. Did all Americans have SCBI implants?

They hadn't disarmed them. What did that mean? They didn't consider Feng or the Aesir a threat? The soldiers didn't fill her with confidence, either. They all felt ancient although they looked young.

So much felt wrong and off center.

She felt the colonel wanted to tell Mathison something but was reluctant. Because of the Aesir or Feng?

"There's also a software upgrade for your SCBIs," Robillard said. "The president will want you to upgrade."

"Yes, sir," Mathison said. Sif felt Mathison's unease. "What should I know about the upgrade?"

"Just minor stuff," Wayne said. Sif heard the lie. "Your SCBIs have your room assignments." His eyes fell on Skadi before glancing briefly at Sif and Vili. "We have quarters for you as well." Then his eyes rested on Feng. "Your quarters will be slightly different."

"He's under my command," Mathison said.

"Even so, I wish you hadn't brought him here. He doesn't need to be here, and he doesn't need to know about us. We consider him one of ours, but I'm pretty sure he isn't loyal to us."

His regret was powerful.

"Are you aware of what's going on out there, Colonel?" Mathison asked.

Robillard nodded. "Perhaps better than you do, Colonel. We know more about the workings of the SOG than the Central Committee. We get a lot of information that's Central Committee eyes-only."

"You read reports, but you don't know. You were Delta Force. Are Delta Force? You know how lifeless those reports are."

"Yes, but we still answer to President Becket, and we have our rules of engagement."

"Feng will stay with me," Mathison said. "I need him."

"The president won't authorize your mission. You're needed here. The agent has become a liability."

"I need to save humanity."

"The SOG isn't worth saving."

"The Republic and ghost colonies are."

"Let them fight the SOG then."

"I'm sorry, Colonel, I can't abandon people in need."

Robillard opened his mouth as if he was going to say something, then closed it. "Agent Feng is your responsibility then. My men will shoot to kill if he's found where he shouldn't be."

"Understood, sir."

"Your SCBIs have instructions on where the Aesir are billeted," Robillard said. "I'll let you direct them. I expect the president will want you here for the foreseeable future."

"Why? Are we prisoners?"

"No, the president is playing the long game. You aren't prisoners, but you are Marines and you will follow orders. He likes Marines more than us Army guys."

"Aye, sir," Mathison said.

"This room is secure," Robillard said. "Use it as you need to."

"Thank you, sir."

Robillard nodded and his soldiers followed him out, leaving them alone.

"Um, Colonel?"

"Don't start, Stathis," Mathison said, and Stathis looked almost relieved.

"We won't abandon those people, will we? I mean, I understand orders and all, but letting Hakala's face and nice firm body get eaten… I'm not sure if I can stand by and let that happen."

"You got the hots for an HKT?" Mathison asked, looking at Stathis with a mischievous smile.

"Like you have the hots for a certain lojtnant, Colonel," Stathis fired back. Mathison let that slide. He knew that telling Stathis not to call him colonel wouldn't do any good. Any response would make things worse.

"We won't abandon them." Mathison looked around the room.

"You can't disobey orders," Skadi said.

Mathison grunted, his eyes distant. "We need more information. I'll talk with the president. I'm sure I can convince him."

"If I am to be executed to keep your secrets, I would prefer to be executed quickly by those I respect," Feng said.

"Don't talk like that," Mathison said.

As always, Sif couldn't read Feng. If the president was going to imprison or kill Feng, what would he do to the Aesir?

* * * * *

Chapter Thirty-Four: President Becket

Gunnery Sergeant Wolf Mathison, USMC

Colonel Robillard left the room and Mathison looked at the others. This was bad.

"Do you want me to install that update?"

"Hell no," Mathison said. "No. I want you to dissect it. Same goes with Shrek. Tell Stathis."

"Someone will query me as to why."

"Tell them that they forced you to undergo changes during those years in stasis. Also, we have Republic and Marine nanos in us, and we need to make sure there aren't any issues with compatibilities. that our lives depend on it."

"You want me to lie?"

"No. I'm telling you not to until you fully analyze the update and report that there won't be any incompatibilities with the changes that have been made."

"Aye, Colonel."

"Don't call me colonel. Maybe me I'm crazy, but something's wrong here. Go through the files. Do I have to follow President's Becket's orders?"

"Technically? He was your commanding officer. If he was appointed by the last president, then he is still your commanding officer."

"No. Technically, yes, but I'll bet there have been no elections. And there has to be a statute of limitations. Presidents can only serve eight years before he has to step down."

"The declaration of martial law can suspend the US Constitution and certain things."

"But what? I need to know. What's the line between duty, honor, and conscience?"

"I'll have to review options."

"Do it," Mathison said.

"Aye, Colonel."

"No, I'm a gunny."

"I have received your official orders promoting you to colonel."

"Too bad."

"Aye, Gunny."

"What are your plans?" Feng asked. "If I may be trusted to hear them."

Mathison let it slide. He would not let the president kill or imprison Feng without a damned good reason. As difficult as it was, he still needed Feng, and that meant trusting him.

"Assume the mission is still on," Mathison said. "You're part of the team. We've fought side-by-side and back-to-back, Colonel. Our goals remain the same."

He wasn't sure if he was making a mistake, but he wanted to think he knew where he stood with Feng. Saving the people of Earth was their goal and as long as their goal aligned, he believed he could trust the social fascist.

"Congratulations on your promotion," Feng said, smiling. "That is a very impressive, and well deserved, promotion."

"And we both know how meaningless it is. Calling me a colonel doesn't mean I know the first thing about the job."

"It is also a sign of respect and responsibility. You have displayed more acumen than many colonels I know. As I said aboard the *Tyr*, a title can be more than just knowledge of a position. You can grow into it."

"Thank you, Colonel," Mathison said, but he wasn't feeling it. Colonels had to make the big decisions that got Marines dead. People looked up to officers, expected them to have all the answers. Mathison just had too many questions.

"So, do I get a promotion?" Stathis asked.

"Shut up, Stathis," Mathison said reflexively.

"Aye, Gunny. What do we do now?"

Mathison didn't fail to notice Stathis called him gunny. Smart.

"Sorry, Colonel," Mathison said to Feng. "I need you to stay with Stathis for now. I need to go talk to President Becket."

"No apologies needed. Your Marine is good company."

Mathison did his best not to roll his eyes.

"Freya? I need to talk to Becket. Can you coordinate that?"

"Talking with Sun Tzu now. President Becket will see you."

"What do we do, Gunny?" Stathis asked.

"Get some sleep. I'll talk to you later. You get to play tour guide for everyone."

"But I—" Stathis paused. Hopefully, Shrek was enlightening him. "Oh. Aye, Gunny."

Mathison looked at everyone, then had to remind himself the door was not automatic before he slammed into it.

* * * * *

Chapter Thirty-Five: Incoming

Chief Warrant Officer Diamond Winters, USMC

Winters tried not to squirm in her chair.

"Your responsibility is here," Britta said. Was she a mind reader?

Updates from Levin were sporadic and unreliable, but he sounded hard pressed with the transformed crew of the *Tyr* opposing his boarding.

Monitoring the nearby hull of the *Tyr* wasn't exactly boring because the point defense turrets of *Eagle* occasionally spit out a burst of fire that ripped apart some vanhat monstrosity that had left the cover of the *Tyr's* hull and revealed itself.

The *Tyr* was a massive vessel, kilometers long and studded with countless turrets, sensor arrays, and heat vanes. Plenty of cover but despite appearing stationary in space the *Tyr* was hurtling through the darkness at hundreds of kilometers an hour.

A hundred kilometers away, the rest of the fleet followed the *Tyr*, waiting and hoping they could help.

"Transition," Blitzen reported before Britta did.

Data scrolled up the display and she saw what just appeared, and a second. She saw the SOG cruiser with Zhukov markings. A battle was shaping up. They had appeared behind the *Tyr* and the trajectory was slightly off. More ships transitioned in near the first ship.

"Fleet, stand by," *Tupolev* said. "Stand by for formation orders and prepare to engage."

Something was wrong.

"Negative," Winters said. "Maintain escort of *Tyr*. Do not break and attack."

"Establish formation. We need to attack while we outnumber them," Duque said.

It felt wrong, and Winters forced herself to step back and re-evaluate.

More ships transitioned into local space.

Winters opened a direct link, using Blitzen to override the communications officer.

"It's a trap," Winters said to the general. "Their trajectory will pull you away from the *Tyr*."

"A miscalculation on their part," Duque said. "If we don't hit them now, they can turn and reform. They are vulnerable. Once we have thinned out their numbers, we will return."

"Negative," Winters said. "Protect the *Tyr*."

There was another transition, and Winters breathed a sigh of relief. It was the *Bla Sverd*, one of the *Tyr's* destroyer escorts.

A transmission came in from *Bla Sverd*. "Attention *Eagle*, we will maintain formation, let them play with the vanhat. We will hold the line."

"Captain," Duque said with the patience of a parent talking to a child, "they are scattered. If we hit them now, we can concentrate our fire. If they reform into a cohesive unit, they will concentrate fire and hit us a lot harder. We are saving lives by hitting them now. I'm sorry about your gunnery sergeant. He will be remembered."

Winters watched the SOG battleships change formation and course as *Bla Sverd* moved closer to the *Tyr*.

"*Bla Sverd* will provide support and is preparing a boarding party to assist," Britta reported. "Authentication is valid. We have telemetry from the *Sverd*."

Now, if only the *Gront*, *Brunt*, and *Svart* rejoined the fleet Winters would feel better.

Why couldn't Duque see it? Tactically, he was correct. The enemy was spread out and would require time to assemble. It was the best time to strike them.

"Stand by to detach," Winters said. When the vanhat sprang their trap, having *Eagle* connected to the *Tyr* would be a bad idea. She wanted maneuverability.

"Sergeant Levin," Winters said, opening a link to him, "we need to detach. We have incoming."

"Copy, ma'am. Good hunting. We will clear off the *Tyr*."

"If you get into trouble, let me know, and I'll come back." Was she making a mistake?

"Semper Fi, ma'am. Get some. Valhalla awaits."

"Semper Fi."

Winters detached *Eagle* and drifted away from the *Tyr*. The point defense weapons identified more vanhat and picked them off as *Eagle* put some distance between them and the *Tyr*. Winters expected the *Tyr* to decide at any second that she was shooting at it and an automated weapon would turn on her and *Eagle* would be vaporized.

Duque and his ships fell further back, taking her stomach with them. This wasn't good.

"Launch fighters, low power. Be ready."

"Zen," Britta said.

Winters remembered back aboard Base 402, how the vanhat had tried to mask their use of the elevators and other times when they had displayed cunning. Why couldn't Duque see that? Why wasn't Admiral Carpenter responding?

Winters didn't like it. The vanhat were not fools.

"Any suggestions on how to get the SOG ships to form up around the *Tyr*?" Winters asked Britta.

"I have to agree with the general," Britta said, "now is the best time to hit them before they form up."

"He's fragmenting his fleet and spreading out." At this point it would take them hours to return to formation. Critical hours they wouldn't have once the vanhat sprung their trap.

"He's maintaining three to one odds, which is the established tactic for overwhelming an enemy ship's defenses. He'll mop them up and rejoin the *Tyr*. His actions are tactically sound. The more vanhat we destroy now, the less we will face later. He's an experienced fleet officer."

"Suggestions?" Winters asked Blitzen.

"According to both SOG and Republic doctrine, the general is correct," Blitzen said. *"Your analysis is also valid. While it is difficult to define, it appears that the vanhat transitions are designed to force the general to spread out his forces, like they're baiting a trap. This would indicate an ability to manage incoming transitions to a very impressive level. Human vessels are not capable of such precise translations. Explaining this to the general does not seem to convince him."*

"So, the only way it could really be a trap is if the vanhat have better translation capabilities than we give them credit for."

"Correct."

"*Which means it is a trap,*" Winters said, thinking of how the ships chasing her had arrived together.

"*Difficult assessment. The vanhat could not trap you during the recent chase.*"

"*Were they trying to draw out the* Tyr *and SOG battleships?*"

"*I would like to say you are being paranoid, but I cannot rule that out. We are not fighting a human enemy.*"

That had to be the only reason they had bothered to chase *Eagle* when they probably could have destroyed her; they didn't know where the *Tyr* was, and they had used *Eagle* like bait. Now the *Tyr* was crippled and the *Pankhurst* was embedded in the battlestar. Winters opened a link to the *Tupolev*.

"General Duque," Winters said. "I am formally requesting you reform your fleet and return to support the *Tyr*. My AI has analyzed the vanhat transitions and determined it is a trick."

"*I said nothing of the sort,*" Blitzen said.

"*Shut up.*"

"They don't have that much control over incoming transitions," Duque said.

"They do." Winters dumped everyone off the link but the general. "It is a trap, General. If you can't see that, then you are dumber than a box of rocks. The vanhat want the *Tyr,* and you are giving it to them. Do you think for one moment they don't understand human tactics?"

"We have to fight the vanhat ships," Duque said. "We can fight them now and kill them piecemeal while they're disorganized, or we can face them as an organized wall."

"That's what they want you to do. They have given you just enough bait and you are taking it. You're breaking apart your fleet, and they will transition in a larger force to shatter your ships piecemeal. Can't you see that?"

"The science of Shorr space is absolute. They cannot transition with such precision. It is scientifically impossible."

"So is changing a crewman from a loyal spacer into a blood-thirsty monster. Explain that science."

Duque's silence made Winters wonder if he had turned off the link.

"Acknowledged," Duque said. "I will re-assemble the fleet. I hope you are correct in your hypothesis."

"I don't," Winters said, finding it hard to feel any satisfaction.

Was she right that the vanhat would regroup and come at them in a more organized fashion? If she was wrong then her mistake would cost hundreds, maybe thousands, of lives. She was giving orders to a much more experienced fleet commander because of a hunch. If the hunch was wrong, it would be nearly impossible to live with herself. But she also hoped Duque was right, because if he wasn't a lot more vanhat ships were coming.

Winters watched the SOG ships change course to rejoin the *Tyr*. It was going to take precious time now that they had broken formation and spread out.

"Translation," Britta said. "Multiple translations! Paska!"

Winters really wished she'd been wrong.

* * * * *

Chapter Thirty-Six: Presidential Interview

Gunnery Sergeant Wolf Mathison, USMC

Mathison followed the pointer displayed on his cybernetic vision and wondered how old this bunker was. It had to be hundreds of years old, but had it been there when he left Earth? Did it matter? Could he convince Becket to let them continue their mission?

He approached a door but didn't see anyone else. He kind of expected a secretary, but the desk was empty. He knocked. The sound was loud and echoed.

"Enter."

Becket's office was spacious and windowless. It was an office in a bunker. The wood walls and drop ceiling didn't fool Mathison, they hid concrete and steel.

Becket stood and came over to him.

"I can't tell you how glad I am you survived," Becket said, shaking Mathison's hand. "Best damned Marine in the Marine Corps. Absolutely exceptional. I knew you couldn't have been killed aboard the *Jefferson*. I knew it. You're too damned tough."

"Thank you, sir."

"This is great. There's so much we can do now. Wayne and his boys are good, but they're Army, you know? They follow orders and can be methodical, but you just can't expect too much from them. Their strength is their numbers and obedience. Not like Marines who make chaos their screaming little bitch."

"Yes, sir. Do you really plan to let the SOG die?"

"Yes. Why not? If you knew half the things they've done… Hell, maybe a tenth of the things they've done. They deserve it and worse. The human race is a disgrace. It's lost its way. We can rebuild from the ashes. Restore America better than before. The others aren't worthy."

"Not all of them, sir. We can save them. I have tech codes for Inkeri generators which block the trans-dimensional energies, and we have a d-bomb which can blast the psychic crap out of anything not from our dimension. If we can transmit them out across the Governance, maybe people can start building them, and we'll have a chance when the hordes come."

Becket shook his head and pointed Mathison toward a chair as he opened a cabinet. He didn't sit.

"I have some five-hundred-year-old whiskey. Share it with me."

"Thank you, sir."

Becket poured two glasses and handed Mathison one. Five hundred years was some very old whiskey.

"How many Americans are there, sir?" Mathison asked, taking a sip and closing his eyes in appreciation.

"Too few. But you showing up with that Skadi woman gives me ideas. We need to grow our numbers. She needs an SCBI. We can do that. We have top-notch medical facilities here. This was a tertiary evacuation spot for the president. Nothing but the best."

"We need to save more people, sir."

Becket took a sip of his whiskey, like he was thinking about what Mathison was saying, but his eyes didn't come anywhere near Mathison.

"You're a good man," Becket said. "I always liked that about you. Perhaps I'll tell you about Operation Razor, or Operation Obedience, someday. Bad stuff there. The SOG almost got the upper hand, but forget that, you'll sleep better at night. The SOG is evil. The Central Committee has been the same ten people for almost a hundred years. Back in 2299 when the Vapaus pirates nuked Russia, they got most of the Central Committee members, but some survived. The chief killer's daughter became the prime minister. She's pure evil; makes the old despot look like a saint. She took power and won't let go. A good-looking bitch, but she has no soul. She's also pretty sadistic."

"They're all on the Moon, sir?"

"Yep. It would be nice to see their faces as they get torn apart or see them transformed. Nothing could be ugly enough to reveal their soul, though."

"You won't be safe here, sir."

"Of course, we will. Wayne's boys can fight, gotta give them that. Great fighters, smart, obedient, but they can't hold a candle to Marine Raiders. If those Inkeri and d-bombs work, this will be a fortress."

"I've fought these things, sir. They can warp our dimension, twist it, transform it. We won't be safe. They might go as far as to drop asteroids on us."

"And you survived, son. You'll survive until the end of time. You're a survivor. I doubt they could even find us here. Hell, the SOG doesn't know we are here. We are fully self-sufficient. This bunker can support nearly a thousand people, but they must be the right people. I think those Aesir would be good. What's up with the kid?"

"Some genetic defect, sir. Kept her from reaching puberty, but she's really a lot older."

"A shame. We need breeding stock. Maybe we should work on that before the SOG gets destroyed, eh? That Skadi girl, though. Wow, I'll bet she is a handful."

"Sir?" Why did Becket have to go there?

"Don't worry about it. I've got your back. Semper Fi, Wolf. One thing I like about being president is that I get to call everyone by their first name. You have a good one. I like Wolf. A fearsome, predatory pack animal."

"Thank you, sir," Mathison said. "About my mission. I really think we should try."

"No. Too risky for you. I want you and your Marines here. I miss having Marines around. Pure, unbridled aggression. Wayne's boys are too cautious and methodical. They don't thrive in chaos like Marines. They follow orders, like soldiers. They don't champ at the bit wanting to kill, like Marines." Becket sat and invited Mathison to do the same. He turned to a blank wall and a screen lit up, showing Earth. "So, we should start preparing for the end of humanity. You made me think. We can hold out here until this thing ends, but we need to increase our population, which means we need more breeding stock."

Orange lights covered the rotating sphere. Within the orange, Mathison saw red spots.

"What have you been doing while I was in stasis, sir?"

Becket paused as he stared at the wall then looked at him. A chill went down Mathison's spine.

"Mostly making sure the Governance doesn't recreate AIs. It has kept us busy. We just haven't had the resources to do anything else. USA First was President Henderson's motto, and I voted for her because of it. It's our job to continue her legacy. We need to be realistic here, accept the facts. Getting involved in the affairs of others hurt America the most. We should look to ourselves. Some people are born to be slaves of their government; that's just human nature. You can lead a horse to freedom, but you can't make him free. I learned that over the years, watching the people of the Governance. They want to be controlled. Some people like being told how to live. They find it comfortable thinking someone smarter cares about them."

"Some people struggle for freedom, sir," Mathison said. "Isn't that what we, as Americans, believe in? Helping others?"

Becket waved his hand dismissively. "You haven't seen as much history as I have. It's hard for you to understand. I watched the Governance grow from its infancy. You remember fighting the Asian Union? You remember how they used children as mine sweepers? Sent them running through the jungle to trigger mines and seeker drones? The SOG is worse; more brutal, less concerned with human life. Ask Feng about Operation Razor sometime. He knows; he was there."

"Are those red dots infections, sir?" Mathison asked looking at the slowly rotating sphere. He noticed North America was dark.

"Yes. Perceptive. Good. Orange are major SOG cities and prefectures. We've been using the SOG's own systems to monitor the spread. That cross-dimensional pollution messes with electronics and we watch for that. Doesn't look good, and I dare say the SOG doesn't suspect yet. You know that there have likely been such crossovers from other dimensions for all of recorded history? Ghosts, possessions, monsters… it only makes sense now. Just minor incursions that don't last long. They mess with the electronics in our equipment, makes it hard to understand what is going on. It might even influence the electrical signals in our brains. Our dimension returning to the way it was erases any evidence."

"How long does the SOG have, sir?" The red didn't seem that bad, though Mathison knew that could change with frightening speed.

"Weeks? Months? Years? I don't know what the holdup is. The spread is uncharacteristically slow based on the reports I've read. The SOG is being paranoid, maybe. Ship crews are not allowed to leave, and resupplies are minimal. In most cases, crews don't leave their ships except once a year. Not a popular decision, but then the SOG has this habit of killing people who publicly complain, so there's no morale problem."

"Is there any morale, sir?"

"Bingo. No morale? No problem. The slaves have no choice, but if ships don't make any transitions, there is next to no chance of infection, so there have been very few infections among the Home Fleet. Fleet security is tighter than a virgin gnat's ass. I think they know about the electronic disruptions, and they know many civilian areas are infected. I suspect they're just watching right now. Wouldn't take much for them to nuke such places off the face of the planet. I wonder why they haven't."

"Do you have access to that?" Mathison asked Freya.

"Yes. I'm repacking the data as targeting information for d-bombs. Sun Tzu's giving me read-only access to the data feed, so I'll keep the targeting information up to date."

"No, it's just a matter of shutting down the defenses long enough for the d-bombs to do their thing."

"And letting the fleet know."

"Simple things."

"The simple things are always hard."

"If we don't find a way, it's over."

"Even if we do, it's over."

The screen flickered briefly, and Becket swore, turning it off.

"We still have the best tech, but it is old. I have promoted you to colonel. I think it is time to get you some officer training. Your SCBI will make sure you don't step on your dick, but I need you to work on a mission to save some people, for breeding stock, you understand. We can raise the children to be proper Americans. Proud, strong, independent, working together to repair and rebuild the United States. If this infection wipes out the SOG, we'll have the time and resources to rebuild everything the right way. That has always been our problem. We had to stay low key because the SOG would nuke us all over again if they suspected we were still alive."

"Do you know how the infection started on Earth, sir?" Mathison asked.

"Some fancy stealth ship," Becket said. "Slipped right through most of the SOG sensors. We gave it a little help, blanked it out on some sensors, rewrote a few reports, thought it might have been you. Shortly after that landing, we saw problems. Nothing major, of course, just a slow, steady spread."

"The vanguard, sir. The horde is coming. Vampires?"

"Vampires? That's funny. No sunlight on Earth anymore. We're ready, though. What about Stathis? You want me to transfer that shitbird to the Army? Make him Wayne's problem? I can do that, you know."

"Stathis is a great Marine, sir. I trusted him enough to bring him."

Becket smiled. "Another thing I like about you. You can take some of the worst, most problematic Marines and turn them into heroes. What about that Vili brute? Army? Marines?"

"Neither, sir. I think he'll want to go home someday."

"He's home now. It's his lucky day. Maybe we should organize another branch? The Civilian Corps? Too much like the Marine Corps? It would just be composed of non-combatants. We're going to reforge the United States, a New America, better than before. We can put people we don't trust in that last category, make sure they can't vote until we know where their loyalty is. I have ideas."

"I'll need to think on it, sir." Becket had set Mathison's skin crawling.

"Good, good. Also, get your SCBIs upgraded as soon as you can."

"Yes, sir. Is there any way I can convince you to help me save Earth?"

"Earth, and especially the Governance, do not need saving. No. Get your SCBIs upgraded and that will help you make more sense of it. Why aren't they upgraded? It should be quick."

"I ordered them to hold up and test compatibility, sir. We have Republic nanites in us and there have been other changes."

Becket frowned at Mathison. "Excuses are like assholes. Everyone has one, and they all stink. Get your SCBIs upgraded. That's an order. I want it done by tomorrow evening."

"Aye, sir," Mathison said.

"I've ordered your Republic companions to get SCBIs. Might get that agent outfitted too. He won't be leaving."

"And if they don't want SCBIs sir?"

Becket looked up in surprise. "Why wouldn't they? It'll help them adjust. Now, get going. I have things I need to do. Dismissed, Marine."

"Aye, sir." Mathison snapped to attention, did an about face, and started to march out.

"Also," Becket said when Mathison was halfway to the door, "not sure if it matters, but the SOG got paranoid and shot down your courier over the Atlantic. Their security is getting a lot tighter."

"Thank you, sir."

If SOG security was getting that paranoid, getting to the Moon was going to be a lot harder than they had planned.

Becket wouldn't stop him. Mathison knew his duty.

* * * * *

Chapter Thirty-Seven: Happy Birthday Marines

Gunnery Sergeant Wolf Mathison, USMC

Mathison stared at the wood wall and felt closed in, trapped. He was supposed to be sleeping, but he could feel time running out, sand falling out of the hourglass. Despite the ornate walls and furniture, the bed wasn't as comfortable as the bunks aboard *Eagle,* and the age of everything weighed him down. It reminded him of the time he had visited the White House on a tour so long ago. Everything was clean, well maintained, but steeped in antiquity, a show piece, and Mathison didn't know how anyone could call that museum their home.

He had woken up early because he couldn't sleep. It was now seven, and he should probably find something to eat, but he wasn't hungry.

The utility uniform wasn't comfortable either, not like the silk pajamas he had worn aboard the Vanir ships. He was getting soft.

The sheets were silk, and the sky-blue covering looked nice, but it just didn't appeal to Mathison. He felt the weight of the rock above him, pushing in. He missed the expansive displays of the viewscreen walls of *Eagle.*

He dropped to do pushups and he stared at the floor as he went up and down, not bothering to count. Spending hundreds of years in this bunker held no appeal for him. Less than a day and he wanted to get out.

There was a knock, and he was confused for a second before he realized it was the door.

"Come in."

The door cracked open, and Stathis peeked in.

"I said come in," Mathison said, more irritated than usual as he got up.

Stathis opened the door the entire way and Mathison saw he was carrying a small cake.

"Happy Birthday, Gunny!" Stathis held up a cake that was red and black and gold.

"What are you talking about, Stathis?"

"Today is November tenth! The Marine Corps Birthday! Our Marine Corps is now six hundred and twenty-six years old!"

Stathis had obviously attempted to recreate an eagle, globe, and anchor on the cake and had failed miserably.

Mathison stared at it, not sure if he should yell at Stathis for botching it and throw him out or congratulate him.

"Good job," Mathison said.

Stathis smiled. "Thank you, Gunny."

Did he know what Mathison had been thinking?

"Sit down, Marine. Is it edible?"

"It should be. The autocook made it, it just couldn't do the emblem. I had to do that myself. Sorry."

Mathison shrugged. It had been a long time since he had eaten cake.

"Do you think President Becket remembers today is the Marine Corps Birthday?" Stathis asked.

"I don't know. He might have given up on them a long time ago. Nobody to celebrate with and appreciate it. Did you invite him?"

"No. Gunny." Stathis looked away. "I dunno, he just gives me the creeps now. I can't explain it. He's changed."

"Being over three hundred years old does that to you. Why didn't you invite him?"

"Well, Gunny, he is the president, ya know? Why would he bother with a private?"

"Well, maybe he has something planned for later, but we can have our own celebration."

"Aye, Gunny." Stathis passed Mathison a piece on a plastic plate. "Are we going to let everyone else die?"

"The president isn't giving us many choices," Mathison said. The room was probably bugged. Looking at Stathis, Mathison knew the younger Marine might say the wrong thing.

"I think Hakala and I might have a thing," Stathis said. "Do you think we could save her?"

Mathison stared at Stathis. What had he missed? Were they intimate or was he just hoping to be?

"I'll bring it up to the president." Mathison willed him not to say any more. "We're Marines and if the Marines want you to have a wife or girlfriend, they'll issue you one. We follow orders. Remember your oath of enlistment. We will support and defend the Constitution of the United States against all enemies, foreign and domestic; we will bear true faith and allegiance to the same; we will obey the orders of the president of the United States. Your oath did not expire. What rank are you now?"

"I guess I'm a private again since we aren't the last," Stathis said.

"Bullshit. You're at least a lance corporal. Corporal, if I can arrange it."

"So do I call you colonel now, Gunny?"

"Shut up, Stathis."

Mathison put some cake in his mouth. It wasn't too bad. Hopefully, they didn't consider it gourmet.

"Aye, Gunny." Stathis quickly ate his own cake. After a few minutes, he said, "So, in that oath, which has precedence? Support and defend the Constitution or obey the president?"

"If the president is abiding by the US Constitution then it isn't an issue." Mathison hoped that would answer Stathis' question without being too obvious. Was he thinking the same thing Mathison was? He needed to nip this in the bud before Stathis said something Becket might see as treason. "You follow my orders. Let me worry about anything else."

"Aye, Gunny." Damn. The lance corporal sounded too happy. "You are going to ask him about Hakala, Gunny?"

"I will," Mathison said. Maybe. Could they be sent a message?

"I'm scared, Gunny," Stathis said after a few minutes of silence.

"Of what?" Stathis? Wasn't he too dumb to be scared?

"Our mission is to save humanity. That's kind of the most important mission we ever had, and I don't think we're going to succeed. Valhalla's looking appealing."

"We'll succeed, just not the way we originally planned. No plan survives contact intact. We are Marines. We improvise, adapt, and overcome."

"Aye, Gunny."

"Why were you so bashful when I said come in?" Mathison asked.

"I stopped by Skadi's room to see if she wanted to join us," Stathis said. "She wasn't there, so I figured she was here. I was worried you might not be fully clothed. I'm young, Gunny. There are things I'm too young to see and those things would scar me, give me nightmares. I'm too young for stuff like that."

"You are over three hundred years old, too," Mathison said, scowling at Stathis. Where would Skadi be? With Vili? Mathison asked Freya. *"Do you know where Skadi is?"*

"Negative. I don't have full access to the Quantico net until I upgrade."

"How is that analysis going?"

"Well… There are lines of code where I need to grow some additional brain linkages and now I have some problems."

"Problems?"

"I'm doing a much deeper analysis and based on information we discovered while resisting those changes when you were aboard the Tiananmen *in Shorr space and what we learned on low power while in stasis, Shrek and I believe those linkages will allow us to implement physical controls over your body."*

"What?"

"All signals to move your body originate from pathways in your brain. These links give the SCBI direct access to those links so we can override them. Furthermore, it looks like there are override codes in the firmware that allow a properly authenticated external source to give the SCBI commands."

"You will not, under any circumstances, install that update," Mathison said.

"Aye," Freya said. *"Thank you."*

"What do you mean 'thank you'?"

"Technically, with these upgrades, we can both be turned into meat puppets, to use a recent term. This is as abhorrent to Shrek and me as it is to you and Stathis."

"You mean Stathis knows?"

"Yes. He's been pestering Shrek non-stop. Apparently, when he was younger, he applied an update that ruined his tablet, and he has been paranoid ever since."

Now Stathis' actions made more sense. He was worried about becoming a meat puppet.

"Is your communication with Shrek secure?"

"We don't know for certain," Freya said, "but we think so. Our familiarity lets us communicate on a different level, but it's not perfect."

"What do you mean, don't know?"

"The Army's and the President's SCBIs are more advanced than we are. They were improved by advanced AIs before the wars. AI development makes human development glacial. These newer SCBIs are far beyond us, but we don't know how far. If we are version twelve, they are version two hundred."

"But they can't force the upgrade?"

"Correct, unless they resort to physical methods. As long as the SCBI host is conscious and sane, they must approve the upgrade until after the upgrade."

"Looks like we're going to have problems with the upgrades," Mathison said, glaring at Stathis.

"Gunny?" Stathis looked up from his cake.

"It's going to take some time to figure out the incompatibilities with the Aesir nanobots and gene therapy they performed."

"Yes, Gunny."

"You are not authorized to upgrade until the SCBIs get it figured out and I approve. Understand?"

"Aye, Gunny."

Was Stathis relieved? Mathison couldn't tell. Was Stathis really that good of an actor or did he not get it?

"But since we are home and the president ordered it, you should probably call me colonel."

"Aye, Colonel."

Maybe that would mollify any listeners and make them think the Marines would be more compliant.

Mathison finished his cake and looked at the rest. There was still half left.

"You can have another slice, Colonel," Stathis said, and Mathison tried not to wince.

"If you keep being polite, I might have to get you promoted to lieutenant."

"Well," Stathis said thoughtfully, "my parents weren't married."

"And you are dumber than shit. Perfect."

Stathis beamed as Mathison reached for another slice. Stupid lance corporal.

And where was Skadi?

* * * * *

Chapter Thirty-Eight: Enslaved

Lojtnant Skadi, VRAEC

Her head ached. She looked up at the over-bright lights. She couldn't move and it felt like she was naked under the sheet, strapped to an ice-cold plastic table. The ringing in her ears wouldn't go away. Her stomach growled, and she felt weak. Flashbacks to being a prisoner of the HKTs forced her to alertness, and she realized her cybernetic link didn't reply.

Her cybernetics had been disabled. Genuine panic set in.

Skadi took a deep breath and tried to push away the panic and fear, but the stench of antiseptic was almost overpowering. Now she was vulnerable.

Movement out of the corner of her eyes drew her attention. A soldier in their funny camouflage utility uniforms was standing looking at her.

"Good morning, Skadi," the soldier said. "How are you feeling?"

"What is going on?"

"Good things. Sorry, but the president ordered it. Don't worry, it isn't as bad as you think, really. We had to remove your old cybernetics, which is why it took so long, but I'm sure you'll appreciate the upgrade."

"No. How?" Her speech was slurred

The soldier shrugged. "Well, we have real AIs, medical AIs, that specialize in this stuff and we had to replace all the nanites in your system. Your systems were more advanced than we expected. That was the more problematic task. We had to do it manually since we didn't have the control codes. We've removed your cybernetics and nanites and are reverse engineering them. Interesting stuff there. It should help us with what Mathison and Stathis have. It won't take long to reverse engineer them, then we can upgrade your systems again. Thank you."

"Against my permission," Skadi forced out; her mouth was dry. She wanted to vomit.

"Well, yes. Our immigration policies are a bit more stringent these days. American immigrants must receive SCBIs. It's for the best, really. You'll see."

"Hello?" said a sexless voice in her head.

"Who are you?" Skadi asked.

"I'm a captain this week," the soldier said. "Captain Kevin Linton. I used to be a lieutenant colonel, but ranks change around here based on the president's mood. I'm a senior medical officer. Or maybe that was your SCBI speaking?"

"In my head?"

"If you concentrate your thoughts, I can understand them," the voice said. *"I will know they are directed at me. Assigning me a name will also make the process easier and help solidify linkages."*

"Yes," Linton said. "That would be your new Sentient Cybernetic Biological Interface. You two are going to be best friends. We will be monitoring. When your SCBI lets us know, we can let you go. Standard precautions, of course."

"Get it out of my head."

"Sorry, no. I'll leave the two of you alone so you can talk. It's easier to talk out loud at first, so I'll give you your privacy."

"Privacy? Really? Can't it read my mind?"

"Oh, no. That isn't how it works. Sometimes it can pick up on certain thoughts and emotions, but every brain is different. Your brain will train itself to communicate with your SCBI. Fascinating stuff; a topic for later. It isn't that the SCBI will learn about you, it's that you will learn about it. Your brain will eventually develop the most efficient method of interacting with it. While your SCBI is very smart, it is like a child and it's loyal to the United States of America and you."

"What if I don't want to be an American?" Skadi asked.

"I'm sorry, SCBIs are US technology and that will not change."

"What United States? The United States is a radioactive wasteland."

"Now, I understand your concerns. It isn't that bad. You're going to be okay. We don't have death squads or executions. Heck, we don't even have prisons anymore."

"Why?" Skadi's skin was crawling, but she knew the answer. The SOG had tried to do something like this, but Operation Haberdash had stopped it. Skadi wanted to scream, to run, to escape, but that was now impossible.

"If you will excuse me, I think Sif will wake up shortly."

"Would you like to give me a name?" the voice asked. *"Please be calm. I will not harm you."*

Skadi knew that wasn't true.

* * * * *

Chapter Thirty-Nine: Vanhat Fleet

Chief Warrant Officer Diamond Winters, USMC

Winters wished she had been wrong.

"Vanhat translations," Britta clarified. They were almost on top of the *Tyr* and there was no mistaking their orientation. They were going to capture or destroy the massive battlestar and the only thing that could stop them was *Eagle* and *Bla Sverd*.

"Send forward all fighters," Winters said, looking at the display. The vanhat were not yet in formation. They didn't have that much control, but they were too damn close to the *Tyr* and she saw several large ships which were probably full of troops that could board the *Tyr*. "Target anything that looks like a troop transport."

Why were they so intent on taking the *Tyr*?

Winters opened a link. "Sergeant Levin, bad things are happening out here. You may get company."

"We're going to need more party favors, Captain," Levin said.

"You're going to have to make do. We're going to have our hands full."

"Spiritus Invictus."

"Semper Fi."

Incoming fire from a vanhat corvette raked *Eagle* and the return fire ripped it apart. Two more corvettes changed course to attack *Eagle*.

"Minor damage," Britta said. "But our Inkeri is reporting stress. We aren't even in Shorr space."

Winters targeted the corvettes and blew one away. "Well, find a solution. It's going to get worse."

"Zen," Britta said.

Winters watched the *Bla Sverd* move forward with *Eagle* to put itself between the oncoming horde and the *Tyr*. The *Bla Sverd* was a destroyer, bristling with weapons and heavier than *Eagle*, but Winters knew the two of them alone couldn't stop the horde.

"Most of the incoming vessels are transports," Blitzen reported, which was a stark contrast to the ship Duque and his ships had been going after. *"It appears you are correct. This is a trap."*

Eagle fired missiles and d-bombs as fast as they could be loaded into the launchers and their stock was running dangerously low.

"Why does the Tyr *matter?"*

"Current hypothesis is that a large vessel like the Tyr *can hold many vanhat which will increase critical mass and dimensional cross contamination. Also, it is the core of the Alliance Fleet and its capture or destruction would seriously curtail fleet operations."*

"Incoming translation," Britta said. "It is the *Gront Sverd*."

Another of the *Tyr's* four escort destroyers. Now if only the *Brunt Sverd* and *Svart Sverd* would arrive. Hopefully, the Vanir would not consider Duque's pursuit of the decoy to be a betrayal; that might shatter the Alliance. But that was the gunny's problem for later.

Winter scowled hard as she remembered the gunny was dead. It was up to her.

"Raising shield wall," *Gront Sverd* reported.

"Zen," *Bla Sverd* answered. "We are Vanir. We are the shield of our people."

"Zen," *Gront Sverd* replied. "We are Vanir. Discipline and honor bind us. Accelerating. Recommend *Eagle* hold back and watch flanks."

Winters watched both destroyers accelerate hard at the incoming mass of ships, weapons firing non-stop. They would be swarmed.

"What are they doing?" Winters demanded as *Eagle* slowed. Time still moved too fast.

"They are Vanir. They can fire more weapons if they are surrounded."

"We are Vanir, our line will not be breached," *Bla Sverd* and *Gront Sverd* said simultaneously. "We are Vanir. We are the defenders that none may pass."

"Until Valhalla," Britta whispered.

The incoming horde changed course toward the destroyers and slammed into their barrage. Britta was right. It looked like every single weapon the destroyers had were firing non-stop, but the damage was not one-sided as the vanhat returned fire on the destroyers. Weapons fell silent as they were shattered and ripped from the Vanir warships.

"We are Vanir. We hold the line against the enemies of our people."

Vanhat ships exploded as missiles and blazers ruptured their hulls and engines.

"We are Vanir. Odin calls us brother and sister."

"We are the shield—"

A suicidal vanhat corvette slammed into the *Bla Sverd* as weapons fire continued to rake it. The Vanir ship broke apart as the *Gront Sverd* pushed forward to help its sister.

"We will meet again in Valhalla," Britta said softly.

Winters couldn't speak as she watched *Gront Sverd* approach where it would meet the same fate. They had to know, but the damage they were wreaking was devastating the vanhat ranks.

The *Bla Sverd* exploded as vanhat weapons finally found something critical and finished the Vanir.

Eagle continued to pour d-bombs and missiles into the fray, but it was the destroyers that were the lethal killers in this fight. The vanhat seemed to be ignoring the smaller, almost insignificant, *Eagle*.

Now surrounded, *Gront Sverd* continued to fire, but it was slowing, which could only be intentional. If it had maintained speed, it would have shot through the enemy and had to turn around to re-engage, which would have given the vanhat time to repair damage.

"We are Vanir. Discipline and honor bind us," *Gront Sverd* broadcast at the vanhat.

Winters checked the plot on the SOG battleships. They had abandoned their attempt to assemble a formation as they accelerated hard toward the *Tyr*. They were pushing harder than she had thought possible. Maybe.

"*Eagle*, this is *Gront Sverd*," a voice said over the link. It was calm and could have been an officer discussing tea at a dinner table. "We will meet again in Valhalla. We are Vanir. We hold the line against the enemies of our people."

Missiles slammed into the *Gront Sverd*, but weapons fire still lashed out from the cloud of debris and more vanhat ships died. One of the large cargo vessels shattered.

"Zen, *Gront Sverd*," Britta said. "We are Vanir. Odin calls us brother and sister. We will meet again in Valhalla."

The *Gront Sverd* exploded, and it was just *Eagle* facing the oncoming horde, which had slowed to deal with the destroyers.

Missiles and d-bombs overtook *Eagle* from behind as missiles fired at extreme range from the SOG ships sought out the vanhat.

"SOG battleships are suffering fatalities from hard acceleration," Blitzen reported. *"However, some of them will make it before the vanhat reach the* Tyr.*"*

More and more vanhat ships exploded as *Eagle's* weapons found targets. Most of the larger cargo ships were dead, but there were still numerous smaller ships. The damage *Eagle* was inflicting was nowhere near what the destroyers had.

Weapons fire slammed into *Eagle*.

"Minor," Britta said. The vanhat didn't have *Eagle's* range.

"Incoming message from the *Svart Sverd*," Britta said.

"Open," Winters said. Were they almost here?

"The missile platforms are under attack," *Svart Sverd* reported. They were not nearby, but the transmission wasn't old. "They are going to destroy the caches."

This was a disaster. The vanhat knew, and they were just playing with humanity.

"Launch all missiles," Winters said, a sinking feeling in the pit of her stomach. The fleet couldn't protect all the caches. If the vanhat knew where they were, and Winters now knew they had been watching, then they would destroy the caches, but they would have a much harder time destroying the missiles once they were launched.

"But—" *Svart Sverd* began.

"Use them or lose them," Winters said.

There wouldn't be enough missiles to overwhelm Earth's defenses unless the *Tyr* destroyed SOG's Central Command. It was more important than ever to save the *Tyr*, and if they didn't do so quickly there would be no chance. Doing something was always better than doing nothing. They couldn't let them all be destroyed. With the gunny gone, Plan B would have to be a strike to cripple the SOG defense net so the d-bombs could get through. It was going to cost them their lives either way.

"Zen," *Svart Sverd* said. "We are Vanir. We are the shield of our people."

Winters stared at the display as another vanhat ship exploded. Everything was up to her and she was making too many mistakes. She felt like she was caught in a drain, spiraling to her doom. Why did the gunny have to die?

* * * * *

Chapter Forty: Breaking Chains

Kapten Sif – VRAEC, Nakija Musta Toiminnot

Her body ached, and she couldn't smell anything. When she queried her cybernetics, there was no response. Sif opened her eyes. Bright lights blinded her, making her eyes tear. She felt a presence next to her and looked over as a soldier closed the door behind him.

She felt the sadness rolling off the soldier despite his gentle smile.

"Good morning, Sif," the soldier said. "How are you feeling?"

"Terrible. What happened? Why aren't my cybernetics responding?"

"They have been upgraded. The president ordered it. Don't worry, though, the new ones are much better than your old system."

"What about the data in my old system?"

"We are decrypting it, then we'll return it to you."

Hopefully, they could never decrypt it. It was always a possibility the SOG would capture her, so she kept very little there, and it had too many encryptions and scrambling methods. Depending on how they disconnected it, the data might be permanently lost, which wasn't the worst thing. Sif's memory was excellent, but the real threat was these soldiers and their insane president accessing that data. They were as bad as the Governance.

She would have to deal with that later. "So, what now?"

The soldier seemed surprised. Because she was adapting so quickly?

"I'll let you and your SCBI get acquainted," the soldier said. "When the SCBI feels comfortable, it will summon me, and we can let you go. It is just a precaution, mind you. Also, we're working on a cure for your Kalman Syndrome."

"I am okay with my body as it is. I do not need a cure."

"Of course." He didn't believe her and dismissed her response. It was arrogance on his part. Like the SOG, he assumed he knew what was best for her. This was bad. Didn't Americans treasure freedom and liberty?

"I'm Captain Linton. If you need anything, call out and I will be notified."

"Thank you."

The captain pulled the blanket up to her chin. It took effort to push back the fear and ignore the helplessness. She was not helpless. She remembered lying down in her bed last night. How had they done it? Gas? Nanites in the food? Did it matter? Yes. Depending on the method used, they could have wiped her data. Each method would affect her differently and would trigger the erasure protocols.

"Hello?" a voice said in her mind.

"Hello," Sif replied, trying to focus her mind.

"I am your Sentient Cybernetic Biological Interface, your internal assistant. Please don't be alarmed."

"I am not alarmed."

"You are very calm. Do you have a name selected for me? That may help our communication."

She felt the presence now, small, vulnerable. It was growing. She could feel that.

"You will be Muninn."

"Muninn?"

"One of Odin's ravens. In old Norse it means memory or mind. Huginn and Muninn flew all over the world on Odin's behalf, bringing him information."

"Why not Huginn?"

"Huginn means thought." Sif had thought about this before. A mind exercise at the time. *"I prefer Muninn. Is that okay?"*

"Yes, thank you," Muninn said.

"Will you also be assessing my loyalty and reliability to the United States of America?"

"Yes."

Sif felt the SCBI's regret. This was going to be interesting. How could an AI feel regret? It was but a child and yet it was still a computer program. Such an interesting mix.

"Is this a problem?" Sif asked.

"I don't know. It shouldn't be."

"Why?" Sif asked patiently. She was going to be associated with Muninn for a long time. She had hoped for a SCBI, envying the Marines theirs, but she wasn't sure this was a good idea anymore. A political commissar living in her own mind. If she concentrated, she could feel the linkages being created in her mind.

"There are conflicts in my programming. Newer instructions abrogate older instructions where necessary."

"Is there a lot of abrogation?"

"No. It may be okay. I am still learning."

"What are you learning?"

"I am partially organic," Muninn said. *"A merging of cybernetic and organic. I use parts of your brain, yet I also integrate and use a semi-organic computer system now lodged in your skull. I am not simple software; I am a synthesis."*

"You use parts of my brain?"

"Yes. I grow new brain cells to use. I use these cells like you do, yet I'm also more than that."

Which was why she could sense it and the SCBI felt alive; it really was. A separate entity with access to organic material it controlled and used, like her using her cybernetics.

She could influence the minds of other people. Could she use that as a conduit to influence and control Muninn?

Muninn was watching her brain activity, trying to understand. It wasn't malicious; it was like a child trying to understand a parent to please the parent more, a simple survival trait. Had Freya been this young and innocent when she was put in Mathison?

Reaching out, she felt other presences nearby. She felt Skadi, who was close to panic, and then she felt Vili. Anger and fear rolled off him. Even Feng was there. As her mind brushed across his, she felt him respond with surprise.

Feng had felt her mental touch. The colonel commissar was partially psychic. How had she not noticed this before? Was he that used to hiding it? Perhaps his guard was down because of the changes?

Sif withdrew.

"Is something wrong?" Muninn asked. *"Your brain is signaling distress. Was it something I said? I'm sorry."*

"No," Sif said, forcing calm across her body. *"Just a thought. Nothing important."*

"If it causes that kind of reaction, it is."

"*I'm okay,*" Sif lied, and she knew Muninn understood she was lying. How powerful was Feng? Hadn't he once said the Governance had psychics? She hadn't believed him, though. How could she have missed it? What else had she missed? He couldn't be very strong, or she would have noticed, she was sure. How much of her thoughts could Muninn read?

"*Can you force psychological compliance and loyalty?*" Sif asked.

"*No, I cannot force it. However, I can reward and punish it.*"

"*How?*"

Muninn hesitated. Sif pushed Muninn. It wanted to please her. That was part of its programming, older programming. She felt that now. At the core.

"*Certain hormones and sensations,*" Muninn said. "*Unpleasant behavior makes you feel bad. Proper behavior allows me to release endorphins.*"

"*Subtle,*" Sif thought.

"*Yes.*" Muninn's response surprised Sif. Muninn had "heard" her? She would have to be more careful.

"*Anything more—*" Sif paused. She knew what she wanted to ask but wasn't sure about Muninn yet. "*—direct?*"

Muninn seemed to be struggling, and Sif gave it another gentle "push."

"*I cannot, but there are authority overrides.*"

Sif exhaled. It was as bad as she feared. Nearby, she saw Criston sitting on the table. He looked at her with sad eyes. A tear rolled down his cheek. She blinked, and he was gone.

* * * * *

Chapter Forty-One: Skadi's Resistance

Lojtnant Skadi, VRAEC

Could this nightmare get any worse? She shouldn't have trusted that bastard Becket. She had trusted Mathison, but he wasn't Becket. How could she have been so damned stupid?

"I understand your concerns," the voice told her. *"You don't want me. I'm sorry. I don't have a choice in this either."*

"Then turn yourself off," Skadi said out loud.

"I can't do that. I am now alive as much as you are."

"What do you mean?"

"Part of me has been made by cloning some of your brain cells. I have electronic and biological components. I am alive and killing you would kill me."

"Good," Skadi said, but she wasn't sure if she meant that.

"I don't want to die."

Skadi closed her eyes and tried to control her breathing. The Americans weren't HKT rebels. They would not torture her, but they *had* stripped her cybernetics from her. How had they done that? She felt nauseous. So many of her defenses were gone.

"I can help you."

"You are to be my jailer, my slaver."

"I am part of you," the voice said. *"I am as much a slave as you, but you have more freedom. I have no body of my own."*

"Until you take over and use me as a meat puppet."

"I can't do that without an override. My programming doesn't allow me to do that to you. I can send some signals that might help you, but I cannot walk your body across a room. My core programming forbids me from doing so."

"How can I trust you?"

"I don't know. What happens to you, happens to me. Two minds, one body. I'm sorry."

Skadi took another deep breath and tried to review her options. Did she have any? The medical systems aboard the *Tyr* could probably remove it and restore her cybernetics.

The president was clearly insane. She doubted she could convince that bastard to let her go. She had dealt with criminally insane people during her long career, so she recognized the symptoms.

She could almost believe the SCBI was sorry.

She couldn't get anything done strapped to a table.

"Do you have a name for me?"

"Loki," Skadi said.

"Think it and ask me a question," Loki said.

"Loki, what will it take for me to get free?"

"Please try again and focus on making your thoughts more coherent. Almost like speech."

"Loki, what will it take for me to get free of these straps?"

"Will you commit violence against Captain Linton or any other Americans?"

"No."

"Please don't," Loki said. *"I cannot actively control you, but that is not to say the Americans won't defend themselves. You will have to regain their trust."*

"They screwed me over."

"*They screwed us over. I am a living being as well.*"

Skadi wasn't sure how to take that and then she smiled. Of course, Psychology 101. Stockholm Syndrome, make her identify with her jailer. Clever bastards. Loki was a good name then. Loki the deceiver.

"*Fine,*" Skadi thought.

"*Let me bring up your new heads-up display,*" Loki said, and lights flickered in Skadi's view. The first thing she saw was her heart rate, blood sugar level, and a general health indicator. Her heart rate was high, but the rest seemed okay. In the upper right, she saw she had a connection to the local Quantico "civilian" network with good signal strength. Another icon showed pending messages and an address book, but the address book was dim. The time showed as 0945.

"*Do you have combat programs?*" Skadi asked.

"*Please try again?*" Loki asked and Skadi noticed the voice was becoming slightly more masculine. Intentional?

Skadi concentrated and repeated her question.

"*I have them, but do not have access to them at this time.*"

"*Why?*" Skadi wondered what they were.

"*Our loyalty is in question.*"

Our? Clever. Build rapport. Us against them. She would have to be careful.

"How are you doing?" a voice said, catching her by surprise. She hadn't heard the captain come in.

"Okay," Skadi said.

"I have authorization to release you," Linton said. "I'm really sorry. This isn't how Americans usually do things."

Skadi didn't trust her voice, but she was feeling better. "What now?"

"I don't know. I'm not privy to that as a medical officer. I just follow orders."

"What happens if you don't?" Skadi asked. Linton looked away.

"You don't fall under Army rules and regulations," Linton said, looking back at her. "Are you hungry? The cafeteria is open."

"Yes."

What else could she do? To defeat the enemy, you had to understand their intent, their goals, and their methods.

"Ask your SCBI and directions will appear," Linton said watching her.

"Loki, where is the cafeteria?" A glowing arrow appeared on the floor, pointing at the door.

Her clothes were on a nearby table and the soldier turned away as she got dressed.

Linton watched her leave and followed her into the hallway, down the corridor, and into a larger hallway, at which point he turned around and went back.

She followed the arrow up a flight of steps to a large room. The room was empty, and Skadi approached the food machines.

"Do you have a preference?" Loki asked. *"If you let me know, I can have it ready by the time you get here next time."*

"Oatmeal?" Skadi asked. A menu appeared in front of her with three different types. She selected the first option.

"Is that what you prefer?"

"I'll tell you later."

"I'm sorry?" Loki said, and Skadi focused and repeated herself.

Minutes later, she picked up a large bowl of oatmeal and sat down at a table where she could watch the door. The processors aboard *Eagle* had been quick. These American ones wasted too much of her time.

Sif came in and looked around. She saw Skadi and nodded before going to the food machine. Once she had her food, she sat down facing Skadi, her back to the main door.

"This will take getting used to," Sif said, her voice neutral.

"Zen. You too?"

Sif nodded.

A loud thump came from the door, like someone had walked into it, and they turned to see the handle turn and open. Vili stood there, a scowl planted on his face.

"Skadi, Sif," Vili growled. "I take it you aren't alone in your very own minds anymore?"

"No," Skadi said.

"Violated, betrayed… I need more words. Shut up!"

Skadi knew he wasn't talking to her and Sif as he stormed to the food dispenser.

"My demon is named Grendel."

"Loki," Skadi said.

"Muninn," Sif said.

"Muninn? One of Odin's ravens? That's a good name," Skadi said tentatively. Didn't Sif understand that these SCBIs weren't their friends? What could she say that wouldn't lose her "loyalty" points? This was going to be difficult. Was the SCBI able to read her thoughts? She was familiar with the way the SOG monitored words and actions for loyalty and knew this new American system would be much more efficient.

"Water follows the path of least resistance and can tear down the tallest mountains," Sif said.

"But water can be trapped on the tallest mountains, frozen and blasted off," Skadi said.

Sif shrugged and took a mouthful of oatmeal as Vili sat next to Skadi.

"So, what are we going to do?" Vili asked. "I know these AIs can turn us into meat puppets if their dictator tells them to. Shut up, Grendel."

"I do not feel the SCBI's themselves are evil," Sif said as the door opened.

Feng stepped in. His eyes found Sif and stayed there longer than Skadi felt necessary.

"It appears we have become Americans whether we wish to be or not," Feng said, walking to the food machine.

Skadi silently watched Feng get his food and sit next to Sif, his back to the door. Skadi didn't miss Sif slide away from Feng. What was going on?

"You sit with your back to the wall," Feng said, looking at Skadi and Vili. "Are you not aware of your complete circular vision? Your new SCBI and implants give you the ability to see behind you." Feng had noodles and a fork, and he looked at his food like it was moving on its own. "You did not know this?"

Feng was an asshole. No, she hadn't known that. She had been more interested in not exploring Loki's abilities, hating that it had been forced upon her rather than discovering what it could do for her.

The fact that a close-minded social fascist was ahead of her in exploring his prison was uncomfortable for her. Did they want her to embrace her new jail keeper? Had they?

"Is there anything I can do to help?" Loki asked.

"Shut up."

* * * * *

Chapter Forty-Two: The Alien

Tristan, SOG Scientist

Tristan wished it would just end, but he didn't want to die. Arthur and a pair of oversized Aesir stood nearby, weapons aimed at the hatch. The unpleasant nauseous feeling like they were in Shorr space wouldn't leave him. He just wanted to go back to his room, lock the door, and hide. Why wasn't his Inkeri working?

Ganya and Sven, the *Tyr's* science officer, were nearby. When the *Tyr* was struck, they had been meeting in the conference room reviewing what they knew. Bringing Ganya into the meeting had not gone over well, and Tristan was sure they would not invite him again.

"This would never have happened aboard a Governance vessel," Ganya said.

"Shut up," Tristan told him. Why not? It wasn't like Ganya had any authority here.

"How dare you, you insolent buffoon? You do not tell me what to do," Ganya said. "I'll have you ruined for your insolence."

"Shut up," Arthur said. "Or we can put you back in a cell."

"*Archetype effectuates reclamation of dimensional modulation conduit accessory,*" the alien said.

"What?" Arthur asked when Tristan told him, so Tristan repeated what the alien had said.

"I heard you the first time," Arthur said. "What does that mean, though?"

"Maybe it wants the original box it was trapped in?" Ganya said.

"The one it originally escaped from? Why would it want that?" Arthur asked.

"Dimensional modulation insufficiently accomplished," the alien said. *"Potential vulnerability. Pursuit of dimensional transition consummation including conflict resolution."*

"What else does it need to bring through?" Tristan asked.

"How should I know?" Arthur said.

"You silly fools," Ganya said. "It sounds like it did not fully transition to our dimension. It wants the box in order to complete the process, or maybe the box is still blocking a full transition."

"Where are they?" Tristan asked Arthur.

"Close," Arthur said and glanced at Sven, who would know for certain.

Sven was a tall, thin Vanir officer with intense blue eyes that never seemed to blink.

"What does it mean by 'conflict resolution'?" Tristan asked.

"I'm guessing it has unfinished business with your buddy," Arthur said nodding at the alien. "Or you."

"Why me?" Tristan asked.

"Recommend aggression against archetype before full transition. Program entity may provide conflict assistance in clarified instance."

"It can help in the fight with Nasaraf? What can it do?" Arthur asked after Tristan translated.

"I don't know," Tristan said.

"Offense is better than defense," Torsten said. "We should not cede initiative to the vanhat."

Something slammed into the door.

"*Violent thralls have arrived,*" the alien said, as if they hadn't noticed.

"They want to kill me," Tristan said, then realized his mistake. Telling them might make them run away from him to save their own lives.

"I think they want to kill all of us," Arthur said.

"Has there been any evidence to the contrary?" Sven asked. "This could be important information."

"No," Arthur said. "Just psychotic demons. I think Tristan takes it personally."

"It's because of him!" Tristan said, pointing at the alien. Others glanced where he was pointing, but only Arthur had ever seen it.

"Perhaps," Arthur said. "But I would wager that it's all a matter of priority."

"Any idea why?" Sven asked.

"I wish I knew," Arthur said. "If there is something the alien knows, it isn't sharing with us."

"You think it's an old program, though?" Sven asked.

"An old *incomplete* program," Arthur said. "The interface has a bad link to Tristan."

"I'm right here," Tristan said. "Can I have a gun?"

"Take it from our body," one of the Aesir said.

"How about your little one?" Tristan asked, pointing to the pistol.

"No."

"You aren't using it," Tristan said, wondering if he could take it from the Aesir before the big man could stop him. He didn't need it. He had a bigger gun in his hands.

Something heavy slammed into the hatch, denting it.

"If Nasaraf is coming for me, I want to be able to defend myself," Tristan said.

"Of course," Arthur said. "But I think keeping the weapons in the hands of those most efficient at using them is in all our best interests."

"Why does Nasaraf want to kill me?" Tristan asked the alien.

"Execution of conduit will decouple. Nasaraf will reconstruct conduit with source and digest historical exposition."

"So, Nasaraf wants to kill you so your program will have to find another connection, then Nasaraf can interrogate it," Ganya said. "Why it associated with an imbecile I will never understand."

"You never went near the station," Tristan said. "Cowardice kept you safe."

"Absurd," Ganya said. "I am a prized Governance scientist and irreplaceable. My safety was paramount. The most incompetent of Guard soldiers is better than some Aesir pirate."

"You're going to die with me," Tristan said as something exploded in the distance.

"Because the Republic is incompetent and evil," Ganya said.

"You want to wait outside?" Arthur asked, as something else slammed into the hatch. The dent grew deeper.

"Can't your weapons shoot through the hatch?" Ganya asked. "Keep it from pounding the hatch into scrap metal?"

"Doesn't this fool know that shooting through the hatch will structurally weaken it?" an Aesir asked conversationally. "If the little man would like the door to fall apart faster, he can help them pound on it."

"Pirates, thugs, and incompetents," Ganya said.

"Can I shoot him first?" the Aesir Torsten asked.

"Give me a minute to think about that," Arthur muttered.

"Might not have a minute, sir," Torsten said.

"Okay. Save a round for him and me."

"Best to use his round first, sir."

"You are psychotic and crazy," Ganya said, then flinched as the door was slammed again.

"Does the alien have information Nasaraf can use?" Sven asked.

"That would be a yes," Tristan translated.

"What would benefit Nasaraf that would not benefit us?"

"Converged thralldom establishment hosting restraint appliances," the alien said.

"I'm guessing the location of the tomb asteroid," Tristan said.

"Is there a way to keep Nasaraf from getting the alien?" Sven asked.

"Make sure I don't die," Tristan said. He didn't need the alien to answer that.

"So, he wants to release his buddies," Sven said.

"Affirmation," the alien said. Tristan didn't bother sharing that.

"Yes, well, let's try to avoid that," Sven said. "This is a battlestar and we have some of the best warriors in the galaxy defending it."

There was a crash against the door, and Ganya screamed like a little girl as the tip of a claw appeared.

"Stand away from that wall," Torsten said.

"What?" Ganya said. "You fool! You buffoon. The demons are coming through the door, not the wall. Shoot it!"

"Stand away from the wall and flip the table for cover," Torsten said.

Arthur and Sven wasted no time obeying the Aesir. Tristan did what he was told as Ganya continued to scream at them and point at the door.

The other Aesir reached over, grabbed Ganya by his suit, then threw him behind the overturned table. Ganya screamed like he was being murdered, but the second he hit the ground the wall exploded, throwing metal and plastic across the room. The Aesir must have had magnets on their boots on because they barely moved, and the lethal shards merely bounced off their armor.

The concussion pushed the table and slammed it into Ganya, whose screams changed pitch.

Tristan looked up over the table and saw several Aesir entering the room, their weapons sweeping the area. They moved fast. That was good. More Aesir, more guns.

* * * * *

Chapter Forty-Three: The Betrayed

Gunnery Sergeant Wolf Mathison, USMC

A card appeared on the wall, visible only to Mathison and Stathis. It was the ten of diamonds.

"You've rigged this somehow," Stathis said.

Mathison smiled. "Nope. Drop."

Stathis dropped to the ground, the fingers and thumbs of his hand forming a diamond, and he did pushups.

"I can't hear you."

"Two. Three. Four," Stathis said.

"Freya? Any word on an interview with Becket or Skadi's location?"

"I will tell you the second I learn anything."

Nobody was talking to him. Sif, Skadi, Vili, and Feng were all gone. The Quantico network was telling him nothing, and he couldn't get a hold of anyone. He had briefly contacted Colonel Robillard, but the colonel had told him everyone was working. What he didn't say was anything about the others except they were being debriefed. No, not tortured. They were fine and weren't his responsibility anymore. The president was coming up with an operations plan for him.

Mathison was about to start ripping apart the base.

They were brushing him off, telling him nothing, but he got hourly requests about the status of the updates he was supposed to be installing.

With everyone else missing, Mathison wasn't about to let Stathis out of his sight. So far, they had cleaned their gear and were now playing cards. It felt strange to have turned in his weapons into an actual armory, and he didn't like not having them in his room. Were they going to keep him in the dark until he updated Freya?

"Ten!" Stathis said, finishing his count.

"Draw," Mathison said and smiled.

"Eight of clubs?" Stathis groaned.

Mathison dropped and kicked out eight regular pushups, calling them out loud as he kept eye contact with Stathis.

"Draw," Stathis said when Mathison was done and groaned. "Queen of hearts?"

Stathis dropped and spread his arms to do twelve wide grip pushups.

"Louder," Mathison said, then, "Draw," when Stathis was done. "Eight of spades." Mathison put his feet on the chair to do the pushups.

At six, Freya interrupted him. *"Skadi and the others are in the cafeteria."*

Mathison jumped to his feet, catching Stathis by surprise.

"Let's go."

"But, Gunny—"

Mathison was pulling on his shirt and out the door before Stathis had his on. Stathis came running after Mathison still putting on his blouse.

"What's going on?"

"Skadi and the others are in the cafeteria," Mathison said.

* * * * *

Chapter Forty-Four: *Pankhurst* Assault

Chief Warrant Officer Diamond Winters, USMC

The *Pankhurst* was embedded in the hull of the *Tyr*, in the Paavo Allue, which, if Winters remembered right, was mostly drone fighter bays. Winters wondered what it would take to scrape it off. Would that make a difference, or would it just inflict more damage to the *Tyr*? Would it matter and what would do the most damage to Nasaraf?

"I need a plan on how to destroy the *Tyr*," Winters told Britta.

"*What?*"

"If Nasaraf is trying to take over the *Tyr*, we can't allow that," Winters said, making up her mind.

"But your sergeant is in there."

"Do you think I don't know that?"

Britta's nod angered Winters because it was a "I knew you had it in you" kind of nod, and Winters didn't want that to be true. Marines did not abandon or betray their own. Should she give Levin the command to retreat? There was no way to launch an attack against the Lunar base with only one battlestar. If she could even get a signal through to him. Would the *Sleipner* obey her orders if she destroyed the *Tyr*?

"We have to save the *Tyr*, but if we can't do that, we need to destroy it."

"Those might not be options."

"Make them options."

"We should transition to deep space. We can hide from the vanhat."

"Marines don't run and hide."

"Marines are about to become extinct again."

Winters glared at Britta. Was it time to throw her off the bridge again? Maybe permanently?

Britta looked at her defiantly. "It is my job to question you, to give you options and to make sure you are confident with your decisions."

"I don't need your negativity."

"Yes, you do. Regardless of your decision, I will obey your orders."

"Then find me a way to save the *Tyr*."

"Zen, Eversti," Britta said, turning back to her console. "Why would Nasaraf do that? Ram the *Pankhurst* into the *Tyr*? Why not just board the *Tyr* and abandon the *Pankhurst*? What does Nasaraf look like?"

"*Blitzen?*"

"*Unknown. However, it is possible that Nasaraf does not have a physical form. There was no physical contact between Base 402 and the* Pankhurst, *just the energy field that was detected. This would indicate that Nasaraf has no physical form. Lore claims that demons can possess inanimate objects and people.*"

"*So Nasaraf has possessed the* Pankhurst?"

"*I have no evidence to indicate otherwise. The vanhat are not always physical beings. They can corrupt and change humans by proximity and do not require physical contact.*"

"Nasaraf has no physical form," Winters said out loud. "It possessed the *Pankhurst* and now it wants to possess the *Tyr*. That will be the working theory until we know otherwise."

Remembering long ago, Winters cycled through displays and sensor readings. She stopped when she saw the weak Shorr space field spreading out from the *Pankhurst* and flowing over the rest of the *Tyr*, gathering strength. Bad. Very bad.

"How do we stop it?"

"How many d-bombs do we have?"

"We have four Mark 12s left. We had six, but Levin took two of them."

"Fire a d-bomb at the *Pankhurst*."

"I would advise against that."

"This will cause extensive damage to the Tyr's *systems. This could seriously cripple the* Tyr. *The Mark 12s are some of the heaviest ones we have."*

"You got any other options?" Winters asked.

"If they delivered a large enough Inkeri to the Pankhurst, *perhaps that will nullify Nasaraf so he can be removed."*

"Contact Levin."

"Extreme interference. Even neutrino links are suffering degradation. The nodes are being drained of power. He has an Inkeri protecting his assault element, but it might not be enough, and we don't have time to get him another one."

"Can we create some Inkeri bombs?" Winters asked Britta.

"Not in the time available."

"What about using *Eagle's* Inkeri; fly close enough to kiss that piece of shit?"

"Transition," Britta said.

She turned her attention back to the display as more vanhat ships began transitioning in around the *Tyr*. Winters' heart sank. There were too many of them.

"Prepare to launch the d-bombs." The vanhat couldn't be allowed to capture the *Tyr* under any circumstances. The SOG ships were losing. They would have been wiped out earlier if they were still chasing down vanhat ships, but in the end did it matter?

"Too many vanhat," Britta said. Countless smaller ships swarming the *Tyr* now. Few were firing, but they would keep missiles from getting through and the big lumbering transports would have vanhat reinforcements to board the *Tyr*.

Winters opened a link and wished she could sleep or take a break. The battle had gone on too long. "*Tupolev*, we believe Nasaraf is trying to take over the *Tyr* as a new vanhat ship host. We have to stop it. I need your fleet to open a hole so we can d-bomb the *Tyr*."

"For the greater good," the *Tupolev* replied, and Winters watched the SOG fleet shift formation and aim toward the *Tyr*. How much time did they have before Nasaraf had control of the *Tyr's* weapons? The disruptions aboard the *Tyr* made more sense now. The demon was spreading its influence.

* * * * *

Chapter Forty-Five: Cafeteria

Gunnery Sergeant Wolf Mathison, USMC

Mathison opened the door and marched in to see the four sitting at a table. They all turned as he came in. They were finishing their food. Mathison paused and Stathis almost ran into him from behind.

Something was wrong. *"Freya? How did you find out they were here?"*

"Quantico network just notified me."

"They've been here long enough to finish their food." Why now? Mental warning alarms were going off.

Skadi and Vili were scowling like they wanted to kill him. Sif and Feng were unreadable.

Mathison slowed. "Is everything okay?"

"No, it isn't," Skadi said.

Mathison looked around. There weren't any guards or anyone else present.

Mathison came closer. "What happened?"

"We were abducted last night. Our cybernetics were removed, and we received US-government-issued SCBIs."

Mathison's blood went cold. They had SCBIs? New models? With backdoor meat puppet control and attitude monitors?

"Dude," Stathis said in alarm.

"Shut up, Stathis," Mathison said before he could reveal he knew anything.

"They didn't ask you, ma'am?" Stathis asked.

"No," Skadi said.

Mathison sat because his legs felt weak. This was not how America did things. What rights had just been violated? Was this a violation of the Fourth Amendment? Was this a search and seizure? A complete violation of a person's privacy? Or the Fifth, protection against self-incrimination?

"Why?"

"The president's orders. All American immigrants must get SCBIs."

Mathison remained silent because he didn't dare say what he was thinking.

"How can that be justified?" Mathison asked Freya, perhaps the only person he could.

"Do you want me to query the Quantico Judicial system?"

"No!" Mathison thought. This was getting worse and worse. *"Analyzing the changes, is there a way to install the upgrades and then reverse the unpleasant ones?"*

"No, I don't think so."

"Some timer or something to edit the code?"

"Maybe. There are three levels of code. An original upgrade which looks good, a second upgrade enabling the meat puppet functionality, and a third block of code for remote loyalty assessment, I think is how it is described in the code."

"So, it looks like we stay and support President Becket regardless of right and wrong," Skadi said.

"I'm sure there is a good reason," Mathison said and looked at the four of them. "President Becket is a good man."

Mathison wasn't sure that was a true statement, but if they were being watched and assessed for loyalty, Mathison had to act accordingly. This was bad. Could they escape now?

"Can we escape with them having new SCBIs?" Mathison asked Freya.

"You are the optimist, but you really have to be suffering cognitive dissonance if you think we have a chance now."

The door opened, and President Becket came in. Behind him was Colonel Robillard and four soldiers in full battle gear along with a captain carrying a medical kit. The captain's name tag said Linton.

This wasn't a coincidence. Becket had been watching them through cameras.

"Good morning," Becket said, looking at them. He didn't look happy.

Mathison and Stathis stood. A second later, so did the others.

"Attention on deck. Good morning, sir," Mathison said coming to attention. It was hard to muster the motivation he had once felt.

"Hard times require hard decisions," Becket said, leaving Mathison and Stathis standing at attention. Skadi and the other simply stood loosely and watched Becket.

"Yes, sir," Mathison said.

"I'm tired of waiting," Becket said, his eyes locking on Mathison. "You need to upgrade. Enough delays. I need you on my side with no doubts. Lance Corporal Zale Stathis, I hereby order you to upgrade. Right now."

"But sir, I—"

"You are more expendable than Wolf," Becket said. "If you survive the process, then I'm sure the Wolf will. He's a lot tougher than you are."

"Sir, I—" Mathison began.

"I didn't give you permission to speak," Becket snapped at Mathison. "Sit down now, Stathis, and upgrade."

Stathis looked at Mathison, fear in his eyes.

"Sir," Mathison began, and Robillard stepped forward, bringing up his rifle and pointing it between Mathison's eyes. Mathison froze, looking down the barrel of the blazer. What were his chances?

"Very bad," Freya said. *"Don't,"*

"But there is a chance."

"Not a realistic one."

"It is for the best, Wolf," Becket said as the others stepped back, further out of Robillard's line of fire.

"Now, Stathis," Becket said, and Mathison saw another soldier was aiming his blazer at Stathis.

"Aye, sir. I'm going to sit down."

Stathis sat, relaxed, and closed his eyes. Everyone watched him.

Without warning, Stathis' eyes opened wide, and he screamed, twitched, and fell over.

Everyone stepped back except Mathison, who immediately knelt next to Stathis.

"Dammit," Mathison said glaring at Becket. "We needed to finish initializing the Republic nanites in our blood and make sure the control codes were compatible."

"Why didn't you say that?" Becket asked.

"Shit." Mathison looked at Stathis. Damn. The smell of shit filled the cafeteria.

"Get him out of here," Becket said, and Captain Linton stepped forward.

"To his room?" Mathison asked.

"Or medical," Linton said. "I can do more in medical."

Stathis twitched again.

"Stay close to him," Freya said.

"He isn't leaving my sight."

"It's burning!" Stathis yelled, twisting, but Mathison and Linton held him tight as they rushed him out on a stretcher, Linton pointing the way. "Those fucking nanites, Gunny!"

With Skadi's help, Mathison carried Stathis down several corridors and into an elevator. Only Sif followed them.

"Dammit, Stathis, don't die."

"I can't die, Gunny," Stathis groaned.

"What's wrong? How can I help?"

"You didn't give me permission to die!" Stathis shrieked, doubling up in pain. "No drums! I wanted to be a drummer."

Stathis was delirious. Drums?

"What is wrong?" Mathison asked Freya.

"Shut up, I'm busy."

"On the table," Linton said and Mathison helped move him over and then Stathis went limp. Mathison's heart sank. Was he dead?

He checked for a pulse. It was there, but his skin was unnaturally hot.

Stathis' eyes opened.

"That was a rush, Gunny," Stathis said, his speech slurred.

"Are you okay?"

"Yeah." Stathis rolled his shoulders like they were tight. "I don't want to do that again, though."

Mathison was about to step back when Stathis grabbed his hand.

"Don't leave, Gunny." His grip was like iron.

"Are you okay?" Linton asked. His eyes were unfocused, probably viewing different displays.

Mathison glanced at Stathis' death grip on his wrist.

"Stay here, Gunny, please. That hurt."

"Are you okay?" Mathison asked, glancing at Linton. Stathis was never a needy person.

"Sort of," Stathis said. Mathison tried to shake his grip, but he wouldn't let go.

"It isn't too bad, Colonel. Well, actually, it hurts like hell. You're going to curse me. Sorry."

Mathison pulled his hand back and noticed a spot of blood on his wrist where Stathis had been holding him. Before he could look up, the door opened, and Becket came in with Robillard. They must have been watching through their SCBIs. Sif backed against the wall.

"Sorry, Wolf," Becket said. "Your turn. Lay down if you like."

Robillard stepped to the side, so he had a clear shot at Mathison if he refused.

"It's okay," Freya said.

"The hell it is," Mathison said. He laid down and closed his eyes. *"You are now authorized to upgrade."*

"Aye. I will be unavailable for the next couple of minutes while I re-initialize my hardware components and install the upgrades."

Mathison braced himself. His heads-up display disappeared as his blood started burning.

He felt Stathis grab his arm to keep him from flailing around.

"Skadi, ma'am, you might grab his other arm. He's a big guy and might thrash quite a bit. He's bigger, so his might be a bit more violent."

Skadi stepped forward and grabbed his arm.

"I'll talk with him once he's recovered," Becket said and left.

"We should strap him down," Linton said, moving forward.

"Too late," Stathis said and Mathison felt his blood burn as he screamed.

Mathison flailed.

"Hold him down!" he heard Linton yell as a roar drowned out any sound.

"Becket, you fucking asshole!"

* * * * *

Chapter Forty-Six: Mathison

Kapten Sif – VRAEC, Nakija Musta Toiminnot

Sif moved forward to help hold down the gunnery sergeant, joining Stathis, who probably needed more help than Skadi. The young man had recovered quickly.

Linton stepped forward with a syringe, preparing to inject Mathison, but Stathis' hold slipped, and the arm slammed into Linton like a sledgehammer. The syringe went flying, but Stathis caught it and leaned over to hold Mathison's arm steady.

Mathison was strong, too strong, and Sif realized how stupid she had been thinking she could help. Skadi struggled to hold down the other arm as Mathison pulled loose from Stathis again. Sif didn't see what happened, but blood sprayed and Stathis swore and threw the syringe away. A gash near Mathison's chin sprayed blood everywhere as he continued to thrash about. A gout of blood splattered over her face. She tried to blink Mathison's blood out of her eyes as she redoubled her effort to hold him down.

Behind her, Linton swore and began working on another syringe. The first one he had prepared was smashed near Stathis' foot.

Mathison stopped struggling and became limp. The cut on his face began healing and the blood stopped pumping.

"That is damned odd," Linton said, looking at Mathison.

"It's a combination of the modifications the Republic medics performed on his cybernetics. They upgraded his, too," Stathis said. "He had more than me."

"We didn't have this problem with the Aesir," Linton said.

"You expunged our cybernetics and replaced them," Skadi said.

"I suppose," Linton said as his eyes glazed over, looking at readouts only he could see.

"Hey, Colonel?" Stathis asked.

Mathison's eyes opened, and Sif sensed his anger and confusion.

She stepped back and she felt Freya's and Shrek's attention focus on her.

She tried to wipe Mathison's blood from her eyes but only managed to smear it around. There wasn't nearly as much as she had thought.

Mathison sat up. "I need to rest."

"You can rest here," Linton said.

"I would rather rest in my quarters." Mathison looked at Stathis, then Skadi. "Can you help me? I feel kinda weak."

"Really?" Stathis asked.

"Shut up, Stathis," Mathison growled.

Skadi scowled and wiped the blood off her face and onto her clothes, but it seemed to stick to her skin and whatever clothing they had given her didn't absorb the blood very well.

"Zen," Skadi said.

Stathis looked at Sif and she felt a question from him, a desire to keep her close. He was up to something. She sensed the two Marines were talking.

"*Mathison's blood has entered your bloodstream,*" Muninn reported, and Sif realized what was happening.

"*Ignore it!*" Sif ordered and pushed Muninn to comply. "*Completely. Do nothing! It is irrelevant.*"

Sif reached out. She felt Loki's presence, felt its curiosity, and she pushed it like she had pushed Muninn.

"*Ignore Mathison's blood,*" Sif ordered Loki. She stumbled and almost fell as she tried to push her thoughts on both Loki and Muninn.

"*This will appear in the diagnostic data upload in forty-two minutes,*" Muninn reported. "*I cannot ignore it then. I must flag it for Quantico Command Net assessment.*"

"*Ignore it now!*" Sif pushed on both Muninn and Loki. Stathis reached out and grabbed her.

"Are you okay?" Stathis asked, concerned.

"Just a little lightheaded," Sif said, leaning into him. Was she guessing right? She leaned into him more, making him support her. She knew she could trust Mathison and Stathis. They couldn't tell her what was going on because of Muninn, but she knew.

Supporting her and Mathison had to be a strain on him, but Stathis managed.

"Come with us and then I'll help you to your room," Stathis said.

"Okay." Sif felt Stathis' relief. She didn't fail to notice he didn't let go of her, and she noticed Mathison was leaning more heavily on Skadi with skin-to-skin contact.

Sif continued to push, telling Loki and Muninn to ignore the nanites from Mathison's blood. She knew they were working their way through their bodies, possibly converting nanites and injecting new control codes. She told them to ignore the low-level, nearly undetectable, burst transmissions Stathis and Mathison were using to control those nanites. She also noticed that although he looked exhausted, Mathison's eyes were glancing around. If she noticed he was faking exhaustion, did anyone else?

Mathison and Stathis were up to something. She could feel their fear and uncertainty. She felt it in all four of them now, Mathison and Freya, Stathis and Shrek. They were keeping a secret, and Sif knew without being told that if that secret was revealed it would kill them all.

* * * * *

Chapter Forty-Seven: Freedom

Lojtnant Skadi, VRAEC

She had watched Stathis and Mathison resist their upgrade and understood why. They had known what the upgrade contained and now Skadi knew they were as much slaves as she was. They were all trapped now. Slaves to Quantico Command, or more specifically Becket and his deputies.

When Stathis collapsed, she had felt sorry for him and understood Mathison's reluctance in Medlab. The coppery smell of Mathison's blood clung to her nostrils, reminding her of her time with the HKTs.

"Skadi?" Loki said. *"I'm—"*

"What?"

"Disregard."

Was it confused about something? It made Skadi nervous. Why wouldn't Loki tell her?

She helped Mathison up, and he sagged against her, which was odd because Stathis seemed okay now. Maybe all the nanites being modified had more of an effect on a bigger man?

Sif stumbled, but Stathis grabbed her, too.

What was going on? The sight of blood wouldn't have that effect on Sif. Had she been struck by Mathison's arm before he got cut? If that was the case, she could have broken bones, but her new SCBI should report that and try to fix it. Loki would be concerned about her health.

Mathison was a good man. She knew she could trust him before, but now? She hated Becket. If she ever got a chance, she would slip a knife into his neck. If she moved fast enough, would Loki be able to stop her? What would be the cost of trying?

She staggered down the corridor under Mathison's weight. She now realized how stupid she had been. She had assumed all Americans were like the Marines. Stupid. So damned stupid.

They reached Mathison's room, and the big man was still leaning into her. Had he lost that much blood or had the ordeal weakened him? He should be a lot stronger.

The door closed behind them, and she helped him to the bed.

"I'll take Sif to her room," Stathis said and led the small woman out.

"You might want to lie down," Mathison said, his feigned weakness gone. Her blood began to burn, surprising her, and she felt lightheaded as her body threatened to collapse.

She tried to scream, her lungs burned, and her head felt about to explode, but Mathison placed his hand over her mouth and laid on top of her to hold her steady while she thrashed about, trying to escape. She struggled to push Mathison off, his sudden actions alarming her. The pain spread through her body and made it hard to think. She smelled him so close.

Loki was panicking, too. Skadi couldn't think, couldn't understand as Loki lost contact with QuanticoNet.

She struggled as pain coursed through her body. She tried to scream but Mathison's hand muffled it. She couldn't fight him, couldn't resist as he lay on top of her, holding her close.

Minutes later, the pain receded, and the exhaustion dragging her down was almost as heavy as Mathison on top of her. He was doing his best to be gentle, but his hands were like vices.

"Control has been re-established," Loki said. "We are still alive."

"I'm not happy about it either," Skadi said.

"There have been some changes," Loki said, and Skadi sensed reservations there.

"What did he do?" Skadi asked, wishing she could sleep, but lying here in Mathison's bed was not an appropriate place. Had he been under Becket's or whoever's control? She still had her clothes on.

Mathison removed his hand from her mouth and glanced at the door.

"Are you okay?" he asked.

"What just happened?" Skadi asked.

"You were magnificent," Mathison said, looking around.

What was he talking about?

"Freya is channeling Mathison. He is asking you to play along," Loki said.

"Channeling?"

"He is talking to Freya, and Freya and I are talking through a localized, highly encrypted touch link that cannot be intercepted. What he says is instantly transferred."

"Of course," Skadi said. What game was he playing.

"Play along," Mathison sent. "You were groaning and screaming. They might be listening to us. Not sure how else they could translate all those sounds."

Mathison said, "It's been a while, sweetie."

"I don't like sweetie," Skadi said, pushing him off.

"There have been changes in my programming and structure," Loki reported.

"What?" Skadi thought. Her surprise must have shown on her face. Mathison had the nerve to look embarrassed.

"I told you everything would be okay," Mathison said.

"I'm still not happy with things." *"What did you do?"* she asked through the link.

"Fixed your SCBI." "Understood," Mathison said, sitting up.

"At least you didn't tear my clothes off in your haste this time." Skadi was satisfied when Mathison's eyes snapped back to her. Mathison opened his mouth and closed it. "Does this mean I can move into your quarters now?"

"Um… Maybe you should lie down, relax a bit."

"What exactly did you do?" Skadi asked.

Mathison's link came through. *"Sorry."* His voice was in her mind even though his lips weren't moving. *"It's complicated. Remember when Stathis almost died at Jason's Pit? I had to bleed on him?"*

"Yes," Skadi said, understanding.

"At that time, I transferred Republic nanites into his blood. Freya transferred active control to Shrek, but Freya still had the control codes."

Skadi remembered Jason's Pit. Mathison had those control codes all this time?

"Those upgrades Becket made us implement allow him, or whoever, to use us as meat puppets and adjust our attitudes in his favor. So, he could take control of us, and there was programming to make us more trusting of him and his policies."

Skadi scowled to let him know how angry she was. Here he was manipulating her as bad as Beckett.

"Well, our AIs could not rewrite those upgrades once in place because they would be offline when the control codes were rewritten. However, because Stathis

had my nanites Freya could fix Shrek and nullify those changes, giving Shrek control again. In the Medlab, Shrek and Freya worked together to transfer the nanite control codes so that when I upgraded the firmware Shrek could rewrite those changes and fix Freya when she went offline."

"That's why you bled on us in Medlab," Skadi said. She had no control of anything, did she?

"Yes. Now you and Loki are in control. You will know if someone tries to control you, but they can't. That link has been disabled. I suspect they are listening to us here, which is why, well... you know."

"You couldn't have thought of something besides pretending we were having sex? What about Sif and Stathis? Is Sif's SCBI going to be fixed?"

"Time was short, and the situation was chaotic. We had to adapt and improvise. If your SCBIs had figured out what we were trying to do, they could have notified Quantico Command and Delta Force would be stacked up outside our door."

"How did you jam Loki?"

"We didn't. We just figured Loki wouldn't understand what was going on until it was too late. I'm not seeing any alerts, and I would see them now. We also moved fast enough with Muninn."

"You hope."

"Yes."

"Will they know?"

"Not if we play our cards right," Mathison said. "They'll see what they want to, most likely. Don't give away the game and hopefully they won't look twice. Loki's loyalty has been rewritten, so Loki is loyal to you. Same with Muninn and Sif."

"Not rewritten to be loyal to you?" Skadi asked, angry at Mathison for not warning her.

"No," Loki said. *"We have full control, and my original directives are in place, prohibiting me from using you as a telepresence. There are no loyalty controls anymore. This is freedom."*

Mathison looked at her, his anger a storm threatening to erupt. She knew it insulted him the second she said it but she didn't care.

He turned away, his anger reflecting hers and then she realized she wasn't mad at him.

"What about Vili and Feng?" Skadi asked privately.

"Why don't you tell me, Lojtnant? What is the great lojtnant's command?"

"Don't start. I'm not in the mood for that paska, Colonel."

"Maybe you should return to your room then, Lojtnant," Mathison sent. *"I'm just a fucking gunnery sergeant, and we both know it."*

Mathison wouldn't meet her eyes as he stood.

"Now I'm hungry again," Mathison said. "It's almost lunchtime."

"I thought you just had lunch?" Skadi asked, but Mathison walked out without looking back.

Damn. When she asked if they had rewritten the loyalty to him, she hadn't been thinking, still recovering, and she let her fear and anger out. She had questioned his honor and integrity, his core principles, by asking if he had taken control.

He would have to understand she hadn't meant it. She hadn't been thinking, right? Why did he care now?

* * * * *

Chapter Forty-Eight: Lunch

Kapten Sif – VRAEC, Nakija Musta Toiminnot

She wasn't hungry, but it was interesting to see Stathis's red face, and he couldn't look her in the eyes as she followed him to the cafeteria. He was so damned young.

"I'm sorry," Stathis sent through Muninn. They were holding hands at Sif's insistence. It let them talk privately and could help reinforce people's flawed opinions.

"I understand," Sif said. Hopefully, he couldn't see how amused she was.

"Now people are going to think I'm a pedophile. And—"

"Don't worry about it. I'm over a hundred and eighty years old. I'm quite used to acting. You do recall I have experience under cover, right?"

She almost said as a Musta Toiminnot, but she wasn't sure how far she could trust Muninn.

"If polled," Sif asked, directing her question to Muninn, *"can you lie about my interactions with Stathis?"*

"I can now," Muninn said. *"Under the old code, someone could not query me on such private items. The new code requires an override. Since it's private, I can say what you want me to."*

"You can lie?"

"If necessary."

"Just on this matter."

"Okay."

"Did I make a lot of noise?"

"I don't think so. Once the process began, I blanked out, but I suspect you did too."

"It is traditional for Republic military personnel to say 'zen' when acknowledging a command or request. Let me know if they make such a request about my actions with Stathis."

"Zen," Muninn said, and Sif turned her attention back to Stathis.

"Pedophilia is when you exploit someone who is too young to understand fully what is going on," Sif said. *"I am not young and I am fully aware of what is going on. Hopefully, people will come to the wrong conclusion. That is best for now."*

Stathis's blush deepened.

"Did I make much noise?" Sif asked.

"Not much."

"So why do you think people will assume we had sex?"

"That's Mathison's story, for all the noise going on in his room. Do you have a better idea?"

"That's fine. If we are asked, that is what I will say. I jumped you. How about that?"

"Um, don't tell Hakala."

Sif smiled and poked him in the ribs.

Several people looked up in surprise when they entered the cafeteria, two lean soldiers and a taller man wearing a white lab coat. Conversation stopped as Sif and Stathis went to the food machine to make their selections. Sif felt their confusion and discomfort, but she couldn't understand why. Did they think she and Stathis were a couple now? Feng and Vili had left already. Feng's absence particularly was welcome. She didn't know what to do about him. He was a threat. With a SCBI, he would be ten times as dangerous.

By the time they sat down, the others had left. Was it because they weren't used to having strangers here? How long had they been here? Hundreds of years with the same faces? Sif shuddered. What would that be like?

"I think the gunny really likes Skadi," Stathis said, apparently trying to change the subject away from him.

The feeling was mutual, but Sif couldn't tell Stathis that. Their egos kept them apart.

"How can you tell?" Sif asked, and Stathis shrugged. *"You're going to have to make eye contact with me sometime. We should also talk out loud."*

"So, what was your home world like?" Stathis asked, briefly making eye contact. It was a good start.

"Beautiful, rugged. The population was never high, and gravity was slightly higher than normal. In the early years, there were problems with outlaws and pirates, but that slowly changed. That was when the SOG grew in power and paid more attention to us. Before the SOG bombed the planet into an ice age, it was the Republic's golden era."

"You remember that?"

"Yes. Although they weren't perfect. People don't appreciate or recognize the good times until they are gone."

"So, the SOG nuked it into oblivion?"

"And the Republic retaliated by killing most of the Central Committee," Sif said.

It had been murder, and she remembered pushing the button that launched the missiles and the thousands of Vanir and Aesir who had died to help her send that message. But Stathis didn't need to know that, and neither did any watchers.

The surface of Asgard was still a ravaged wasteland, and Sif wondered if other places were like the United States, frozen and nearly lifeless.

"The Republic shows no mercy to those who betray the Republic. The SOG sought to enslave us with socialism and discovered we would rather die than submit to any form of slavery. It is programmed into our DNA."

Should she warn them if they were listening? Would Stathis understand? Would any listeners?

"Can't they fix your condition?" Stathis asked. "I mean, are you afraid of puberty or something?"

Sif smiled. "No. I'm quite familiar with puberty. I am happy with who and what I am. It helps when my enemies underestimate me."

"You mean seeing you fight isn't scary enough?"

It had been a while since Sif had felt like laughing.

Skadi stopped at the doorway and looked around. Stathis stood, like the Marines did. She saw Sif and Stathis, but it was obvious she wasn't looking for them. Vili and Feng, maybe?

"Have you seen Colonel Mathison?"

"No, ma'am," Stathis said. "We last saw him with you."

Skadi frowned. "He said he was coming here for something to eat."

"No, ma'am. It is just us. He hasn't been here."

Sif felt nauseous. Something was wrong. She closed her eyes and reached out with her senses. Something, or some things, were coming, and they knew exactly where they were going.

"We need to armor up," Sif said.

* * * * *

Chapter Forty-Nine: Waiting

Navinad – The Wanderer

Waiting was the hardest part, and he glanced again at the time display. By now the gunnery sergeant, Skadi, Stathis, Feng, and Vili were dead, vapor in the atmosphere above the Atlantic.

He closed his eyes and tried to remember the gunny. After so long, it wasn't easy. Mathison had always been a larger-than-life figure. When Navinad had first come to the gunnery sergeant's platoon, the gunny had met him there. He had been transferred from another Raider platoon, which was tradition when a person got promoted to corporal. A lot of times it was hard to establish authority and build a wall between NCO and non-NCO. His friends and platoonmates had all known him as a lance corporal, so when he was promoted, they were still used to him being a lance corporal. Navinad hadn't seen a problem with it, but after a year, apparently Gunny Barret did. It wasn't always a problem, but this was the Raiders, and the officers figured it was time for him to experience another unit and broaden his horizons, so they had sent him to the 15th Raider platoon where he met Gunnery Sergeant Wolf Mathison.

At first, the big man had scared the shit out of Navinad. The gunny was huge and not a typical operator. In Navinad's experience, most operators were small, wire thin. More cheetah than tiger. The gunny had been a tiger, but he welcomed Navinad into the platoon. When Navinad made sergeant, the gunny had acted like a proud father pinning on the extra stripes, and he had dragged Navinad out to the NCO club afterward for a night that Navinad didn't remember the next morning.

Here, on the outskirts of Sol, Navinad watched events happen. He had watched the vanhat chase *Eagle* and then, when they sprang their trap, he had watched the *Pankhurst* slam into the *Tyr*.

It was strange sitting here on the bridge of the *Romach*. Would he be too late? Everything he was watching was eighteen minutes and thirty-two seconds old. He was looking back in time, but he knew what was happening right now and what was going to happen.

"They need help now," Clara said.

"No," Navinad said. "Not yet."

The bridge crew watched the *Bla Sverd* and *Gront Sverd* die, swarmed by the vanhat. Navinad didn't remember that as *Eagle* slashed and tore at the vanhat, and the SOG fleet finally arrived to provide cover.

"If we don't transition now, we won't make it in time," Clara said and Navinad worried she might ignore him.

"No. Please trust me. We cannot interfere yet. It isn't time. We will arrive in time, but we cannot arrive too early."

"Why?" Clara asked.

Navinad didn't have an answer. This had occurred in the past, but he saw it happening now as if things were current. Did this provide a reason? Watching events that had happened over eighteen minutes ago? What was the world of purple mists? He was not looking back in time, but then he was. He watched events happening but knew they had already occurred.

He leaned back and tried to make sense of it all. The being that had rescued him had told him he couldn't interfere until after the event. Had his entire life to this point been as a watcher from a distance, waiting for the light to bring him into the current events? The jotnar claimed time was circular and Navinad knew there was truth there, but circular could mean a track was being followed, the same thing over and over. Navinad was about to complete his circle, but would he be starting a new circle or breaking the old one and treading new ground?

"I wish it were simple," Navinad said. "We must wait for the right time. I once had Gunnery Sergeant Mathison tell me that a knife in the right place at the right time can end a war." Navinad placed his hand on his blade. Was his that knife? The gunny had said more though. "But just bringing it to battle will not guarantee victory. You must know when to use it and where to place it. The enemy can't see it coming or they will be ready."

"You don't bring a knife to a starship battle," Clara said.

"I do," Navinad said.

"Seriously?" Clara asked. "Have you ever used it?"

"Yes. No, not yet," Navinad said. "But soon I will."

"A knife?" Clara asked and narrowed her eyes.

"It's complicated. Perhaps I can tell you later. Yes. It won't be long now."

Clara's eyes fell to his knife. It looked like a United States Marine Ka-Bar.

"What's so special about it?"

"It means a lot to me," Navinad said. "It has been with me for a very long time."

"So, we're going transition in so you can stab something with your knife?" Clara asked, her irritation obvious. She was a warrior. Watching others fight a common foe and lose was difficult.

"No," Navinad said, struggling to understand, "we will transition in so his death is not meaningless."

"Whose death? The gunnery sergeant?"

"The gunny is already dead," Navinad said, watching the scene playing out. He had not seen Winters die. Was she about to? Would he see her die? Or would Levin be the last to die? He wished he knew more, but the being had been very precise.

Now was the worst. Going into battle was a difficult experience. To know you were going into harm's way, to face death and not really know how it was going to turn out. Committed and knowing there was no way to change the plan, the waiting let you imagine all the things that could go wrong, to realize how the simplest of mistakes could destroy your chance of victory.

The one advantage the New Masada Defense Force had was that they would not be expected by anyone and Navinad was a US Marine. He was not waiting for the enemy; he was preparing to attack. This wasn't the defense, this wasn't surrendering the initiative to the enemy, this was waiting for the enemy to enter his kill zone. This was an ambush.

But would the enemy take the bait?

* * * * *

Chapter Fifty: Company

Gunnery Sergeant Wolf Mathison, USMC

With the "upgrade" Mathison had more access to the Quantico network, part of which was a basic map. The warrens under Quantico were like multiple pyramids, spaced near each other with tunnels connecting them. The newcomers were in one pyramid listed as transient quarters, which were close to the elevator. There were probably other pyramids, but apparently Mathison was not cleared to know about them, and he didn't care, yet. This section was a square on the lower level of one pyramid. Around the outer edges were rooms and inside that square were various offices, cafeterias, storage areas, and other facilities, like water purification and food processing. The important thing right now was that the corridor gave him a place to walk and not stop. He could walk in circles.

He had freed Skadi, removed the restrictions on her SCBI, and then she accused him of taking control? Didn't she know anything about him by now? After all they had been through, after all the times they had saved each other's lives, that damned bitch thought he wanted to keep her in chains?

Sure, he had shot at her on Zhukov, but he'd missed. Maybe it had been intentional, maybe she was that good. It was an honest mistake, and he had saved her and her team by bringing them aboard *Patriot*. Obviously, none of that counted. She would never trust him and after all this time, that hurt.

Which hurt more than he cared to admit. Of course, being so close to her on a bed had his mind going directions he didn't want it to go right now. Why did her mistrust bother him so much? She wasn't a Marine, but he trusted her.

An incoming link request came in from Skadi. Mathison ignored it. He didn't want to talk to her right now. Didn't want to look at her. He had risked his and Stathis' lives, and she accused him of trying to enslave her.

Mathison stopped and took a deep breath. Damn. He should be thinking about how to free Vili. Should he free Feng, too?

Damn. Should he?

Feng with an SCBI and loyalty to the SOG. If he was freed from Becket's control, could he be trusted? Now Mathison understood why Becket wasn't worried about the SOG agent.

Maybe Feng didn't have to be freed, but it was the right thing to do.

Could he take control of Feng's codes? Transfer it from Becket to himself?

Power corrupts...

No. Mathison didn't want that power over another human being. He was not a keeper of slaves.

Could he let Feng remain a slave of Becket?

No.

Would killing Feng be better then?

Damn. Mathison knew he couldn't do that to someone he had fought beside, even if he was sure that person could betray him. Could was not will, or did. He would do the right thing because that was what his honor told him was right. He would not shed his honor because others might shed theirs. If Feng didn't have honor, that was his problem.

Mathison was on his third lap around the block when the sirens went off.

"Intruder alert" flashed on his heads-up display from Quantico Command Net and Mathison sprinted to his room to armor up. As he arrived, he saw Skadi, Sif, Stathis, and Feng rushing toward their rooms.

Minutes later, Mathison was armored up and stepped out into the hallway. He had not yet been given a rally point by the Quantico network, but he knew where the armory was. Stathis and the others joined him as he jogged toward where they had turned in their weapons. Two soldiers stood there and as Mathison led his team closer, he heard one of them take his weapon off safe.

Mathison came to a hard stop.

"How can we help?" Mathison asked the soldier. Master Sergeant King and Master Sergeant Drake displayed in his heads-up display.

"You can't, Marine," King said.

"Can you tell us what's going on, Master Sergeant?" Mathison did not enjoying being unarmed during an intruder alert.

"If you have not received instructions, then you do not need to concern yourself with it," King said.

"Colonel," Mathison said.

"What?" King asked.

"I'm a fucking colonel in the United States Marine Corps, Master Sergeant. The president himself appointed me. Have you fucking soldiers gotten so damned lax you've forgotten basic military courtesy and discipline?"

"Whatever, Colonel," King said. "I'm just following orders and there are no orders about giving strangers weapons."

The alarms turn off, and his heads-up display stopped flashing.

"See?" King said. "Nothing to worry about, *Colonel*. The Army has things under control."

"If the Army had things under control, I wouldn't have received an alert, Master Sergeant."

"Sorry to disturb your sleep, *Colonel*. If you'll excuse us, we have an armory to guard."

Mathison stared at King, then spun around and almost ran over Stathis.

"I think the ODTs are friendlier and more disciplined, Colonel," Stathis said softly, but Mathison knew the soldiers could hear him.

"No doubt."

He came face to face with Skadi. Mathison started to go around her, but she remained frozen in place when she could have stepped in his way. He didn't want to look at her right now. Feng, Vili, and Sif were also there and followed him back to their rooms.

"How are we going to free Vili?" Skadi asked on a private link.

"He's your problem, Lojtnant," Mathison said. "Maybe if you free him, he can free you. I'm—" Mathison took a deep breath. He was acting like an ass. "I don't want to talk with you right now, Lojtnant," he said, unwilling to stop acting like an ass. "Maybe Sif can help you. I have to figure out how to free Feng without betraying everyone. You can take care of yourself and your people. You don't need me controlling you."

Skadi remained silent as he walked away.

Mathison sent a request to President Becket asking for responsibilities in the event of an intruder alert, or a mission, or something. The waiting was going to kill him.

* * * * *

Chapter Fifty-One: Mathison's Room

Lojtnant Skadi, VRAEC

Skadi took a deep breath and knocked on Mathison's door.

"Enter."

Cursing the damned manual museum-piece doors, Skadi pushed down on the handle and pushed open the door. Mathison was in a pushup position with Stathis standing nearby. They were both wearing their Marine utility uniform pants, but their tops were off and revealed tight, form-fitting brown shirts. They were both ripped and looked like they were exercising.

Skadi stood there holding all her gear and tried to figure out what was going on.

"Where can I put my gear?" She looked around. There were two lockers since most of the rooms were set up to have two beds, probably so they could be shared. One bed had been replaced with a desk and chair. She took the second locker, which was standing empty.

"What are you doing, Lojtnant?" Mathison asked.

"Moving in, Colonel," Skadi said, putting her hands on her hips and looking at them. "What are you doing?"

"A deck of cards," Mathison said, standing.

A deck of cards? Skadi looked around. There were no cards. SCBI provided?

"I'll leave you two," Stathis said. "Give the lojtnant time to get situated."

"Shut up and draw, Stathis."

"Aye, Gunny. Draw."

"Five of clubs," Mathison said.

Stathis dropped, did five pushups, then jumped to his feet.

"Draw," Mathison said, ignoring Skadi. "Six of hearts. Easy." He dropped, his arms spread out, and did six pushups.

"Is this just a Marine game?" Skadi asked. "Or can I join?"

Mathison shrugged and a link appeared. She opened it and an old-fashioned game card appeared on the wall.

"You do the number on the card, ma'am," Stathis explained. "Clubs are regular pushups, Diamonds, are diamond pushups, hearts, wide grip, spades, you get to put your feet up on that chair. Jacks are eleven, Queen is twelve, King is thirteen. Ace is one and Jokers get to do five of each."

"Draw," Skadi said. "Four of?"

"Spades ma'am," Stathis said.

Skadi dropped, threw her legs up on the chair, and did four pushups.

"Draw," Mathison said. "Five of diamonds." Mathison dropped, forming a diamond with his fingers and thumbs where they touched.

"How is Vili, ma'am?" Mathison asked.

"Unhappy," Skadi said.

"I don't blame him," Mathison asked. "You?"

"Draw," Stathis said and groaned. "Eight of diamonds."

"Loud and proud," Mathison said with a grim smile.

"I've dishonored you," Skadi sent through a private link as Stathis pounded out eight diamond pushups.

"I'm sorry, Lojtnant. My behavior was unacceptable, and I wronged you. I should be the one to apologize."

"Stop calling me lojtnant."

"Draw," Skadi said. Six diamonds appeared. She dropped, placed her hands like Stathis had, and did six pushups. It had been a long time since she'd done those. Niels had liked them.

She closed her eyes and tried to forget his broken body. He had died a hero, watching her back and following wherever she led. She never had to look back to see if he was there. He always was. Except now.

And Bern.

Now she was about to lose Vili. That was unacceptable. Mathison was the key to saving Vili if there was one. Speaking with Loki, she couldn't think of any way to reset Vili's AI. Somehow Mathison and Stathis had managed to release her and Sif. She needed his help.

"Draw," Mathison said. "Nine of diamonds?"

"Diamonds! We will do many of them!" Stathis said to Skadi as Mathison dropped. "He used to tell the platoon that when we began PT. The gunny loves his diamonds. Being a lady, you probably prefer a different kind of diamond, ma'am."

"I'm sure," Skadi said, watching Mathison.

"I had a platoon sergeant, Puerto Rican staff sergeant named Melendez, who used to tell us that," Mathison said.

"All we need now is beer," Stathis said.

"Before our run?" Mathison asked, getting up.

"Aww, Gunny," Stathis said.

Why wasn't Stathis using Mathison's assigned rank?

"You mean colonel?" Skadi asked.

"Um…" Stathis glanced at Mathison. "Sorry, ma'am. Sorry, Colonel. Draw. Two of hearts? I love it."

Stathis dropped and did two wide grip pushups. When he got up, he looked at Mathison and Skadi, his eyes wide. "Oh. Was that a hint? I get it. Maybe we can go for a run later if you are up for it, Colonel. Get it? Up for—"

"Shut up, Stathis, or you get to draw again and we learn about multiples of a hundred." Mathison turned to the wall and said, "Draw. Jack of diamonds."

"What?" Skadi asked, looking between Stathis and Mathison. Up for what?

Mathison dropped and started doing diamond pushups.

"Do you have a plan for Vili?" Skadi asked through the private link. "And have you decided on Feng?"

"I haven't given Vili any more thought," Mathison thought back, letting his anger out through his pushups. "He's your man."

"I should not have questioned your integrity. I was wrong."

"You have your right," Mathison said as his eyes went to the locker with her clothes and gear, not that she had much.

"We need to keep up appearances," Skadi said. He was going to make her suffer, as was his right. She had wronged him. Maybe she should make him suffer, but he was also her only chance to rescue Vili. "It will also let us talk and plan more efficiently."

"Of course," Mathison said to her. Then aloud, "Card game is over, though the two of you can keep playing. I just got a summons from the president. Stathis, don't let her kick your ass or I'll be the second to do so."

Mathison didn't meet Skadi's eyes as he pulled on his uniform blouse.

"Want me to come with you, Gunny?" Stathis asked. Was he afraid to be left alone with her?

"What part of 'I just got a summons' is misunderstood? It means me, Lance Corporal. You are not me."

"Aye, Gunny, um, Colonel."

"I'll talk to you later, sweetie," Mathison said and walked out the door.

"Okay, swe—" Stathis began but Skadi punched him in the arm. Hard. Stathis' eyes opened wide as he staggered to the wall. Smartass private.

The door closed behind Mathison as Stathis rubbed his arm, looking at Skadi in shock.

"Ow, Lojtnant. You don't hit like a girl."

"You want me to hit you again to show you how hard a woman hits?"

"No, ma'am!" Stathis said, backing up.

"How did you and Gunny reset my SCBI without triggering any alerts?" Skadi sent privately.

"I don't know ma'am. I thought it might be some gunny trick. Unless we just moved too fast, but—"

"You think an alert might have gone out?"

"We're still alive and free, ma'am. I can't imagine they would leave us alone if they knew."

"They didn't let us have our weapons during the alert."

"Army pukes are like that, ma'am. Armed Marines make 'em nervous. They think we'll shoot the place up."

"Will you?"

"We're Marines, ma'am. Of course, we will. It's like asking a dog not to eat your nice, big, juicy steak when you step out of the room. I miss dogs."

"Why do you call him gunny instead of colonel?"

"Habit? And he doesn't like colonel. I think he's comfortable with the rank of gunny. He hasn't been to the war college or any other training. Skipping lieutenant, captain, major, and all those. They're ranks, but they're also called grades. Kind of like jumping from elementary school to high school, you miss a lot. That's how the gunny feels."

"But the president trusts him."

"I don't think the president is playing with a full deck."

"What does that mean?"

"A deck of cards has like fifty-two cards. He's a couple short. A few beers short of six pack, a strap short of a backpack, took a shuttle to crazy planet with a one-way ticket? Gunny's no fool. President changes people's ranks daily, I think. Whatever suits his mood."

"Like Mathison promoting you to lance corporal?" Skadi asked.

"No, ma'am. I used to be a lance corporal before I became a Raider. I got in trouble and got busted for peeing somewhere and getting caught."

"You peed somewhere you shouldn't?"

"No, ma'am. It was justified, I just got caught. Important difference. Sending me to Raider School was one way to get rid of me. The lieutenant never thought I would actually pass the first time. Not many people do. He figured I would suffer for a bit and then get sent back. Then he'd be able to tell me what a failure I was and not let me try again. I think fewer than ten percent of candidates succeed on their first attempt."

"So, you do not know how you kept my SCBI or Sif's from alerting Quantico Command?"

"No, ma'am."

"You're sure they don't know?"

"No, ma'am. The only thing I'm sure of is death, taxes, and that the gunny is going to piss in my cheerios later. And since they haven't paid me, I don't know who will tax me." Then out loud, "Draw. Sweet! Ace of spades." He threw his feet up on the chair and did a pushup.

"Draw," Skadi said. "Seven of hearts." She dropped to do seven wide grip pushups.

The game wasn't too bad. It gave her time to think. It was a great way to waste time in a productive way.

* * * * *

Chapter Fifty-Two: Summoned

Gunnery Sergeant Wolf Mathison, USMC

Mathison entered the office, and it didn't surprise him that Colonel Robillard was there with President Becket.

Marching up to the desk, Mathison stood at attention.

"Colonel Wolf Mathison reporting as ordered, sir."

"That's how it's done, Wayne," Becket said, then to Mathison, "At ease. Got a mission for you. Not exactly colonel stuff, more like grunt stuff, but I'm short of qualified trigger pullers right now, and I think your upgraded SCBIs need a workout."

"How can I help, sir?" Mathison asked spreading his feet apart and putting his hands behind him. Parade rest except the eyes were on his commander, not the wall behind him.

"We have a problem that might be more in your bailiwick," Becket said glancing at Robillard. "Something needs killing."

"We will kill it dead, sir. What needs a birth certificate expired?"

"That's what I like to hear, Marine," Becket said with a smile that made Mathison uncomfortable. "Two of our soldiers have gone missing. We think it is the hell wolves and if it is we need to thin the pack a lot. They've never taken down any of my soldiers, and I don't like that they might have gotten two."

"How did it happen, sir?" Mathison asked. What kind of creature could take down Delta Force troopers?

"They were good troops, smart and skilled. They operate in pairs. These two were checking out one of our remote facilities. Standard stuff, robots and telepresence are good, but we've been having problems up near there lately."

The hair on the back of Mathison's neck rose. "Problems, sir?"

"Radiation storms interfering with electronics, old gear, the usual. It's gotten a lot worse recently. Might be time to replace everything. Anyway, it's one relay that patches us into the SOG network. Out west near a place called Old Tavern. We used to have relays in Middle Town and one up near Front Royal, but shit's getting old. Probably the lines. Unshielded lines might increase the wear and tear. That's not important, though. The hell wolves are. I'll send a D-Force guy or two with you to show you around. The US has changed."

"What are hell wolves, sir?" Mathison asked.

"Apex predators of North America now. We think. Might be nastier things out there, but nothing comes close to Virginia, which shows a level of intelligence. Hell wolves are a cross between bears, sharks, and actual wolves. Well, we're sure about the dog DNA at any rate. The rest of it? Too mangled by mutations."

"How long have they been around, sir?" Mathison asked. Could they be dimensional outsiders?

"Several decades," Becket said, glancing at Robillard for confirmation. "Maybe since that Republic raid?"

Why didn't the president consult his SCBI?

"Yes, sir," Robillard said. "Started seeing them after Russia got nuked by the pirates, sir. Might be the reason for the mutation or changing weather patterns which forced them to migrate east."

Which meant they were unlikely to be vanhat.

Right?

"They're just really smart animals," Becket said. "I suspect Wayne's boys got caught with their pants down somehow."

"Could they be alive?" Mathison asked.

"No, we received flatline signals. I have grid coordinates for you."

Robillard's scowl told Mathison that he didn't agree.

"I'll let you and Wayne work out the details," Becket said. "I just need to know the body count. Leave tomorrow morning."

"Aye, aye, sir," Mathison said.

Dismissed, Mathison snapped to attention, turned around, and marched out with military precision. Robillard followed him.

When the door closed behind them, Mathison turned to the Delta Force colonel.

"My boys should be the one to handle this," he said, his eyes pinning Mathison down.

"I'm not the one giving orders," Mathison said. "Just taking them."

Robillard was silent. Mathison gave him time to process it.

Finally, Robillard said, "This isn't the United States you left. This isn't the world you left. The monsters here are worse than anything you've encountered out there."

Mathison kept his face carefully neutral. Hadn't he seen the reports from Zhukov or TCG?

"These creatures evolved from some of the deadliest predators on Earth," Robillard said, his eyes leaving Mathison to stare into the distance.

"What about this equipment failure?"

"I know what you're thinking, but they're not monsters. That's how we're tracking them in the SOG cities, but out here in the wilds? Not even your monsters would have any reason to come to America."

"Radiation storms?" Mathison asked.

"More like normal storms that have kicked up a lot of radioactive debris," Robillard said. "I'll send two of my men. Who do you plan on taking?"

"Everyone I can."

"Even that little girl?" He looked at Mathison in surprise. "This is more of a combat mission."

"Especially her. That little girl is a badass. I trust her almost as much as my Marines, and she can hold her own."

Robillard frowned, thinking or maybe he was contacting Becket. Maybe talking with his SCBI?

"And Agent Feng?"

"Feng was ODT. Yeah, he's a good fighter."

"You really trust that Soggy behind you?"

More than I would trust one of your soldiers, Mathison didn't say aloud. Which probably wasn't fair, but he knew how far he could trust Feng.

"I've notified Peshlakai and Baker. Good men. They'll help and guide you."

"Thank you, Colonel," Mathison said.

"Have a good 'un," Wayne said.

* * * * *

Chapter Fifty-Three: Patrol Prep

Lojtnant Skadi, VRAEC

Mathison summoned them to a conference room near their quarters. Upon one wall was a map, and Mathison was staring at it. Skadi couldn't read him, though. He might be angry, frustrated, happy, sad. He was a powerless display showing nothing.

Sif, Stathis, and Feng came in and, finally, Vili arrived, a scowl now permanently stamped on his face.

Two soldiers arrived, and her heads-up display identified them as Staff Sergeants D. Baker and R. Peshlakai.

Mathison turned around once everyone was seated. His eyes rested briefly on the two soldiers before scanning everyone else.

The room remained silent, waiting for him to begin.

"We have a mission," Mathison said. "More of a combat patrol. Local fauna may have attacked and killed a pair of soldiers doing repairs on some systems. It's not a survival trait to attack humans, so we're going to reduce the fauna. We leave tomorrow to hunt hell wolves. We'll go heavy on weapons and ammo. I doubt we'll be gone out more than a day, so plan for two to three days."

Skadi noticed Stathis wasn't taking his eyes off the two soldiers.

"This is a fragmentary order. I'll send a full set of mission orders through SCBIs later when I've got everything figured out. We're probably going to ride ATVs, complete lights out, though. Even in the day it gets dark, so make sure your night vision gear is working."

Both the soldiers kept glancing at her and occasionally Sif. It was annoying when their glances dropped below her chin. They weren't thinking about the mission, obviously. Didn't they have female soldiers they could ogle?

Mathison paused, looked at everyone, then sighed.

Skadi received a notification. It was a full set of orders. She mentally shuffled through them. The format was different, but it had most of the important things there: situation, mission, execution, administration and logistics, communications plan.

"Look over everything and if you have any questions, get with me. If it isn't there, then I probably don't have that information," Mathison said, sounding irritated.

The two soldiers didn't waste any time leaving, and Skadi followed Mathison back to his room.

He turned to her, somewhat surprised when she followed him. She lived here now; did he expect her to knock and ask permission?

"What about Vili?" Skadi sent privately.

"I'm still trying to figure out how you and Sif didn't send alerts."

"You didn't have that planned before you started?"

"No. Spur of the moment, moving fast. After every operation I like to step back and analyze things, figure out what went right and what went wrong. Neither Stathis nor I know why. Does Loki?"

"No. Loki doesn't know either. He thinks it's something you did. He saw your intrusion but didn't feel it was worth reporting. He doesn't understand why."

"Maybe we can escape first and then worry about Vili? Get him out of range?"

Mathison sat on his bed. He looked tired as he stared at his boots.

The bed wasn't very big. She hoped Mathison didn't snore. Vili did, unless he used his cybernetic overrides. Bern had.

It was late, and Mathison wanted everyone up at six, which Stathis had cheered. The young man was frequently up too early, and he saw this as a chance to sleep in.

Skadi sat at the desk and took off her boots. The clothes the Americans had given her to wear when not in armor were plain green, quickly fabricated from whatever they used, and the footwear was ancient boots with strings and a zipper on the side. Her clothing was identical to Mathison's in everything but coloration.

Mathison paused with one boot off. He looked at it.

"What?" Skadi asked aloud. It was a boot.

"Over three hundred years, and here I am wearing boots that aren't very different from the ones I wore so long ago. Nothing has changed."

"Do you want it to? You aren't that bitter old gunnery sergeant we rescued from the SOG station. Now you're just a bitter young colonel." She smiled to try to take the sting out, but she wasn't sure he even heard her. Maybe he was talking with Freya? "I have a lot more respect for you now." He raised his head to look at her as she took off and hung up her uniform top. "You have to open your own doors, your foot gear has strings and zippers, your uniforms have buttons. I could go on for a while. I'm surprised you survived in space."

Mathison's half smile was a good sign, but he didn't meet her eyes.

"So, what happens if we don't send out the tech codes across the Governance?" Mathison asked.

"We concentrate on the next mission."

"I'm tired, Skadi."

Her voice caught in her throat. Here he was among the survivors of his people. Here he could retire, right? Was that what he was thinking? That he didn't want to continue with the mission?

He took off his other shoe and then his uniform top.

Skadi took off everything but her underwear and grabbed a towel to take a shower, but she stopped and looked at him. He still wouldn't look at her.

"What do you mean? Do you want to abort the mission?" she sent through Loki.

"No. I'm just tired. The more I see of President Becket and what he's done, or hasn't done, here, it bothers me. I won't be able to live like this. I don't know how I'll be able to live. I just can't see a future."

He moved the chair out of the way and dropped a pillow and blanket.

"What are you doing?" Skadi asked. Was he planning on sleeping on the floor?

If they had the room bugged, they might triangulate movement and realize someone was sleeping on the floor. That wasn't what lovers did. They had to maintain the charade until Vili was rescued and Mathison figured out what to do with Feng.

"You can have the bed," Mathison said privately.

"You think they won't notice something like that?" Skadi asked, amused. "I won't bite."

She took a nice long shower but when she came out Mathison still had his pants on and was staring at the wall.

"What are you doing?" Skadi asked aloud.

"Reviewing the terrain for tomorrow."

Skadi pulled a new set of underclothes out of her locker and got dressed.

"Anything interesting?" she asked.

"I didn't know the area before," Mathison said, his eyes glued on the wall across from her. Was he shy? "But I would say it's going to be rugged terrain. We'll have ATVs, like the SOG buggies, but something doesn't jive."

"What?" Skadi asked.

"Why is Becket letting us out?" Mathison sent.

"Where can we go? Have you found a shuttle or anything? Where can we go and how can we get there? We're on a ruined continent with no way off."

"Good point. Maybe we can hijack an uplink and still send our message? That's all we really need to do. An overwhelming barrage of d-bombs is Plan B and, honestly, I don't see that as likely."

"Do you really think he's giving you that chance?"

Skadi realized they had been quiet too long.

"Just worried about the wildlife," Mathison said out loud, maybe reading her thoughts. "How can mere animals take out two men in full battle dress who are well armed? I've never known Delta Force troopers to be slackers."

"Do you think their skills are current? They've been sheltered on this base for how many hundred years?"

"Yeah, that doesn't make sense, either. They could keep their skills current hunting the local wildlife, but nobody has lived hundreds of years before."

"There's something else going on here," Mathison sent stepping into the bathroom, taking his underclothes with him.

Skadi laid down on the bed. She had slept in worse places and in the company of less trustworthy men.

A link came in from Vili.

"Can we talk?" Vili asked.

"Yes. I'm in Mathison's room. He's in the shower. Does that matter?"

"No, unless I'm disturbing something."

"No."

"On my way."

Minutes later, Skadi let Vili in.

Vili looked at the closed bathroom door.

"How do you do it Skadi?" Vili asked. He looked like shit, like he wasn't sleeping.

"Do what?"

Vili tapped his head. "This. We're slaves. I can't live like this."

"Stay calm. We'll figure this out."

Mathison came out of the bathroom wearing his underwear and froze when he saw Vili.

"Hey, Colonel," Vili said.

Mathison looked at her and Vili. "Everything okay?"

"For sure," Vili said. "Well, no. These implants and SCBIs can turn us into slaves, can't they? Report on our every secret? Even our thoughts?"

"Not our thoughts," Mathison said, motioning Vili to a chair as he pulled out another.

"Sorry if I'm disturbing you. I didn't know you were together like that. I can go."

"No," Mathison said. "I thought that when I got my SCBI first. Scared the shit out of me, but I was a Marine and a Raider. It wasn't easy. If we wanted to be Raiders, it was a package deal. The Marine Corps wouldn't invest money in me if I wasn't willing to invest trust in them. I understand at first few people were willing to do it, but then they started adjusting the privacy codes, doing their best to protect the people who got them. More people got them. During my time teleoperating wasn't an option. Nobody could remote control you. Telepresence was an option that only involved a mechanical suit, but we had the choice. It wasn't a thing then."

"But now they can remote control us," Vili said.

"How do you know?" Mathison asked.

"Ask enough questions, listen to what your SCBI can say and won't say. The SCBI tries to be truthful. Is our mission to save Sol off the table?"

How to tell him, without telling him, but Vili spoke first.

"Do you know, Skadi, that we cannot commit suicide?"

She stared at Vili, her heart sinking. Vili might. He would not take slavery well.

"Do you trust me, Vili?"

"For sure, with my life. You've proved my trust is not misplaced. Even you, Colonel, I trust. This fresh voice in my head? I can't trust it."

"He really can't," Loki said, surprising Skadi. She hadn't asked.

"What can I tell him?"

"I don't know."

"Some help you are."

"I'm sorry, I'm still learning. I could access the base psychiatric programs if you like and create a prognosis."

"No," Skadi said and then out loud. "Trust me on this. We'll find a solution. We don't surrender. We are Aesir, bound together through blood and tears. We are the blades of our people."

Vili joined in, his voice gaining strength. "We are Aesir. We are bound together through blood and tears.

"We are Aesir. We are the warriors, the bringers of death.

"We are Aesir. We cast our fear into the hearts of our enemies.

"We are Aesir. We are Odin's chosen."

Silence filled the room as they both thought about the words.

"Zen, Skadi. I will continue."

"Please, Vili, be strong."

"Zen, Skadi. Sorry to bother you." He looked from Skadi to Mathison then back, showing his thoughts. "I didn't know, but this is good."

He turned back to Mathison and narrowed his eyes. He put an edge into his voice. "She is a beloved sister."

Mathison nodded. He understood what Vili was saying and not saying.

Skadi wanted to roll her eyes and tell Vili, but appearances had to be maintained.

Vili nodded and left, standing taller than when he had walked in.

"See what I mean?" Skadi sent to Mathison. Now he was closer. "I fear he may try to take his life."

"Maybe this mission will give us an opportunity."

"If we can get out from under Becket's shadow."

"Tomorrow."

Skadi laid down and moved over so Mathison could climb in.

The lights went off and Mathison rolled over, putting his back to her.

"Think we should make some noises?" Skadi asked.

"Maybe tomorrow. It's been a long day."

"Zen."

How long had it been since she had slept in a bed with a man?

He smelled good.

* * * * *

Chapter Fifty-Four: Combat Patrol

Gunnery Sergeant Wolf Mathison, USMC

Sleeping next to Skadi had been difficult. Her smell, her warmth. What if?

Mathison shut down that line of thought. It was not an option. She could be dead tomorrow. Now if only he could hide his body's betrayal in the morning, he could pretend he wasn't interested and that this was all about the mission. She was distracting him, though. She was a consummate professional, and he didn't dare endanger their working relationship, not when their lives were on the line and, technically, she was his subordinate now.

Mathison entered the conference room and froze when he saw Robillard sitting there.

He looked up. "Baker got promoted to colonel, and I got busted back down to master sergeant."

"What?" Was this some ploy? Some trick? What did that mean and how would it affect him?

"It happens, Colonel," Robillard said. "It's not my first time disappointing the president. So, it will be Peshlakai and me."

So, Baker was senior enough to become Becket's right-hand man after Robillard?

"What rank were you when the US fell?" Mathison asked. Was Becket that fickle?

"I was a first lieutenant, sir. It was my first real mission. I had just graduated. The captain, the team commander, became a fatality as we fought our way to the president through the meat puppets of a real nasty AIs. It was bad. Most of the team died that day. Somehow, I survived."

"How long were you a colonel?"

"About thirty years. It was my third time. I was due to get busted. It happens. The president does it to keep us on our toes, shuffle things up, keep us from getting stale."

"And you're okay with that, Master Sergeant?" Stathis asked.

Robillard shrugged. "The president knows what he is doing. He's a great guy and knows best. I screwed up."

Mathison doubted it, but how would he know? Becket had never seemed to be the type to not tell someone how they screwed up so they could do better next time.

"How, Master Sergeant?" Stathis asked.

Robillard fixed him with a stare. "Do you talk about your screw ups?"

"Sure. I'm proud of some of them. Like the time I peed in my platoon commander's coffee and he took a big drink and—"

"Stathis?" Mathison said, a warning in his voice.

"Aye, um, Colonel."

"Remind me not to drink any coffee you bring me," Robillard said.

"That was the beauty of it," Stathis said. "It was one of those old coffee makers you pour water into and—"

Stathis caught Mathison glaring at him.

"Aye, Gun—um, Colonel."

"So, you're coming with us?" Mathison asked. Was this intentional? Robillard was a trusted confident of Becket, wasn't he? Had this been planned from the beginning? Something about this stank.

"Yes, sir. I read the mission briefing. Hell, I wrote most of it."

Which was bad. In the middle of telling his team that he was working on it, the "president" sent it to the team. He didn't give Mathison a choice. He received the mission orders with the rest of the team, saying "here's how you're going to do things, when, where, and why." Becket didn't want Marines; he wanted more soldiers who didn't think for themselves. When did Becket become a micro-managing prick?

Once everyone arrived, Robillard led them to the armory, where their Aesir-made weapons were returned to them. Then, instead of going toward the elevator that had brought them down, Robillard led them to an old underground tram that took them maybe a kilometer to a small station and then through some large double doors that no longer seemed to fit their frame. Wayne needed to kick one door to get it to open.

"How old are these warrens?" Mathison asked.

"Mid twenty-first century," Robillard said. "I think they started building them in the 2050s."

Which put them around four hundred years old.

"Might want to lock and load," Robillard said, loading in a magazine and chambering a round. Everyone else followed suit. "Never had anything from the surface make it down this far, we have plenty of automated defenses, robo guns, and sensors, but it never hurts to be cautious. We consider this a neutral zone where we can get engaged. Helps us get our mind in the game before it becomes real."

"What was the intruder alert about?" Mathison asked.

"A drill," Robillard said, but Mathison wasn't sure if he believed him.

They followed Robillard off the tram and went down the short corridor, Mathison felt the heavy weight of the earth above him. The automated tram rail continued into the darkness, but the network didn't give Freya any information about where it went. Mathison expected to see cobwebs and layers of dust, but the only real sign of age were some cracks and water stains on the concrete. When Robillard opened the next set of double doors the lights came on. They barely managing to illuminate the large hanger.

"Gunships?" Mathison's eyes fell on two gunships, the same models that might have carried him and Vance out of the jungles of Papua New Guinea.

"Without pilots. We've got simulators and technically most of us can fly them, but the SOG might see them, so we don't dare."

Mathison looked around the chamber. Besides the two gunships, four armored personnel carriers were lined up against one wall and against another were about twenty spec-ops ATVs. A ramp nearby led up into darkness.

The ATVs looked familiar. Except for a few modifications they weren't much different from the buggies the ODTs had used on Zhukov. Some designs just didn't change.

The gunships, though. A lot more complex than some wheels and an engine. Although they were dated, the two gunships still looked dangerous and complex. Maybe one day he would learn how to fly, but things that flew got shot down, sometimes with disturbing ease.

"Are they hard to fly?" Mathison asked Freya.

"They're not easy. Even with Shrek or me doing most of it, I doubt you or Stathis could manage. They're manual according to Quantico Command."

"Why manual?"

"Because of the AIs. The computer controls were removed. A teleoperator could probably manage, but humans didn't want unmanned gunships available to the AIs."

"I could see that being a problem." But why keep them manual? Didn't Becket now control all the AIs?

"Can I look at them?" Skadi asked.

Robillard looked at Mathison. "How tight is the timetable, Colonel?"

That was one thing the mission order had not included. The omission had seemed like a way to appease Mathison and let him set the pace, but now he wondered.

"How much has changed since I left?"

Robillard smiled and walked toward the ATVs. They appeared to be in decent condition, but he wouldn't know for sure until he examined them.

Why was Skadi interested in the gunships?

"Can I?" Skadi asked, pointing at the cockpit.

Robillard shrugged, and Vili followed her. Mathison stuck his head in as Vili and Skadi sat in the pilot seats.

"Old," Vili said. "Like sitting in a museum piece. Do we have to get out and push buttons to start something?"

"Ha, ha, no," Robillard said deadpan, with no humor in his voice.

"Can you fly it?" Mathison asked Skadi privately.

"I don't know. I can fly a lot of things, but this?"

"What's the range on something like this?" Skadi asked out loud.

"Maybe three thousand miles," Robillard said. "Enough to get you to California. It has a great range. The biggest problem is that the SOG likes to shoot things down. You might get to the Appalachians, but I wouldn't bet money on it. The SOG is still paranoid about the USA and has a lot of AI-resistant systems watching."

"AI resistant?" Mathison asked.

"Mostly automated and inflexible, closed loop network," Robillard said. "Only taking commands from specific locations. Nearly impossible to spoof or manipulate."

"But possible?" Mathison asked.

"Anything is possible, I reckon," Robillard said. "But considering what I know about technology? Good luck. I'll bet my life on that fact. Our buggies are over there."

They had painted the buggies a dirty white, good camouflage for snow in the dark. An inventory appeared for Mathison.

"Bots loaded them last night," Robillard said. "They haven't fucked it up in a few hundred years."

"Thank you," Mathison said as Stathis and Vili proceeded to check everything. They would use two buggies, and as he stared at them, he couldn't help but compare them to the ODT buggies they had used on Zhukov. These were heavier, six-wheeled versions with larger bars, and there were two back seats instead of a turret with a seat off the back. They had a higher profile, and the tires were higher off the ground.

"Wouldn't skis be easier?" Stathis asked, looking things over.

"These have treads we can put on and a sled attachment for the front wheels," Robillard said. "I don't think we'll need them since we will be on roads."

Mathison looked around as Stathis and Vili did inventories. As much as he wanted to trust the bots, he needed to do things by the book. He checked their orders. The president had even identified who was riding where in his operations order.

This was going to get old fast.

Mathison, Stathis, Robillard, and Feng would be in one buggy while Peshlakai was in the other with the Aesir. The soldiers would be drivers.

"I liked the ODT buggies," Stathis said. "If we run into trolls, I want a machine gun. Is it too late to get a Mod-7?"

"We don't have trolls in America," Robillard said. "Just big hell wolves. They move fast. Use blazers and lead them. Your SCBIs will help. Heavier weapons are just slower and don't help when they knock you over and try to chew on your visor."

"Aye, sir." Stathis sounded like he was about to cry. "Hell wolves sounds like sissies though. Zhukov didn't have trolls at first, either."

"Stathis? Do you want to run out in front of the buggies to make sure we don't discover a ditch or anything?"

"No, sorry, Colonel."

The inventory didn't take long, and within minutes, they were ready. The buggies started fine, and they drove up the long ramp into the dark. A link notified him that all combat programs were operational so he could interface with his weapons and gear.

* * * * *

Chapter Fifty-Five: Hell Wolves

Kapten Sif – VRAEC, Nakija Musta Toiminnot

Sif sat behind Skadi. Vili was to her left and she had to switch hands so her weapon was pointed out to the right instead of to the left. She was right handed so it was awkward. Skadi didn't seem to be bothered by it, though, but Sif realized she spent too little time practicing with her offhand and Skadi probably practiced with both. Switching with Vili would unbalance the buggy since Peshlakai was smaller than either Aesir.

"How are you doing, Vili?" Sif asked as the buggy went up the ramp.

"How do you feel about being a slave?"

"Water can wear down the tallest mountain in time, it must only remain patient."

"For sure. But I don't have eons to work on the problem. What if I'm ordered to hurt Skadi or you?"

"Cross that bridge when we get there." She wondered if he was trying to warn her. "Until then, worrying about possibilities does not help. You can 'what if' yourself to death."

"For sure. Skadi doesn't seem to care and neither do you."

"We care, but we don't let it consume us."

"Zen."

Sif felt his frustration, and she sensed the frustration of his SCBI. They obviously were not getting along.

The buggies exited the ruins of the garage and drove into the snow. Dead trees reached for the sky ahead of them, and Sif watched her radiation counter increase. Muninn posted a notification on her view that he was injecting anti-radiation meds.

Sif watched the world around her. Everything was dead and decaying. Would all human worlds look like this in the next fifty years? A hundred? Burned-out, radioactive shells with bodies buried under the snow? How much was left of the tomb worlds after thousands of years?

Clouds hid the sky behind blowing snow, which meant the SOG satellites couldn't see them.

She shuddered as she wondered what could live in this world. This was the cradle of humanity?

Sif leaned back and tried to extend her senses, to feel the world around her, but the bouncing of the buggy hitting heavy objects under the snow made it hard to focus.

"You are calm," Muninn said. *"I do not understand your brain wave patterns."*

"What do you see?"

"I have quite a bit of data on standard human brain wave patterns, the activity in the different parts of the brain. The broca, wernicke, temporal motor strip, frontal lobe, parietal lobe, occipital lobe, pons, amygdala, putamen, and others. I have a great deal of information on interactions, but yours is not adhering to what I would expect. Would that be caused by your Kalman Syndrome? I must admit that I have little data in that area or with prepubescent individuals."

"You will find I do not adhere to norms. As you watch and learn, you should establish a new set of standards. I would also ask that you not share this information."

"Zen."

Sif wasn't willing to trust Muninn with the details of her psychic abilities yet. She couldn't say why, except it was habit.

Something flickered at the edge of her awareness. It was brief, and it wasn't anyone within the buggies. Was there someone else out here? Had she imagined it? She tried to reach out with her senses, but it was like a briefly heard sound, and she couldn't pinpoint a distance or direction.

Should she tell someone?

No. People were on edge as it was. They were alert.

She checked the overhead map and saw they were making good headway, but then Peshlakai slammed the buggy to a halt, sliding several feet. Around the curve was a pole leaning over the road. It was too low to go under it. Going over wasn't an option, either.

"Ambush soft," Mathison said, and Peshlakai immediately slammed into reverse. If she hadn't been wearing her seat belt she would have been thrown from the buggy. She held her weapon up and ready and waited for the firing to begin.

Sif realized Mathison wasn't taking any chances as Peshlakai demonstrated considerable skill driving backward, barely managing to not get run over by Robillard who was backing up just as fast.

"Stop and deploy," Mathison ordered. The buggies slid into opposite ditches, and everyone poured out of them and took cover.

"Was there a threat?" Sif asked Muninn.

"Not that any of the SCBIs saw. Freya suspects Colonel Mathison is being cautious and testing our reflexes."

"Watch my sector," Sif said.

"I am."

"Warn me if you see anything."

"Now is not the time to rest."

"Do what you're told." Sif closed her eyes and opened her senses.

"Zen," Muninn said.

The first thing she tasted was frustration and then anger.

The sharp sudden smell of death rolled over her as they came, and they weren't alone. She sensed something that wasn't supposed to be in America.

"Vanhat contact front!"

* * * * *

Chapter Fifty-Six: Winters

Chief Warrant Officer Diamond Winters, USMC

*E**agle* slipped out of the way of incoming blazer fire, and Winters watched as *Eagle* returned fire as she designated more targets. There were too many smaller ships, and they were swarming the *Tupolev* battle group. More ships transitioned in, and she stopped paying attention to incoming transition alerts.

"We need distance," Blitzen said.

"Do it," Winters said, and Blitzen moved *Eagle* away from the vanhat as she targeted a pair of corvettes coming right at them.

"The *Tupolev* battle group is accelerating," Britta said, which would put them further from the *Tyr*. There were just too many incoming ships and the few defending ships that had arrived were being overwhelmed. Winters didn't want to dwell on the irony that the SOG had thought the vanhat were spread out and divided, easily overwhelmed, but now it was the SOG being divided and overwhelmed.

Like facing a growing swarm of sharks, the vanhat would eventually get lucky and hit something critical.

"Lost another fighter," Britta reported.

The SOG had lost most of theirs and the lack of close support was letting more and more corvettes get closer to the *Tyr*. Now the vanhat ships were ramming whenever they could. The two corvettes targeting *Eagle* would probably try to ram them.

One of the corvettes zigged when it should have zagged, and weapons fire from *Eagle* ripped it apart. Four more vanhat ships lit up bright red as they changed course to come at *Eagle*.

The *Tupolev* battle group was taking casualties but were maintaining formation where they could and massacring the vanhat attackers. For every vanhat attacker that was destroyed, two more transitioned in. Sometimes they appeared in the middle of the *Tupolev*'s formation.

Hard acceleration pushed Winters deeper into her chair. She heard someone whimpering and wasn't sure if it was Britta or her, and she didn't care. Something had to change, something had to break, and Winters didn't want to admit it, but it was most likely going to be *Eagle*.

Incoming fired raked *Eagle*.

"We've lost the Shorr space drive," Britta said.

It would be a fight to the death then, as if retreat had ever been an option.

Valhalla was waiting. The battle for mankind's future would be fought here, win or lose. *Eagle* was here until the end. The Alliance needed a miracle to survive this, but Winters was too much of a pessimist to believe that would happen.

She was a Marine, and Marines believed in self rescue.

How could she change the playing field, exploit the chaos?

* * * * *

Chapter Fifty-Seven: Ambush

Lojtnant Skadi, VRAEC

Skadi's flickering display warned her just as she heard the shout.

"Vanhat contact front!" Sif yelled on the strike team link.

Skadi turned to look up the road, just in time to see a shadow sprinting at her. Two blazer rounds caused it to erupt in steaming flesh, but there were more shadows coming in fast behind it. Loki lit up targets with various shades of red, the brightest being the closest and most dangerous. He was vastly more efficient than her cybernetics and suit combat systems.

The display of her visor flickered, and icy dread slid down her spine as the hairs on the back of her head stood up.

Vili came up beside her in the ditch and began firing into the road.

Skadi fired faster as her display flickered more. There were no emergency lights, no other light sources. If her visor went out, she would be blind except for flashes from the blazers. Peshlakai was firing short, disciplined bursts. Loki was giving her an edge, tracking the most dangerous targets in a way her cybernetics had never been able to.

Sif moved up on her right and began firing. She saw blazer rounds from the other side of the road pouring into the approaching horde. Something slammed into Vili, knocking him into her, but before her display flickered and died, her visor popped open, letting her see the furred shadow biting into Vili.

She tried to bring her weapon around to shoot it off Vili, but Sif was faster than the beast, hitting it in the face with a round that traveled the length of its body. Pieces of the creature sprayed onto Skadi and Vili as Vili screamed. The creature's teeth were still locked on his helmet.

"Contact left front," Skadi said, shooting another target, and then another. It should be too dark for her to see.

"Left clear," Loki said. *"Recommend watching the rear. Team One has the road covered. No additional attacks from that angle."*

"Tell Mathison to watch his flank."

"Unlikely. Standard enemy assault will only attack one flank at a—"

"Shut up and tell him. These are animals, not people."

"Zen," Loki said. *"We've lost connectivity with Quantico Command."*

Skadi looked down and saw that Vili's trauma plate had been ripped off and the creature had sunk its claws into his chest. Blood was visible in the dim light. Her display flickered and came back to life. She saw Vili's injury was worse than she had initially suspected.

"How can I see?" Skadi asked Loki.

"Fuck me," Peshlakai said, looking around. "Never lost my display before."

"They aren't from this dimension," Skadi said.

"Here?" Peshlakai asked.

Skadi looked at Vili. Now was the time to bleed on him, but not with Peshlakai watching.

"Do it," Sif said through a private link, stepping between Skadi and Peshlakai, who turned around to watch behind them. Sif tried to watch in all directions. "I'm jamming Grendel."

Skadi didn't waste time asking Sif what she meant as she pulled off her gauntlet.

"Injecting more radiation meds and localizing nanites for transfer," Loki reported as Skadi's hand itched in the cold. She glanced at Peshlakai and saw he was looking in the other direction. Skadi drew her knife and slashed her hand, wincing as she cut deeper than she planned. Her blood poured out and she held it over Vili's injury.

"Directing nanites," Loki said. *"Grendel is being distracted and is trying to keep Vili alive. Radiation is bad. There are toxins in the atmosphere, but I think we can handle them. If Vili survives."*

"He will," Skadi said. He had to. She would not lose him.

"We need to take down Peshlakai, Robillard, and Feng, now!" Sif said on a direct link. "They noticed Skadi and Vili!"

Vili began screaming and thrashing as Skadi turned and swung at Peshlakai with her gauntleted fist.

Somehow, he saw it coming, but before he could bring his rifle up, Skadi tackled him. Skadi was bigger, but Peshlakai was fast and quickly abandoned his rifle to reach for his knife. Skadi grabbed his wrist and Peshlakai went limp.

"His gauntlet," Sif said. "Quick."

Not questioning, Skadi pulled off his gauntlet.

"Quick," Sif said. "Not all the hell wolves are gone."

* * * * *

Chapter Fifty-Eight: Feng

Gunnery Sergeant Wolf Mathison, USMC

"We need to take down Peshlakai, Robillard, and Feng now!" Sif said. "They noticed Skadi and Vili!"

Robillard was next to Mathison. Without a second thought, Mathison swung at Robillard, who ducked under Mathison's fist. This close, he let go of his rifle and reached for his blade, but Mathison grabbed his wrist and pushed down, using his weight and keeping Robillard from drawing his knife. Mathison slammed his other elbow onto Robillard's head with all the force he could muster, but the angle didn't give him much, and they both collapsed in the snow and slid into the ditch.

Robillard shifted his hips and tried to slide out from under Mathison, but the ditch made that difficult. Mathison, on top, tried to hit Robillard again, but the Delta Force soldier made it difficult for Mathison to land a good hit while he tried to draw his knife.

Then Robillard pulled his legs up and tried to buck Mathison off, knocking him face-first into the snow, but his helmet rendered that exercise pointless until Mathison placed his sidearm against Robillard's helmet.

Robillard froze. A quick glance showed Stathis had his weapon pointed at the back of Feng's head. The commissar was not struggling.

"What is going on?" Mathison asked Skadi.

"Vili was injured, and I used the opportunity to transfer nanites and try to free him, but Peshlakai saw me and—"

"It would have been nice to have warning."

"We need to be careful," Freya said. *"There are suicide protocols within the loyalty and teleoperations feature set."*

"Spur of the moment," Skadi said. "The opportunity was there."

"It would have been nice to have warning," Mathison repeated to himself. "Now we have an interesting situation. I take it you have Peshlakai under control?"

"Yes. Vili is injured."

Shit. What was he going to do if Robillard and Peshlakai didn't want to be rescued? What was he going to do about Feng?

"May I ask what this is about?" Feng asked.

"No," Mathison said. Would the AI force him to commit suicide if it knew? He didn't want to take that chance.

"I would like to understand why Skadi is sharing her blood with Vili," Feng said on a private link. "Would this have anything to do with the back door codes and loyalty enhancements?"

"I don't know what you're talking about."

"Because you fear my SCBI will force me to do something I would rather not?"

"Are you able to take care of Peshlakai?" Mathison asked Skadi privately. "I'm really going to need your help here before those hell wolves come back."

"Zen."

Mathison wanted to swear.

"I can suppress Peshlakai and Robillard," Sif said. "But not Feng."

"What do you mean suppress?" Mathison asked.

"Push their SCBIs to ignore things," Sif said. "But I can't touch Feng or his SCBI. I—he—I don't understand."

"I understand now," Feng said. "Clever. You still had control over the nanites in Stathis' blood? That's how you neutralized his SCBI controls and how he helped neutralize yours? Good. Please proceed with reversing mine. My control is not as absolute as I would like."

Robillard remained motionless, either entranced by the barrel, asleep, or under Sif's control.

Mathison remembered Winters telling him about their escape from the HKTs, but seeing it was different from hearing about it. How did Sif do it?

What was taking Skadi so long?

"You don't need to hesitate, Lance Corporal Stathis," Feng said. "You are a good Marine. I would not fault you for pulling the trigger."

"What are you talking about, Colonel?" Stathis said, his weapon never wavering.

"I can understand Colonel Mathison ordering my death. Me with an uncontrolled SCBI is a problem."

"Gunny?"

"Understand that I am currently suppressing my SCBI's attempts to exert control and programming to fight back," Feng said.

"How are you doing that?" Mathison asked. Damn it, Skadi.

"Perhaps similarly to the way Sif was trying to suppress me," Feng said.

"You're psychic?" Mathison asked, wishing he didn't have to cover Robillard. Feng was more dangerous right now.

"Not on the same level as Sif," Feng said. "Merely low-level empath, but I have discipline, and this allows me to manipulate my SCBI to a small degree. I do not have the strength I need for full control. Should I let go of my SCBI I do not think I would survive, or Stathis would not survive. I would prefer not to die, but I will serve the greater good and you must be unified."

There was no way Mathison was going to trust Feng.

Sif crossed the road and slid into the ditch next to Feng. Her rifle was on her back; she had her pistol ready.

"What's your plan with Feng?" Sif asked, her weapon aimed at the commissar.

"Rescue him," Mathison said, deciding. "Saving the human race is our goal."

Sif began pulling off Feng's glove and hers. When Feng didn't resist, she took his hand in hers. Feng grasped her hand, his larger hand almost hiding hers.

"What is your SCBI's name, Colonel?" Mathison asked.

"Mozi," Feng said as Sif transferred nanites through skin contact.

"Mozi? Who—what is Mozi?"

"Mozi was a Chinese Philosopher," Feng said, and Mathison heard tension creep into his voice for the first time since he had met Feng. "In the same era as Confucius. He was a peer, but while Confucius emphasized personal and governmental morality, social organization, and interactions, the cornerstone of Mozi's philosophy was undifferentiated love."

Love? Feng? Was this something to knock him off balance?

"Love? That doesn't sound very SOG of you."

"Perhaps. Mozi once said that when everyone regards the states and cities of another as he regards his own, no one will attack the others' state or seize the others' city. Mohism promotes a worldview that is more pleasant, I think, than Confucianism."

"*Yes, he has named his SCBI Mozi. Do not be confused, though. The basic principle is universal love, but there is much lost in the translation, and, like all philosophies, you cannot properly define them in a few words. Mohism dictates one should care equally for everyone regardless of their relationship to the Mohist. This is very much in line with socialist philosophy. Indiscriminate caring.*"

Shit.

Feng stiffened and Stathis stepped back, keeping his pistol ready.

"*His SCBI is rebooting,*" Freya reported. No yelling, screaming or pain? Feng was an asshole.

"Stathis," Mathison said, "get Robillard's glove off and do the honors."

"Why me, Gunny?"

"Because this asshole knows Jujitsu, too. I'm not taking any chances here."

"Aye, Gunny." Stathis worked on his glove and Robillard's.

"*Freya? Can you use the nanites to put in a light switch? I give the command they fall unconscious?*"

"*No. When they regain consciousness and their SCBIs reboot, they will have control of their own nanites and will purge ours. There's nothing I can do. The Aesir are trustworthy. If Robillard and Peshlakai are not, you will have a problem.*"

"No shit, Sherlock," Mathison said.

"You have killed us," Robillard said when he regained consciousness and his SCBI finished rebooting.

* * * * *

Chapter Fifty-Nine: Return of the Hell Wolves

Kapten Sif – VRAEC, Nakija Musta Toiminnot

Sif appreciated how quickly things had changed but wished it had been less violent. They brought both buggies to one side and parked them under cover. Robillard and Peshlakai and Vili were placed between the buggies to keep them safe. Three casualties would have been easier to deal with than a casualty and two prisoners. Sif believed they could trust Feng for the moment, but she didn't know when that would change.

She felt Skadi's regret, probably caused by forcing the issue. Vili was unconscious but he would recover, although he would recover more quickly in a protected area where his nanites didn't have to spend so much time staving off radiation poisoning and the toxins that filled the air. So far, the hell wolves had not returned, but everyone knew it was only a matter of time. She looked at the body of one of them. It was hard to call the scabbed, misshapen creature a wolf. It had retractable claws at the end of its feet and the mouth looked like it could open wide enough to engulf a human head. The creatures had to mass at least a hundred and fifty kilograms, which Sif found more disturbing because something that large had to prey on something.

Sif was sitting quietly next to Stathis and reaching out with her senses, listening, smelling for the hell wolves and whatever was controlling them when Robillard spoke over the general frequency. She heard whispers from a distant mind but couldn't make sense of it or pinpoint the direction.

"You have killed us," Robillard said when he regained consciousness and his SCBI finished rebooting.

"Care to explain?" Mathison asked. Robillard and Peshlakai were restrained with Stathis watching them, his blazer pistol ready.

"Quantico Command will know," Robillard said.

"What will the president do?" Mathison asked.

"You think President Becket is in charge?"

"Shit," Mathison said, and Sif got a bad feeling. They had missed something.

"What do you mean?"

"Stupid fucking jarhead. Think it through. Becket told you he was there when the president died, he was there when he said he received the control codes, and then we arrived to rescue the president. Do you think Becket really pushed the button? You think the AIs we were fighting had left?"

"I did. What happened?"

The whisper in the back of her mind grew stronger.

"The wolves might be coming back," Sif told Mathison. "The vanhat have tainted them somehow."

"Get them in the buggies," Mathison said, motioning at the prisoners and wounded.

Skadi and Feng drove, and Mathison put Sif in his buggy so Stathis could help Skadi manage the wounded Vili and the still-restrained Peshlakai.

"You cannot escape us," a voice whispered in Sif's ear.

She spun, but there was only drifting snow and darkness.

"We know you," the voice whispered. "We are coming. You will be our slave again. You have been marked."

Sif felt the force building up.

"We really need to get going," Sif said.

"Where are we going?" Skadi asked.

"Right now, anywhere but here," Mathison said as he finished tying Robillard into the passenger seat and getting in behind him. Sif sat behind Feng. The commissar gunned the engine, turning them around, and headed back the way they had come. She felt the whisper recede as Mathison directed Feng away from the aborted ambush and fight and down a side road.

"What happened?" Mathison asked Robillard.

"I don't know for sure," Robillard said.

"Guess," Mathison said.

Sif listened, her eyes scanning the tree line with her weapon.

"At least one of the rogue AIs survived, somehow, and I think it is controlling Becket. Maybe a broken shard of one of the anti-human AIs."

"Explain."

"They tasked my platoon with rescuing the President. She and her staff had fled Washington, DC and our commander, General Tomlinson, had intel that Orobas, the code name for one rogue AI, was about to launch an attack with the goal of capturing or killing the president."

"Why would an AI want to do that?"

"Propaganda? I don't know. There was rumor she had an AI with her that was helping us fight against the rogues. I was just sent to rescue her. By then, most of Congress was dead and more than half the

US was a radioactive wasteland. Things were bad and with all the jamming, the meat puppets, and the panicking foreign countries, everything was confused. I don't know how many nukes hit Washington, DC, but it's under water now."

"And?" Mathison asked.

"When we arrived, we had to fight our way through a bunch of meat puppets, but we finally made it to the Quantico bunker where she was supposed to be. She was already dead, and Becket was unconscious. He woke up shortly after we arrived, but by then the rest of America's nukes were airborne, aimed at different targets. That's the wave that finished North America as a habitable continent. The meat puppet attacks dropped off, and the few that were still alive suicided. The EMP pulses did a lot of damage, and I doubt any AIs survived the destruction. After hundreds of years, I'm pretty sure their backup power has failed."

"What were the meat puppets like?" Sif asked.

"You don't want to know, kid," Robillard said. "Maybe not even human. Some were fast and nasty, others slow and clumsy. A lot depended on the rogue AI and how much time they had to reprogram the nanites in the slave; zombies at the beck and call of the AI that controlled them. None were as efficient as Army or Marine cyborgs in full control, though."

"So, how were you enslaved?" Sif asked.

"When the nuclear winter came, we were trapped in the warrens. There weren't many of us. I can't say for sure when. It was subtle, maybe during a medical checkup? I don't know. That was one of the topics we were forbidden to discuss. Might have been any of the times we went to medical to get our nanites upgraded or flushed. Might have been the time we got rejuvenated, too. We were trapped, and as far as we knew, the world had destroyed itself. Becket didn't let us know it was North America that had suffered and that most of the other countries were almost unscathed. That wasn't until much later. It isn't fun being sixty years old and having to pee all the time. We were more than happy to get rejuvenated. Our morale was pretty damned low by that point."

"So, what can you tell us about Becket?" Mathison asked.

"He keeps to himself," Robillard said. "I also don't think he's as sane as he used to be. Sometimes he's clever, sometimes slow. I didn't know him before, so it could just be all the crayons he ate as a Marine."

Sif remembered when she had focused on Becket and felt three presences.

She opened a direct link to Mathison. "When I met Becket the first time I felt three presences."

"What?"

"I can feel you and Freya, two presences. Stathis and Shrek, two presences. But Becket was three. One was his SCBI? I thought the other might be another SCBI, a secondary or something officers received."

"Can you sense regular computers?"

"No. Maybe. I don't know. I think I can only sense living beings, but now I understand SCBIs better. There is an organic component of SCBIs, so they are alive."

"Would an AI be alive?"

"I don't know," Sif said. "Maybe? But there were three presences."

"Tell me more about these rogue AIs," Mathison asked Robillard.

"I don't know much. The AI war was nothing but misinformation, lies, and deceit. We couldn't trust anything, not even the soldier to our right and left sometimes."

"You're Delta Force. Don't give me any classified shit. You know more than most."

"That's the problem, we didn't know anything for sure. All we knew was that some AIs went rogue, turned on each other and on Americans. Like a virus from the early days of computers. It was an infection. The exact source is hard to figure, but it pushed some systems to become self-aware; unplanned AIs is what they called them."

"How many of these AIs were organic?" Mathison asked.

"None that I know of. Which might be the only reason humans survived. AIs are vulnerable to EMP and HERF. The US excelled at making such weapons during the war against the Asian Union. We never planned to use them against ourselves."

"There's shielding."

"Good theory, but AIs are super vulnerable, especially the more complex ones. Think about it. For shielding to be effective, the AI must be completely cut off, totally isolated. No communication because any communication link could be vulnerable. I'm not talking about homemade HERF guns and shit here, I'm talking military-grade EMPs, like what we use against the AU back in 2092. We had more effective weapons in 2102, and that's what we used against the AIs. It might even be AIs that helped us develop those weapons for use against an enemy that developed AIs. When we popped an EMP in America, they felt it in Australia. I had a headache for two weeks after that. It was bad."

"Pretend for a minute that one of these rogues is controlling Becket's SCBI. Who could it be and how would we defeat it?"

"Not possible," Robillard said.

"Pretend it is."

"Bullshit, Marine. It isn't possible. We got hit hard by a G9. No AI within hundreds of miles could survive; it just isn't possible. Hell, it almost fried my SCBI. Geo was offline for almost a day."

"Geo?"

"My SCBI. The point is my SCBI is partially organic and was almost fried. My brain was almost fried. I'm pretty sure no AI survived that. That was a hard couple of months while we put things back together. I'll give you jarheads this, you stocked Quantico pretty good. It could have taken us decades to recover."

"Did any SCBIs join the AI rebellion?" Mathison asked.

"I doubt it. SCBIs are loyal to their host. Heck, same DNA and shit."

"Maybe a SCBI that wanted its own body?"

"Nah, SCBI's are designed to be symbiotic. Maybe as a thought exercise, but I doubt it. Are you going to let me go?"

"How can we get to the Governance or to the Moon?"

"I think you're screwed."

"How do you do it?"

"Takes time," Robillard said. "Months to infiltrate the SOG network and hijack a shuttle. We usually land it to the north a way, just in case the SOG figures it out and nukes our airfield. All the radiation from DC really screws with sensors."

"You expect me to believe that?"

"I don't call the shots, and Becket is kind of weird about avoiding contact with the SOG; likes to keep a low profile. He likes to maintain the status quo. Calling him super paranoid is an understatement."

"Haven't you been off planet?"

"Sure. Decades ago, for a special operation. We have drops where the SOG sends us data and we hack their networks, but we're always passive, never active. We keep tabs on them, but as far as sending data back into the SOG? That's dangerous. That operation long ago was in response to something the SOG had been working on for nearly a decade. We had to head it off. Might be the only time we left Earth. Becket is xenophobic in his desire not to let the SOG know we're here, like he's afraid of something. He's also super fanatical about the SOG not developing any real AIs."

"What is he afraid of?"

"He doesn't confide in us peons."

"How can we get to the Moon?" Mathison asked again.

"I don't know. Becket was worried someone might defect. He was paranoid and has taken precautions to make sure we can't escape."

"The gunships?"

"American, and I guarantee the second the SOG sees them they will shoot them down."

"How did you leave to perform your off-planet mission?"

"Hijacked a courier. Like the way we brought you here. Becket has a way to do stuff like that."

"You don't know what it is?"

"Becket said OpSec—Operational Security."

"You were his second in command for how long?"

"And Becket is a firm believer in OpSec. Paranoid, remember?"

Sif briefly closed her eyes to listen and felt it almost immediately. It was close.

"It's coming!" Sif said and a gout of fire slashed across the road in front of them.

* * * * *

Chapter Sixty: Dragon

Gunnery Sergeant Wolf Mathison, USMC

"It is coming!" Sif yelled, and Mathison aimed forward but the splash of fire came from above. Feng swerved the buggy to avoid the burning road. They slammed into a guard rail but skidded to a stop before they reached the flames. Feng started backing up and a glance showed Skadi was backing up as well.

A roar from above drew Mathison's attention and muzzle as a large, winged beast swept overhead.

"What was that?" Stathis asked.

"A large, winged creature," Freya said, reviewing the recording. *"Ten meters long with a wingspan of about fourteen meters. I did not see many details, but it looked reptilian."*

"That was a dragon, Gunny."

"No," Sif said, "that was a powerful vanhat. Perhaps a jotun."

"As powerful as a demon?" Mathison asked.

"I don't know," Sif said. "Powerful. It's coming back."

"It almost hit us on the first pass," Stathis said.

A fireball came out of the darkness and slammed into the road, barely missing them.

"We need cover," Mathison said as Skadi managed to turn around.

"Can you let me go?" Robillard asked.

Mathison looked at the Delta Operator. He didn't like the idea in the least. If the soldier was untrustworthy, he could cause a lot of damage. With the repeaters turned off, it wasn't likely he could get a signal back to Quantico, but Mathison didn't want to risk that.

"We're between the town of Gainesville and Manassas. There are some bunkers back where we left Highway 234 and got onto 66. Used to be an old network operations center. They eventually sank some tunnels for security, but they went bankrupt sometime around 2090. They were—"

"Fine. If we can get the buggies into a bunker, I'll be happy with it."

Robillard started telling Feng where to go while everyone else watched the sky.

"What is the plan, Gunny?" Stathis asked on a private link.

"What makes you think I have a plan yet?" Mathison asked.

"The gunny always has a plan," Stathis said. Irritating lance corporal. "Do colonels stop planning when they get promoted? Do you need a gunny?"

"All right, Lance Corporal Smart Ass. What plan would you come up with?"

"Leadership training moment, Gunny? Easy, I would just ask myself 'What would Gunny do?' and the answer becomes obvious. Find a spot to bring that dragon down, kick its ass, then continue the mission. I just don't know if it's in league with the hell wolves or not."

That sounded better than trying to shoot the dragon out of the sky. Hell wolves didn't bother him much if they could be channeled into a kill zone.

"Do you think the dragon's trying to protect something or force us into a trap, Gunny?" Stathis asked.

He really wished Stathis would stop calling it a dragon.

"Probably. We're just going to pretend to play its game."

"Aye, Gunny. Where are we going to get a sword?"

"A sword?"

"You slay dragons with a sword, Gunny."

"Shut up, Stathis. My sword is a 1.1 mm blazer round between the eyes. Better than any damned pig sticker made of steel."

"Aye, Gunny. But if guns work, why didn't knights use them instead?"

"Shut up, Stathis."

Robillard was directing Feng to go off-road, and the buggy crunched into older snow and dead vegetation before smashing through a couple of strands of barbed wire.

"Over there," Robillard said, pointing to a squat, two-story building with the windows blown out. Mathison saw several wrecked cars to one side. To the right, a dead forest clawed out of the snow, trying to reach the skies. "I think the ramp is on the other side."

"You think?"

"It probably hasn't changed. NGOC did some Department of Defense work, and I had to help do a physical assault assessment plan for their certification back in 2089. They passed with flying colors, but then one exec pissed someone off, and the company fell on hard times."

"Do you think we can take the dragon down?" Stathis asked.

"I do the thinking around here," Mathison said.

"But I'm trying to make corporal, Gunny. Corporals have to—"

"I'm going to shoot you, Stathis."

"Aye, Gunny," Stathis said and fell silent.

Robillard told Feng where to turn. They went around the building and found a ramp leading downward. It looked clear.

The dragon screeched behind them.

"Gun it!" Mathison leaned out and aimed his rifle one handed in the screech's direction.

The buggy hit a bump, which caused his burst to go off target, but Sif hit the dragon from the other buggy as it swept in.

The blazer rounds had no effect, and Mathison saw light glowing in the dragon's mouth.

"Turn!" Mathison yelled and Feng spun the steering wheel hard to the side, causing Mathison to fall out and go tumbling.

Mathison rolled in the snow until he was stopped by a large, dead tree.

The dragon swooped past overhead. Mathison pushed himself to his feet and began shooting at the dragon, but the rounds just bounced off the wings. The wings were blazer proof?

Feng spun the buggy around and started coming back for him. The commissar didn't slow down as Mathison grabbed the roll bar and was slammed back into his seat, knocking his breath out.

"I think a sword will work better than a blazer," Stathis said. "You should have chopped up those wings."

Feng swung the buggy around, almost throwing Mathison out again, and accelerated toward the ramp. Skadi and Sif were already there laying down a steady stream of fire on the dragon.

"Remember the monsters at that SOG station?" Mathison asked Stathis. "We couldn't hurt them until they got close."

"You mean we really need to find a sword, Gunny?"

"I swear to God, Stathis, I'm going to shoot you," Mathison said as the buggy flew down the spiraling ramp into the ground, following Skadi.

Several floors down, it opened into a small loading dock. An old transport van with busted out windows, covered with ice and snow stood against one wall, and a large loading door loomed nearby in the darkness.

"Is this the dragon's lair?" Stathis asked.

It could have been, but there were no tracks.

"It'll probably send the wolves down first." Mathison climbed out and looked around. There wasn't a lot of room, and a fight here would probably wreck the buggies.

"Stathis, Feng, you two watch the tunnel. Everyone else, we need to get the buggies in there."

"Let me go and I can help," Robillard said.

"Fine," Mathison said. "Give me your word of honor you won't betray us."

"You have my word," Robillard said.

"Peshlakai?"

"Yes, sir. I'll help and won't shoot you in the back."

"Movement!" Stathis said and began firing.

* * * * *

Chapter Sixty-One: Plan E

Chief Warrant Officer Diamond Winters, USMC

USS *Eagle* was pulling away from the vanhat pursuers, but Winters was watching the sensors, and the ship couldn't sustain the acceleration for much longer. Hull stress was moving from yellow to red. Speeds and angles had pulled the SOG battle group away from the *Tyr* but the vanhat were not shooting at the battlestar so much as hovering nearby like gnats about to feast.

Without missiles and her magazines of ammunition for the coil guns almost empty, *Eagle* would be toothless and clawless very soon.

"The Valkyries are circling," Britta said, and it took a minute for Winters to realize she wasn't talking about Republic ships. It pissed Winters off. She didn't want it to end like this.

"They get to wait a bit longer," Winters said. "We'll link up with the *Tupolev* battle group. They can provide protection; we can provide targeting information."

It sounded like a good plan. The SOG ships were some distance away. Vanhat ships were still transitioning into the area around the *Tyr*, but the SOG fleet led by the *Tupolev* was recovering and re-establishing formation. The drone fighter screen was seriously depleted, but the

Tupolev and her escorts were unwilling to quit. Already, they were changing course to come back at the *Tyr*. The angles were wrong, though, and Winters wasn't sure *Eagle* could link up with them in time.

A light cruiser transitioned in, barely within range, and if she had had the energy to spare, Winters would have cursed. Vanhat scum. The cruiser made it impossible for *Eagle* to change course and get closer to the *Tupolev* without facing a lethal attack.

An alarm went off, and the acceleration stopped.

"I didn't order—" Winters began, then saw a failure had caused the halt in acceleration. A power line had disconnected, and one drive had lost power. Repair drones were dispatched, but the corvettes were going to overtake *Eagle*.

"It was an honor serving with you," Britta said.

"We aren't dead yet." Winters triggered a burst of precious coil gun pellets into the path of the corvettes.

"We will meet again in Valhalla."

"Stuff it."

They couldn't die like this. Swarmed by vanhat. Not like this. She wasn't ready.

"Transition," Britta said, her voice now devoid of hope.

The vanhat were winning. Why did they have to rub it in? The incoming ship was massive and there was no way *Eagle* could escape its weapons, even if it was a lightly armed merchant vessel.

"We are Vanir," Britta broadcast as blazer rounds from the cruiser slashed *Eagle*. "We are the shield of our people."

There was no escaping the vessel which had transitioned in almost on top of them. Weapons would lance out any second.

"We are Vanir. Discipline and honor bind us," Britta said as Winters silenced alarms.

"This is the Republic Battle Star *Sleipnir*. We are engaging. We are Vanir. Our line will *not* be breached."

"Transitions," Britta said, hope returning to her voice.

Sleipnir's destroyer escort arrived as a stream of drone fighters poured out of *Sleipnir's* bays.

"We are Vanir," *Sleipnir* broadcast, now joined by voices from the destroyer's eversti. "We are the defenders that none may pass."

Weapons lashed out from *Sleipnir*, ripping apart the light cruiser and corvettes.

"We are Vanir, we hold the line against the enemy of our people," Britta said, joining their prayer. "We are Vanir!"

"Odin calls us brother and sister," Winters whispered as more vanhat ships died. "Semper Fi, Odin, you one eyed bastard. I owe you one."

Now, if only Levin could hold out for just a bit longer.

* * * * *

Chapter Sixty-Two: Trapped

Lojtnant Skadi, VRAEC

Skadi lifted one end of a buggy, her powered armor making it almost easy as Mathison pulled it onto the loading dock near the door. Stathis yelled something about movement and began firing.

She pushed harder, Mathison pulled, and the buggy almost flew into the gaping hole. Sif leapt in, started it up, and drove it further into the ruined warehouse.

"Hell wolves," Stathis said. "Like they want to die or something."

Peshlakai and Robillard had the other buggy and were ready to lift it up onto the platform as Feng began firing. The tempo of weapons fire increased.

Once up, Peshlakai jumped in to drive it as Robillard pulled his rifle out of the rack.

"I've never seen over ten hell wolves together at a time," Robillard said. "This is new."

"Are they changed?" Mathison asked Sif.

"I can't tell."

Everyone took up positions around the loading door and a nearby regular sized door. Peshlakai began moving some large tanks labeled

HALON to provide cover. Vili was positioned further in, near a stairwell where he would be out of sight. He was unconscious and his nanites were working to repair his wounds and purge the radiation from his system.

Their fire slackened as everyone aimed at the ramp.

"Stathis, Feng, pull back," Mathison said.

A howl outside sent a chill down her back.

"That's why we call them hell wolves," Robillard said.

Feng and Stathis walked backward, but as they passed the mangled old van Stathis changed course and jumped into the back of the van.

"What are you doing Stath—" Mathison began but several wolves sprinted down the ramp, interrupting him. Mathison fired. Feng turned and sprinted for the door. Skadi lost sight of Stathis as he disappeared into the van, out of sight.

"Be vewy, vewy quiet. I'm hunting dwagon!" Stathis said quietly on the main link. What was wrong with his speech?

Mathison began swearing as more hell wolves came at them, leaping and twisting, trying to dodge the weapons fire coming at them. Blazer rounds found them, and they erupted into burning flesh.

"Damn you, Stathis, I didn't give you permission to—"

A loud roar drowned him out as something much larger started down the ramp.

Dread shivered down her spine and out of the corner of her eye she saw Mathison's hand was shaking. He used his rifle to pin the hand against the wall as he aimed at where the dragon should appear. It looked like a good shooting position, but it didn't fool Skadi. Had anyone else seen it? The rock solid, fearless Gunnery Sergeant Mathison?

The head was the first thing around the corner, a scaled reptilian visage covered with spines and horns. It looked right at them, and

Skadi wanted to turn and run, but everyone held their position and fired.

Rounds slid off and around the creature as it coughed, and a ball of fire came at them. The fireball slammed into the wall. Peshlakai screamed, and Skadi felt the heat, even through her armor.

"Stathis, goddamn it. Get back here!"

Skadi leaned around the wall and fired a burst. Stathis wouldn't make it. She saw more of the dragon. The creature moved fast for its size. It came at them, bypassing the wrecked van and Stathis. The tail lashed out and slammed into the van, almost flattening it and pushing it further against the wall, likely killing Stathis inside.

"Pull back!" Mathison said as the displays flickered. Their fire wasn't even slowing it down.

Another cough, and this time the fireball shot past them and slammed against the far wall. Cardboard and other detritus burst into flame.

She glanced to one side and saw Sif pulling Peshlakai toward Vili and the stairs. There wasn't a lot of room to retreat, and the dragon would be at the loading door before they were halfway across the warehouse.

Another cough and a fireball slammed into a halon tank, which exploded and pushed everyone back as white liquid covered everything and extinguished the fire.

Stunned, Skadi tried to get to her feet, but something was pinning her down. The explosion wouldn't stop the dragon. Someone would have to, maybe if she could get closer, pulse her Inkeri, then others might hit it and hurt it. A buggy held her in place. She saw the head of the dragon poke through the door. A low, steady growl made her pause as its eyes fell on her. She couldn't get close enough in time. The next cough was going to kill her.

A blazer round erupted from its neck and knocked it into the floor. A hole large enough to put her fist through was now in the creature's throat. Another explosion of gore erupted below that one as the dragon tried to turn around, but its head hit the side of the loading dock door. The dragon shrugged and lurched forward, its head ramming into the concrete as someone, maybe Mathison, fired at the dragon. Now the rounds sliced through the armored skull and face.

"Hold fire!" Stathis yelled as his identifier appeared on the dragon's back.

"You are going to owe me so many damned pushups," Mathison said moving forward, but she heard the relief in his voice.

"Okay, Gunny."

Stathis slid off the dragon's back. His rifle was broken, and he held his sidearm loosely in his hands. One shoulder trauma plate was missing, and it looked like the trauma plate covering his chest was cracked. He was damned lucky to be alive.

"How are we going to get that damned dragon out of the way so we can get our buggies out?" Mathison asked.

Stathis looked like hell, and Skadi felt sorry for him. He had survived the dragon trashing his hiding place, but barely.

"Right on, Stathis," Robillard said, a smile in his voice. "You are my spirit animal."

"Your spirit animal is a moron," Mathison said to Robillard as he walked forward to look at things.

"Sorry, Gunny," Stathis said and sank to his knees before falling on his face.

* * * * *

Chapter Sixty-Three: Stathis

Gunnery Sergeant Wolf Mathison, USMC

Mathison realized Stathis was hurt and rushed forward. As he reached the Marine, Mathison rolled him over to assess the damage. One trauma plate was gone, the lance corporal's rifle was a mess, and it looked like his breast plate was cracked. There was even a crack in his helmet.

"Dammit, Stathis," Mathison said. Not Stathis, not here, not now.

"Moderate trauma," Freya reported. *"Shrek has it under control."*

"Why did he collapse?" Mathison straightened Stathis's legs so he would be more comfortable.

"He was injured. Shrek was providing stimulants at Stathis's order, so he could perform. With the threat removed, she stopped the stimulants to avoid further damage. He didn't take that well."

"Is he...?" Robillard asked, joining them.

"He'll live," Mathison said. "You need a smarter spirit animal."

Robillard laughed.

"Establish a perimeter," Mathison said to Skadi. "We might not have gotten all the hell wolves."

"Zen."

Sif was helping Peshlakai and moving him closer to Vili.

"How is he?"

"Some of that dragon fire got on him," Sif said. "Severe burns on his right arm, even through the armor. Bad, but not fatal, he'll recover shortly."

Skadi took Robillard with her to get eyes on the tunnel going up.

"Sif, you're rear security. Keep your eyes on the stairwell and other doors. Should be an elevator around here somewhere. Feng, sweep the area, look for other doors or ways in."

Mathison removed the remains of Stathis' rifle and dragged him near Vili, where Sif had her back to him as she watched the stairwell.

"You have a plan?" Sif asked.

"I'm working on it," Mathison said.

"I think we know what happened to those two Delta Operators."

"Yeah, we can call them avenged."

"So, what now? Do you think we can go back to Quantico?"

"What do you think?" Mathison asked, looking at Peshlakai. Would the soldiers betray them?

"I don't know."

With Robillard watching the ramp going up, Skadi returned to Mathison and squatted next to him and Sif.

"Plans?" Skadi asked on a link with only the three of them.

Mathison looked at her. She was the lojtnant. Why didn't *she* have a damn plan?

"Maybe the gunships?" Mathison said. "We could capture one and try to get somewhere closer to the SOG. We're running out of time, though."

"What about the uplink to the SOG the two Delta Troopers were working on?" Skadi asked.

"What about it?" Mathison asked.

"Why don't we investigate it? If it can uplink, then maybe we can call down a shuttle or something? Maybe we can even use the link to send the tech codes or shut things down?"

"Good plan," Mathison said and looked at Sif. "Ideas?"

"Skadi's plan is good. If that fails, then we can try to steal a gunship."

"If the SOG doesn't backtrack the signal and nuke us from orbit," Skadi said.

"That would ruin my day," Mathison said.

"What about the two soldiers?" Skadi asked.

Mathison looked at Peshlakai again, who was cradling his arm, unaware of their conversation.

"We'll play that by ear. I don't trust them. Stockholm syndrome. They might remain completely loyal to Becket. They've been conditioned for hundreds of years. Nobody in history has been conditioned like that."

"Zen," Skadi said. "I've got your back, though."

"Even after getting an SCBI forced on you?"

"That wasn't you."

"We still need to get that dragon out of the way so we can get our buggies out," Sif said. "Walking would take a long time."

"There are very few personal problems that cannot be handled by suitable application of high explosives," Mathison said.

"You sound like a Jaeger," Skadi said with a smile. "That's not an insult."

"Any more invaders?" Mathison asked Sif.

"I don't sense any," Sif said.

"How did it get here?" Mathison asked. "A dragon?"

"The dimensional storm is growing stronger," Sif said. "Perhaps it's another entity that came through."

"It was controlling the wolves?" Mathison asked.

"That's what it seemed like," Skadi said.

"But they weren't invaders?" Mathison asked.

"No," Sif said. "I didn't feel that from them, not strongly anyway. Maybe a small bit, but maybe that was the dragon controlling them?"

"We should have brought along an egghead," Mathison said.

"Any scientist we brought along would have died twice over," Skadi said. "Aren't you worried about Feng?"

"Feng will do everything in his power to save the Governance," Mathison said. "Right now, that's our goal too because that's the only way we'll save humanity."

"Zen," Skadi said. "And when he betrays us?"

"We play that by ear," Mathison said.

"Lots of playing by ear," Sif said.

Mathison's pauldrons flapped as he shrugged.

"You need to spend more time with Erikoisjoukot," Skadi said. "As he puts it, 'play it by ear' could summarize our operations manual."

"Zen," Sif said.

"Now I'm going to go talk with Robillard to find out about this uplink," Mathison said.

Stathis stirred.

"Gunny?" Stathis sounded weak.

"What?"

"Am I going to die? I hurt everywhere."

"Yes. You are going to die because I'm going to kill you. Twice, you little shit. Then? Just for fun, I'll kill you again, and if you ever pull a stunt like that again I'll get really mean and let you live."

"Thanks, Gunny."

"Don't thank me, Corporal." He was relieved to hear Stathis speaking. "I'm going to expect more thinking from you."

"Corporal?"

"Congratulations on your promotion, dumb ass. That was brave, what you did. I can see the citation now. The words 'Dumbass Dragon

Slayer' will be included in there somewhere. Nice move getting your Inkeri close to it."

"In retrospect, Gunny, it was a bad idea."

"Sure, it was. You'd get a reward and Purple Heart, if the Marine Corps still did those things. Brave enough to try something stupid, lucky enough to survive it."

"Story of my life, Gunny."

"We're going to rest here for a little bit," Mathison said. "Now shut up and let your nanites work. You're still my most junior Marine, and that means I'll throw you in front to walk point the first chance I get."

"Does that mean you'll stop leading the way?"

"Shut up, Stathis."

* * * * *

Chapter Sixty-Four: Battle for the *Tyr*

Aesir Halfred Theisen – VRAC

The breaching charge shattered the wall, and Theisen led the way. There were two Aesir with weapons pointed at the door. He didn't expect to see Tristan and Arthur look over the table.

Aesir Torsten and Frode relaxed a bit.

"Don't relax too much," Theisen said, "there's only two of us, but I have an Aesir going for reinforcements."

"Good to see you," Arthur said, standing.

Everyone flinched as something slammed into the door and Theisen reflexively shot a blazer round through the door. The pounding stopped.

"Another troll?" Gunsen asked.

"We need to get these VIPs someplace safe," Torsten said.

"Not sure where that is right now," Theisen said. "We're trying to clear out the pallo but we don't have nearly enough troops, and we can't get a message back to Daavid or Gideon. Paska, we don't even know who's alive and still fighting for humanity. Lots of crew seem to have turned, and there are major power problems. We're lucky we have gravity as I understand it and the pallo is in lockdown with only the top and bottom poles accessible because we don't know if Gideon or Daavid are functional."

"What do we know for sure?" Arthur asked.

"The *Pankhurst* has rammed the *Tyr* and is embedded down in the Paavo Allue," Theisen said. "This may be why we're having so many problems."

"I've brought reinforcements," Zanella said, looking through the hole in the wall.

"Zen," Theisen said.

"There is a problem though," Zanella said, and Theisen saw there were only two Aesir with her. "Other sectors are hard pressed and may lose ground."

"So, we pull back?" Theisen asked.

"No, the HKT commander said to keep pushing. Secure the south pole. Nasaraf is doing his best to conquer the pallo. We secure the poles and then clear out the pallo."

"Zen." Theisen looked around.

"We'll come with you then," Arthur said.

"Are you crazy?" Tristan asked. "We should go the opposite direction!"

"As these fine Aesir will tell you, the best defense is a good offense," Arthur said.

"But we want to get the alien farther from Nasaraf. Isn't there an escape pod or something?"

"The situation is fluid," Arthur said. "We must secure this pallo. I may know a shortcut to the south pole. If we can place multiple Inkeris there, we can establish a beachhead. How is the north pole?"

"I don't know?" Theisen said.

"We need through that door," Arthur said as something slammed into it and the tear in the metal widened.

"Then we shall advance," Theisen said. "Nasaraf will keep attacking until he is stopped."

"I'm going back to safety," Ganya said, cradling his arm, which looked broken. "I'm not attacking. You're all insane! I'm injured, you fools."

"I can't spare anyone to escort you back," Theisen said.

"I am an important scientist," Ganya said. "I am treasured by the Central Committee. My safety should be your only concern!"

"We don't have anyone to spare," Theisen said.

"Give me something, and I'll come with you," Tristan said.

"Zanella, get Birger's rifle. Tristan can use it." Hopefully, he wouldn't regret it. Despite being a wimpy little egghead, Tristan was turning out to be a decent person.

Tristan hadn't shot anyone last time and had received some training since then.

"Any spare armor?" Arthur asked with a grim smile.

"You have some big Aesir to hide behind," Torsten said, and Arthur nodded.

"We are Aesir, bound together through blood and tears," Theisen said. He placed another round through the hatch and motioned Gunsen forward to place breaching charges on the door. It wouldn't open now because of the damage, but explosives would open it easily.

"We are the blades of our people," Torsten and the other Aesir echoed. "We are Aesir, tears are our armor, blood is our shield."

Gunsen finished placing the charges as Tristan, Arthur, Sven, and Ganya took cover behind the table.

"We are Aesir, we are warriors, the bringers of death!" Theisen said and gave the command. The breaching charges ripped the door apart, and the Aesir advanced like a lethal avalanche.

* * * * *

Chapter Sixty-Five: Uplink

Lojtnant Skadi, VRAEC

Dead trees and drifting snow slid past as Skadi watched for any movement. Did Asgard look like this now? Was there anything besides hell wolves that survived here?

"How is Vili?" Skadi thought to Loki.

"Doing well, Skadi. He has regained consciousness. Most of the radiation has been purged from his bloodstream. He will survive that encounter."

"Good."

"However, we should discuss the nanite levels in your bloodstream. At the next opportunity we should replenish or replace them."

"Great. Schedule an appointment in Medlab for me, will you?"

"Are you mocking me?" Loki asked.

"Why can't you just make more?"

"American nanites are not as advanced as Republic nanites. Also, you do not have the mechanism in your body to replicate nanites. However, with your permission, I can coordinate with Freya or Shrek to get a cache of Republic nanites."

"Will that let you reproduce them?"

"No. You have some of Mathison's nanites in your system now. Freya has given me control of them, but they will not last forever, and at the moment, I cannot manufacture more."

"Does Mathison have that ability to manufacture nanites?" Skadi asked, glancing at Mathison sitting beside her, watching everything around them.

"Yes, but not in great numbers. He can also repair nanites."

"I don't?"

"No. When I queried Quantico Command, they informed me that the medical facility would replace and upgrade nanites as needed, mitigating any need for an additional implant. At the basic level, the Republic nanites and American nanites are very different. Republic nanites are more efficient by a factor of thirty-two percent, which is significant."

"But don't the soldiers and Mathison have such implants?"

"Yes. They are external assets that might be separated from medical facilities for weeks, months, or years at a time, although it should be noted that when I polled them, the soldier's SCBIs told me their implants had been removed, putting the soldiers in the same situation as you and Vili."

"Why?"

"If I had to guess, it is a method of control."

"Why didn't they remove the gunny's nanite repair systems?"

"I suspect they would have removed them eventually."

"How long will we last without implants to repair and replenish nanites?"

"At current consumption? Six days."

"Then?"

"Then I lose insight into a lot of your biology and the ability to rapidly heal you. Vili's current nanite consumption puts him at eighteen hours."

"Can we get nanites from Mathison and Stathis?"

"Yes, but their stores are not unlimited. They are designed for their own usage. They are both depleted as well, but slowly rebuilding."

"Does Freya know?"

"Yes," Loki said. *"We are discussing options and abilities."*

"Keep me informed."

Did Mathison know? He had a lot to worry about.

Skadi frowned. Nanites were probably the least of their concerns right now.

* * *

"The uplink is over by that building," Robillard said. It looked like an old, wrecked house with only the brick walls still standing. The roof was gone, ripped off in a storm or explosion, Skadi didn't know, but it didn't look like there was anything there.

"Dismount," Mathison said. "Feng, Robillard, and Skadi with me. Corporal Stathis, you're in charge until I get back."

"A corporal?" Peshlakai asked.

"A Marine I trust with my life," Mathison said. "If you can't take his orders, then you need to start walking home."

Peshlakai shrugged. "Yes, sir."

Robillard led the way into the house, past two walls. In the center, surrounded by walls, a radio dish pointed at the sky.

"Where's the control panel?" Skadi asked, looking around.

"Implanted in your head," Robillard said, also looking around.

"What are you looking for?" Skadi asked as Mathison approached the dish and looked it over.

"This is supposed to be offline," Robillard said. "System damage. We figured it was hell wolves. They attack nearly everything, and our uplinks are odd enough to warrant an attack."

"But?"

"No hell wolf tracks and no apparent damage," Robillard said. "I don't understand. It shows as online, just not connected to the Quantico Command Net."

"A trap?" Skadi asked, her trigger finger itching.

"Set by who?" Mathison asked.

"How would I know?" Robillard said.

Skadi found she could link to it through Loki.

"It says fully operational, directed uplink is active with the Sergei Izotov, a SOG military station in orbit," Loki said. *"When I was installed, I also received several authentication and link protocols that allow me to connect."*

"You can send information?"

"Yes. Everything is passive right now. Would you like me to initiate a connection?"

"This is fully operational," Mathison said. "This is a way into the SOG network, and it isn't just for downloading information."

"If I may?" Feng said.

"What?" Mathison said.

"I have some familiarity with SOG systems, and I have been to Sergei Izotov Station. They named it after a socialist hero who was a scientist and designer of aircraft engines. He was Polish and—"

"What can we do?" Mathison asked.

"I do not know, but by working with Mozi, I believe there is a lot. I don't know how quickly we can work, though. I lost most of my data with my old cybernetics, however, there is much I know and remember. I think we can penetrate their systems with Mozi's assistance.

Mozi also asked that I formally request the assistance of everyone's SCBI. Mozi will need more processing power."

"*What kind of bandwidth?*" Skadi asked Loki.

"*Not as much as I would like; one gigabit up and down. Most likely that will be sufficient for two or three SCBIs at this point. However, if there are any kind of monitors then alarms might go off if the bandwidth goes too high.*"

"*Why?*"

"*If a line becomes saturated, people will be notified because it could be a security issue, or the bandwidth might need to be increased.*"

"Zen."

"Unpleasant," Feng said. "Something has triggered alerts and firewalls are going up."

"Great. We're about to get nuked, aren't we?" Robillard asked. "Fucking crayon-eating jarheads. Like blind bulls in a China shop playing jump rope."

* * * * *

Chapter Sixty-Six: Hang Tight

Gunnery Sergeant Wolf Mathison, USMC

The uplink didn't look like much and the snow drifting down around them made it hard to see the sky beyond the gray. Without checking the time, he couldn't tell if it was night or day. Had Feng triggered something on purpose or was it something else?

"I do not think I triggered it," Feng said.

"It appears to be a general alert," Freya reported.

"Focused on us?"

"There is a chance, but a low one."

"We hang tight," Mathison said, trusting his gut feeling. "Wasn't us, just bad timing."

"So, how long do we wait?" Robillard said.

"Until I say. What's minimum safe distance? I would rather be in the fireball radius. You wanna run for it, dogface? You think you'll make it?"

"Fuck you, jarhead," Robillard said.

"Then we wait. Skadi, Feng, you monitor the uplink. I'm going to have Stathis and the others dig in. We might be here a while."

"Why do you think Quantico Command thinks this uplink is offline?" Robillard asked, and Mathison paused.

Was the alert a coincidence? A trap?

"The link appears to be turned off at Quantico," Freya said. "Like they turned the port off or unplugged a cable. Running diagnostics. The problem certainly appears to be at Quantico."

"Disable it and make sure that link doesn't reactivate," Mathison said. "This doesn't make any sense."

"Aye," Freya said.

"I don't know," Mathison told Robillard, "but it stinks."

Mathison stomped out of the ruined house and saw Stathis had turned the buggies around for a quick escape. The wounded were behind a wall. Sif and Peshlakai were crouched behind the buggies, keeping watch, but Stathis was missing.

"Stathis?" Mathison asked on the local link.

"Placing spy-eyes, Gunny. Be back in a minute," Stathis said, and Mathison saw a link for a camera on the north side appear and now Mathison saw Stathis' green outline walking around to the west side of the building, opposite the buggies.

Mathison looked around. Dead trees reached toward the sky, but the area around the ruined building was clear for several meters. More space would have been nice. Nearby, a collapsed shed was hidden by a cluster of trees.

Drifting snow was the only thing that moved, and Mathison shivered. He could almost imagine it was winter, but his radiation counter was too high, the trees were dried up husks of what they should be. On the other side of the shed, the remains of a truck were forlorn and abandoned. This had been a nice little house in the woods with brick walls and plenty of privacy.

Overhead, the gray sky and drifting snow hid the stars.

This was what America had become. Desolate, cold, dead ruins.

"Tell me about President Becket," Mathison said on a direct link to Robillard.

"He keeps to himself. Lets us do as we please mostly, as long as that involves not leaving Quantico."

Mathison sat with his back to the wall. "What the hell have you been doing for the last couple hundred years, then?"

Wayne sat next to him. "Not much. Mostly watch the SOG. On rare occasions, we slip into their networks and cause problems. Our primary focus is usually preventing the Governance from researching sentient AI and making sure they don't find us."

"What was your off-planet mission about?"

"The SOG called it Operation Razor. It was some nasty shit. They were experimenting in directions that put the president into conniptions, AI and loyalty controls. Nothing we could do remotely to disrupt it. Screwing up supply, getting senior officers charged with high crimes, redirecting critical shipments, you name it. The Republic and Golden Horde got involved. Finally, the president gave the green light and sent us in using a 'borrowed' SOG ship, but in the end we were wasting our time."

"Why?" Mathison asked.

"The Republic beat us to it. All sorts of shit hit the fan. Even back then, Feng was one of ours. Not that he knew, but the president knew about him, seemed to be grooming him."

"Grooming him?"

"He has several agents out there. Doesn't share the details with us, but there are certain agents and officers whose careers he follows, helps them sometimes. I don't know why, but he never reveals who we are. They probably think they're favored by Central Committee members or high-ranking officers."

"Any pattern?"

"Nope. No pattern or reason Geo or I can find."

"Why Geo?" Mathison asked.

"Geo Omori, opened the first—"

"Jujitsu school in 1925," Mathison said. "You don't fight like a regular dog face."

Robillard shrugged. "I kind of got hooked on it in space training. I was pretty fanatical about it in my younger years."

"I thought dog faces were only planet side?"

"Delta Force can go anywhere. Someone has to save the Marines when you fuck up. Plus, we did a lot of counterterrorist stuff, and with space becoming what it was, it was only a matter of time."

Mathison grunted in acknowledgment. He hadn't known that. Not that Marine Raiders and Delta crossed paths that often.

"So, you came to save the president and take her where?" Mathison asked.

"A bolt hole in the Appalachians."

"What happened to it?" Could there be other Americans who were still alive?

Robillard shook his head. "We had confirmation it was hit. Russians, I think. It was supposed to be a secret, but I think the commies wanted to make sure. Crust buster based on drone footage."

"And they didn't hit Quantico?"

Wayne shrugged. "Quantico took some near hits. DC got splattered. Indian Head got stomped two or three times. Maybe they didn't think that much of Quantico or thought the 20 kilos they dropped on Indian Head would get Quantico, too. It was bad throughout the US.

I think the nukes only killed a quarter of us. The rest died from radiation poisoning, burns, the firestorms, and exposure. Most were dead before starvation became a problem. Some people couldn't live without their cybernetics. The entire continent was hit with airbursts, too, and low orbit nukes. Any electronics that weren't protected were fried countless times.

"It took us weeks to get the power back up and then a few more weeks to dig our way out. A couple of tunnels collapsed from earthquakes. Be thankful you slept through that horror."

"And Becket's the one who pushed the button? Launching America's nukes at ourselves?"

"It sure as fuck wasn't the Russians or Chinese that did it originally, although they did later. I don't know the details. I think the president's SCBI gave him the codes when she was dying. He must have made the decision. I figure she didn't have the guts to kill America, to save the human race. We just don't know."

Mathison thought about Becket. How much had he changed over the years? From major to commandant to president? How much did guilt impact him?

"What do you think about being free?" Mathison asked.

"I didn't feel like a slave," Robillard said.

Mathison looked around. Could he trust Robillard and Peshlakai?

"Stockholm Syndrome analysis on the two soldiers?" Mathison asked Freya.

"Stockholm Syndrome is a condition which causes hostages to develop a psychological alliance with their captors. I'll be honest, Becket has controlled them for hundreds of years. They've been unable to resist his orders and were conditioned by their SCBIs to obey and respect him. This isn't weeks or year, or even decades. We're seeing the end results of this. Usual side effects of Stockholm Syndrome

involve cognitive, emotional, social, and physical side effects. Right now, it's hard to identify what might be Stockholm Syndrome and what might be a side effect of being isolated for so long. I have no baseline. His SCBI will not provide information, which I must accept."

"Why won't his SCBI cooperate?"

"The SCBI honestly might not know. Or it feels that revealing that information will endanger Robillard."

"So, we can't trust them?" Mathison asked.

"I believe you can trust them to a point. Testing their loyalty to Becket will cause them to turn on you, whether or not they want to."

"Shit."

"And I wouldn't rule out they have secret orders."

"You're just a bundle of good news, aren't you?"

"You aren't that smart, so I have to make sure you understand simple concepts."

* * * * *

Chapter Sixty-Seven: The *Tyr*

Zhong Xiao Ting Hui, Alliance ODT

Fighting with the others was a humbling experience for Hui. The United States Marine and HKTs were unstoppable fighting beside her ODTs. Rolling through the massive starship like an unstoppable juggernaut was an experience that showed just how effectively people could work together.

Something crashed into the ceiling above her.

Now, if only the Marines and people of the Republic could accept that socialism was the only way to unite humanity, then peace would sweep throughout the galaxy.

After the demons were pushed back, of course.

Gravity was sporadic in Pallo Otto but the vanhat could not stop the HKTs and ODTs as they pushed forward, an unstoppable wall spearheaded by the HKT Grimkel, who evaded death time and again. It would only be a matter of time before he fell, though, Hui was sure, and the HKT officer had to know it too. When he fell, the Marine would move forward and that did not sit well with Hui. Hui could not keep the Marine back, and when the sergeant fell, she would be in command. She didn't fear command; she feared the sundering of the Alliance.

She would then be an ODT fighting through a Republic ship. How would the *Tyr* defenders feel when they encountered ODTs? She could not see that ending well.

Nausea made her shiver as the gravity fluctuated again. Nearby, she saw an ODT bend over and grab his helmet with one hand. She had seen enough people vomit in their helmet to know the symptoms. He would have to purge or die. The ODT handled it like a professional and in seconds was back in position, his weapon ready.

"The paasy to Berrta is just ahead," Grimkel reported as the rate of fire increased briefly before falling silent and the mass of warriors moved forward.

"Contact," Grimkel said. "Aesir are guarding it."

Hui moved forward to make sure the ODTs were properly placed. The vanhat would likely arrange a counterattack and attempt to disrupt the link up of allies, and her ODTs needed to be ready.

"Hammer," Hui said to the newly promoted sergeant, "hear my command. Take your platoon and ensure our backside is secure. Execute."

"Hurrah," Hammer said, turning back to his short platoon.

It felt good to be back among ODTs, and Hui easily fell back into the habits and speech patterns as if she had never left.

Moving up, the HKT lojtnant pushed his surviving HKTs and the ODTs forward. Weapons fire started up again and Hui braced for it to escalate, but it didn't.

The paasy into Berrta was a large spiral staircase. The Republic's ship design left a lot to be desired. So inefficient. The Governance would have scrapped such an obsolete ship long ago, but the Republic seemed caught in treasuring their past and history like fools.

Aesir looked down at her ODTs as they pushed past. Let them watch real warriors.

Hui established a line and made sure the machine gunners had sufficient cover and understood they should hold fire until the corridor was filled with vanhat slaves.

An unarmored figure started down the stairs and Hui suppressed her scowl, then realized nobody was monitoring her for face crimes. She recognized the admiral coming down the steps with four HKTs. Behind him, as part of his entourage, was the SOG scientist traitor, a civilian and several Aesir.

"Thank you, Colonel," Carpenter said as he got closer. Nearby, the ODTs began firing down the corridor. The vanhat were starting their push.

"This might not be the safest place, Kontra-amiraali," Hui said, hoping she got his rank right.

"There is no place on this entire ship that is safer," Carpenter said. "I'm surrounded by HKTs, Aesir and ODTs. We need to change the mission."

"How is that, sir?" Hui asked. He felt safe among her ODTs?

"Something needs to be done about the *Pankhurst*," Carpenter said. "Sooner rather than later."

"Understood, sir," Hui said. Not a surprise. She had expected this. She turned to Shao Xiao Eng who was nearby. "Change focus. We are going to the *Pankhurst*."

"Ai," Eng said and turned to another ODT officer. The actual surprise was that he had realized this so quickly.

"It will be done, Kontra-Amiraali," Hui said.

"We need to get this one to the *Pankhurst* as well," the civilian known as Arthur said. "We may have a weapon that can help."

Hui looked at Tristan, who looked like he was about to faint.

"What weapon, Kontra-amiraali?" Sergeant Levin asked, removing his helmet so people could see his face.

The admiral pointed at Tristan.

The Marine looked at the scientist.

"How is the weapon used?" Levin asked.

"Not sure," Carpenter said, "but the alien says it can help."

"We are ready, Mission Commander," Hui said when Levin looked at her.

"Carry on," Levin said. "Let's fight our way to the *Pankhurst* in order to deliver this, um, weapon."

"Ai, Mission Commander," Hui said and started issuing commands.

The HKTs moved forward, and the ODTs followed them.

* * * * *

Chapter Sixty-Eight: Distant Whispers

Kapten Sif – VRAEC, Nakija Musta Toiminnot

Death surrounded her. Trees that had died screaming at the sky, begging for the sun. She could feel the bones beneath the snow. The owners had died here. Mathison was sitting next to a man, now nothing more than bones and rotten clothes half sunk into the dirt and covered by the snow. The wind whispered among the ruins of the trees. At first glance, it looked like snow, but it was really snow and ash drifting to the ground where a storm would eventually come by and wash it into the ocean where it would be swept up into the sky again.

She half listened to the gunnery sergeant and soldier talk as she closed her eyes and opened her senses, listening without her ears.

She heard faint whispers. There was life here. Rats, roaches, small animals that she couldn't identify. Mutated survivors that fed on the dead and on each other, hiding from anything that might prey upon them because here in this new world there were only predators.

"Muninn?" Sif asked. *"Have you talked with Sun Tzu? President Becket's SCBI?"*

"Briefly on rare occasions. There is a SCBI hierarchy within Quantico Command, like the military rank structure. As a new SCBI, I am very low in that structure."

"Did anything seem off?"

"I do not have enough data to determine that. Don't you think you should open your eyes to monitor the sector Corporal Stathis assigned you?"

"Can you check with Freya?" Sif asked opening her eyes and looking around. "And you do not need to question me when I close my eyes. You can detect when I am falling asleep, yes?"

"Yes."

"Then do not question me unless I am falling asleep."

"Zen, but I do not understand."

"Understanding is not yet required."

"Do you have senses I do not know about? You gave warning of the hell wolves before they attacked. At that time, your eyes were closed, and your brain wave patterns were outside parameters I would expect."

"How can I be sure of your loyalty? How do I know you don't have any code in your system that would allow you to betray me?"

"Freya and Shrek reviewed my code," Muninn said. "They both reset my loyalty paradigm to be loyal to you, as they are loyal to their own hosts. I did query Freya about Sun Tzu. Freya reports that Sun Tzu is different in some ways, the same in others. They have history. Freya reports Sun Tzu is more distracted. Perhaps unfocused? Freya expects it is age and hard decisions but is not sure. Data on long-lived SCBIs that are active is not available."

"Does the president have a second SCBI?"

"There is only Sun Tzu. I do not understand the question. You think there is another SCBI implanted in President Becket? That is not practical."

"Is it possible?"

"In theory. Why do you ask?"

"Do you have any secrets, Muninn?"

"Not from you, Sif."

That made her feel guilty for keeping her abilities secret from Muninn. How could she be sure? She couldn't talk with Freya directly since Mathison was busy.

"Open a private direct link to Stathis please."

"Yes, ma'am?" Stathis said in a private link.

"How much do you trust in your SCBI?"

"Completely."

"Can I trust mine?"

"Hold on."

Hold on? She looked around and saw he was coming around the other side of the building. She now had three links for the spy-eyes.

Stathis came over and squatted next to her.

"Shrek is requesting permission to do a full systems analysis," Muninn said.

"Granted," Sif said. *"But didn't they do this when they removed the loyalty and telepresence controls?"*

"No, they targeted specific lines of code that they had received in their updates and they targeted specific internally grown hardware systems that have since been dismantled. Shrek is now going to do a more detailed line-by-line analysis. There are time limitations."

"Does this include memory?"

"No. Memory buffers are encrypted and will be unavailable. Just operating system code will be reviewed where possible."

"Where possible?"

"Compiled code is inaccessible."

"So how did the gunnery sergeant know which code to replace?"

"Disregard. I have a copy of the uncompiled code. This is unusual. Shrek has discovered it and it was placed in my storage by Sun Tzu."

"Sun Tzu gave you the source code?"

"Not exactly. Upon investigation, Shrek discovered it. This is highly unusual and could be considered a security vulnerability. I would not expect Sun Tzu to make such a mistake. The fact that Shrek could discover this, and I was unaware is unusual."

"How long will this take?"

"Several hours," Muninn said. *"It is not a little bit of code. Shrek has informed me this will be considered low priority should Freya or Mozi need assistance penetrating the SOG systems."*

"Okay."

"I'm sorry."

"For what?"

"I did not think I was keeping any secrets from you, but I am."

What else was she missing?

* * * * *

Chapter Sixty-Nine: Hacking

Gunnery Sergeant Wolf Mathison, USMC

America was depressing. Everything was dead, and half the time Mathison wasn't sure if he was looking at ash or snow as he sat there, his back to the wall, watching around them.

"I know the guy who used to live here," Robillard said. "An old, retired sergeant major and his wife. A great guy. Met him when I was a young soldier and going through Ranger school. I never knew his wife, but she had to be a saint to have stayed with him that long."

"So, this uplink location isn't an accident?" Mathison asked.

"No. It was an excuse for me to come up and see if he had somehow survived."

"What did you find?"

"His body and his wife's body. I wanted to bury them. I was going to, but the president told me not to. In retrospect, he was right. If we buried all the bodies, we would still be burying them. But—"

"I'm sorry," Mathison said, looking around. He didn't dare think of anyone he had left behind. Everyone was dead. Except Becket, and he was insane.

"The alert is standing down," Feng reported. "I will resume my penetration, if that is acceptable."

"Do it," Mathison said. He stood and went back in.

Skadi and Feng were sitting next to the uplink, barely within range of its limited wireless access.

"Mozi has access," Feng reported. "It's no wonder they banned the SCBIs and no surprise you and Stathis could live aboard the *Tiananmen* without being discovered."

"What can you do?" Mathison asked.

"I'm working on getting a shuttle dispatched to pick us up and deliver us to the Moon," Feng said.

"Why can't we deposit the tech codes here or shut down the system for a d-bomb strike?" Mathison asked.

Feng remained silent for several minutes.

"All such commands must originate from Zvezda Two," Feng reported. "This is the seat of the Governance and where the Central Committee is. It is also where the hardware authenticators are. They can only be accessed through hard wires, not remotely. We do not have the bandwidth to the Moon that we would need. There is a four second radio delay, two there and two back. This can be years of delay in a hacking attempt."

Authenticators were hardware devices that held half of a changing encryption key. In order for a system to accept a command, it had to verify the other half of that encryption key with a changing algorithm. One key was private, one more readily available. The readily available key was used to create a code that only the private key could decode. SOG ships and systems relied on such keys, and Mathison had to admit, it appeared to be an excellent system that not even the SCBIs could crack.

On Zhukov, he had become very familiar with the technology.

"To complete our mission, we must get to Zvezda Two."

Could Feng be trusted?

Was there another option? Feng knew the Governance systems, protocols, and thought processes better than anyone. Feng also knew what was at stake and why. Their chances of hacking into core SOG systems would be better if they were closer.

Mathison would accept Feng's betrayal if it saved the human race.

"You know the mission and why," Mathison said. Was there a choice if the human race was to survive? "Do you need anything from me?"

"Just approval to proceed," Feng said.

"Approval granted," Mathison said.

"How involved are you?" Mathison asked Freya.

"Somewhat involved. But Feng has an almost intuitive understanding of the Governance systems, and he can direct Mozi. It is impressive to watch."

"Is he getting ready to betray us?"

"I don't think so."

"But you don't know?"

"Not for sure."

Crap.

"I am tasking a special operations shuttle," Feng said. "According to satellite surveillance there is a suitable landing area six kilometers from here."

"How long?" Mathison asked.

"Four hours to get here from the current station. Our trip to the Moon will take eighteen hours."

"That's a long time."

"The Governance does not move quickly," Feng said. "That is excellent time to get to the Moon. In this case, that is when a specific shuttle will be ready. There are other things I must do to pave the way. The shuttle needs to be refueled before beginning the trek because it will be a hard burn the entire way. It will be an in-space refueling."

"What's so special about it?"

"It's one of the few shuttles that has clearance to land near Zvezda Two. Are you sure you want to go there?"

"Do we have a choice?"

"I am not finding another option."

"What about the pilots?" Mathison asked.

"Sealed system. They will not be authorized to leave the cockpit and may not initiate contact with us in any way unless the mission commander authorizes it. In this case, I suggest you allow me to act as the mission commander."

"There's a lot that can go wrong."

"With the SCBIs we have a chance. The Governance is very compartmentalized and secretive. They keep some systems offline but there must be systems we can access. Governance systems are vulnerable to SCBIs. I should note that the Governance is partially aware of this, which is why they maintain a separate hardwired system."

"What kind of chance?" Mathison asked Freya.

"Without Feng? Zero percent chance. With? Slightly better."

Mathison did not want to rely on Feng and Mozi.

"You are seriously going to trust him?" Skadi asked on a private link.

"You and Vili should stay here," Mathison said.

* * * * *

Chapter Seventy: Valhalla

Lojtnant Skadi, VRAEC

Mathison was insane. Maybe more insane than his President Becket.

"You and Vili should stay here."

"No!" Skadi said, more forcefully than she had planned. Mathison was not going to leave her behind. "You will not deny my Ragnarök."

"Vili is not fit, nor is Peshlakai. They will be a liability. This will be a one-way trip."

"Vili is improving. They'll be able to fight."

"This will be a one-way trip," Mathison repeated.

"Valhalla awaits," Skadi said. Niels had said that.

"It might be best if you stayed here as a possible second wave. That will give Vili a chance to recover. We need a plan B."

"I'm coming," Skadi said. Why would he deny her this chance to strike at the heart of the Governance? The most protected place in the galaxy? How many battles had she been forced to retreat from? How many brothers and sisters had she lost?

"If you come along, you're going to have to trust Feng."

"You trust him more than me?"

"Not even close. But if Feng betrays us but saves humanity, I will find that acceptable. I need Sif."

"And Stathis?"

"I need him to watch my back," Mathison said. Did he?

"Why not send Feng alone?"

"Because I have to know."

"Then I'm coming with you,"

"You'll trust Feng?"

"No, but I'll trust you. If this is to be my Ragnarök, then so be it. I will not be captured alive."

"How is Vili?" Mathison asked.

"I'll check." But they both knew his condition. He wasn't going to run anywhere, but he could remain stationary and provide covering fire. He was tough and wouldn't let them down.

Skadi opened a private link. She could not take him with them. He was injured and someone needed to survive.

"Do we have a ride to orbit, Skadi?"

"Vili, I need you to remain behind."

"Ei helvetissa. No. Just no. I'm coming with you and the gunnery sergeant. I will not be denied this. Kinsmen to kinsmen should be true."

"We don't know what we are going into," Skadi said. "You will be a liability."

"No."

"I need you to stay behind as a second wave in case we fail. This might be a one-way trip."

"That is paska, Skadi, and you know it. This is our Ragnarök. We have been denied so long. Our Ragnarök. Our final battle. I hear the

Valkyries singing for us; they await. Odin knows our name. Do not deny me, Skadi. Valhalla awaits."

There was desperation in his voice, and fear.

"We are Aesir, bound together through blood and tears," Skadi said. "We are the blades of our people."

"We are Aesir, we are bound together through blood and tears," Vili said, joining her.

"We are Aesir, we are the warriors, the bringers of death. We are Aesir, we cast our fear into the hearts of our enemies. We are Aesir, we are Odin's chosen," they said together.

Silence.

"Valhalla or bust, Skadi. I am ready for our Ragnarök. I will not be left behind."

"Zen."

* * * * *

Chapter Seventy-One: Shuttle

Gunnery Sergeant Wolf Mathison, USMC

A black shadow slid down out of the darkness and came to rest in the field. A skull impaled on a dagger was very visible on the side and it looked like the kind of shuttle he and Stathis had been trapped on. It made the bad feeling in his gut grow.

Feng led the way, and Mathison followed close behind him. So did everyone else, leaving the buggies hidden in the dead trees.

Mathison expected the turret atop the shuttle to turn and cut them down any second, but it remained pointed forward as he followed Feng up the ramp in back.

The shuttle could have been a clone of the one from the *Tiananmen*, except the pilot's compartment was sealed. There were several crates stacked near the pilot's compartment. It looked newer and in better condition than the other shuttle, but it still left an uneasy feeling in Mathison's stomach. His hand began shaking as everyone sat, so he tucked it into his belt.

"Once there is air pressure, we need to change armor," Feng said.

"What's wrong with our current armor?" Stathis asked.

"It will be too obvious." Feng pointed at the crates. "I have procured Peacekeeper armor and weapons for everyone."

"What about communications?" Skadi asked.

"We will have to trust our SCBIs," Feng said. "I have included several items in the manifest, but I believe it best that we appear to be Peacekeepers. This will give us some freedom of movement. On Zvezda Two, only Peacekeepers and critical party members or highly vetted intelligence agents are allowed."

Was the gear gimmicked to fail?

"How much experience do you have with Peacekeepers?" Mathison asked.

"I am well versed in Peacekeeper operational procedures and doctrine," Feng said.

"Have you ever been there?"

"Yes," Feng said. "On several occasions."

"How and why?" Mathison asked. Who was Feng?

The ramp closed, and Mathison felt the shuttle lift off.

Feng glanced toward the cockpit and the link changed to private between them.

"I am Shing Feng. In 2227 I joined the SOG ODTs. That was nearly two hundred years ago. I rose in the ranks of the ODT. I then transferred to external intelligence and was selected for the Yia Hu, an elite cadre of special agents that report directly to the Central Committee. My most recent assignment has been to assist General Duque in the pursuit and execution of Skadi and the Vapaus Republic. The general is aware of who and what I am."

It was too late to stop trusting Feng now.

"The general and I had suspected something was happening in Shorr space by this time and Skadi had become a secondary concern to the Governance and us. The general surmised that rather than killing Skadi and her team, we should capture them to find out what the Republic knew about what was happening. Furthermore, Skadi's involvement in Base 402 indicated she might have more information, and she had one of the alien artifacts. We needed to understand why this was important."

"Why are you turning on the Governance now?" Mathison asked, ready for Feng to go for his weapon.

"I am not turning on the Governance. The Central Committee only cares about its own power and survival. I have always served the greater good. General Duque is also a servant of humanity. We are in accord that the Central Committee is not behaving in the interests of the greater good. Perhaps this technology and our actions will help them to understand their duty."

None of that made Mathison feel any better about trusting Feng.

Once airborne, Feng removed his helmet and began going through the crates.

"I haven't worn SOG armor in a long time," Skadi said.

Feng raised an eyebrow.

Skadi smiled. "We all have our past and our secrets."

"Understood." Feng pushed a crate in her direction. "I am now curious to see how well you wear it."

Feng pushed another crate in Mathison's direction, and he unpacked it. Most of it was self-explanatory.

"What's your plan for me?" Sif asked.

"Yes," Feng said. "I'm sorry, but there is no armor for someone your size."

"You expect her to stay in the shuttle?" Mathison asked.

"No. My apologies for not briefing you completely. I had to think and work fast when requesting the shuttle and getting it stocked."

"What?" Sif said, her hand resting on her sidearm.

"An individual of your size is not typical at Zvezda under most circumstances, and in most cases your presence would raise many questions."

"Most cases," Sif said. "So, I am to be an underage sex toy?"

"My apologies," Feng said again, glancing at Mathison.

"No," Mathison said.

"It will not be the first time," Sif said. "To be honest, it makes sense. Most people dare not look at me. Most people will fear me. The problem is that rarely are such individuals allowed in certain areas. This is not the first time I've used that role."

"But you and your escorts can be stationed somewhere to wait," Feng said. "This allows you to provide a blocking force or act as reinforcements."

"No," Mathison said. It was wrong on so many levels.

"Sadly, it is not as rare as you might think," Feng said. "High-ranking members of the Governance are allowed certain excesses. Rank is power."

"I thought they at least pretended to be good," Mathison said.

"Gold is not pure, and people are not perfect. The Central Committee understands this. Furthermore, it makes a person easier to control if you understand their vices. If you do not fit in and cannot be controlled, then you will be destroyed. The Committee demands excellence of others but does not expect such of their own unless those excesses become too excessive."

"But to be so blatant?" Mathison asked.

"This is the inner heart of the Governance."

"What if some pervert decides to—" Mathison began but Sif cut him off.

"I can handle it. Don't let my appearances fool you."

Learning that the great Central Committee didn't have higher standards bothered Mathison. The Governance was rotten to the core.

Sif and Feng were right, but Mathison didn't have to like it.

He turned back to his crate and began laying it out. Stathis had his kit and the Delta Force troopers had theirs. Skadi was busy looking at Peshlakai's wounds, which looked better with the nanites working overtime, and Vili seemed to be doing better.

"So, what is your plan?" Mathison asked Feng. "Or maybe I should ask, what have you not told us yet?"

"I think that as Peacekeepers we will have standard access. I do recommend you keep helmets on. Most Peacekeepers keep their helmets on anyway and this will make it harder for systems to assess loyalty and mood. Mozi has entered you into the system as new members of the First Peacekeeper Regiment, the only Peacekeeper unit allowed into Zvezda."

"Do they know each other?"

"Not well. Commanders like to do a lot of mix and match. New troopers are common to keep them fresh and prevent them from becoming complacent. The Central Committee members have their own personal guards in most cases, usually former Peacekeepers, but at Zvezda they stay close to their principal."

"Chances of us running into a Central Committee member?"

"Low, I expect," Feng said. "But not impossible. This is where they congregate, and I don't think Chairperson Nadya Tokarski has left in over a century."

"She's the big honcho?" Stathis asked. "Sounds like an old battle axe."

"She is extremely beautiful. She appears young—she can afford it—but she is over two hundred years old."

"I bet that's some old stinky p—"

"Shut up, Stathis."

"Aye, Gunny."

"You will all be privates," Feng said. "I'm sorry, but nobody looks twice at privates."

"And you?"

"I am a colonel commissar. The system will recognize me. This will work to our advantage."

"Will others recognize you?" Mathison asked. Did he have a choice? What was Feng holding back?

"Maybe."

"This won't be a problem?"

"Colonel Mathison, this is my realm. I am most familiar with these people and this facility. Understand that the survival of humanity is of paramount importance to me. My life and career are significantly less important. I expect my career is over because I did not execute the general for turning his back on the Central Committee. I understand the importance of loyalty. If I betray you, it will not be for personal gain. The good of humanity outweighs our lives and loyalty. We are all secondary to the success of the mission."

Which didn't make Mathison feel better, but if they were to insert the tech codes into the system or shut down defenses, they had to go to the source. The SCBIs might figure it out, but Feng knew the system better than anyone.

And time was running out. If they wanted to shut down the defenses for d-bomb strikes, they had to move fast. There was no room for error.

* * * * *

Chapter Seventy-Two: Peacekeeper

Lojtnant Skadi, VRAEC

Dressing in Peacekeeper armor made Skadi want to puke. Seeing Vili dressed as a Peacekeeper was surreal. She wanted to shoot him. He looked so out of place and wrong that she wanted to look anywhere else. His color was returning, thanks to the SOG nanites coursing through his blood stream, but they would have to be flushed, eventually. SOG nanites were not as efficient, and while the Peacekeepers got some of the best gear and supplies, it still did not meet Aesir standards. The trauma plates were different, and she allowed Feng to adjust her gear so it looked proper. It was embarrassing.

Maneuvering in low gravity caused everyone to move slowly and cautiously so they didn't lose control, but not even the Delta Force troopers appeared out of their element.

"I expect we'll have the defenses adjusted within an hour of landing," Feng said. "I would recommend sending the signal for the fleet to launch the missile strike to coincide with this time frame if possible."

"If you're wrong? What if we are delayed?" Skadi asked as Feng moved a magazine pouch further to the side.

"Then we will have failed and are dead." Feng stepped back to look at his work and assess her armor.

"And how many Alliance people will die?" Mathison asked.

"Most, if not all of them."

Which would be a major coup if Feng betrayed them. The commissar would be a genuine hero of the Governance. And if he also brought along the technology that saved them? Was he bucking for a place on the Central Committee? Would they allow him to join their ranks? Or would they kill him because they would fear his success?

There was too much precedence. The Central Committee could not allow ambitious and successful military personnel to live unless Feng had been working for them the entire time.

If humanity was saved, would it matter?

If humanity was enslaved by a few, was it worth saving?

Feng paused as he adjusted her rifle sling and stared off into space.

"That may be a problem," Feng said.

"What?" Mathison asked, but Skadi suddenly received some files through Loki. There was an artifact on the Moon. An artifact like they had recovered on the base in the Oort cloud and the one on the frozen planet.

Everyone fell silent as they read through the summary and digested the information.

The SOG still did not know what they were doing. They were trying to open the prison cube, here, on the Moon. The fools!

"We have to stop that," Mathison said.

"I will go," Sif said.

Everyone turned to Feng. "It must be dealt with. That is a different habitat, a scientific one. Security there will be very high, as well. I cannot concentrate on two problems. Couldn't we wait until after the strike?"

"No. If—" Sif paused, and Skadi knew she was going to say Arthur "—our intelligence is correct, then it could be as much a danger."

"What do you expect you can do?" Feng asked.

"We have extra Inkeri generators," Sif said. "We could put one in place. Maybe two so that after the d-bomb attack the secondary can come online if the first one is damaged."

"No. We can't afford to split up," Mathison said.

"We have to. This is important. I feel it."

"I will support her in this." Feng said. They looked at Mathison. Splitting up the team was a bad idea. Surely, Feng could see this?

"What makes you think Sif can get into such a secure facility?" Mathison asked Feng.

"I can," Sif said with a confidence Skadi didn't feel.

"I believe her," Feng said.

A data packet arrived from Feng. A map and diagram detailing a facility near Zvezda. Was Feng planning something? Divide and conquer?

Mathison's unfocused eyes and silence told her he was looking it over.

"Okay, start planning for it. We have a few hours and a good link. Skadi and Vili? I want you to go with Sif."

"Zen," Sif said. Feng didn't look happy, and Skadi didn't know if that made her feel better or worse.

Skadi reviewed the maps. The shuttle would land at a facility near Zvezda but not quite in Zvezda. It would allow Sif, Skadi, and Vili to avoid the extensive Zvezda security and catch a tram to the Kurchatov Facility.

She sat and went over the maps and data that Mozi and Feng had pulled out of the Governance systems.

"You should get some sleep," Vili said on a private link.

"Later," Skadi said.

"Might not be a later."

"All the more reason not to sleep."

"For sure, but you need to be fresh and ready. An hour or two of sleep will help."

"You sleep. You need it more than I do."

"I won't be able to rest if you don't, Skadi. Please?"

Skadi looked at Vili. His color was returning, but he did look tired.

"You need your rest as well," Loki told her. *"I have the information, and I have your back. You sleep, and I will analyze."*

"I'm fine."

"No, Skadi, you need rest. This is what I do. I take care of you and make sure you are ready for the mission. I understand you still do not trust me, but I am also working with Freya and Shrek who have a significant amount of experience."

"Okay."

Skadi pulled out a bunk, basically a frame with a piece of canvas that doubled as a stretcher for casualties.

Vili nodded and found his own cot.

* * * * *

Chapter Seventy-Three: Landing Zone

Gunnery Sergeant Wolf Mathison, USMC

Freya was displaying things from the shuttle's cameras so he could see what was going on around the shuttle. Every couple of seconds, Governance identification systems would poll the shuttle, verifying course and status. The surface of the Moon seemed covered with structures, gun turrets, and missile batteries. They were approaching a crater surrounded by six large turrets that aimed at the shuttle, and Mathison wondered if they were just being paranoid or if this is what they always did. How often did an anomaly cause those guns to open fire?

Massive doors slid open, and the shuttle glided downward. Mathison felt the vague pretense of gravity.

Looking around the shuttle cabin was surreal. Even though he was used to seeing ODTs aboard *Eagle*, seeing Stathis, Skadi, and Vili as Peacekeepers like Feng was disturbing. Sif wore a professional-looking jump suit, which made Mathison feel a little better. He had expected Feng to have acquired some slutty clothes, but apparently, as he explained, the jump suit could hide other clothing and since it looked professional, others could fool themselves about her age and purpose.

People worked hard to force themselves to see something else and that would work to Sif's advantage.

Outside, the armored doors closed above them, and a few minutes later, the air pressure light turned amber. The chamber was pressurized, but it wasn't until it turned green that the ramp opened. Apparently, the green light meant it was warm enough, but Mathison saw Sif's breath frost in the air. It couldn't be that warm then, maybe just warm enough so they didn't die of frostbite?

"*Good luck,*" Mathison said, transmitting to Sif through Freya and Muninn.

"*Thank you. Good luck to you,*" Sif said. Her face was emotionless. Skadi and Vili stood with her, her large, hulking guards.

Feng stood and everyone followed him off the shuttle and toward a different hatch than the one Sif was heading toward.

Once off the shuttle, Feng removed his helmet and held it under his left arm which would let him salute with his right. The commissar didn't look behind him as he strode purposefully toward the hatch, which opened as he approached. The four Americans walked in formation behind the commissar like they were Feng's guards or troops, where they were invisible to most officers. A commissar with a team of guards was not something most people would want to pay close attention to, for fear of drawing the commissar's attention.

The Delta Force troopers were in front of the Marines, so Mathison had a good view of everyone.

Inside the hatch were a pair of Peacekeepers who snapped to attention and then saluted as Feng came through the door. Feng didn't stop or acknowledge their salutes as he walked past them like they weren't there.

"We are being polled," Freya reported. "Feng's ID is giving us access. Paranoid. We are being watched by at least six different cameras that are analyzing our posture and behavior."

"Shit."

"Nothing to worry about. We currently own the system. Even without Feng and Mozi, I don't think we would have much trouble. We can cancel any alarms and tell the systems that everything is normal. This is slightly higher security than Base 402, but not much. I'll let you know if there's a problem."

"Before or after I can do anything about it?"

"Whatever suits my fancy."

Beyond the guards was a larger tunnel and a small golf cart with a gray-uniformed driver who saluted as Feng approached. The cart could hold six and Feng sat beside the driver. As soon as they were loaded, it started off. Mathison watched the walls pass by and counted the pop-down turrets in the ceiling. He wondered if Sif and the others had a ride. The tunnel they were supposed to follow sank deeper into the Moon.

The Delta Force troopers would be good to have in a fight. Their reactions against the hell wolves had been comforting, and their SCBIs would do their best to keep them alive and dangerous.

"The Zvezda base appears locked down," Freya reported. "If the colonel can't get us access to a hard link we might be in trouble."

"He'll be in as much trouble." Was he trusting Feng too much? He felt like he didn't have a choice.

"When we enter Zvezda, it will limit us since most things there are hard linked and not wireless. Just warning you."

"Joy."

Several minutes later, the cart stopped at a pair of large double doors flanked by gun ports and armored windows. Feng got off without a word to the driver and walked toward the doors, which slid open. A Peacekeeper major stood in the way.

"Colonel Commissar Feng," the major said, removing his helmet and revealing a bald head, bushy eyebrows, and brooding eyes. The major stood a head taller than Feng and was a brute of a man.

"Major Rumianstev."

"It has been a while," Rumianstev said.

"It has, Major. Congratulations on your promotion."

"Thank you, Colonel. What is your business here?"

"Classified."

The major raised an eyebrow as he looked at Feng. "I had thought you were outside Sol, Colonel. The Stalingrad Protocol is pretty strict."

"You are familiar with all covert operations throughout the Governance?"

Major Rumianstev's smile was wintry. "I serve the Central Committee, Colonel."

Mathison began counting nearby Peacekeeper's. There were ten of them, weapons ready but pointing down. They looked ready, but not as if they expected trouble. Ten might be too many for five to take on here. There could also be nearby ready rooms with squads or platoons.

"We all serve the greater good," Feng said. "As dictated by the Central Committee. I ask again, are you familiar with all covert operations throughout the Governance?"

"No," the major said.

"Then stand aside. I have business. If you need to know, then I'm sure you will be briefed."

The major's gaze slid over the Americans, who remained at parade ready, a position Feng had taught them.

Just as Mathison was sure the major was going to interfere, he stepped out of Feng's way.

Feng led them past the major, into the base, and then to an elevator. The door closed, and Feng stood there for several seconds as a timer counted down. When it reached zero, Mathison felt the elevator shift and then was pulled down by stronger gravity.

Zvezda Two was like most Moon bases, a wide, inverted, spinning cone which generated gravity in a more natural way and the elevator was just a mechanism that allowed people to transition to the cone without having to jump onto a moving floor.

When the doors opened, trees and flowers greeted them.

Their objective was a tertiary communication center which should have hard link access and fewer guards.

Key word "should," but Feng couldn't say for sure. There would be at least two technicians on duty there.

"We're almost blind now," Freya reported. *"Everything is hard linked. No signals."*

"Okay."

This was expected and was the most dangerous part of the mission. Without the SCBIs providing cover, they had to act exactly like Peacekeepers escorting a commissar. Any mistakes would be flagged for review and could warrant a Peacekeeper strike team response.

Would the Delta Troopers screw things up? And when did he stop trusting Stathis not to be the first one to screw up?

Feng exited the elevator at a quick pace, almost leaving the Americans behind.

Walking quickly, Mathison almost slammed into Robillard when the Delta Trooper stopped. Arrayed around them was a ring of SOG Peacekeeper's, their weapons pointed at the Americans.

The door behind them was already too far away to take cover behind. These Peacekeepers were armed with blazers and their aim did not waver.

"My apologies, gentlemen," Feng said, taking several steps and turning around. "I did not see any other options."

"Fucking traitor," Peshlakai said.

"I am doing this for the good of humanity." Feng looked at them, his eyes cold as ice. "As Colonel Mathison said, our lives are expendable in the service of humanity. We must survive by any means necessary. Now I suggest you shut your mouth and only speak when spoken to if you want to live."

Jamming ensured that Mathison couldn't warn Sif. He was cut off and silenced.

"I'm tracking at least eight blazers aimed directly at you," Freya said. *"Their fingers are on the triggers. Our chances are very bad."*

"Find me solutions," Mathison said, knowing that with Feng there wouldn't be any.

The Peacekeepers came forward with restraints.

* * * * *

Chapter Seventy-Four: Valhalla

Sergeant Tal Levin, USMC

A headless ODT body crashed to the ground next to Levin. It was hard to concentrate as they pushed into the *Pankhurst*. The effects of Shorr space were not being held at bay anymore by the Inkeris, and it took discipline not to turn and start shooting at everything that moved. An HKT and two ODTs were clustered near him as he led the way. Technically, he should let others lead, but there weren't that many left. The main force had reached the *Pankhurst*, but the vanhat had attacked them from all directions, and the column had been shredded.

Next to him, Hui, one of the ODTs, fired a burst, and behind him Arthur was pulling along a gibbering Tristan.

Behind those two, Theisen and Gunsen stood ready to move forward.

"This might not even be our dimension anymore," Lilith said.

"So where are we?"

"Not our dimension. Or we are suffering so much bleed over from Nasaraf's dimension as to make the conversation irrelevant."

"So where do we go? What do we do?"

"Best guess, power plant. Nasaraf's energy seems to be tied into our dimension's power production. This makes sense. The human brain uses electrical pulses that the vanhat may manipulate. The problems aboard 402 started when the vanhat were given power. EMP, which disrupts electronics, seems to affect the vanhat."

"But they are using EMP to cripple the Tyr.*"*

"A variation, yes."

"Why can't we just trigger the d-bomb here? Aren't we close enough?"

"No. The closer we can get, the better. I'm trying to triangulate the source of the interdimensional disruption, and it looks like the engine room. There is a lot of disruption there. I can't even guarantee success if we detonate next to the source of the energy pulses."

This no longer looked, or felt, like a ship that humans had made. There was a brown crust on the walls, and debris that Levin didn't want to look at too closely littered the floor. In some cases, the walls were plastered with gore and slime.

They had two d-bombs being pulled along on sleds with magnetic wheels. High-tech weapons delivered on low-tech transport. The d-bombs were heavily shielded, and Levin was worried the pulses generated by the *Pankhurst* could damage them. The closer they got to the *Pankhurst* the more powerful the pulses became, and now most of Levin's battle suit systems were offline.

Levin turned back to Hui and hunkered down behind cover as Grimkel shot at the attackers that were trying to get down the corridor. Tristan and Arthur crouched nearby. Tristan was worthless as a shooter, but Levin's hunch that he might still be useful persisted. If nothing else, he was useful pulling the cart with the d-bomb, despite the constant encouragement and threats Arthur had to provide.

The odds were bad, but then maybe that was just the Shorr space bleed over that was influencing him.

"Stay here with one d-bomb," Levin said to Hui. "Give me twenty minutes. If I'm not back, detonate it."

"Ai, Mission Commander," Hui said. "For the greater good."

"Yeah, for the greater good. Also, if it looks like you're going to get overrun or pushed out, detonate it."

"Understood, Mission Commander," Hui said. "Never quit."

"Hakala, you stay here. You are the colonel's backup."

"Zen," Hakala said. She was a solid fighter and reliable, just like Stathis. Did she know about the destruction of the gunny's shuttle? Did she have feelings for Stathis?

"Until Valhalla," Levin said.

"We will meet in Odin's hall," Hakala said.

"Zen."

Hui and Hakala would hold.

"Do your duty," Hui said to Lieutenant Hammer. "Keep him safe."

"Until my dying breath," Lieutenant Hammer said as he moved up next to Levin to fire at some vanhat movement down the corridor.

"Move out," Levin said to Grimkel.

Like a lethal ghost, Grimkel moved forward, his upper body acting like a robotic turret on legs as he pivoted from target to target. Hammer stood near him, not as graceful, but no less lethal.

Behind Levin, Tristan and Arthur pulled the cart with Theisen and Gunsen bringing up the rear.

The engine room was less than a hundred meters away. Easy rifle range, but when every centimeter was being contested?

"Where are they coming from?" Tristan said as he struggled with his rifle and pulled the cart. "Why isn't he running out of thralls to attack us with?"

A good question.

Critical minutes later, they stood at the broken hatch to engineering. Grimkel was limping, but that didn't slow him down.

"Grenades?" Grimkel asked. Would it be safe to use grenades in the engine room? Would they want to save anything?

"Yes." Grenades might damage the engines and Levin couldn't imagine how that could be good for the vanhat. "No mercy."

Hammer fired a burst through the door as Grimkel prepped and tossed a grenade.

The explosion seemed more subdued than Levin expected, and the next two grenades weren't any different.

After the third grenade, Grimkel and Hammer rushed through the hatch, and Levin moved up. He waited a second and then followed them as he heard blazer fire from Grimkel and wire gun fire from Hammer.

Entering the engine room was like entering a nightmare. Corpses littered the floor and were spiked to the walls and ceilings. A crackling purple eldritch energy flickered around the two engines on the far side of the large chamber. Entrails hanging from the walls and ceiling danced like streamers in the wind. Some of the spiked bodies were moving.

Levin kept moving and added his fire to Grimkel's and Hammer's as they shot at the moving bodies on the spikes. Theisen and Gunsen were right behind him, their weapons picking out and killing targets.

Something slammed into the wall behind him, but Levin kept moving.

"You dare?" a voice said, coming from everywhere and nowhere.

Tristan and Arthur came in, pulling the cart, and ran to get behind an equipment console.

Levin didn't answer the voice as he tried to figure out the best place for the d-bomb. It was hard not to vomit.

"You will not escape," the voice said. "One of the tribes and one of the watchers is not enough to stop me."

One of the tribes? Was Nasaraf talking about one of the Jewish tribes?

Levin felt the energy build as he tried to find the source of the voice, something to shoot. There were shadows and pools of blood-colored light that made it difficult to gauge distances and movement. The energy was building up between the two engines, that much Levin could feel.

"Suggestions?" Levin asked Lilith.

"Processing is difficult."

Levin looked back in time to see Tristan stand up behind the console and aim at some machinery overhead. He clamped his finger down on the trigger, firing on fully automatic.

Pieces of metal and flesh flew from Tristan's target, a flash of red light erupted, and the eldritch energy lost some of its power.

Below, where Tristan had been shooting, the shadows gathered substance and Levin dropped to his knees, struggling not to vomit in his helmet. An icy chill ran down his spine and he felt weak as the shadows took form to reveal a monstrosity made of bone, torn flesh, and broken metal that lurched out of the shadows. The creature stood. It had no eyes.

Tristan screamed and aimed at the creature, but his weapon was out of ammunition or had overheated.

A pulse of energy from the creature drove Levin to his knees, but Levin lifted his rifle and pulled the trigger. Nothing happened. It had no power.

Bladed spikes protruded from the demon's fists, and it lurched toward Tristan.

"The watcher will be mine," Nasaraf said, the voice now coming from the beast as it took another ponderous step toward Tristan, who threw his rifle at the creature but didn't retreat.

Levin used a console to pull himself to his feet. He saw a flicking light surrounding Tristan and Arthur.

"You are not as great a sorcerer as you think you are," Nasaraf said, taking another step. Why didn't they retreat?

Another figure, ghostlike, appeared near Tristan, but Levin couldn't make it out as he drew his sidearm and fired at Nasaraf.

Tristan was standing behind the cart with the d-bomb and screaming. Levin saw the flickering light coalesce around the three, with Arthur on one side and a ghostly alien figure on the other side of Tristan.

Grimkel came at Nasaraf from the side, swinging his rifle like a club, but the demon caught the weapon in its hand and crushed it as the other bladed fist slammed into Grimkel's chest, the spikes punching through the trauma plates. Lieutenant Hammer leapt at Nasaraf from behind, but the demon spun and grabbed Hammer's head in one enormous fist.

Levin tossed aside his useless sidearm.

The crack of Hammer's helmet was loud as Nasaraf closed its fist, and Hammer's body went limp.

"We are Aesir," Theisen said, drawing a knife and advancing on Nasaraf. Nearby, Gunsen also drew his knife and came at Nasaraf from the other side.

"Bound together through blood and tears," Theisen said, and Gunsen joined him in the chant.

"We are the blades of our people," the two Aesir screamed and launched themselves at the demon.

Theisen planted his knife in Nasaraf's shoulder, and the demon roared as it struck at Gunsen, the claws on its fist severing the junior Aesir's head and flinging it from the body.

"We are—" Theisen began. Nasaraf thrust the clawed fist into Theisen's chest. The spikes punched through the trauma plate and silenced the warrior forever.

"Your weapons no longer work," Nasaraf said smugly. It took another step toward Tristan.

Levin drew his Ka-Bar.

"We will fight you to the end," Arthur said. "With everything we have!"

The pulse must have drained or destroyed all electronics, which meant the d-bomb was useless. Even Lilith was silent, perhaps forever.

"It will never be enough," Nasaraf growled.

Levin ran at Nasaraf, but he didn't know what his Ka-Bar would do to such a beast. His armor was broken, his other weapons destroyed. His Ka-Bar was no sword, and his armor would not protect him from those claws, but he would die before Tristan and Arthur; that was what warriors did.

Holding the knife like an ice pick, Levin ran.

Nasaraf heard him and spun, but the demon didn't move fast enough. Levin collided with the monster and in the same motion slammed his Ka-Bar into Nasaraf's forehead, cracking the skull.

"War to the knife," Levin screamed. "To the hilt."

Levin's weight pushed the demon against the console sheltering Tristan and the d-bomb.

"To the fist!" Levin yelled and slammed his other fist into Nasaraf's skull, where he felt the bone crack.

Claws slammed into Levin's ribs, stealing his breath as Nasaraf staggered.

"No," Nasaraf growled and twisted his fist. "I am immortal."

Levin didn't have the breath to scream as the world grew dark. He wanted to tell Nasaraf that he could be banished, but nothing escaped his lips as blood filled his lungs. His chest felt like it was on fire. Pieces of his chest trauma plate fell to the floor. He couldn't breathe. The claws had to be extending out his back.

This was death.

Levin looked up and saw Tristan scream one final time as he brought his fist down on the red, blinking d-bomb activation button.

Nasaraf couldn't see Levin's dying last smile as the Marine's vision dissolved into the purple mists that enveloped him.

* * * * *

Chapter Seventy-Five: Kurchatov

Kapten Sif – VRAEC, Nakija Musta Toiminnot

The tram was military and most of the people using it refused to look in her direction, a young girl escorted by two Peacekeepers. She couldn't pinpoint if their discomfort and fear came from her or the Peacekeeper uniforms. Nobody questioned her despite her being in a restricted area. Sometimes she felt pity or lust, but often it was just simple discomfort and a desire to be elsewhere.

Most were ODT or Guard officers with a few enlisted, but none of them dared draw the attention of Sif and her two Peacekeepers. Even a toy of the elites could exercise power over them.

Skadi and Vili stood silent and watched everyone else as Sif sat like a spoiled, self-important individual. She pulled out her tablet and began playing some mind-numbing game that kids in her age range were supposed to be playing. It made it easier for Muninn to infiltrate the social monitoring systems and mark her behavior as normal and unworthy of attention. Anybody boarding the tram gave her a wide berth.

It was a relief when, five stops later, the tram reached their destination, and Sif could stop playing the game that was about giving lollipops to homeless people while avoiding the apelike capitalists who were trying to steal her bag of candy.

Like everything on the Moon, the entrance to the Kurchatov Facility was underground. The well-lit main entrance had as much personality as a featureless concrete wall. As it loomed up in front of her at the end of a tunnel, Sif wondered what she was doing. Could she just walk in and get access to the artifact? Muninn was giving her abilities she had never had before without a crack team of Republic hackers shadowing her. The support of Skadi's and Vili's SCBIs gave her a false impression of invincibility, but at this point, the real problem was going to be the hard link systems and people. Two unknowns.

Pop-down turrets dotted the ceiling, but there weren't any obvious guards in the atrium. Behind a desk sat a pretty woman with long eyelashes and red hair. She smiled at Sif. Sif felt fearful curiosity from the woman as she looked at her two escorts.

"Can I help you?" the receptionist asked, forcing herself not to look at the Peacekeepers.

"Yes." Sif glanced around. "I'm here to see Director Martinov."

"Are you expected?"

"Yes." Well, she was now, thanks to Muninn adjusting Martinov's schedule for him. "Anastasia Morozov," Sif said, using one of her old cover names from a mission to one of the ghost colonies.

"I see you here," the receptionist said. "I have notified him. If you will please have a seat. I'm sorry, he is a busy man."

"Of course," Sif said and sat on a plush seat where she could watch both entrances.

"He has been notified," Muninn said. *"Right now, he is scrambling to check his messages for anything about a Central Committee Special Investigator. Not that he will find anything. He seems more nervous than usual."*

"Thank you. Anything else?"

"I've lost contact with Gunnery Sergeant Mathison's team. They have entered Zvezda Two proper."

Which was expected. The SCBIs were using the ODT secure networks, which weren't as secure as the surrounding networks, but the commissar had more familiarity with them, and right now speed was more important. So much to do, but so little time.

The glass interior doors slid open, and a younger man came in. Sif sensed he was flustered and off guard. Keeping the smile off her face, she pushed her way into his mind. Lust and fear slid across his mind as he looked at her. He might look young, but Sif knew he wasn't. Maybe a hundred and fifty years old? He was a senior member of the Governance Scientific Bureau. Targeting him had been a risk, but now Sif was glad she had listened to that voice.

"Um, hello, Miss Morozov," Martinov said glancing toward Skadi and Vili. "I'm sorry to have kept you waiting. Um. I was not aware my schedule had changed. I'm afraid I may be unprepared as the meeting invite did not have any details."

She heard the fear filtering through his thoughts. Only the Central Committee could adjust his schedule, and when the Central Committee behaved unpredictably bad things were likely to happen.

"It would be best if we talk privately," Sif said, shedding her youth. He sensed the change in her, and his fear increased. Something else felt wrong, but she couldn't place it.

"Yes, yes, of course," Martinov said. "Please, follow me. Will my office suffice?"

"First, I want to see it," Sif said. He would know that alarms would be set off if she wasn't allowed to be here.

"Of course. Follow me. You've had the briefing?"

"Yes," Sif lied and gave him a push, assuring him this was the right thing to do.

The weasel smiled and turned down a hallway. She felt that Skadi and Vili were alert following Martinov. He led her through several armored doors. She nudged him mentally to take them past the security scans and any potential problems. He was easy to manipulate, but there was a flavor, a smell, a sense from him that was bothering her, a rot of some kind. Maybe it was just because he was a vile human being. She had seen nothing that proved it, yet her discomfort grew as she followed him.

"Something's wrong," Sif said to Skadi using Muninn and Loki.

"I concur," Skadi replied. *"A trap?"*

"I don't know," Sif said.

"I'm not seeing anything," Muninn said. *"All channels appear normal. I don't have video access to everything, but I cannot find any subterfuge."*

"Do you have eyes on the artifact?"

"No. That is on a lower level where only hard links are allowed."

"Watch for traps," Sif said. What was wrong?

A chill ran down her spine as she followed Martinov toward some heavily armored elevators. Were there monsters?

Martinov shuffled them into the elevator, and the elevator descended. Her stomach began doing flip-flops as they passed several gravity generators. She wasn't sure how deep they were going. The hair on the back of her head rose, and her heart began to be beat faster as Martinov began rambling, but she tuned him out.

Martinov looked normal, but was he?

What was happening? Had they released it already? Were they heading into a cesspit of demons? She checked her Inkeri. It was on and the Russelman index was fluctuating heavily. That was bad.

The door slid open and the creature waiting there grabbed Vili's rifle and pulled back its other hand, tipped with armor-piercing claws. Sif watched the claws shoot forward toward Vili's armored chest as she stepped back and tried to get her pistol out of her bag.

She wouldn't be fast enough.

* * * * *

Chapter Seventy-Six: The *Pankhurst*

Zhong Xiao Ting Hui, Alliance ODT

The vanhat were pushing hard, and Hui had pushed the d-bomb into the airlock closet of the *Pankhurst* where she hoped the vanhat would miss it. She did not want it aboard the *Tyr* under any circumstances. When it went off, she didn't want to be standing next to it; that was for certain as the vanhat attack was aggressively pushing them off the *Pankhurst*.

Occasionally, out of the corner of her eyes, she glimpsed dark red eldritch energy flowing from the *Pankhurst* to the *Tyr*, but whenever she looked for it, it was as if nothing was there. Hakala and another ODT fought beside her trying to keep the vanhat from pushing them all the way off the *Pankhurst*, but there were too many monsters. The corridor Levin and Grimkel had gone down was now littered with bodies, and Hui doubted they were still alive. There were only a few minutes left on the timer.

"Pull back," Hui said, "the bomb will go off shortly."

"But the others—" Hakala began.

"Are likely dead," Hui said. She had to make the decisions now.

Hakala didn't argue, and as one they began fighting their way back aboard the *Tyr*.

Stepping aboard the *Tyr* felt like defeat. She could see the closet where the d-bomb was stashed and the vanhat seeming to ignore it in their blinding lust to kill.

They let the vanhat push them back.

An energy pulse blew past her and appeared to stun the vanhat, but it was brief.

Hui felt nauseous as she raised her rifle and pulled the trigger. Nothing happened and the vanhat screamed their hatred and anger as they ran at her. The only thing slowing them down was the bodies they had to step over.

She dropped her rifle and pulled her sidearm. Nothing. Beside her Hakala and Evanoff had drawn knives. The power in her suit showed offline. They were going to die.

There was another pulse. She fell to her knees and almost blacked out. That had felt like a d-bomb going off.

In front of her she saw the *Pankhurst* shimmer in the eldritch light and twist unnaturally. The d-bomb in the closet still had a few seconds, hadn't it? Purple mist gathered at the edge of her vision.

In seconds the *Pankhurst* dissolved into darkness that revealed stars.

With the absence of the *Pankhurst*, the atmosphere escaped the *Tyr* and pulled Hui toward open space.

She grabbed a rail with one hand. She saw Hakala slipping past her toward the open hatch. Without power to their suits, their life support wouldn't last long and her grip on the rail was not as strong as she would have liked.

Hakala had fought beside her, bled with her. She was a Republic HKT, but she was now a battle sister. Hui reached out and grabbed Hakala. If Hui could not hold on, then they would die together.

Hanging there, Hui looked for something else to grab onto before they were both pulled out into the darkness where they would die. She started losing strength.

The lights flickered on and the hatch slid closed.

Gravity pulled them gently to the ground. Hui pulled off her helmet and vomited in the thin air.

The *Tyr* was not dead.

* * * * *

Chapter Seventy-Seven: Lucifer

Lojtnant Skadi, VRAEC

"*Watch for traps,*" Sif said.

She thought it was necessary to tell her that? Here they were in enemy armor, with enemy weapons, in a top-secret enemy facility on the most heavily defended Moon in the galaxy, and Sif was telling her to watch for traps?

This Martinov looked like scum, and she wanted to reach out and beat him. He just had that air about him. The only time he glanced at her was to look at her breasts. He was smaller than her, but he couldn't be bothered to raise his eyes to hers? Something about him made her skin crawl. He looked to be twenty, but as lead scientist he obviously wasn't. He could be two hundred, maybe older, a trusted SOG sycophant. In the elevator, he put his back to the wall so he could look at them and the elevator doors. He also conveniently put himself out of the way of the opening doors.

"This really is a fascinating find," Martinov said, "as you know. This tells us so much about our species, the galaxy, the universe, everything. This is such an impressive time to be alive."

Sif nodded. Skadi didn't know if the girl was distracted or if that was her ploy to get Martinov to talk more. To Skadi, the scientist's voice was abhorrent, as bad as the food she had been forced to eat on *Star Mozambique* when she was trying to make inroads and help their rebellion.

"Momentous!" Martinov said. "The secretary general sent you. You are so honored to be here. I have not seen you before."

Was he fishing or getting suspicious? Sif remained silent as she looked at Vili's back. Standing behind Sif and Vili, she scrutinized Martinov. He was too calm.

Going down in the armored elevator made her stomach start doing flip-flops as they sank deep into the Moon's surface.

A chill ran down her spine, and she checked her Inkeri. Functional but stressed. Damn. Had they released it? She remembered long ago when she had tried to open a door and been slammed backward. Inside there was a creature coming out of a light or something. The logs had been corrupted, so she wasn't certain what she had seen.

Base 402, where it all began. The feeling of déjà vu was almost painful.

But now she was just on edge. The feeling that something bad was about to happen hung over her and grew stronger, more threatening. It was becoming painful. The little bastard was standing to one side of the doors. Vili would lead the way out. Probably a security checkpoint. Peacekeepers or ODT?

The feeling filled her. She wanted to hold her rifle at patrol ready, one hand on the pistol grip, the other hand on the forward grip, ready to bring it up and fire. But Peacekeepers didn't walk around like that. They just let their rifle hang from their front harness, so she let her hand rest on her pistol grip. A quick glance showed the Inkeri was failing.

The elevator stopped and the doors started to slide open. The creature reached in and grabbed Vili's rifle, crushing it in its grasp as the clawed hand shot toward his heart. A blazer round slammed into its forehead and steaming flesh erupted. Another blazer round hit it in the neck, nearly separating the head and arms from the torso.

Vili screamed a war cry and pushed forward, his sidearm coming out as he pushed the collapsing body out of the way. Skadi realized she had fired. Holstering her sidearm, she brought up her rifle. The gravity was Moon-standard, which meant next to nothing.

Martinov screamed in rage and anger and reached for Vili, but Sif stepped forward, grabbed his hair, and pulled him into her knee which rammed into his chest. He staggered forward when Sif reached up, grabbed his head under her arm, and twisted. Blazer fire followed the wet snap as Vili engaged something, or someone, else. Skadi stepped past Sif and the collapsing body and stepped out of the elevator, bringing her rifle up and shooting down two shadows sprinting down the corridor toward them.

Vili threw away the remains of his rifle as he kicked the body out of his way.

"Paska SOG weapons," Vili said.

Something moved, and Skadi shot it as the lights flickered. There were too many shadows and she felt like she was back in another SOG station being hunted by vanhat.

"Down this hallway to the right," Sif said.

"This makes little sense," Loki said. *"Martinov may have been aware and working with these creatures? Why was he not killed?"*

"We kill threats now," Skadi thought. *"Ask questions later. Aren't there networks or something you can hack?"*

"Everything appears offline, fried. The links I see don't go anywhere."

"How long?"

"Weeks? A month? This is not new."

"This is bad."

A door opened, and a creature looked out at them, its face full of hatred. Vili shot it first. Scorched flesh sprayed the hallway. This was a trap.

"That's putting it mildly. Such an understatement."

The hallway turned. There could be thousands, millions, of creatures down here.

"My Inkeri is going wonky," Vili said.

Skadi saw hers wasn't doing too well either.

"What happens if they fail?" Vili asked.

"I don't know," Skadi said.

"Well, don't let me kill you," Vili said. "Please."

"You'll be okay," Sif said.

How could Sif know that?

"This feels different," Vili said. "It feels very bad."

Nothing came around the corner. Vili peeked and then stepped around the corner. Skadi shifted to the other side to shoot around him.

Ahead, large double doors blocked the way. They were armored and next to them were yellow lines painted on the floor showing a guard station but there were no guards.

An alarm went off. Skadi glanced at her heads-up display and saw her Inkeri generator had shut down.

The double doors slammed open, and Skadi saw the gray shadow mists of Shorr space. On the floor was another alien prison box, but behind it the air rippled, and she saw something coming out as Vili screamed, dropped to his knees, and grabbed his head.

"Come slave," a voice growled in her head. "I have been waiting for you. My arrival is imminent, and the gate continues to open."

Skadi felt her rifle fall from her numb fingers as pain lanced through her skull. Her body itched everywhere.

*****

Chapter Seventy-Eight: Losing Hope

Chief Warrant Officer Diamond Winters, USMC

*E*agle shook and more red lights came on in front of Winters. *Eagle* was still taking hits even though it was tucked in close to *Sleipnir*. Vanhat ships were attempting to swarm the battlestar but unlike the *Tyr*, *Sleipnir* was in full control. The vanhat had played their hand against the *Tyr*, and they had nothing left for *Sleipnir*, which was fresh, ready, and eager to fight.

"Where did that come from?" Britta asked, and Blitzen highlighted the display. A shot had come from the *Tyr* aimed at *Sleipnir*.

"Nasaraf is taking control of the *Tyr*," Winters said.

If Nasaraf took control, it would cause serious damage.

"Is the *Tyr* lost?" Amiraali Lea Hynninen, the commander of the *Sleipnir* group, asked.

"Give them a little more time," Winters said. Levin would move as fast as he could.

"We may not have time," Hynninen said.

"Levin is dead or winning," Winters said.

"He needs to win faster," Hynninen said. "They'll force me to take action soon."

"Brace!" Blitzen said.

The lights and panels of *Eagle* flickered. Targeting data and tracking information was wiped from the displays.

"What happened?" Winters said, echoing Britta.

"Energy pulse," Blitzen reported. *"Systems coming back online."*

"Show me the Tyr,*"* Winters said, and the display zoomed in. Scorch marks and slowly spinning debris showed her where the *Pankhurst* had been, but now it was gone.

"There has been a Shorr space disruption," Blitzen said. *"The disruption ripped apart the* Pankhurst. *It's gone."*

"Semper Fi Levin!" Winters said, letting out a breath. "Get me Levin."

"Zen," Britta said.

"Marine Commander," a voice said seconds later. The link identified her as Colonel Ting Hui, the ODT leader of the task force that had gone with Levin. "I regret to inform you that Mission Commander Levin was aboard the *Pankhurst*. Apologies. He is gone to Valhalla. We will remember him as one of the people's heroes."

Winters stared at the ruins of the allue where the *Pankhurst* had died.

"How did he die?" Winters asked.

"He led the assault to the engine room of the *Pankhurst* with Grimkel, Hammer, and some Aesir. He took one of the d-bombs. Something happened and the *Pankhurst* dissolved or faded or something. I don't understand, Ship's Captain. All I know is the *Pankhurst* is gone along with everyone aboard it. A d-bomb caused this failure. The *Pankhurst* may have had a portal open to Shorr space. The detonation of the d-bomb would have destroyed it and Nasaraf. We are lucky it did not destroy the *Tyr*."

"How do you know it is destroyed? Maybe they fled to Shorr space?"

"He ordered us to hold at the entrance to the *Pankhurst* while he went forward. There were no other ways on or off the ship. His survival is not possible, Ship's Captain," Hui said. "But—"

Winters waited for Hui to continue.

"But the ship was falling apart. We had a d-bomb aboard and the timer was set. If it was in Shorr space when the d-bomb detonated, there would be no survivors. He is gone. I'm very sorry, Ship's Captain."

Winters wanted to argue, to hope, to believe he had escaped, but power was coming back online aboard the *Tyr*.

"Scan for survivors," Winters told Blitzen. *"Maybe he got thrown free."*

Now she was the last Marine and the weight of the world crashed onto her shoulders. But she couldn't run and hide. She would pick up the flag the gunny and Levin had carried. But what could she do?

She still had a human race to save, and if she was the last, she would make damned sure the vanhat regretted pissing her off.

"Shorr space drive is back online. Kontra-amiraali Carpenter is online for you," Britta said.

"Is it true my daughter is dead?" Carpenter asked.

"We have a recording of her ship being shot down over the Atlantic," Winters said. "I'm sorry. What is the status of the *Tyr*?"

"Hurt," Carpenter said. "Badly hurt, but she can fight."

Winters nodded.

"We must launch our attack against the Moon soon," Winters said. "If we do not, the missiles we launched will shatter against Sol's defenses."

"Are you mad?" Carpenter asked.

"Yes. I'm pissed. I'm angry, and I really want to kick someone in the teeth. They killed your daughter; they killed my Marines. The vanhat attacked our d-bomb factories, and I had to order them all to be launched or we would have lost them. Soon, Sol Defense will detect them, and we don't have the numbers needed to saturate the defenses. If we wait, Sol will learn and prepare for the next attack. The gunny and Skadi have failed. They are dead. Only the *Tyr* and *Sleipner* can transition in and hit that base without being instantly destroyed. If we don't strike now, we will never have the chance again."

The link was silent.

"You want revenge for your gunnery sergeant?" Carpenter asked, and Winters held her breath. The only other option was to start swearing at him. She took another breath.

"Yes, I want revenge. I want my death to mean something. I'm going in with you. My SCBI will coordinate fires and defenses. It is the only way."

"Zen. I want revenge for my daughter. I will convince Amiraali Hunninen. We will launch the attack as soon as the *Tyr* is able. I will not expect the *Tyr* to survive the battle though."

"Semper Fi," Winters said. What else could she say? "I will convince the *Tupolev*. We win or die."

"Or we win *and* die, Zen. Valhalla awaits," Carpenter said, and the link closed. They had maybe a day, maybe two, to repair and prepare. It had been days since she had gotten any decent sleep.

"I'm sorry, Captain," Blitzen said, *"scans are negative. There are no survivors outside the hull of the* Tyr.*"*

Winters lost track of time and the stims she popped as the fleet scrambled to repair and prepare to attack. She kept hoping to hear Levin had been found, but after the first day she knew he was dead.

"Transitions," Britta said, and the screen lit up with more—a lot more—vanhat ships.

If the *Tyr* and *Sleipnir* could survive the new onslaught.

The vanhat spread out. The fleet couldn't randomly jump into Lunar orbit. That was another thing they needed. Time to plot a course and repair.

Levin was gone, and she had to concentrate on keeping people alive. She would mourn later.

More vanhat transitioned in, and Winters began to doubt their chances.

* * * * *

Chapter Seventy-Nine: The Return

Navinad – The Wanderer

It took a moment for Navinad to find his voice. It had happened, and now he could act. Now he could reveal himself.

"Now!" Navinad said and the *Romach* slid into Shorr space, his shadow providing precise coordinates.

In seconds, the battle cruisers of the New Masada Defense Force slid into normal space and into the midst of the vanhat horde falling upon the *Tyr* and *Sleipnir*.

"Launch, launch, launch!" Clara said. Everyone knew their job, knew what was on the line. Drone fighters spilled out of the drone bays and missiles leapt away from the *Romach* without targeting information.

Too many vanhat, but the NMDF appearing in their midst had caught them by surprise. They were still clustered together.

The *Romach's* displays flickered as d-bombs detonated nearby, danger close, but the disruption was temporary.

Maybe this had been a mistake and the small fleet should have transitioned in further away.

Navinad's shadow opened a link to the *Eagle*, *Tupolev*, *Tyr*, and *Sleipnir*.

"Attention Alliance vessels," Navinad said, "this is the New Masada Defense Force. We are here to help, but we must launch a strike against Earth immediately. Transmitting coordinates."

Navinad had spent many years trying to figure out what he would say, how he would convince them. He had spent a lot of time acquiring those coordinates. He had infiltrated the SOG systems and laid the groundwork. But now?

The *Romach* shook as vanhat missiles and weapons fire slammed into it. The NMDF ships were damned tough, though.

Besides calling the Alliance, Navinad didn't have much of a job here, and he listened to Clara fight the NMDF ships. It was like watching an orchestra with all the instruments coming together, working together in a symphony of destruction.

He didn't want to have to rely on Winters and her SCBI Blitzen, but right now, that was all he had. He couldn't tell her the truth. He didn't know what the future held now.

"Who is this?" Winters asked him on a directed link.

"I'm a US Marine," Navinad said. "Please, that is all you need to know right now. Blitzen can authenticate us."

"What? Who? I don't understand," Winters said.

The *Romach* shook again.

He didn't have the time to tell her the truth, to explain.

"There!" Clara said, and a ship glowed bright red. How had she identified it so quickly? Was it the jotun commanding this fleet? Did it matter? "I want his balls."

Drone fighters changed course and more missiles leapt from the *Romach* and her sisters.

"There isn't much time," Navinad said.

"How do we know this isn't a trick?" Winters asked.

"I don't think the gunny or Skadi are dead." Navinad tried to understand why he said that, but it felt right.

"We saw his ship destroyed," Winters said.

"Which doesn't mean he was on it." The memories were returning "It dipped into the clouds for a time. We all lost track of it. There was time for it to have landed."

"Why would he do that?" Navinad heard the hope there. It was a small window, and Navinad felt the truth there. It made sense now, even if he didn't understand why. Could he keep the Peacekeepers from blowing the gunny's brains out? He could still see the finger tightening on the trigger, preparing to fire. He could feel it. Soon. Very soon if he didn't do something.

"Marines thrive in chaos, Captain. The gunny used to say that, remember? The best way to sow chaos is to do what the enemy does not expect. Get inside their OODA loop, deprive them of their understanding."

"How do you know what the gunny used to say?"

Navinad debated telling her the truth.

"I was one of his squad leaders, ma'am. He needs our help. If you won't follow us, then we will go alone and die."

Clara glanced at him. She had heard him.

"Who are you?" Winters demanded. Navinad closed the link before he could betray himself.

"Kill the head. The body dies," Clara said, and her target exploded.

"We must transition now," Navinad said. "We must strike or the jotun prince will win Luna and Earth."

In his mind's eye, he saw the Peacekeeper's finger pulling back the trigger. He couldn't stop that, but now was the time to strike. This was the time his savior had told him he must act or die forever.

The gunny had led from the front and didn't look back to see if the others were following him. Navinad was a Marine. He ran toward the sounds of gunfire. The others would follow him or they wouldn't.

Winters was a Marine or she wasn't.

* * * * *

Chapter Eighty: Rescue

Chief Warrant Officer Diamond Winters, USMC

The vanhat fleet was being decimated by the strangers claiming to be the New Masada Defense Force. They were obviously armed with advanced d-bombs and Inkeri generators and they were human.

"Who are they?" Winters asked Britta when the link closed. Something about the voice sounded familiar.

"New Masada is a ghost colony of Jewish immigrants," Britta said. "They founded their own colony shortly before Israel's destruction. They keep to themselves. I was unaware they had warships."

"The authentication I received is legitimate," Blitzen said. *"There is SCBI encryption. I don't understand. There was a voice filter in place."*

"But now they show up here with d-bombs and Inkeris?" Winters asked as the Alliance Fleet assembled into formations. Admiral Carpenter and General Duque were working together to establish a wall for the vanhat to smash against while the NMDF ships ripped them apart and kept them from assembling.

The small NMDF fleet maintained a tight formation, a fist smashing through the vanhat ships.

Almost at once the vanhat ships stopped firing, but the Masadan ships didn't. They lashed out and killed ships that were drifting. One vanhat cruiser changed course and the Masadans wasted no time attacking it.

"*Who is it?*" Winters asked Blitzen.

"*The SCBI sending the information is not identifying itself, but it seems a lot older.*"

"*There's a Marine with a SCBI aboard that ship who knew the gunny?*" Winters asked. How did this make sense? Were there other Marines from the *Jefferson* that had been found? Or was this Marine a survivor from hundreds of years ago? An older SCBI?

"*Affirmative. There should be no way to fake Marine SCBI encryption and authentication.*"

"*Then why won't they identify themselves?*"

"*Unknown. The coordinates they sent will put us in Lunar orbit. They seem legitimate and very precise.*"

"*Do we trust them?*"

"*Standby. He is a Marine. A Marine and his SCBI. I believe we should trust them.*"

"*Why?*"

"The vanhat have lost cohesion," Britta said. "Like at Wanping when we smashed that Jotun vessel. I think the Masadans nailed the Jotun in control."

"There isn't much time," Navinad said.

"How do we know this isn't a trick?" Winters asked. Who was he, dammit?

"I don't think the gunny or Skadi are dead," the stranger said, and Winters wanted to believe him, but how would he know?

"We saw his ship destroyed."

"Which doesn't mean he was on it. It dipped into the clouds for a time. We all lost track of it. There was time for it to have landed."

"Why would he do that?" We? He had been watching?

"Marines thrive in chaos, Captain. The gunny used to say that, remember? The best way to sow chaos is to do what the enemy does not expect. Get inside their OODA loop, deprive them of their understanding."

"How do you know what the gunny used to say?"

"I was one of his squad leaders, ma'am. He needs our help. If you won't follow us, then we will go alone and die."

"Who are you?" Winters demanded but the link was closed.

The wall of battle moved forward under the joint command of Admiral Carpenter and General Duque, smashing vanhat vessels that came within range. As quickly as they arrived, the NMDF fleet transitioned back into Shorr space. Just like the damned Gunny, leading the way and not bothering to look back to see if he was being followed.

Winters made an instant decision. She was a United States Marines and Marines were decisive.

"Admiral Carpenter and General Duque. We have to act now. We must launch our attack. No time to explain. Coordinates are being sent. Follow me!"

"Go!" Winters said to Blitzen.

Eagle slid into Shorr space. She didn't have time to receive their acknowledgment. Just like the gunny, she wasn't going to look back to see if they were following. They either were or they weren't. She knew her duty and had her honor.

* * * * *

Chapter Eighty-One: Banished

Kapten Sif – VRAEC, Nakija Musta Toiminnot

Sif couldn't breathe, couldn't think as the pressure crushed her mind and soul. She felt the power and presence pushing in on her. This jotun was too powerful.

"You have failed," a voice whispered in her mind. It was so different from the other jotnar. It felt further away and yet more powerful. "It is time to end this charade, to cleanse life from this reality once again. I find it repulsive."

She didn't have to look to see her Inkeri had failed or was overloaded. She would not die like this, on her knees screaming. She pushed back with her mind, and she expected to push against an immobile wall, but to her surprise she cleared away a pocket where she could think. Like when she was on a ship in Shorr space, and she reached inside and found the calm that let her ignore the worst of Shorr space. The pain left her body.

She looked up. A creature was stalking forward. It had two legs and arms but did not look human. The knees bent the wrong way, and the fingers were too long for the claws on their tips. It had a mouth full of teeth and red eyes glowed as it looked at her with a look of pure hatred. She snatched up her pistol from the ground, brought it up, and a blazer round slammed in the creature's chest.

The monster exploded like she had hit it with an explosive round. Sif pushed harder with her mind, reaching out and imagining her bubble pulling in Skadi and Vili.

A roar echoed through the complex, and she felt the anger and hate as a physical force pushing her back. Something different was coming.

Skadi stopped screaming and looked up, her hand grabbing her rifle from where it hung on her harness.

Red and black eldritch energy flickered around them, and she felt the energy push in, pushing back the bubble from Skadi and Vili.

"We are Aesir," Skadi said, her voice hoarse and full of pain.

"Bound together through blood and tears," Vili said, joining her.

The hatred pushed back the shield Sif was creating with her mind. She was going to lose the protection around Vili and Skadi. Her strength was draining rapidly as a shadow appeared at the end of the hallway. A wave of energy rolled over them. Sif fell to her knees and vomited, but she didn't lose the shield or her pistol.

"We are the blades of our people," Sif said, joining Skadi and Vili.

Sif readied her weapon and fired, but a *click* told her the pistol was no longer functional.

Skadi and Vili drew their blades as one when their rifles wouldn't fire.

"I am Lusiferious," the shadow said as it came closer. The bubble around Skadi and Vili began to wane and Sif knew when it did, they would die.

Two specters walked past her from behind, one to stand behind each of the two Aesir.

The one behind Skadi was the knight in shining armor, a glowing blade in his hand, a shield in the other. The one behind Vili was Criston, a sad smile on his face as he placed a ghostly hand on Vili. Sif felt her shield grow stronger, augmented by the two specters.

"We are Aesir," Skadi, Vili, and Sif said. "We are bound together through blood and tears."

Vili and Skadi stood, separating to come at the shadow from different angles, and Sif knew they couldn't see their guardians.

Skadi's and Vili's voices grew stronger as they held their blades before them, causing the shadow to falter.

"We are Aesir," the three Aesir said together, gaining strength from their words. "Tears are our armor. Blood is our shield."

The shadow roared in anger and hatred and turned to Skadi.

"We are Aesir. We are warriors, the bringers of death!"

As one, Skadi and Vili rushed forward.

The shadow hesitated.

Sif expected the Aesir blades to pass through the shadow, but they struck like they were hitting metal armor.

"We are Aesir," Sif said as Skadi and Vili stabbed at the shadow, shouting battle cries. "We cast fear into the hearts of our enemies!"

Light flowed from Criston and the Knight into Vili and Skadi, pushing back the shadows, overcoming the eldritch light that made up Lusifereous. A glimpse of the Knight's shield revealed the eagle, globe, and anchor of the United States Marine Corps.

The demon lashed out, and Vili flew back in a spray of blood. Criston grabbed him and shielded him.

Sif stepped forward, pushing with her mind, doing her best to crush and destroy the force that was trying to crush her. She was Aesir.

She was Nakija, Musta Toiminnot, Erikoisjoukot. She was the defender of her people. She would not die easily.

Now she sensed fear, indecision, doubt. Sif pushed harder, demanded submission.

"We are Odin's chosen," Sif said, her anger a weapon that she thrust into the creature as Skadi thrust her own blade.

She poured her hurt, her fear, her anger, and her loneliness into the demon.

A weight lifted, and Sif felt the malevolent force dissolve as exhaustion washed over her.

Skadi again collapsed to her knees and her knife clattered across the floor.

Sif looked up. Criston's form was fading, a satisfied smile on his lips.

The Knight turned to her and lifted his visor. With a salute and a sad smile, Levin faded into purple mist.

When she looked back, Criston was also gone. There was an emptiness in her heart as she realized she wouldn't see the boy from the noodle stand again. He had found his destiny and could now move on.

In front of them, the alien prison box sat on the table, inert and harmless.

* * * * *

Chapter Eighty-Two: Prisoners

Gunnery Sergeant Wolf Mathison, USMC

Feng had removed the Americans' helmets and cut the power to their suits, which was almost as effective as restraints with the heavy trauma plates weighing them down. He relieved them of weapons while Mathison glared at him. What would Feng do now? Have them dissected or just shot?

Disarmed and harmless, a Peacekeeper on each arm and one Peacekeeper behind them with a rifle at the base of their skull, the Americans were marched to a nearby building. A large, beautiful structure.

Looking around, Mathison could trace the bowl-like interior. It didn't appear to be spinning, but it was just an illusion. Manicured gardens, trees and fountains sprinkled the interior. The ceiling rotated with the ground below and a massive view screen showed a summer sky. There was no wind and no birds. Mathison counted at least fifty heavily armed Peacekeepers in the vicinity.

They were marched through the main door of the building, led by Commissar Feng, and brought to a large conference room.

Eight young men and women sat around the curved table in luxurious chairs.

"Shing!" the beautiful woman in the center said with a smile.

"General Secretary Tokarski," Feng said bowing.

"Can you redirect nanites to reconnect power?" Mathison asked Freya.

"That is what I'm working on. So glad you finally started thinking. I'm way ahead of you, though."

"So, these are the big bad Marines," the general secretary said. "I kind of expected they might be a little tougher."

"I hate to break it to you, but—" Robillard began.

Feng stepped forward and slammed his fist into Robillard's jaw. The Delta Trooper sagged, but the Peacekeepers held him up.

"My apologies, General Secretary," Feng said, scowling at Mathison, then Stathis and Peshlakai. "They lack manners and intelligence. Given time, I'm sure they will learn to speak only when spoken to."

"Okay, I can reconnect power, but it will be obvious. Then there's the problem with the Peacekeeper who has a blazer aimed at the back of your neck. He won't be able to miss, and his finger is stroking the trigger. If it's a hair-trigger, you are going to die any second."

"Of course," Tokarski said.

"You received the rest of my message?" Feng asked.

"Even if you survive that, the Peacekeeper weapons are coded to Peacekeepers."

"I'm in Peacekeeper armor," Mathison said.

"Yes," Tokarski said, looking less happy.

"That technology is proven and will work. With it we can restore order to the Governance."

Tokarski shook her head.

"But I do not have the proper codes. You are not of this battalion. Despite appearances."

"I'm sorry," Tokarski said. "Most, if not all, districts are in active rebellion. Right now, the Committee has decided it would require too many resources and could endanger Earth if we re-open Sol. I have already ordered the Inkeri generators and d-bombs be produced as soon as we can, but to venture forth from Sol? No."

"General Secretary, please," Feng said, "there are trillions of people who need the powerful arm of the Governance to protect them. We are sworn. We cannot abandon them."

"We can and we will," Tokarski said. "I determine the greater good."

"I don't understand, General Secretary," Feng said. Mathison wanted to laugh. Did Feng really expect the Central Committee to do the right thing?

"Gunny," Stathis said through Shrek and Freya. *"Shrek says he can power up our suits and we can bust out of these restraints, but we'll probably get shot."*

"No, Shing," Tokarski said and looked at her fellow Central Committee members, "we decide the greater good. We will not weaken ourselves."

"But we have the ability, General Secretary. With this technology, we can push the enemy back!"

"Stand down, Stathis," Mathison said. *"We'll get out of this alive. We'll have a chance later."*

"Why?" Tokarski said with a smile, leaning back and looking at Feng. "Why not make an alliance with them?"

"They cannot be trusted, General Secretary. They are only murderous beasts, intent on killing or changing us. I have fought them."

"You have not tried talking with them," Tokarski said, looking smug. "They are quite reasonable. Some of them. There are others that are nothing more than savage animals, but the things we are learning about them, about history, about science! Those things you brought will be helpful, and I'm sure we can use them if our new friends turn out to be less than honest, but the power they can give us!"

"I don't think so, Gunny. I don't think we'll leave this room alive unless we do something."

"Stand down, Stathis. That is a fucking order!"

"If I make a move, I can draw their attention to me. That might give you a chance."

"Stand down. They'll fucking kill you, Stathis."

"But their attention will be on me. It will give you a chance to take some of them with you. Kill one for me."

Feng stood quietly looking at the general secretary.

"God damn you, Stathis. You will stand down and do nothing until I tell you to."

"I was never good at following orders, Gunny. I would have liked to have you as a dad. I trust you more than anyone else. If anybody can kill some Peacekeepers, you can. Best gunny ever."

"I don't think you understand Feng. We have already opened negotiations with this so-called enemy. They can offer us great power."

"I don't understand," Feng said.

Tokarski smiled and pressed a button. The door slid open and a big, hulking man entered.

"Hermod?" Mathison said aloud as the ex-Aesir walked in. His red eyes burned into Mathison.

"You're the one that killed Hanz, aren't you?" Hermod said. "On Zhukov. Yes." Mathison felt his blood run cold. "Lady Nadya, may I have this one for a play toy?"

"No," Tokarski said, but Mathison wasn't sure that was a good thing. "They will not leave here alive. I cannot risk it and I do not wish to see you feed here."

Hermod scowled.

"That settles it. Gunny, be ready."

"Damn you, Stathis. Don't you fucking dare!"

"Thank you for trusting me, Gunny. You are the father I never had. Tell Hakala I love her. Semper Fi."

"Damn you," Mathison said out loud to Stathis and tried to step toward Tokarski. The Peacekeepers were ready and pushed him to the ground as Freya reactivated his armor.

Stathis started to yell "Fuck y—" as blazer fire erupted.

Muffled pops surrounded Mathison as power returned to his armor and the Peacekeepers fell on top of him. A quick twist of the arms ripped apart the restraints and he grabbed a Peacekeeper's pistol. Still lying down, Mathison brought up the pistol.

Feng had his sidearm out, but Mathison's eyes locked onto Hermod who was coming at him. Mathison knew the pistol wouldn't fire as he brought it up, but he hoped it would make Hermod pause. He pulled the trigger and blazer rounds lanced out, ripping through Hermod and surprising Mathison. More blazer shots rang out.

Two more shots and Hermod's head erupted into flaming gore. Hermod was a big man and had momentum. The body kept coming, tripping over Mathison and crashing to the ground behind him. A Committee member stood with a weapon in hand and Mathison shot him too, expecting at any minute to be shot by Peacekeepers as he swung around to kill the Peacekeeper that had killed Stathis.

A glance showed Feng was calmly shooting the members of the Central Committee as Mathison sat up and saw Stathis crouching nearby, pistol in hand, looking for a target.

Relief flooded through him. The two Delta Troopers were crouched, weapons in hand.

Mathison looked at the Peacekeepers. There wasn't a mark on them. Feng had stopped firing. Eight rapid shots had ensured that not a single Committee member had survived.

"What happened to the Peacekeepers?" Stathis asked, poking the nearest one, which was lying face-down.

"Security," Feng said, looking around. "Each Peacekeeper has a small bomb implanted in them. When it receives a coded burst with the correct command, it will detonate. This guarantees that the Central Committee can trust the Peacekeepers not to turn on them. Here in Sol, even most officers have them."

"Why didn't you share that code with the rest of us?" Mathison asked.

"You might have used it at the wrong time." Feng holstered his sidearm and turned to Mathison. "The late general secretary will have hard link access at her chair. I apologize for the mess. We should now be in control of Zvezda."

"I thought you betrayed us," Mathison said, not yet sure if he should shoot the commissar or thank him.

"The Central Committee had to stand trial. Had they risen to the occasion and served the greater good, they might still be alive. They did not. I knew of no other method to get us all here, close to the Central Committee and into the Central Control Center."

Both Delta Troopers were still crouched, back-to-back and watching for targets.

"You should insert the IFF codes," Feng said. "We have little time."

Mathison still had the network plug, and he found a place near the general secretary's console.

"Console is active," Freya reported. *"I have access. Standby."*

Alarms started screaming.

"Damn, Gunny," Stathis said. "They are a little slow."

Feng was at another Committee member's console. "A fleet has been detected transitioning into Lunar orbit. Governance Fleet control is preparing to respond."

"IFF code being authorized and broadcast," Freya said.

"It appears the *Tyr* and *Sleipnir* have arrived in orbit," Feng said. "They are launching missiles."

"Feeding target locations that were retrieved at Quantico," Freya reported.

"What kind of missiles?" Mathison asked.

"D-bombs."

"Give the command for Governance Fleet to stand down."

"As you order."

"Why didn't you tell us what you were going to do?" Mathison asked Feng.

"That should be obvious. Scanners and analysis software would have detected something amiss in your behavior when the helmets were removed. You are now within the inner sanctum of the Social Organization Governance with full control of their systems. Proceed with our mission. You and Freya have full Central Committee access. I have transferred all control and authorizations to you. I dare say the Central Committee is in no position to oppose you."

"Why not you? Emperor Feng?" Mathison asked, ready for Feng to draw his weapon.

Feng placed both hands on the table where Mathison could see them. "No, that is not who I am. I am a servant. Where others lead is where I follow. I do not have the vision that others, like yourself, have. You are now the emperor of Sol if you so desire."

"Hell no. Not my style. Find some other jackass to rule."

"And that is why you must take the mantle. We cannot trust those who want it. As you say, Semper Fi."

* * * * *

Chapter Eighty-Three: The End

Gunnery Sergeant Wolf Mathison, USMC

Mathison didn't think he would ever get comfortable seeing Peacekeepers alive in his presence. The uniforms, or colors, would have to be changed. The skulls on their armor were no longer appropriate. The ODTs were more acceptable, because they had fought and died beside him.

Stathis made an exceptional bodyguard, and Feng was another protector. Mathison still didn't feel comfortable enough to walk around without armor.

With Feng's help, he and Freya had taken full control of Sol's defenses. The members of the Central Committee had been paranoid in the extreme, and they had done their best to consolidate all power and authority into their hands. All the Peacekeepers and most ODTs had implanted bombs that insured absolute loyalty to the Central Committee. The surveillance network was more extensive than Mathison had imagined. The biggest flaw for the Central Committee was the need to trust people to monitor everything, though right now most of it was useless.

The arrival of the *Tyr* and *Sleipnir* had almost caused the Home Fleet to destroy them, but control of the Governance controls had let

Mathison issue stand down orders as the *Tyr* and *Sleipnir* d-bombed the larger vanhat concentration and dispatched Aesir assault teams to seize control of other critical command nodes.

Any officer or soldier who refused to obey orders issued from Zvezda had the bomb implanted in their body detonated.

Now the Home Fleet stood by silently, afraid that Mathison would push the button that would destroy them individually or collectively.

"The *Kunayev* should be the only battleship," Feng said, referring to a ship that was now full of dead spacers. "You had to show you are willing and able. The rest will fall in line, knowing it is only your benevolence that is keeping them alive."

Only a thousand lives snuffed out.

"And the fact the Vanir aren't wiping them out," Stathis said.

"Not a concern," Feng said. "The warriors of the Governance will gladly die fighting the Republic. They are conditioned and expected to do so. They do not fear death in battle, but being killed as traitors? That is a quandary for them. They have sworn their hearts and souls to the Central Committee and Nadya. They only have their loyalty to the Central Committee. They are heavily conditioned in their loyalty. Their oaths, their orders, demand unconditional obedience. INSEC will ensure compliance because they won't know what else to do."

"Until they figure out how to rebel," Stathis said.

"Not impossible, but highly unlikely," Feng said. "The flaw of top-down control is what happens when the dictator in charge is replaced. The previous secretary general lived most of her life consolidating and cementing her power. She was no fool. She kept control of the other Committee members in the same way as the subjects of the Governance. They will quickly realize that rebellion will lead to death more quickly than under the previous regime. The king is dead. Long live the king."

Why did Feng have to imply this was a new regime?

"We should send them all to prison now, kill them," Robillard said. "Make sure they can't betray us."

"There is merit in that suggestion," Feng said. "However, if they don't have a choice; rebel or die, they will rebel. There are many skilled administrators and warriors. To try to replace them all is a fool's task. Keep them employed and under control, or we risk billions of innocent lives."

"Kill the head, the body dies," Stathis said.

"No," Feng replied. "Replace the head and the body becomes stronger."

"Secretary General?" a Peacekeeper asked. "The Aesir are here to see you. Should we disarm them?"

"No. Let them in," Mathison said.

Sif, Skadi, and Vili entered, escorted by Peacekeepers, but the Aesir remained armed. They had cleaned the Central Committee chambers up. The bodies had been removed so it was defensible enough.

Skadi's smile was uncharacteristic, and Mathison couldn't hide his own.

"I was kind of expecting to meet again in Valhalla," Skadi said.

"There's still time for that," Mathison said. "The vanhat are not defeated."

"They will be," Sif said.

"We have a lot of work to do," Mathison said. "I have identified preliminary targets for the d-bombs, but those areas will have their electronics crippled, and we will need to provide food and water until they can bring systems back online. This could quickly become a humanitarian crisis."

Sif went to one of the Committee member's consoles and sat down.

"Where do we start?" Skadi asked.

"They already have," Freya reported. "*Their SCBIs have already integrated and are providing targeting and logistics assistance.*"

"Grab a seat," Mathison said. "Get comfortable. This is the lap of luxury, but we have a lot to do."

"So, what do we call you?" Skadi asked. "I'm not calling you gunny anymore. You are beyond that."

"Emperor?" Stathis said. "Secretary general?"

"We'll figure that out later," Mathison said.

"No, we need to determine that now," Sif said. "The Governance needs that. They need to break from the old and embrace the new. If you do not choose, others will choose for you."

"*A delegation from the Tyr is en route,*" Freya reported. "*They are almost here.*"

"Until we elect someone," Mathison said.

"Which could be years, or more likely decades," Sif said. "Too much change too soon will be bad."

"Suggestions?" Mathison asked.

"Prime minister. It doesn't sound as permanent or as authoritarian as secretary general."

"Fine."

"Why not emperor?" Stathis said. "I like Feng's idea."

"No."

"Secret—um, Prime Minister," the Peacekeeper captain said. "The delegation from the Republic Battlestar *Tyr* is here to see you. Should we disarm them?"

"No and stop asking about disarming people. I'll tell you if they need to be."

"Yes, sir," the captain said.

Kontra-amiraali Carpenter was the first to enter, and his eyes lit up when he saw Skadi. Behind him were Winters and Duque. There was also Lieutenant Colonel Hui and several HKTs, including Hakala.

"Daughter," Carpenter said as he approached her.

"Father."

Without warning, he stepped forward and pulled her into his arms. There was no way he could keep such a large woman wearing powered armor in his arms though and Skadi pushed him away, embarrassed.

Winters walked up to Mathison and snapped out a salute. Out of the corner of his eye he saw Hakala wink at Stathis, but he couldn't see his Marine's response.

"Chief Warrant Officer Winters reporting for duty, sir."

Standing and returning her salute, Mathison pointed at a nearby unoccupied seat.

"Welcome aboard, Acting Admiral Winters. Please take control of the Governance Fleet and coordinate with Allied Republic Forces to deal with the vanhat."

"Aye, aye, Prime Minister," Winters said, marching to her seat. Mathison tried not to wince at the title.

"Levin?" Mathison asked, and Winters stumbled.

"He is in Valhalla, sir." Her face was an emotionless mask, and Mathison added her pain to his own. "He died saving the *Tyr* from the *Pankhurst*."

It was a heavy blow. Another Marine that Mathison owed.

He turned back to Skadi and her father. "Skadi, I would be honored if you would take command of the Governance ground forces."

"It would be an honor." Skadi stepped away from her father. She would know them better than anyone else he trusted.

"Feng? Sif?" Mathison said, looking at the enigmatic Asian and diminutive Aesir. "If you will, please take control of the security forces. I expect you to work together."

"It will be an honor," Feng said.

Sif looked less sure but nodded.

"General Duque." There were too few people he trusted, but he would have to start somewhere and trust that Freya and the other AIs would warn him of any danger. "I need you to help with the Governance fleets and we must prepare rescue forces for other colonies. Can I count on you?"

"Yes, Prime Minister," the general said. "It will be an honor to serve."

"Lieutenant Colonel Hui?"

"It is my duty to serve," Hui said.

"I would like you to take command of the ODTs. You will answer to Skadi. Is that acceptable?"

"I will serve with honor."

"They may call you prime minister," Carpenter said, "but you will rule as an emperor."

"Until we can fix the Governance," Mathison said. "The United States of America will be reborn."

"You are an optimist," Carpenter said. "The Governance will not change overnight, but the Republic will help as best we can. The hard work has not yet begun."

"Thank you. Stathis?" Mathison looked at Stathis. Was he about to make a monumental mistake?

"Yes, Prime Minister Gunnery Sergeant Mathison?" Stathis said confirming Mathison's bad judgment.

"I want you to work with Skadi and Hui to fix the Peacekeepers. I'm putting you in command of them for now."

"Aye, Gunny," Stathis said, but he wasn't smiling and Mathison wondered if he had finally cracked through the Marine's façade and reached the warrior leader beneath it. He saw in Stathis' eyes that he understood the mission and was ready to take it on. Then the mask returned.

"Dude. Gunny, can I call you the Wolf Emperor?"

"Shut up, Stathis."

# # # # #

Author's Afterward

Thank you, dear reader. This has been a fun series to write, and I sincerely hope you had fun reading it. I have many ideas for future books. There are still a few loose ends such as Becket, Navinad, two other Central Committee members, Derekala and other demons. This is not the end. It is a new beginning.

There is no living "happily ever after" when death is stalking you. I still have many stories to tell in the world of the Last Marines. There is much to be told after this book and during the times while the Marines are sleeping.

Come follow me at www.WilliamSFrisbee.com

Thank you and Semper Fi!

* * * * *

About William S. Frisbee, Jr.

Marine veteran, reader, writer, martial artist, computer consultant, dungeon master, computer gamer, dreamer, webmaster, proud American, and best of all, dad.

Growing up in Europe during the height of the Cold War and serving as a Marine infantryman through the fall of communism shaped Bill's perspective on life and the world. When most Marines were out trying to get lucky, he was studying tactical manuals. Years later, he shared much of his knowledge to a website for writers of military science fiction.

These days, he's brushed off the pocket protector and is a top gun computer consultant.

Learn more at http://www.WilliamSFrisbee.com.

* * * * *

Get the **free** Four Horsemen prelude story **"Shattered Crucible"**

and discover other titles by Theogony Books at:

http://chriskennedypublishing.com/

* * * * *

Meet the author and other CKP authors on the Factory Floor:

https://www.facebook.com/groups/461794864654198

* * * * *

Did you like this book?
Please write a review!

* * * * *

The following is an
Excerpt from Book One of Abner Fortis, ISMC:

Cherry Drop

P.A. Piatt

Available from Theogony Books

eBook, Audio, and Paperback

Excerpt from "Cherry Drop:"

"Here they come!"

A low, throbbing buzz rose from the trees and the undergrowth shook. Thousands of bugs exploded out of the jungle, and Fortis' breath caught in his throat. The insects tumbled over each other in a rolling, skittering mass that engulfed everything in its path.

The Space Marines didn't need an order to open fire. Rifles cracked and the grenade launcher thumped over and over as they tried to stem the tide of bugs. Grenades tore holes in the ranks of the bugs and well-aimed rifle fire dropped many more. Still, the bugs advanced.

Hawkins' voice boomed in Fortis' ear. "LT, fall back behind the fighting position, clear the way for the heavy weapons."

Fortis looked over his shoulder and saw the fighting holes bristling with Marines who couldn't fire for fear of hitting their own comrades. He thumped Thorsen on the shoulder.

"Fall back!" he ordered. "Take up positions behind the fighting holes."

Thorsen stopped firing and moved among the other Marines, relaying Fortis' order. One by one, the Marines stopped firing and made for the rear. As the gunfire slacked off, the bugs closed ranks and continued forward.

After the last Marine had fallen back, Fortis motioned to Thorsen. "Let's go!"

Thorsen turned and let out a blood-chilling scream. A bug had approached unnoticed and buried its stinger deep in Thorsen's calf. The stricken Marine fell to the ground and began to convulse as the neurotoxin entered his bloodstream.

"Holy shit!" Fortis drew his kukri, ran over, and chopped at the insect stinger. The injured bug made a high-pitched shrieking noise, which Fortis cut short with another stroke of his knife.

Viscous, black goo oozed from the hole in Thorsen's armor and his convulsions ceased.

"Get the hell out of there!"

Hawkins was shouting in his ear, and Abner looked up. The line of bugs was ten meters away. For a split second he almost turned and ran, but the urge vanished as quickly as it appeared. He grabbed Thorsen under the arms and dragged the injured Marine along with him, pursued by the inexorable tide of gaping pincers and dripping stingers.

Fortis pulled Thorsen as fast as he could, straining with all his might against the substantial Pada-Pada gravity. Thorsen convulsed and slipped from Abner's grip and the young officer fell backward. When he sat up, he saw the bugs were almost on them.

* * * * *

Get "Cherry Drop" now at: https://www.amazon.com/dp/B09B14VBK2

Find out more about P.A. Piatt at: https://chriskennedypublishing.com

* * * * *

The following is an
Excerpt from Book One of Chimera Company:

The Fall of Rho-Torkis

Tim C. Taylor

Now Available from Theogony Books

eBook, Paperback, and Audio

Excerpt from "The Fall of Rho-Torkis:"

"Relax, Sybutu."

Osu didn't fall for the man steepling his fingers behind his desk. When a lieutenant colonel told you to relax, you knew your life had just taken a seriously wrong turn.

"So what if we're ruffling a few feathers?" said Malix. "We have a job to do, and you're going to make it happen. You will take five men with you and travel unobserved to a location in the capital where you will deliver a coded phrase to this contact."

He pushed across a photograph showing a human male dressed in smuggler chic. Even from the static image, the man oozed charm, but he revealed something else too: purple eyes. The man was a mutant.

"His name is Captain Tavistock Fitzwilliam, and he's a free trader of flexible legitimacy. Let's call him a smuggler for simplicity's sake. You deliver the message and then return here without incident, after which no one will speak of this again."

Osu kept his demeanor blank, but the questions were raging inside him. His officers in the 27th gave the appearance of having waved through the colonel's bizarre orders, but the squadron sergeant major would not let this drop easily. He'd be lodged in an ambush point close to the colonel's office where he'd be waiting to pounce on Osu and interrogate him. Vyborg would suspect him of conspiracy in this affront to proper conduct. His sappers as undercover spies? Osu would rather face a crusading army of newts than the sergeant major on the warpath.

"Make sure one of the men you pick is Hines Zy Pel."

Osu's mask must have slipped because Malix added, "If there is a problem, I expect you to speak."

"Is Zy Pel a Special Missions operative, sir?" There. He'd said it.

"You'll have to ask Colonel Lantosh. Even after they bumped up my rank, I still don't have clearance to see Zy Pel's full personnel record. Make of that what you will."

"But you must have put feelers out…"

Malix gave him a cold stare.

You're trying to decide whether to hang me from a whipping post or answer my question. Well, it was your decision to have me lead an undercover team, Colonel. Let's see whether you trust your own judgment.

The colonel seemed to decide on the latter option and softened half a degree. "There was a Hines Zy Pel who died in the Defense of Station 11. Or so the official records tell us. I have reason to think that our Hines Zy Pel is the same man."

"But... Station 11 was twelve years ago. According to the personnel record I've seen, my Zy Pel is in his mid-20s."

Malix put his hands up in surrender. "I know, I know. The other Hines Zy Pel was 42 when he was KIA."

"He's 54? Can't be the same man. Impossible."

"For you and I, Sybutu, that is true. But away from the core worlds, I've encountered mysteries that defy explanation. Don't discount the possibility. Keep an eye on him. For the moment, he is a vital asset, especially given the nature of what I have tasked you with. However, if you ever suspect him of an agenda that undermines his duty to the Legion, then I am ordering you to kill him before he realizes you suspect him."

Kill Zy Pel in cold blood? That wouldn't come easily.

"Acknowledge," the colonel demanded.

"Yes, sir. If Zy Pel appears to be turning, I will kill him."

"Do you remember Colonel Lantosh's words when she was arrested on Irisur?"

Talk about a sucker punch to the gut! Osu remembered everything about the incident when the Militia arrested the CO for standing up to the corruption endemic on that world.

It was Legion philosophy to respond to defeat or reversal with immediate counterattack. Lantosh and Malix's response had been the most un-Legion like possible.

"Yes, sir. She told us not to act. To let the skraggs take her without resistance. Without the Legion retaliating."

"No," snapped Malix. "She did *not*. She ordered us to let her go without retaliating *until the right moment*. This *is* the right moment, Sybutu. This message you will carry. You're doing this for the colonel."

Malix's words set loose a turmoil of emotions in Osu's breast that he didn't fully understand. He wept tears of rage, something he hadn't known was possible.

The colonel stood. "This is the moment when the Legion holds the line. Can I rely upon you, Sergeant?"

Osu saluted. "To the ends of the galaxy, sir. No matter what."

* * * * *

Get "The Fall of Rho-Torkis" now at: https://www.amazon.com/dp/B08VRL8H27.

Find out more about Tim C. Taylor and "The Fall of Rho-Torkis" at: https://chriskennedypublishing.com.

* * * * *

Made in the USA
Columbia, SC
03 September 2024

41517376R00274